➵·➴

The Cottingley Cuckoo
Print edition ISBN: 9781789096859
E-book edition ISBN: 9781789096866

Published by Titan Books
A division of Titan Publishing Group Ltd
144 Southwark Street, London SE1 0UP.
www.titanbooks.com

First edition: April 2021
10 9 8 7 6 5 4 3 2 1

A CIP catalogue record for this title is available from the British Library.

Printed and bound by in Great Britain by
CPI Group (UK) Ltd, Croydon, CR0 4YY.

THE COTTINGLEY CUCKOO

A.J. ELWOOD

Titan BOOKS

For Priya and Mark

PART ONE

1

The first thing I notice about Charlotte Favell is that she smells like my mother. The perfume creeps under the door and into the hall and I recognise it at once: lily of the valley, and I am a child again, balancing in her heels while I dab it behind my ears. It is as sweet as it is familiar, and I wonder that anyone would choose to wear it now. It came as a shock to me to learn, later, that lilies are poisonous.

I go in and she is the first thing I see, sitting with her back to the window so that I have to blink to make her out, and the second thing I notice about her is that she doesn't smile. Most of the residents had, wanting me to like them or wanting to like me, because they think we might be stuck with each other for long enough. They don't know that, for me, this is purely temporary.

Charlotte Favell is nothing like them, that's clear. What she is like I don't know, not yet. I wonder if I'll see her smile later, when I serve her dinner or help with her hair, and realise I'm not sure

I want to. Maybe such familiarity would mean I belong here; or perhaps my discomfort is something else, something to do with the sharpness of her eyes.

Her spine is very straight. 'Old school,' Mandy had said. 'Manners, talking proper, all that. You'll get it.'

I wasn't sure if Mandy was telling the truth even then, but I smile at Mrs Favell anyway. She doesn't do anything, doesn't even nod, and for a second I wonder if she's asleep – sleeping with those piercing eyes open – but she shifts her hands in her lap, a gesture that could be rejection, could be a question, and I know I should say something, introduce myself. *Manners*, I think, but somehow my voice isn't there. I can't seem to look away from her. She's wearing what I will learn she always wears: a pastel-coloured blouse that looks like silk: a garment I'd have spilled something on in five seconds flat, a neat, plain skirt; and a string of the most lucent pearls I've ever seen. Later I'll find a succession of those blouses in her wardrobe: pink, mauve, lavender, blue and green, all of them soft, delicate, perfect, and smelling of flowers.

They are not a key to her character. It doesn't matter what Mandy says. I may only have been here a few hours, but I saw the looks when Mrs Favell's name was mentioned and I knew at once there was something amiss. It's not that anyone pulled a face or said anything direct – it might have been better if they had – it was more the way they closed up, as if there were things they wanted to say but couldn't, or wouldn't, because if they did they might have to go to her room instead of me.

Then Mandy told me that when I settle in I could even be her keyworker, that I should *take special care of her*.

The others didn't say anything then either, but I sensed their suppressed laughter, saw their eyes brighten. I wasn't sure if the flush I felt was entirely down to the temperature in the care home, kept up high to comfort old bones.

'It's room ten,' said Mandy. 'You go up and say hello and see if she wants anything, while we sort out all the bedpans.'

Making it sound as if they were doing me a favour – that too was a dead giveaway, but I told myself I didn't care, and they watched as I turned and headed for the stairs. Mandy and the others are a clique, that much is obvious. We went to different schools but I can almost see them smoking in a huddle behind the gym block, bunking off to eat chips, chatting up the same bus drivers and then, somehow, drifting into working at Sunnyside. And they know I'm different. I got the sense they can smell the university on me. I may have only been there a year before I was called back again but I feel marked somehow, and I'd had the urge to tell them; to package up my failure and present it to them like a gift. But my mother's face had floated before me and I'd said nothing.

And so I went to see what was so wrong with Mrs Favell while Mandy turned and cooed over Edie Dawson, everybody's favourite. She'd just finished knitting some tiny garment, soft and fluffy and pink.

'What is it that you want?'

Mrs Favell's question makes me jump. Somehow I still can't speak. It isn't her words or the sharp, clearly incised consonants or her tone that cuts into me but the clarity of it, the bell-like musicality of her voice. It doesn't sound as if it's coming entirely from inside

this room: enclosed, narrow, almost the same proportions as a
student cell in the halls of residence I'd briefly lived in and only a
little larger. She has the usual accoutrements: a single bed, though
hers is ordinary rather than adjustable or fitted with guard rails; a
wing-back chair; and a matching wardrobe and chest of drawers
in anodyne blond wood, not a sharp corner in sight. The walls, as
in all the rooms I've seen, are painted peach, a colour someone
must have imagined would look homely but doesn't. And then,
in the middle of it all, these: a gleaming bureau, well used and
weathered but polished to a heartwood gleam, as if a corner of an
antique shop had materialised here in this room; and above it, her
photographs, not a single one in colour.

I realise I'm staring at the pictures. Their ornate silver frames
reveal a series of faces: all of them women and children, some
of the ladies wearing bonnets. They look stern and impossibly
distant, except one: a smiling girl, her eyes full of merriment and
dimples in her cheeks, shining curls escaping a hat that places her
a hundred years in the past. I suppose she must be long dead. I
wonder how Mrs Favell could have known her, if she'd known
any of them, or if the photographs are just dressing. That's the
word that comes to me – *dressing* – and I don't know why. We're
supposed to talk to the residents about their pictures, their old
lives, the manager told me so, but I shiver and look away.

'Come here,' she says.

Her tone makes me feel like a child and she isn't supposed to
give me orders, not like that, but I don't want to start off on the
wrong foot and so I smile as if I want nothing more than to go
towards her. She holds out one hand like some ladies do in films,

palm down, the fingertips hanging limp. I'm not quite sure how to respond but I touch my hand to hers, just for a moment.

'Charmed,' she says.

I start to step away from her but she leans towards me and grasps the short sleeve of my tunic, pulling it higher, and I squirm. Her fingers are like iron and just as cold.

'Painted,' she says. I don't know what she means until I realise she has bared my tattoo, the one I'm supposed to keep covered: a garland of briars around a central rose, the thorns long and sharp, all in simple black, no colour in it. At once, I am minded of my mother again, the moment she had first spotted it; her bright fury. I'd sneaked off and had it done on my fifteenth birthday, at a parlour that was none too picky about the law or what her wishes might have been, so eager to be *me*, to claim my own skin.

Mrs Favell smiles, as if she's uncovered a treasure. I didn't admit to being inked when I had my interview here, but 'No visible tattoos' was stated in the application pack. It had put me off – what kind of backwater was this? – but then, money's tight and I couldn't afford to be put off. *Not yet*, I think.

'You love nature?' Her voice is arch and there's a flash of impatience or something else in her eyes, amusement perhaps, or maybe she's wondering why I still haven't spoken.

At last I find my voice and say, 'It's my name. Rose.'

'Ah.' She lets out a trill of laughter, letting go of my sleeve. 'Of course.'

The way she says *of course* summons an image of Mandy, grinning and pointing at the ceiling at the thought of how I'm getting on.

I straighten my posture, push back my short black hair. 'I came to see if there's anything you need.'

'*Did* you.' She doesn't say it like it's a question. She stares at me until it becomes uncomfortable. Her eyes are clear as a twenty-year-old's and very blue. Her skin is a little creased and thin-looking but she carries no spare flesh and the overall impression is one of elegance. I have the idea that she'll walk with her head high, with poise, that she'll carry herself better than I do.

'Any help with the stairs, perhaps?' The words feel stupid on my lips, particularly since there's a lift at the far end of the corridor for anyone who needs it, but I want to fill the silence, or offer some reason for my presence, or simply leave.

'Oh—' she puts a hand to her mouth to cover a sudden smile, a gesture that seems purely theatrical, and she lets out another trill of laughter.

Be careful, I think to myself, biting back a retort, sensing hidden depths, a polished surface covering something worm-eaten. Another word springs to mind: *acerbic*. It strikes me that she's a woman who likes to play games and is likely to be good at them. I do not think she would take well to losing.

'Yes, you may help me with the stairs, if you wish,' she says. 'And later, you shall read to me. You'll like that, won't you, Rose? I see that you will.'

She says it as if she really does see, and she's right. To sit away from the other residents and staff, to be immersed in a book – to share dreams and ideas and something bigger, just for a little while – that is a pleasant picture, an ideal, I suppose, of what I imagined life at Sunnyside might be like. I wonder if it's common knowledge that I studied Literature, at least for a time. Mrs Favell has a way of looking at me that makes me feel transparent, as if she can read me too.

I reach out, expecting her to take my arm, but she doesn't. She merely holds out her hand as she did before and places it over mine, as if I were a page and she a queen, and we process down the stairs like that, side by side, our hands held high between us. I don't quite know how to arrange my features as we enter the residents' lounge, the clatter of dice and rustle of newspaper and the murmur of conversation all stopping suddenly like the closing of a door. Mandy and Sarah are over by the tea trolley, scowling as if this isn't what they expected; as if they want me to run from the building screaming or crying. I hold my head higher and glance sidelong at Mrs Favell's sharp little eyes. Then I turn to meet the world with the most genuine smile I've felt on my face in days.

3rd September 1921

Dear Sir Arthur Conan Doyle,

Forgive the impertinence of my writing to you as a stranger and without introduction. I have lately exchanged correspondence with Mr Edward L. Gardner, and he would have been pleased to be our intermediary; but I felt that in view of your current endeavours, I should not delay in laying before you the wonders it has been my lot to discover.

I am aware that you have unveiled upon the world some photographs in which have been captured, by the agency and innocence of children, the little beings that live all about us and are usually unseen, which we have been pleased to name 'fairies'. Naturally, Mr Gardner, whom I had heard of through his lectures in Theosophy, hesitated to admit any particulars of your continued interest in the matter to me. I trust that, when I reveal the reason, you will feel his change of heart understandable, and I hope his only sensible course.

I hold within my hand something that will be of the utmost interest to you, if not the crowning exhibit in the proofs it may be your pleasure to unleash upon the disbelieving world. I will come to it; but first I will explain how it came to me, and say that I myself have undergone the most profound change of view regarding the existence of such beings, so that I hope I may be the model of what is to come upon a larger stage.

I am, I should say, too old for fairies. I am indeed the grandfather to a little girl, Harriet, who is seven years old. Sadly, the war visited me with the deepest grief with regards

16

my son – my wife was spared such misfortune, having gone to a better place some years previously. My son's wife, Charlotte, and his child have done me the honour of abiding with me for the last few years, greatly to my comfort. I gave up my little business in the architectural line soon after the event and moved to a pleasant cottage just outside the village of Cottingley, with which I know you are familiar, for such is where the fairies were apparently captured on a photographic plate.

You may think that such circumstance would mean that Harriet had caught tales of the 'folk' from the local children, and it is true that she has heard tell of them, but little more. She is rather younger than Frances Griffiths and much more so than Elsie Wright, the two amateur photographers who brought the sprites to your notice; and being new to the village, she has often been somewhat rebuffed as an 'incomer' or 'offcumden' by those who should be her playfellows. Furthermore, we have discovered there to be a marked disinclination to speak on the subject of fairies among the residents hereabouts, one which has passed, rather more surprisingly, to their children.

And so it was with much enthusiasm, but nothing in the way of formed notions or expectation, that Harriet persuaded me to go 'hunting for fairies' in Cottingley Glen earlier this year.

Wishing to please her, and to allay in some wise the loneliness in her situation at which I have hinted, I set out readily enough. We had been there often before: she enjoys naming the flowers, and arranging pebbles in the stream, and peeking into birds' nests. It is a pretty place, and hearing her laughter, and her chatter of magical things, is pleasant for a fellow of my more sober years; and I smiled as I went, listening to the babble of Cottingley Beck and child alike.

There is a place – I understand Miss Wright has spoken of it also, though you have not yet found opportunity to visit – where the brook falls in merry little steps into the pools below. All about is verdure, with an abundance of wildflowers and singing birds, and the trees lower their branches as if to provide a resting place for any travellers who wish to pause and admire, and hang their legs over the stream. I did so, being rather more fatigued than Harriet, who busied herself about the water, poking twigs into the hollows to 'seek them out'.

She soon alarmed me, however, with a shriek, and I looked up sharply to see her whitened face, and a flash of light which I took for a reflection dancing in the water.

Tears started into her eyes. She held up a hand, staring at it, and at first I saw nothing; then a drop of crimson appeared at the knuckle and dripped into the pool. I hurried towards her, thinking she would begin to cry in earnest, but she appeared too surprised to do so. I caught her arm, drawing her up the bank, and examined the wound. Thankfully I found only a small, circular puncture, nothing concerning, and indeed she seemed to have forgotten all about it, for she pulled away and slithered down the bank again. She dirtied her dress as she went, and landed with her feet in the water.

I was rather inclined to scold her, but she stood there with her back to me, so intent on something in her view she did not hear my words. I called her name; she remained motionless. This absence of attention was concerning. She was not accustomed to ignoring her elders or disregarding their imprecations, but since she still did not turn I became curious and stepped towards her.

She was peering at a rock that jutted from the beck where it fell a matter of three or four feet to the pool in which she stood. The outcrop was darkened with spray and dressed with moss, though its upper surface remained relatively dry. There, tiny white flowers wavered in the humidity thrown up by the water. I could not see what had so interested my grandchild. I thought to find there some bee or wasp or other stinging thing, and then I blinked, for where the air was misted I thought I caught sight of a hazy form. It was like the tiny semblance of a man, but so indistinct I was certain I must be mistaken.

I forgot myself so much as to take another step, which soaked me to the ankle, but I did not look away until another bright flash caught my eye. This was to the side, and again could have been nothing but sunlight playing on the water, except that when I looked at it directly I saw six or seven of the brightest, smallest, most lovely of beings, floating about us in the air.

Harriet's laughter added to the atmosphere of wonder that came over me at the sight. My eyes are not what they once were, but when I peered more intently I made out the most perfect little ladies, their hair like gossamer and their wings iridescent like those of a butterfly. They captured the light and threw it back, now in lavender, now mauve, now blue and green, now in the palest of pinks.

Harriet called to them and stretched out her hands as if to provide a perch for them to land upon, but they did not; they drew away, and instead she began to follow them. The strangeness – nay, the sheer peculiarity of it, the sense of falling into a dream, was such that I reached out and seized her shoulder. And something – oh, I do not know what, but something made me turn from such gorgeous little miracles and back to the grey stone.

I knew not what it was, but I leaned in closer. And I saw a little man all dressed in green, not six inches high. I did not see if he possessed wings like the others, for his expression caught my attention utterly. His pippin face was unreadable, but his eyes, which were quite black – and, if I may say it of such lovely perfection, somewhat soulless – were brilliant with anger, which deepened when he saw me looking at him.

The sight froze me to the spot, and I became conscious of how cold it was, standing with my feet in the pool; but I peered more closely, because I saw that he was not alone. He stood over a little body lying at his feet. It was another of the females – quite beautiful, but entirely motionless.

I could not help myself: I reached out and he leaped into the air with rage, landing once more on the rock in front of the prone figure. Harriet was beside me again and she let out another shriek at his motion but at the sound he seemed to despair, and in the next instant another bright flash marked his darting away. A series of little clicks, such as might be made by a bat, drew my attention towards where the gaily dancing maidens had been, but as if by some mutual consent, they too had passed from sight.

I fully expected his companion to have similarly disappeared, but she had not. She lay as before, indifferent to everything, for I saw that her breast did not move with any breath, nor did any animating principle enliven her features. Her eyes were closed and I could not doubt that she had gone to whatever heaven awaited such creatures.

That was the moment when I realised I could return home not merely with a fanciful tale, but carrying the proof of what I had seen.

With special care, I bore up the tiny form. I hardly felt its weight. I asked Harriet to draw my handkerchief from my pocket and I fashioned a sling in which to carry it, anxious to avoid crushing her wings. I kept expecting the fairy to vanish beneath my coarse hands or to dissolve into ether, but she did not.

I cannot adequately explain the effect it had upon me. My powers of description pale before your own; I will only say that my wondering was matched by a peculiar sense of fear at seeing something that was thus far out of my experience or expectation. I became concerned at how rapidly my heart was beating – I am no longer a young man – and I had an odd aversion to lingering any longer by the beck. Indeed, I wished to be away from it, and the glen, as quickly as was practicable; and so, stealing away the bounty I had found there, I walked home with Harriet by my side, the child piping questions to which I possessed no answers. And I hope it is not too fanciful to say that as I went, the very sky looked different to me, knowing that such creatures live beneath it.

Now, justly, I am sure you would request of me what became of the fairy. This is the point where the observer of such a marvel should say it has indeed vanished into the air, leaving no trace behind, conveniently leaving their story to the credulity of the listener; but such is not the case.

I placed the frail body into a little wooden box. I somehow did not like to have it in the house, though it constantly preyed upon my mind, so I placed it in an outbuilding to which only I possess a key. Was it that I still struggled to encompass the existence of such a thing? Harriet seemed to feel an odd kind of reluctance too, or I think she did; at any rate, she did not like to speak of it. If I tried to begin on the subject, or even if she observed that I was going outside to check on it, she would close up somehow and slip away to bury herself in a book.

I regularly looked in upon the box, though something prevented me from opening it. It was not until a number of weeks afterwards that I felt I should intrude upon her little casket and see what had become of the fairy. I know little of the process of human decomposition, and regardless, I do not suppose it would be directly comparable; but I rather dreaded witnessing the putrefaction of such a lovely thing, and I must confess, the fear had grown upon me that she might really have vanished. If she had, I think there would have been nothing left for me to do but puzzle over the loss of my senses.

She had not vanished. She had putrefied however, and I suspect more rapidly than a human might, but it was not hideous. It was, rather, fascinating in the extreme. Indeed, I examined the body more closely with the aid of a magnifying glass, feeling as if I had fallen into one of your Sherlock Holmes stories and turned detective.

Barely anything was left of her flesh. What remained had greyed and turned powdery, and there was a smell upon bending closely over it, like stale herbs. And beneath the skin – oh, what a splendid little skeleton! It is a wondrous thing, delicate as a bird's, and easily as weightless. She possesses ribs like a human's, though more steeply angular, as if crushed by the strictest corset. The leg bones seem very like, though I only noticed upon looking so closely that the knees bend backwards. The arms are similar to a woman's in everything but size, as is the skull, if a trifle elongated, like some of the more primitive incarnations of humanity. The wings are incredibly fragile, like those of a preserved insect. They are veined and quite whole, the membranes nearly transparent. My hand shakes as I write of it; it is so very strange and wonderful.

And so I come to the purpose of my letter. I have not told of the fairy to anyone save Mr Gardner and now yourself. Indeed, I scarcely know what to do. This evidence could open the eyes of man to something so momentous it is unheard of in our history, and yet I fear I am not possessed of the skills or wherewithal to do it. And so I write to you, Sir Arthur, most humbly, in recognition not only of your penmanship, which is of course without compare (I have read many of your praiseworthy stories, and even now Charlotte sits at my side, barely keeping in check her ardent admiration and good wishes), but also with regard to your high reputation, your unimpeachable character, and your interest in the world I have so unwittingly stumbled upon.

The skeleton, I am certain, will pass any inspection. It may be photographed; it may be examined, so long as such examination does not press it to destruction, for it is as fragile as may be supposed.

In short, I can only assure you what a singular object it is. I would be greatly honoured to set it before you at any date you require, and at your convenience. I am only sorry I cannot send it to you, but as I am certain you will understand, I fear to move her – she would crumble to dust, I think, or may be mislaid upon the way, and that would be the most tragic and unbearable loss.

For this is something that should belong to the whole world. Of course, the mind of man is such that when faced with an idea so new, the inclination is to see what one will and disregard anything that does not line up with it. But this – it must surely break through any such failure to see. It cannot be denied!

Needless to say – and the times are such that I must address a point that should require no assurances – I seek no monetary gain. I would merely see the remains set before those who may use them best for the advancement of Truth and Knowledge, and such things should never be sullied or brought into question by financial inducement.

I have exhausted my tale. Pray, forgive the length of my letter; having remained silent on the subject so long, I am quite carried away by it. I dare hope you will be as excited as I with the discovery, and I most eagerly anticipate your reply.

Your humble servant,
Lawrence H. Fenton

PS. I should add that Harriet's little hand healed very well;

there were no lasting effects. I do not doubt that she scraped it on a stone as she started away in surprise upon seeing her splendid discovery. Truly, in the realm of fairies, children have proved to be our most visionary and bold adventurers.

2

I had thought I would be able to guess at the contents of Mrs Favell's bookshelf. She would have serious, weighty tomes, something I might have read as part of my degree; peeling linen boards and gilded pages rather than the pink-covered paperbacks they keep downstairs. She's not the Catherine Cookson or Mills & Boon type.

I hadn't expected the thing she placed in my hand. It's a letter, written with fountain pen flourishes on thick cream stock, the ink a little faded, the paper darkened at the edges. Its touch is luxuriant and I'm still half caught up in the magic of the words, though I don't know what to think of them.

Wherever did she find it? It crosses my mind that it must be valuable, that I should be wearing white cotton gloves – after all, it's addressed to Sir Arthur Conan Doyle. And yet the letter isn't *from* Doyle. There's no sign it was ever delivered to him. And if it really had been in the possession of the author who created

Sherlock Holmes, how could Mrs Favell have come by it?

My son's wife, Charlotte, the letter said. I found the line again: *and his child*. I wonder if the name is a coincidence. I look at the Charlotte sitting in front of me, her eyes closed yet with an intensity about her that makes me think she's listening, waiting for my response. I shake my head at the strange idea that comes: that here is the Charlotte spoken of in the letter. But the Charlotte it refers to must be long dead. And she's a Favell, not a Fenton – meanly, I tell myself I can't imagine she's changed it through marriage. Maybe she discovered this in an auction or an antique shop, noticed her own name written there and bought it as a curiosity.

Why ask me to read it to her, here, now? It's bizarre, but then the whole thing is peculiar, more like the opening to a story than a letter. If Sir Arthur Conan Doyle had ever come into possession of a faked fairy skeleton, no matter how cobbled together, people would have heard of it. Plenty have heard of his involvement with the Cottingley fairies, said to have been caught on camera near Bradford. I went to the National Science and Media Museum there once with my mother, saw the prints and the cameras they'd been produced with. It was famously a hoax: two little girls had painted fairies onto cardboard, cut them out, propped them up using hatpins and taken their pictures as if they were playing with them. It was Doyle's belief that escalated a children's game into a situation they could never have anticipated. From what I'd heard, it hadn't done much for his reputation that he'd trusted them. The fairies never had been anything but trouble.

It occurs to me what my old tutor's reaction would have been upon seeing this document, something never uncovered before by academia – the studies I might have built around it – and I feel dizzy.

But perhaps Doyle never received this letter, or issued some scathing reply and disregarded it, or returned it to the sender. That might be how Mrs Favell had come by it – did she have some connection to Fenton? Perhaps she's a distant relative.

I look up and see that she's opened her eyes. She's watching me with interest, her gaze steady and unblinking. When I meet her look she doesn't alter her expression, just goes on glaring until I'm the one to look away.

'Thank you,' she says, and holds out her hand for the letter. 'That will be all.'

I long to question her, to keep hold of it and examine it again, but it's as if she's a headmistress requesting my homework and I hand it over.

I hadn't expected to be so intrigued. I had offered to read to her for a while after my shift ended – there was no time during it, and I hadn't wanted her to think I'd ignored her request. I suppose what I'd really wanted was for us to be friends. Now she's dismissing me, without even thanking me, not really. On her lips, 'thank you' means 'you're done'.

Now I don't want to leave. I look at the letter she clutches so carelessly and I want to ask her about it – how she obtained it, what it means, whether it's a real thing that was sent in the post, on a steam train maybe. Had the great man held it in his hands? But perhaps she'll tell me it's simply some kind of joke. She might even say that, in some odd moment of imaginative fancy, she wrote it herself.

One look at those cold blue eyes and I know she won't tell me. I don't think she needed the letter reading out to her, not really. She doesn't wear glasses. She doesn't have macular degeneration, not like Alf Harding downstairs, pottering about with a cane he doesn't quite know how to use. I don't know what she does want. Probably to see me at her beck and call, lending her a semblance of power in a world in which she must have little. Or she wants me to be intrigued, to give me a glimpse of something fascinating and strange, bait for her hook, only to snatch it away when I bite.

I decide not to bite. I say, 'It was my pleasure, Mrs Favell. Sleep well.'

She stands and turns to the window. It is full of that peculiar light they call gloaming, the perfect word for the radiance coming from beyond the edge of the world. I expect her to say something sarcastic about early nights, since it isn't yet time to sleep, but she doesn't. She focuses on the trees that lie beyond the garden, their crowns shifting and swaying in some breeze, and her eyes go soft. She almost seems to be listening, but for a moment everything is suspended. I can't even hear the television downstairs, on permanently too loud, the clink of teapots or rattle of Scrabble tiles in a bag, the traffic outside.

'I knew you'd like it,' she says. Her voice has softened and I wonder who she was before she came here, whom she might have had in her life. A husband? Children? There haven't been any visitors so far and I can't picture her with anyone, but how would I know?

'Rose. What kind of Rose, I wonder?'

Alarm crackles through me, a sudden electrical charge, and

I wonder what it is about her tone that makes me so overreact.

'Goodnight, sweet Rose.' Her voice is neutral once more, cooler, even cold. 'I shall most certainly see you anon. Pleasant dreams.'

The car park is almost empty. The staff ratio is lower at night and most of the others who work days, as well as any visitors, have already gone. The light is almost gone too, having drained from the world while I fetched my bag and put on my coat. When I start the engine, my car's headlights highlight a patch of hedge, each tiny leaf casting its own black shadow. For a second I imagine diminutive figures dancing in its depths, peering out with eyes that are too dark and blank, and I don't know whether to laugh or shudder. I try for a smile but that little patch of light somehow makes me feel alone and it quickly fades.

I sense the depths of the woods at the back of the building, the fields stretching away beyond them. But I am headed the other way, through the indifferent town with its hard roads, houses full of strangers balancing meals on their knees while their televisions flicker. I remind myself of the future and suddenly I can't wait to get home. I picture Paul in the doorway, grinning at me. The two of us huddled up on our sagging sofa while I tell him stories: how one day, we'll have a big house made almost entirely of glass, with a swimming pool in the garden and a view of the sea. Or an old farm in France, with sunshine every day and goats for fresh milk. Or my favourite: a house in a forest, a turret reaching up amid the branches, a circular room lined with shelves where I'll keep my mother's books.

I can almost hear his voice, his stubble tickling against my cheek: *You know what's different about you, Rose? What I love about you?*

I never answer. He does that himself, and his answer varies, but his meaning never does. Sometimes he uses the word *dreams*, or perhaps *visions*, but mostly he says: *You believe.*

And I do. Someday we'll be out of here. I almost made it once and I will again. I remember Mrs Favell, her failure to smile. Is she the only one who recognises the truth – that this is temporary for me? That I'd sat there in my interview and told the manager all the words she wanted to hear, so that I can earn the money to get out? *Yes, I'd relish the chance to support the residents. I'd love to work in a caring environment – I really do care. I'm sure I'd fit in at Sunnyside.*

But who would stay here if they didn't have to?

For now, I do have to. I imagine Mrs Favell's sneer at the sight of our tiny terraced house; at Paul, with his long hair and arms more tattooed than mine; his irregular work, helping a mate shift unwanted furniture or labouring on building sites. Her disdain would surely make me hate her after all. We're doing okay. At least I got off my backside and found gainful employment. Paul may not be all that driven, not yet – steady jobs never ran in his family – but I reckon that, with a little time and my influence, he'll change.

I think of the other girls. I bet Mandy isn't fretting over what she's done today or what so-and-so said or what anyone thinks of her. She's probably bitching about the new girl, laughing about how we'd marched down the stairs together, Mrs Favell and I hand in hand like film stars going in search of champagne and finding only bowls of Weetabix. I grin and feel better. Sod

Mandy. She's probably never believed in anything in her life. I picture her fifty years from now, still at Sunnyside, still doing all the same things, until finally she gets old and simply moves in.

I let out a huff of laughter as I turn into our street and see the light shining from our front room. Before I've braked fully to a stop the door opens and Paul spills out, his shaggy hair loose to his shoulders, his arms dark with tattoos and strong as a wrestler's – and I see that his hands are full of flowers, bright points of colour plucked from our sorry patch of garden.

He waits while I park our ancient and battered Fiesta between the van belonging to the painter and decorator next door and a shiny saloon that probably belongs to someone just passing through. He opens the car door for me, all gallant, and I jump out and there are kisses and he puts the flowers into my hands. There's the big massy head of a hydrangea alongside limp daffodils and sagging tulips, a frayed stalk of ragwort nestled among the rest, all the petals drooping and damp and smelling faintly of petrol. I tell him I love them.

As soon as I've put them in a vase and Paul's throwing dinner together, I go and sit halfway up our narrow flight of stairs, which is narrowed further by the books stacked along the side of each tread. There's no space in our house for bookshelves, not yet. I run my hands over the worn and battered spines, pushing aside the guilt I'd felt earlier, the memory of my mother's anger about my tattoo. These are the things we had shared; the books Mum had loved, the ones she introduced me to the moment I could read them. All of the dreams, the *visions*, are still here: orange-clad paperbacks, black-trimmed classics, tiny volumes of poetry almost lost among the rest.

Mum did most of her dying when I was away, in silence and in secret. She had so wanted me to be free.

But her books remain. I lean against their spines and close my eyes. When I was tiny, I would curl up on her knee while she read fairy tales to me, the first stories we shared together, that were *ours*. Even before I open my eyes again to scan the titles, as I have so many times, I know I will not find any fairy tales at all and I wonder again where they have gone. Did they vanish into the air? Were they somehow stolen from me? Was the memory even true, or only a sweet fiction I tell myself? Of all the possibilities, the one I can least believe is that she would have thrown those stories away.

I remember that, now, I am to read to Mrs Favell. How very odd that she and I will be the ones to share stories together.

But then, don't they call old age a second childhood?

3

It feels like I've been at Sunnyside forever as I undo the buttons on Reenie Oram's cardigan and re-fasten them. She'd made a good effort but matched them with the wrong holes, bunching it up in front of her. The manager pointed it out, telling me to straighten it before visiting time, concerned about who might see, what conclusions they would draw. It's better than the mop-and-bucket duty I've spent all morning doing, a consequence of being the new girl.

When I finish I smile, knowing that Reenie will keep staring into space with her pale and watery eyes, and she does, but it seems important to smile anyway. There are flashes that make me think her mind is still working: a sudden glance, a grasp at my hand. I wonder what she's seeing now. Family? Times gone by? Whatever it is, she keeps it locked inside.

There's another of the carers going about the residents' lounge, straightening the mismatched chairs with their wing backs and high seats and plastic covers, setting a walking frame neatly aside, drawing back the vertical blinds from the French windows to brighten the room. Nisha has been here a while. She's not entirely one of the clique and has a bright smile and a readiness to laugh that makes everything a bit lighter. She doesn't seem to feel the weight of the manager's frown or the atmosphere hanging in the air like an exhalation of this place: the sense of giving up, of loneliness that is never really dispersed by the false enthusiasm of let's-try-to-keep-interested or let's-play-a-game.

Nisha is admiring Edie's knitting, held out in her shaking hands. White wool shines in the sunlight streaming in, bright and clean as innocence. I imagine soft new skin, tender little feet kicking, tiny hands enclosed by that softness. I'm glad Paul can't see my thoughts. The first time he mentioned kids, I laughed; I honestly thought he was joking. We're not in that place yet. We need the house first, we need to see what lies across the ocean or through the forest or on the other side of the world. We need to see it all.

'She never visits,' Nisha says at my shoulder, and I jump. At first I don't know what she means and she nods towards Edie. 'She knits herself senseless – see her knuckles? Arthritis. It must be so painful for her. She keeps saying her daughter's having a baby, like she's forgotten the kid must be years old now, because she's never seen it. They live in Australia. They never have been back.'

I look again at the snowy whiteness falling from Edie's hands. 'What does she do with it all? Does she post the clothes to her?'

Nisha pulls a face. 'Too expensive. She gives everything to the staff, whether they've got kids or not. You'll probably get something at some point. Most of it goes through the local

Oxfam, I expect. She might as well unravel it and start again.'

I feel a stab of alarm at what Paul would say if I turned up at home with a pair of bootees, then Nisha flicks her eyes towards the stairs and says, 'Has *she* given you anything?'

She doesn't say whom, but I know at once. Mrs Favell doesn't like to come down in a morning, not unless she's going out for a walk. Sometimes she doesn't have breakfast; she eats an apple in her room and then reads, away from the overly loud television, which is currently belting out some inane morning show. She's not that dependent. She needs less support than anyone here. It was as I suspected, she never did need me to read to her, and I still haven't worked out why she asked me. To have a look at the new girl I suppose, the fresh blood, new meat. It's a pity in a way, because I long to hold that letter in my hands again, to touch something from a world so completely removed from this.

I shake my head, though there's something about the way Nisha asked the question I can't let go. 'Why?' I ask. 'Is she likely to?'

I regret my form of words at once. It makes me sound like a gold-digger waiting for gifts, but she doesn't seem to notice.

Leaning towards me, she lowers her voice. 'The girl who was here before you – there was a lot of trouble. Just be careful.'

I want to ask what happened but just then the manager, Patricia Stott, comes in, and we start tidying away the piles of magazines and disarrayed board games, making space to put out tea trays when visitors arrive. Patricia is a stout woman of fifty or so, her eyes veined with tiredness but still vital, still darting about with swift certainty. One of the residents told me that over the years she's had two husbands, four children and a whole pack of rescue dogs, and I imagine her organising them all with the same brusque efficiency. She glances at me, checking I'm doing what I'm supposed to be doing, and sets down the pills she's carrying, already sorted and labelled with names and room numbers. Nisha hurries off to help distribute them, making sure everyone has cups of orange juice to wash them down. She casts a sharp look over her shoulder at me – bidding me to secrecy, or something else?

I realise that Mrs Favell has come in. She stands in the doorway surveying the room, pearls gleaming at her neck. Her hair, like Patricia's, is swept into a bun, but unlike Patricia's there are no stray hairs floating about her face. She's holding a book, though it's tiny and I only notice it when the gold foiled edges flash back the light.

It's obvious that something sets her apart. There's no sense of distraction about her, no staring into space, not a moment's vagueness. I wonder again that she needs to be here, just as her gaze lights on me and she beckons.

'A walk,' she says as I approach. 'Fresh air. Just the ticket, yes?' She gestures towards the French windows with her book, which I see is old, no name visible on its black leather cover. She tucks it away in one hand and reaches for me with the other, her fingers slender, gripping my upper arm tightly. I should be starting on the teas but Patricia doesn't object so I don't either.

I'm not sure if I'm supporting her or being led as we step onto the path that edges the building. A bird trills, high and out of sight, and the world is suddenly sharp slices of sunshine and shade. The garden isn't that large – Sunnyside's not purpose-built and it's clear from the mismatched brickwork that it's been extended a couple of times, encroaching on the lawns to make room for more residents on the ground floor. There are still plenty of benches dotted around. I half expect to see little plaques set into them marking the death of someone's aunt or grandmother, like in the park, though I suppose no one wants to think about such things here. There's a nip in the air, the faint memory of winter, pricking the hairs along my arm. Mrs Favell doesn't seem troubled by it. She stops suddenly, standing in shadow, only the tip of her shoe crossing into sunlight. She closes her eyes and breathes in, long and deep.

'Are you all ri—' I begin, but her grip tightens and I fall silent.

'Do you hear that?' she says.

I try to listen. From somewhere comes a child's brief shout. A distant engine starts up and a door closes. Closer still are the television's meaningless prattle and a guffaw of laughter – that's Jimmy Rees, one of the jollier old men. He calls me 'flower' and I thought it was because of my name before I realised he calls everyone that, including the postman.

'That's a skylark,' she says, 'and the wrens are nesting in the azaleas. Caterpillars are eating the leaves. Do you hear them?' There's an almost dreamy look on her face, though her eyes remain closed.

Surprise – even alarm – jolts through me. Is this why she's at Sunnyside? No one's told me she's losing her faculties, but maybe it's true. How can she expect to hear caterpillars? It isn't possible, but her focus remains, her posture rigid, her expression serious. I actually find myself listening, looking up at the sky, but I see only contrails, the ghosts of other people's journeys. I can't see the bird, not now. I can't even hear it.

When I look back at her, she's waiting for me. Her lips are pressed into a line so thin they've almost vanished, her cheeks sucked inward, her eyes filled with as much amusement as contempt. She holds something out: her book. I reach for it, thinking she wants me to read to her again – no letter this time, more's the pity – and she says, 'This is for you. A gift.'

'Oh,' I say, drawing back from her. 'I couldn't.'

'You will,' she says. 'It's an important poem. I want you to read it.'

'Well, I'll read it to you now,' I say, gesturing towards a seat. 'Then we can pop it back in your room. It's a lovely book.'

'Of course it is. That's not the point. It's for you.' She thrusts it towards me again and I hear the echo of Nisha's voice. *The girl who was here before you – there was a lot of trouble. Just be careful.*

'I really can't.'

'You remind me of me, Rose.'

I start. What can she possibly mean by that? How can she compare the two of us? I'm nothing like her. I realise she's gripping my arm just around my tattoo, as if to underline the difference between us. I try to keep my distaste from showing and instead answer her earlier question again. 'I don't think it's allowed. I'm new here, you see.'

She gives an amused *tsk*, as if to say, *Do you think I could have forgotten?*

'No such rule. Oh, for heaven's sake – read it to me then.' She marches to one of the benches and sits primly, crossing her legs at the ankles. I wonder if she went to one of *those* schools, back in the day – finishing schools or etiquette, establishments for young ladies, something like that. She nods at the space beside her and I lower myself into it, wondering what exactly happened to the girl before me.

This time, when she holds out the book, I take it. I'm no longer certain the cover is plain black: there are hints of other colours trapped within it, blues and purples and greens swimming in its depths. The binding is even softer than I'd expected – it feels as tender as skin and for a moment I think of Paul. Last night we'd had sex, taking our time after a hastily put-together dinner. He hadn't closed his eyes. He looked into mine while he ran his hands down my body, as if taking measure, memorising the way it felt for when he awoke and I'd be gone. I almost feel his fingertips on me again and I shiver.

'Read it,' she says again. Her lip twitches as if she knows what I'm thinking about and I redden as I open the page at a silk ribbon bookmark.

'"La Belle Dame sans Merci",' I begin, hoping the whole thing won't be in French, and I realise it's by Keats: a famous poem, one I might have studied, though I'd come home before that module began. *The Beautiful Lady without Mercy*. It's a poem about fairies.

> 'O what can ail thee, knight-at-arms,
> Alone and palely loitering?
> The sedge has withered from the lake,
> And no birds sing.'

She jabs a finger towards a stanza lower down. As I read, she continues to do so, making me stumble, making me jump ahead, leafing through the wafery pages.

'I see a lily on thy brow
With anguish moist and fever dew,
And on thy cheeks a fading rose
Fast withereth too.

I met a lady in the meads,
Full beautiful – a faery's child,
Her hair was long, her foot was light,
And her eyes were wild.

I made a garland for her head,
And bracelets too, and fragrant zone;
She looked at me as she did love,
And made sweet moan.

I set her on my pacing steed,
And nothing else saw all day long,
For sidelong would she bend, and sing
A faery's song…

She took me to her elfin grot,
And there she wept and sighed full sore,
And there I shut her wild wild eyes
With kisses four.

And there she lullèd me asleep,
And there I dreamed – Ah! Woe betide! –
The latest dream I ever dreamt
On the cold hill side.

I saw pale kings and princes too,
Pale warriors, death-pale were they all;
They cried – "La Belle Dame sans Merci
Hath thee in thrall!"

… And this is why I sojourn here,
Alone and palely loitering,
Though the sedge is withered from the lake,
And no birds sing.'

My words fade, the feeling of them hanging in the air like the contrails above, soon to be gone. I'm not sure what I'm supposed to think. The poem is full of death and melancholy, but there's magic in it too. The words are seductive and as I read a kind of greed swept over me, a longing not only for the beautiful fiction but for the language. I've missed this. I've had so little time for reading since I abandoned my course to return to my mother; and then there was Paul, and now there is Sunnyside. Still, I have no idea why Mrs Favell wanted me to read it. Is she going a little bit mad?

She murmurs under her breath:

A fading rose fast withereth too.

I feel the slightest brush of something on my cheek: her touch? Her breath? I jump and turn towards her, but her eyes are closed and she's unmoving, though she says, 'Yes, that's it. What did it make you think of, Rose?'

Death. Melancholy. 'I don't know.'

She keeps motionless as a statue, as if waiting for the rest. Then she snaps her head towards me, though her eyes remain in deep shadow. 'Do you wish to read more of my letters?'

I open my mouth to speak, to make some instinctive excuse perhaps, or with sudden dizziness at the thought that she possesses more: more lovely artefacts, but most importantly, more of the *story*. I realise how very much I do want to read them and I say, 'Yes please,' like a ten-year-old asking for ice cream.

'Then you need to learn to be honest with me.'

Abruptly, she stands and walks away. Her figure is as slender as a girl's and her silver-white hair looks almost golden in the light. She's as elegant as I'd imagined her to be when I first saw her. It could be a young woman walking away from me and I stare after her. It takes me a while to realise she's left the book after all. The page is still open in my hands and at the same moment I focus on my name printed there I hear someone calling my name. It's Patricia, no doubt wondering why the new girl's slacking already, why I'm not doing whatever I'm supposed to be doing; certainly not this, sitting alone in the sunlight with dreams of fairies floating through my mind. I stand quickly, and for want of anywhere else, shove the little book into the pocket of my tunic. It fits perfectly, almost as if it was made for it.

➤·◄

12th September 1921

Dear Mr Gardner,

It was with great pleasure that I received your letter, with your extremely interesting and exciting news. We were especially delighted that it followed on so quickly from my sending you the approximate copy of my missive to Sir Arthur, who unfortunately has not yet been able to reply, being, as I'm sure he is, extremely taken up with the many demands on his time.

But to hear that we may be included in a book – and one written by Sir Arthur! That is thrilling indeed. Charlotte in particular could scarcely rein in her astonishment and delight.

Naturally, you will wish to view the fairy first, and you are most welcome to do so at any time you require. I am sure you will be satisfied with it. I can only express how pleased I am that Sir Arthur is undeterred by the naysayers all about him and is desirous only of discovering the Truth. In that, I shall remain his servant, most particularly so should he ever wish to visit in person. I believe it is laudable to turn the light of scientific enquiry upon what some would describe as an unknowable world, as well as upon that of touchable things. If he could achieve his wishes, and prove the existence of a spiritual realm—! But I shall try to set aside my excitement, and answer the questions you put, before turning to another thrilling matter.

I believe you are quite correct in your supposition that a sunny day is best for catching a sight of the little folk. It was indeed summer, an especially bright day, and almost noon when we had our glimpse, though both of us felt quite well, and there was no question of our being overwhelmed by heat stroke. There was a little haze in the air over the meadows, but once in the glen it was not especially hot, being pleasantly shaded by trees and with the cooling influence of the beck.

It is an interesting notion that 'higher vibrations' may be detected in the noontide shimmer, and indeed that it was some peculiarity of the day or something inherent within ourselves that made us able to see them. It is possible indeed that fairies lie outside our usual visible colour spectrum, though I must say that the little skeleton is quite visible in the shade of our outbuilding, at least with the assistance of my magnifying glass. Do you think there is something special about that lens, and perhaps that of a camera, that has the same effect?

To your next point, however, that we might have glimpsed some 'thought-form', a type of reflection of our innermost imaginings – I think that is what you meant? – I can say that the little body certainly possesses an objective reality, and I am sure when you visit you will come to the same conclusion.

You also posit that the fairies may be from a different branch of evolution from that of humanity, perhaps even springing from the same line as winged insects. Having seen the remains, I consider that rather likely. Indeed, the fragile wings are veined like those of a dragonfly, although the skeleton itself did remind me rather more of a bird. Perhaps they could be related to both somehow, or indeed neither? Without the examination of someone rather more expert in these matters, I doubt we shall be able to hit upon anything conclusive.

In answer to your last point, your certainty that Harriet's

tender age and innocence will assist in future sightings is very encouraging. As you say, Elsie and Frances are possibly now too old for such things. I am afraid, however, that the question of whether my granddaughter has some loose-knit ectoplasmic material in her body, giving her a special clairvoyant power, is beyond my ability to ascertain. I am also unsure as to whether the Wright girl and her cousin growing up and perhaps even falling in love should entirely end the possibility of their seeing fairies. I saw them myself after all, though no doubt with less clarity than Harriet, whose eyes are younger and sharper. She was certainly the first to notice them and draw my attention to their presence.

I so look forward to being able to discuss these matters in person. Until such time, and spurred onward by your news, I have not been idle. I rather felt that I should renew my acquaintance with the fairies, and attempt to find such evidence of the living beings as I can.

With that in mind I have several times turned my steps towards Cottingley Beck on my wanderings, often accompanied by Harriet's mother, who is most intrigued by the whole matter. We have naturally encouraged Harriet to go with us, being curious as to what she might espy, but we have been a little hampered in this by her own inclinations. I am sorry to report that my granddaughter has taken a sudden aversion to the place. She insists the fairy man stung her, though I am certain I saw no tiny spear or any possible means by which he could have done so. When asked why he would do such a thing, being a dear little creature as he is, she replies only that he did not like being looked at.

Sadly, I have not on any other occasion seen a fairy. Charlotte is the only one among us with anything out of the ordinary way to relate.

She was standing apart from us when it happened, as I had taken Harriet to examine some rather fine fungi that had sprung up at the base of a fallen ash tree. We had persuaded the child to come with us, even to venture close to the spot of her original sighting, but I am afraid she closed her eyes tight shut and refused to open them until I led her a distance away.

Charlotte remained by the beck, and I last saw her settling upon a low branch to better enjoy the cleansing air of the stream, her face dampened by the cold spray. She appeared quite serene, and so I was startled when she began calling for me.

We hurried to her side. I did not like her look; her countenance had paled, whilst her eyes glittered with almost unearthly excitement. For a moment she could not speak, though I kept asking 'What is it?', and Harriet was stricken and pulled incessantly on her mother's sleeve.

At length, Charlotte calmed enough to say 'little dancers!' and she pointed at the rock where I had found the fairy body. She went on to explain that she saw lights playing over the water, and thinking them nothing but reflections had, rather dreamily, half closed her eyes, when suddenly she made out a brighter flash among them, in the most exquisite shade of lightest turquoise. That was followed by one in soft green and another in lilac; and then she saw the swirl of skirts, the gleam of golden hair, and the points of tiny, bird-like eyes, which, she said, were 'quite dark'.

She thought she made out sounds also, as of diminutive pipes almost beyond the range of her hearing, and said she imagined she could have followed that sound all the way to Fairyland. She did admit later that it might simply have been the sound of birdsong combined with the powers of suggestion, but that, of course, is mere supposition.

That was when she had shouted, and the lights vanished at once.

The emotion they engendered was very marked and apparent however, for when she finished relating the incident she covered her face and burst into tears. I felt quite overcome myself. I wonder what the feelings of mankind shall be, when all may share in the certainty of the existence of such extraordinary beings! The thrill of it sounds in my blood!

For a full ten minutes, all my daughter-in-law could add was that they were 'so beautiful'. Harriet said nothing; she stood scowling by with her arms crossed over her chest, and refused to look for them at all. And so, after I had cast about and found nothing, we made our way home, where we scarcely knew what to do with ourselves for the wonder of it. I resolved to note it all down in my diary, so that I should forget nothing and could later, if called upon, recount it fully. It is by my side as I write.

Harriet watched as I made my record, though she continued rather sulky and refused to comment. She would only say that she thought the fairies ugly, and that they did not truly dance at all; and she would not be drawn further on the subject.

That is the whole of our first-hand experience since my last letter. It is not everything however, for I have endeavoured to be your faithful assistant and have made visits to certain of our neighbours to ask their views, concentrating particularly on those with young children or who live nearest the beck.

I recognise that the newspapers made assiduous enquiries following the article in *The Strand* which unveiled the photographs, but the villagers here are not the most forthcoming to strangers, and suspicion is easily aroused. Particularly telling, I thought, was their reaction as related in the *Westminster Gazette* this January (yes, I am rather afraid I saw it). That the local folk dismissed the story as untrue deterred me not at all, since that seemed entirely in character with their bluff way of repelling incomers. Of more interest was the comment that no one else had seen the fairies, but everyone in the village was aware of their supposed existence.

Of course, that could be taken to mean they all knew of the stories put about by Elsie and Frances. But it seemed to me suggestive of some older knowledge, particularly when viewed against their reluctance to speak of such matters, as if some deeper current prevented them.

At any rate, I decided to approach them openly, if not as a local of the requisite number of generations at least as a fellow resident, and ask them directly what I had before only alluded to in our limited conversations. I hoped in this way to overcome any reluctance they may harbour, but I am sorry to say they continued, if anything even more taciturn.

The Wrights would not see me at all, though I suppose I cannot blame them for it. The attention from various newspapers as well as the idle curious and impertinent sceptics must have greatly stretched their patience, and since you have been in regular contact with them yourself, it was scarcely worth placing further pressures upon the family.

But I found an equal measure of reluctance throughout the village. Heads were shaken; others laughed; one old gaffer, only slightly more talkative than the rest, told me to my face to 'have a care'.

Another grandam said not a word and left me standing in the doorway whilst she rustled about within. I had begun to doubt whether she intended to return when she appeared again, as silent as before, and pressed a battered volume into my hand. Then she closed the door in my face. The book was Edwin Sidney Hartland's *The Science of Fairy Tales: An Inquiry into Fairy Mythology*, though it is surely too old in its ideas to be of much use now. I suppose she was at least trying to be helpful, but there's 'nowt so queer as folk', as they say in these parts.

Needless to add, I shall continue my observations until such time as you can come. To that end, and in emulation of your experiments, I have sent for a camera, having made enquiries for the same type as was used by the Wright girl. The Midg quarter-plate should be here imminently, and I shall keep you apprised of the results; I may only hope to be as fortunate as she.

Again, it is a shame that Sir Arthur is unlikely to be able to see our little elfin skeleton in person. My daughter-in-law has a volume she particularly hoped he might sign; but such a great man must be under terrible pressures. We very much anticipate your own visit. To think that you were here in August, and we did not chance to meet! It is a pity that the Wright girl and her cousin had not then the opportunity to get more pictures, as they had the previous summer. As you stated, there was the most dismal rain. And it is true that a small seam of coal has been discovered in the locality, but there is not so very much disruption, I trust, as to prevent our own enquiries.

We shall hope for sunshine, and a steady hand to point the camera, and the good fortune to choose our moment; and we look forward to welcoming you to Cottingley as early as you are able.

Yours sincerely,
Lawrence H. Fenton

4

Once again I stare down, completely bewildered. Mrs Favell had selected the letter from her bureau with care, as if deciding what I might see and what was beyond me, and handed it over as if giving a treat to a dog. *This much, and no more.* Papers rustled enticingly – on purpose? She sat in silence while I read it aloud and she's silent now, but she still manages to convey her disdain. She stares at me staring at the letter, and I feel her gaze. I see the dark shape of her eyes in the periphery of my vision, in shadow, since she's sitting in her place by the window.

What an odd thought it had been, to think she might bear any relation to the lady in the letters. *Charlotte in particular could scarcely rein in her astonishment and delight.* That isn't Mrs Favell. Despite her invitation to read to her again, she remains stern, unsmiling, unbending. It occurs to me to wonder how long she has been alone. Is that why she's like this – is she lonely and bitter? Did she have a difficult life – has she been treated so very badly?

I should try to understand, even pity her. If my mother had lived, she might have one day grown frail. I might have been looking after her like this, or someone else would have. But Mrs Favell is nothing like my mother, and it's not as if I haven't tried; I did ask Patricia about her. She suddenly looked all interested and I waited for some kind of detail, but she only said, 'Perhaps, if you're interested in becoming her keyworker...?' I swiftly backtracked, saying something vague about my current duties, and both of us clammed up. Everyone does when it comes to Mrs Favell. Is it only that they don't like to be reminded of her presence? Whatever the reason, I haven't asked again. I don't want to be saddled with her any more than I am already.

But the letter's weird phrases are circling in my mind like the crows outside the window, pushing all else aside. Mrs Favell's room overlooks the little band of woodland at the back of the home – they pay extra for that, apparently – and there's a column of the birds hanging above it now, spiralling over some death they've found. *A summer's day. Vibrations. Loose-knit ectoplasmic material.* The writer had sounded as if he'd had to rein in his feelings at that part. And Sir Arthur hadn't responded after all – what a great shame.

I'm curious and full of questions, and annoyed because I know she won't answer them. One letter to reel me in, the next to keep me burning with curiosity. I tell myself that at least it's a break. I've been helping housekeeping all morning – one of their team, a young lad called Dan, called in sick – and my back aches from changing beds, the worst of them soiled. Patricia certainly wouldn't have allowed me to spare the time if Mrs Favell hadn't asked her directly, claiming her eyes were tired from the sunlight, although she hadn't even been outside. I was in the lounge with them at the time, but neither of them had acknowledged me and she doesn't acknowledge me now.

They're probably completely fake, I think. Edward Gardner, Conan Doyle's friend, might never have seen the letters either. Lawrence Fenton might have been judged a lunatic, locked away in an institution not that different to Sunnyside, and the letters were never sent anywhere or meant anything.

'Of course he *sent* them,' she says suddenly, her voice peremptory. 'He sent all of them.'

I look up, startled, my mind filling with more questions. Why then hasn't the world heard of the fairy skeleton? How did these letters come into her possession? But none of them are as insistent as: *Did she just read my mind?*

'I have them here now, all of them I think.' Her tone is conversational, as if this was what she had intended to talk about from the beginning. And perhaps she had; she can't be reading my mind, after all. It would be natural for anyone reading these letters to wonder such a thing. It wouldn't be so hard to work out what I was thinking.

'One wouldn't just throw away something of such interest, would one?' she goes on. 'One wouldn't simply leave it all behind.'

I feel a pang at that, remembering my flight from uni, all my possessions hastily shoved into bags. 'Did you know something of these people, then?' I ask. 'Are they your ancestors?'

She doesn't answer. Instead she says, 'Doyle thought you could see fairies until you fell in love. Have you ever been in love, Rose?'

I can't think how to reply and anyway, she doesn't wait for me. She says, 'You're a little different to the others, aren't you – *Rose?*' She puts a peculiar emphasis on the word, as if claiming me somehow, or as if it could mean something other than my name.

Paul's words return to me. *You know what's different about you, Rose?* And his answer: *You believe.*

But how can I?

I shake my head. 'I – well, I'm new here.'

'Such a shame. Still, I expect you'll soon fit in.'

Something inside me rails against the idea. I picture myself far away, in London maybe, or New York or Paris, in some fascinating job: media or journalism, or being a writer, living in a glass house or tucked away among the trees. And I remember something that Paul had said when he helped carry my bags into his house: *Welcome home* – only that – but why should it come to me now?

She must see something of my thoughts in my face because she adds, 'All these *bodies*. Old, sagging, sinking, smelling. All so physical. Cleaning up after us, is that your ambition, Rose? Is that your *dream?*'

She gives a condescending smile. It's easy to see why the other carers don't like her. But then, they probably don't *see* her, not like this. They wouldn't listen or linger to chat to her. Is that what happened to the girl Nisha told me about – did *she* listen to Mrs Favell? I could have returned her book now, of course, but I hadn't expected to be here at this moment. The little volume of poetry is in my locker. I hadn't wanted to keep it in my pocket, since it spoiled the line of my tunic and anyone might have noticed it. Anyone could have asked what I was doing with it.

I remind myself, defiantly, what Nisha had said about everyone getting a share of Edie's knitting, but that doesn't feel quite the same and I suppose it isn't. And so the urge had stolen over me to conceal it – or was it only that I'd wanted so badly to keep it, that lovely little volume with its touch of skin and enchanting words? I wouldn't, of course, but it's almost as if a fairy tale has been given to me to replace all the ones I've lost.

'You'd better get back to it then, Rose,' she says. 'Goodness, you are a quiet little thing, aren't you? Shouldn't you be talking to the residents, helping keep our minds active? God forbid we should all be reliant on *my* conversation.'

She gets up from her chair, lithe as a girl, and I push myself up too. I don't allow myself to put a hand to my aching back. I don't think I could bear the look on her face if I did. I feel I've been judged and fallen short, that there was some response I should have given, and I blush. I remember the essays I wrote for my degree: the social significance of turn-of-the-century fiction. But Fenton's letters feel as if they were formed by an earlier time – and I suppose they were, since he was a grandfather when he wrote them. Still, I know she's right, that I should have more to say, something interesting. It just all seems so very long ago.

'Well, they couldn't have found a skeleton,' I try. 'An interesting hoax, wasn't it? Strange that it didn't become as famous as the Cottingley pictures.' Even as I speak, I imagine her sarcastic response. *Of course* it was a hoax – what did I think, that a fairy skeleton could really exist? I'd stated the obvious, and Mrs Favell has little patience for the obvious.

'I won't keep you.' She replaces the letter in the bureau –

which surely must be her own property, so different from the regulation furniture – closes and locks it. She gives me an odd look as she drops the key into a ceramic bowl, alongside several glossy, ripe red apples. Why bother to lock it if she's going to leave the key so openly? Is it a kind of test? Would the girl who worked here before me have come snooping, to see what she could find? But I'm not like that. Mrs Favell can trust me.

I feel an odd compulsion to bow my head before I walk away, but I resist it. Why does she have such an effect? It's as if she's the lady of the manor, summoning and dismissing me as she wishes. I report to Patricia, not to her, and no matter how she might single me out, or why, I don't need to humour her. I don't have to ask any more questions. I make up my mind to avoid her as much as I can.

And I wonder why Nisha should have felt the need to warn me to be careful, when something about Mrs Favell demands that all by herself.

5

It isn't long before I catch Nisha alone. She's on her break, sipping coffee in the staff kitchen and looking at her watch. Breaks are strictly timed around here. The kitchen is tiny and windowless, situated along a narrow corridor behind reception, accessed via a keycard. The staff office is opposite, which in contrast to the kitchen is a goldfish bowl of sheet glass with a view of nothing but the corridor. Patricia is in there now, sitting at the desk, ready to frown upon anyone emerging from their break even if they're on time. It's her view that carers care, always – why would we want time to ourselves? But no one really loiters in here. There isn't room for loitering. The alternative is to go and sit in the residents' lounge, where social interaction is encouraged by the careful arrangement of the chairs, but right now, I can't stand the babble of the television. It's always turned up too loud, for the hard of hearing who won't wear hearing aids or can't get on with them, and I still haven't got used to it.

Besides, I want to talk to Nisha. I smile and nod at her. I don't need to look around to see there's no one else in here.

'Kettle's just boiled,' she says.

I busy myself with finding a clean mug and teaspoon and say in a casual tone, 'You mentioned the girl who was here before me. Do you mind if I—'

'I shouldn't have said anything.'

The clock ticks, too loud and too fast. I can't be subtle; she'll soon be gone. 'Why did she leave?'

Her face swivels towards me. 'Look, girls are always leaving. Some of them don't see it as a vocation. They just do it as a job, and you really can't. It's never just a job.'

I have no answer to that, and she sighs.

'It's a high-turnover kind of place. With Theresa it just went a bit wrong, that's all.'

'Wrong?'

'There was a misunderstanding. I think that's what it was. Mrs Favell's not so bad. Theresa thought she'd given her something, a gift, only it got reported missing and there was a big fuss. Patricia wanted to search her locker and Theresa wouldn't agree, so the police were called, and they found it in there. It all got a bit nasty. Theresa – I liked her, you know? She seemed nice. Not like a thief, but you can't tell by looking. We do sometimes get those here too.'

I think of the book secreted in my locker and force myself to meet her eye. 'No, I don't suppose you can tell. Like you say, it could have been a mistake. Mrs Favell forgot she gave it to her, maybe?'

Nisha mumbles something under her breath.

'Pardon?'

'I said she doesn't forget, not that one.' She sips her coffee, though she doesn't look as if she tastes it. 'I don't know. Theresa said she gave it to her, but how can you be sure?'

I picture a girl wearing a tunic like mine, leaning against a wall, sobbing. Mandy and Sarah looking on while the police riffle through her locker. Mrs Favell watching too, pressing her lips together so tightly they almost disappear, her eyes bright in the dimness of the corridor, though black – soulless.

'This gift. Was it a book?' I ask.

Nisha looks puzzled. 'A book – what? Who'd want a book? No, it was that necklace she always wears. She said it was taken from her bedside table while she slept.' She pulls a face. 'As if anyone could sneak up on that one. She never misses a trick.'

It's only a book, I tell myself as I get through the afternoon, but the thought of it nestled in my locker gnaws at my mind. Everyone knows that Mrs Favell wanted me to read for her, she asked Patricia about it right there in the lounge, so why shouldn't I have it? I might just have borrowed it for a time. I *was* only borrowing it – I only wanted to look at it again, perhaps show it to Paul, and then I'd give it back. And Nisha was right. Who would want to steal it?

All the same, I'm glad when the clock says I can leave.

The first thing I do is go to retrieve the little volume of poetry. The lockers are situated in a narrow room behind the staff kitchen, narrowed still further by their metal bulk so that it's little more than a corridor leading nowhere. I hear voices as soon as I open the door. One of the carers, Sarah, is in there, talking loudly to Mandy about a new wine bar that's opened in town. She segues smoothly into *Coronation Street*'s latest plot turn and I smile, not wanting to open my locker in front of them. Sarah pauses when she sees me and stands back against the wall, pointedly making room for me, waiting for me to be gone. She watches as I take the key from my pocket.

I block her view with my body, fitting the key into the lock and turning it. I don't see why I should worry about what she thinks. I haven't done anything wrong. Still, I can imagine her expression if she sees the book – something old, its leather and gilding so out of place she would know at once it could never be mine. I hear Nisha's words again, asking if Mrs Favell has given me anything; mine, reassuring her she hasn't.

Resentment squirms through me. I know, no matter what excuses I repeat to myself, that they would gossip. They might even tell Patricia, cast it in a bad light. I can't afford for them to do that, not being new. What would she think? I won't give them the chance – or the satisfaction.

There are other books in my locker, other paperwork. There's a staff manual and a Sunnyside brochure, complete with an entry code for when the front door is locked at night – hardly very sensible to print it out, especially if they're worried about theft, but clearly the convenience outweighed security. There are procedural instructions, care standards, fliers about first aid courses, manual handling, adult safeguarding and others, not forgetting information about the NVQ I'll have to face if I'm going to stay here, as I so blithely promised at my interview. The little book is wholly out of place, its gilt edges gleaming like treasure in a dragon's cave. I grab the navy-blue cardigan that's hanging at the back of my locker and wrap it around the book, feeling like a shoplifter.

'Settling in?' Sarah's voice is loud at my ear.

The cardigan slips from my hands and I catch at it, then let go. The book falls with it and I hope the fabric will cover it. I'm lucky and it does, but the slap of the book hitting the floor is plainly audible.

'Jesus. Jumpy much? That bad, is it?' Sarah's voice is mocking.

My laughter sounds false to my own ears. 'It's fine.' I bend and scoop up the cardigan and the book with it. I half expect a couple of burly policemen to come elbowing their way into the room.

'If you say so.' Sarah sounds like she's trying not to laugh.

I curl my lips into what I hope is a bright smile. 'Well, see you both tomorrow.' I let myself out, feeling their gaze on my back until I can close the door behind me. Nisha's words run through my mind, about *those* people, the ones who only do this for a job; about thieves; her tale of Theresa.

I step out into the evening. All the colours are intensified with that odd, warm light that presages rain, everything draped in long shadows. I refuse to look back towards the windows ranked behind me. I don't want to see if anyone is watching me go.

6

The flowers from yesterday are in their vase by the sink, their heads drooping, petals already falling. There's a note on the fridge: GONE TO PUB WITH MARCUS and a couple of kisses. No big welcome tonight then. Marcus, Paul's brother, lives a few streets away. If they've headed to the White Hart they could be hours – spending money we don't have. I sigh and shake off the bitterness. Everyone deserves a little fun and it's not as if we'll live here for ever; he won't always have the chance. I make a sandwich and eat it standing between the tiny open-plan kitchen and the ratty beige sofa. I think about Mrs Favell's gift. It's a beautiful thing. I find myself thinking it's a pity she gave it to me outside, where no one else could see – if they had, perhaps I really could have kept it. But had she done that on purpose? Whether she did or not, I shouldn't have hidden it. I should have made her take it back; tomorrow, that's what I'll do.

What was it that made her choose poetry as her gift to me? I think of my mother's volumes lining the stairs, all those windows onto other places, other lives. I decide that out of everyone at Sunnyside, Mrs Favell must have thought I'd appreciate it the most. Perhaps I should be flattered. Should I even feel some kind of kinship with her?

You remind me of me, Rose.

I remember the sharp gleam of her eyes and shake off the idea. For a moment I almost think I can smell her scent, so like my mother's, and I pull a face. Tomorrow, I'll go to Patricia myself. I'll report Mrs Favell's attempted gift, get my story in first. That way she'll know I'm honest. She'll tell me to give it back and I'll say it's already done and she'll nod and approve. If Mrs Favell is playing some kind of game, that's checkmate to me.

I find myself rubbing my fingers together, savouring the touch not of an ancient leather book cover but the dry paper of a letter. I picture the sharply slanted handwriting telling of peculiar things, the language of upright gentlemen in darkly furnished rooms, men of respectability and good sense, at least until they decided to believe that fairies could be found at the bottom of a little Yorkshire garden.

You know what's different about you, Rose?

I smile wryly. Perhaps La Belle Dame sans Merci had us all in thrall. When I'd held the letter in my hand, I too felt half bewitched. Or perhaps Mrs Favell really is reading my mind, feeding me the things I want to hear when I want to hear them. I pull a face at that word, *feeding*, but it's the one that feels right.

Perhaps her gift of the poem was a little too apposite. Or perhaps she's just a half-mad old lady telling of mad things, and my mind is running away with itself, far too eager to fill in the blanks.

I'm not quite ready to return to the Keats; that's something to be savoured. Instead I step into the lounge, take my laptop from the cupboard and switch it on. I got it for uni and haven't used it much since updating my CV. It whirrs and the screen lights up and I sit in front of the blissfully silent television, googling Sir Arthur Conan Doyle and the fairies. Myriad links appear and there they are: a row of pictures depicting little girls surrounded by strange forms, figments of their imagination come to life.

I think back to a long-ago day, when I'd stood before a similar picture in a museum, my mother at my side. I had gazed at a young girl in a white dress, half smiling, and the little fairy next to her: too big, too clumsy, too flat, holding out a bunch of flowers as lifeless as she. Even as a child I had been surprised that they ever could have fooled anyone, but then, they hadn't been accustomed to trick photography back then. They were more innocent times. It must have been so much easier to take people in; they trusted what they saw and heard. They hadn't expected that young girls could have concocted such a lie.

I scroll down the screen. And there, listed on a website of copyright-free texts, is a book that Arthur Conan Doyle had written: *The Coming of the Fairies*.

I hadn't heard of it before, although it was hinted at in the letters. I never realised he had gone so far in trying to convince the world to believe. Even his own creation, the relentlessly rational Sherlock Holmes, never would have stood for it. The incongruity makes it even more strange. Doyle surely couldn't have been serious.

I examine the contents page – 'How the Matter Arose', 'Observations of a Clairvoyant in the Cottingley Glen', 'Some Subsequent Cases' – and catch certain phrases: 'dancing goblin', 'wood elves in a ring', and 'I am so glad you like the fairies!'. I dip into the text to discover Doyle expressing his hope that one day special 'psychic spectacles' might be invented, making the unseen visible, enabling anyone to see fairies all of the time.

Then I catch the name E. L. Gardner, and everything becomes stranger still. Apparently Gardner believed not only in fairies but in pixies and goblins too. He thought children really could see them and play with them. He'd had one of the Cottingley pictures enlarged and hung in his hall where he could see it every day.

Yet despite it all, there was some attempt at a scientific approach, at rationality. Doyle wondered if the fairies' colours belonged to a part of the spectrum beyond the ability of the human eye to detect. Hadn't Fenton suggested something of the kind? He'd said Doyle was turning the light of scientific enquiry upon the 'unknowable world'. Perhaps in a way, the author wasn't so very distant from his creation, Sherlock Holmes, after all.

It strikes me that Doyle was also an adherent of spiritualism, that he visited mediums in the hope of contacting deceased members of his family. But it must have been easy to believe in the existence of an afterlife back then, when so many people did. An unbidden picture flashes before me: the residents in the lounge at Sunnyside, the 'departure lounge' as someone in housekeeping had called it, and my mother sitting among them, a book on her lap.

I push the image away. Doyle had sought evidence that the world wasn't bare and desolate and empty, that the afterlife not only existed but could be reached. Perhaps if he could prove that fairies were real, it would be easier to swallow the rest; it would show that life wasn't quite so soulless after all. He'd *wanted* to believe.

I open my eyes and am almost surprised to see the bright screen in front of me. *The Coming of the Fairies* is still there, a real thing – I hadn't imagined it – and I download the file to read later. Then an idea strikes me and I run a search within the text for Lawrence H. Fenton, then Lawrence, Laurence for good measure and then just Fenton. There's nothing. I search for Charlotte and Harriet and come up empty each time.

I frown. This must be the book that Lawrence had hoped to be included in; there surely couldn't be another. Had Doyle realised that the skeleton, if nothing else, was a hoax, and made the wise choice to ignore it? If only he'd done the same with the Cottingley photographs, his reputation would have been intact. Elsie Wright and Frances Griffiths wouldn't have spent their lives being plagued by questions that must have been increasingly hard, perhaps even painful, to answer.

And yet a little bit of magic, one that had entranced so many, would have vanished from the world.

For a second I picture Charlotte Favell, a sly smile marring her features, bending over cream-coloured paper, her elegant hand dipping a pen into an inkwell, smoke-coloured letters flowing across the page. But why would she write such things? It was too elaborate an invention. And I remember there was another book referred to in the letters: *The Science of Fairy Tales.*

I discover that too is real, and freely available, since it was written in 1891. I click 'Download' and it appears on my desktop, an artefact from the past materialising in the present by the wonders of technologies not dreamed of when they were written. Would that too have seemed like magic?

As I close down the various search windows, a familiar word snags at my eye.

Sunnyside.

My mind flashes back to my application letter – *Would love to work in a caring environment* – and I remember googling the home. But this is different. There is the name *Doyle*, together with the word *asylum*, and I click on the link, following this new path. I find something so surreal it's almost like another fairy tale.

Sir Arthur Conan Doyle, it transpired, was born into a family who liked to paint fairies. His uncle, Richard 'Dickie' Doyle, was celebrated for his pictures and they were immortalised in a book, *In Fairyland*. His father, Charles Altamont Doyle, had different fortunes. Frustrated by the demands of his job and the need to support his family, he retreated into alcoholism and the fantasy world created by his art. Eventually he was committed to an asylum that he dubbed, somewhat ironically, 'Sunnyside'.

A self-portrait appears on the screen, showing him surrounded by little figures, engrossed in tormenting him – are they fairies or demons? It's hard to tell the difference. I stare at it. Is his asylum the same as *my* Sunnyside, now a care home? But it can't be. That wasn't even the real name of his institution, and anyway, it was situated in Montrose. It's a strange coincidence and nothing more, even if it feels as if some dark, twisted magic is at work –

but isn't that what coincidences are, really?

It might not even be a coincidence. It might be the very reason Mrs Favell chose to live there. I shake my head at the unlikely idea. Who would choose a place to live just because of its name?

I think of the stories I like to tell Paul, about our home by the sea, or in a great city, or in a forest. I realise that none of those have names, not really. I don't even know where any of them are; they're everywhere and nowhere. Do I really have belief – or do I only have stories?

I dwell on it while the light fades outside the window, wondering what it would have been like to have such a sense of possibility; to really think that little faces might be peeping from the shrubbery beyond the glass. Then comes a loud bang, *knock-knock*, and I half jump out of my seat. A face presses up against the window – pale but human-sized, the mouth distorted into a leer, the tongue practically licking the pane, and I realise it's Paul. He's back, he's drunk, and he thought it would be funny to surprise me. I laugh, though my heart flutters as if something as small and fragile as a wren is trapped within my ribs.

I go to let him in and he grabs my waist, spinning me around. His kiss is clumsy and I push him off.

'Wine,' he announces, brandishing the bottle he's brought back with him, a hunter with his spoils. Distantly, I hear the tuneless singing of other revellers expelled from the Hart. I close the door against it and he plants another wet kiss on my forehead, grabs my hand and pulls me into the kitchen, starts rattling through a drawer for the bottle opener.

He's distracted by something on the countertop. 'What's this?'

It's the book, small, old, out of place and beautiful. I have no memory of leaving it there.

He sets down the bottle and opens it at the ribbon marker. "'Alone,'" he says, "'and palely loitering." Not any more, love. How was work?'

'Fine,' I say, not wanting to talk about it. It would take too long to encompass it, to make him understand how I feel. Anyway, none of it matters; the job won't be for long. It never was meant to be permanent.

I smile as he hands me a too-full glass and clink it against his. The wine is rich and sweet, better than usual, and I smile wider. He grabs me around the waist again and nuzzles in close. He smells of beer and, faintly, of man-sweat.

'Palely,' I hear between the kisses he plants along my neck, 'loitering.'

I laugh for real this time. Even drunk, he can always make me feel better. His arms are around me and they are strong and I lean against him.

'Take me to bed,' he says, gruff and low, his stubble brushing my cheek, 'and read me poetry, you sexy bitch.'

The next minute I'm on the bed but it's him who reads me poetry, bursts of it between kisses that taste of wine. He enunciates each word as if it's the last, grabbing my questing hand, then both of them. He holds them in one of his, inclining his neck to read the better, as if I'm getting in the way of his recitation. I can hear the beginnings of too-loud music booming through the walls from next door, but for once I don't care; I'm caught up by the words, as seductive as his hands, and by the laughter that dances in his eyes.

'She look'd at me as she did love,
And made... sweet... moan.'

He punctuates these words by making appreciative noises against my neck, then moves to undo the zip of my work tunic.

'And sure in language strange she said –
"I love thee true."

She took me to her elfin grot,
And there she wept, and sigh'd full sore,
And there I shut her wild wild eyes
With kisses four.'

He leans over, flutters gentle kisses against my eyelids, each in turn, and then again. He draws back, holding the book in one hand, forcing the spine wide, and I want to tell him not to damage it. But I'm always too careful, with books and probably everything else, and I kiss him instead, nipping the lobe of his ear between my teeth. He makes a show of tearing himself away, wiping his lips on the back of his hand to murmur, 'Sweet... *moan*.'

I laugh. He tosses the book aside and I snatch for it, too late, and hear it land on the floor. I tell myself it's safe enough and close my eyes again; it's as if his words have pushed it all away, Sunnyside with its staff and their cold looks, the girl who was fired, and her: Mrs Favell, banished, just like that.

A fading rose fast withereth too.

He murmurs the words; it almost doesn't seem like his voice and I feel the slightest brush of something on my cheek. My eyes flicker open to see him gazing down, not into my face but at my arm. For a moment he wraps his hand almost all the way around it, gazing down at the tattoo between his fingers. I squirm away from his grip and instead he kisses the rose painted there, and then my lips, and everything recedes again until it's dark and we're spent, and he reaches out for the lamp, hits his wineglass and sends it plummeting to the floor.

I sit bolt upright and lunge after it. The glass hasn't smashed; it's lying on the carpet, only a smear of liquid remaining inside. The book is lying next to it, splayed open with the pages downward. I pick it up and it's too heavy, I feel that at once, and I know it's ruined before I see the pages crimsoned with wine, darkening at the edges to the colour of old blood.

'Sorry, love.' Paul tucks his chin into my neck and his hair brushes my shoulder. The bass thrumming through the wall is louder now, but he doesn't seem to hear it. I push him off. He's waiting for me to tell him it's all right, but I can't. I'm suddenly furious. I jump up from the bed, all of it returning: Mandy's stares, Nisha's words, and most of all, Mrs Favell's withering smile.

'It's just a book, love.'

I turn on him. 'It's *never* just a book.' He should know that. He should know how I feel – yet how can he? Still, I walk around the bed and grab the first cloth that comes to hand – or perhaps I choose it to spite him. I dab at the pages with Paul's shirt, but I know it's useless. Nothing will get rid of the stain.

The book is ruined. I bring it to my face and can no longer smell the old pages, the passage of time; there is only stale alcohol and the trace of Paul's aftershave. There's no way I can give it back to Mrs Favell now. And I feel sad, not only because the option has been taken from me, but because it was such a beautiful thing, and mine for so short a time, and so very quickly spoiled.

7

Under the watchful eye of Sandra, the Activities Coordinator who comes into Sunnyside twice weekly, I shuffle a well-worn pack of cards. I'm not quite sure how it happened but I've got both Edie Dawson and Mrs Favell at my table, one smiling, one not. We're playing rummy, which Sandra proclaims to be inclusive, stimulating and *fun*. It's not an especially difficult activity to organise I shouldn't think, but she took one look at Mrs Favell's face at the suggestion of cushion catch – inclusive, good for dexterity and *fun* – and that was that.

I deal the cards. Edie nods as if I've done something clever and Mrs Favell slides her cards towards herself, holding them close to her chest, giving them an appraising glance. She looks at me in much the same way and says, 'I do hope you enjoyed the book.'

I jump in my seat. I somehow hadn't expected her to mention it in front of anybody else and I wonder if that's because I genuinely thought she'd been setting me up for trouble. I feel relieved, then anxiety bubbles through at the memory of what happened to her gift.

'My mother gave it to me.' She picks up an unknown card and places a diamond on the discard pile with a sharp snap.

An image: Paul holding the book in one hand and me in the other, reciting from its pages and laughing over the words. I shake my head and murmur something about how generous she is. Edie's focused on the table, already befuddled. I don't think she's really listening.

'It *was* very valuable.' She raises her head and stares into me.

She *knows*. I don't know how, but she does. I shrivel under her look, trying to persuade myself she can't possibly, that's it's just a way she has of giving the impression she sees everything. It's a consequence of her superior, brusque manner, something bred into her, a demeanour she's had many years to perfect.

'Why don't you get rid of your heart, Mrs Dawson?' Mrs Favell's tone is clipped. She doesn't call Mrs Dawson Edie, like everyone else. She doesn't really call anyone by their first name, I realise – except, perhaps, me. On the other hand everyone calls her Mrs Favell, even the manager. Not Charlotte and certainly not Char, Lottie, or God forbid, Charlie.

'Oh,' Edie says, fumbling to pick up Mrs Favell's discarded card before casting away one of her own, 'I'm slow – a bit slow. More used to my knitting.' She nods at me over her half-moon glasses.

'She's never coming back, you know.'

Edie hears that all right. We turn to Mrs Favell, both wearing the same expression of dismay.

'Your daughter's glad to have left you behind. They all are, don't you know, after a time. People think their offspring will look after them. So glad I never troubled over it. Some would say I miss out, not having constant visitors, but it's scarcely any different, and I saved myself a world of bother.'

Edie's mouth trembles.

'Of course your daughter's not glad,' I say, patting Edie's hand. Her skin looks dry but it's as soft as draped silk. 'Don't you listen.'

'It'll be the fees next.' Mrs Favell, usually separate, usually silent, will not shut up. 'Too expensive here. Who knows where you might end up? Some places are awful. It's not as if they can go and look them over first. They'll have talked about flying you out there, though not for long.' Her eyes go distant, as does her voice. 'Why linger, like this?'

'Mrs Favell,' I say, unused to challenging her, 'that's unkind, and uncalled for.'

'The truth often is,' she says. She throws down her cards and they land in a fan across the table, muddling what's been played and what hasn't. 'I think I shall go and read what remains of my books.'

'She doesn't know those things.' Edie's fingers grasp at my arm, her grip weak, her skin so very soft and vulnerable. 'Does she? She *can't* know.'

Her eyes are unfocused and tears are welling, running down her cheeks. I'm horrified, then angry. What was Mrs Favell thinking? A part of me knows she was telling the truth, that she's perceptive – perceptive and unkind, even cruel – and for a moment I hate her.

I pat Edie's hand again, feeling helpless. Another tear spills over and rolls onto her cheek. She's rocking herself, her eyes unfocused, looking at – what? I wonder if there's anything so awful as someone old and alone being in pain – and I suddenly realise she might die this way, sorrowing over a daughter who never comes, wishing for a grandchild she never sees, all the gentle lies she shielded herself with stripped away.

The thought is unbearable, but I swallow it down and murmur useless words of comfort. I tell her it's nonsense – I suggest that it's all lies, although I do not use the word. I don't know if Edie's convinced; she doesn't look at me. It takes me a minute to realise that Mrs Favell is standing by the door, having turned to look back at us. There's no remorse in her eyes. They're cold, like everything about her. She *wanted* this. She's enjoying it.

Lies. I can taste them on my tongue. They feel hopeless in the face of the truth.

As if summoned by my gaze she strides back across the room, leaning over the table and resting her bony knuckles on the chaos of playing cards. She's not looking at Edie, isn't concerned with her any longer. 'Life decisions,' she says. 'We make them or we don't. No point in crying over them when it's already too late – is it, Rose?'

I'm too flummoxed by her words to respond, and anyway she's gone, stalking off with her flowery scent and her pearls and her blouse, which today is the softest, sweetest pink.

Across the room, Sandra pushes herself up from her table, watching Mrs Favell leave. She opens her mouth to call out but Mrs Favell's expression must stop her because she shrugs at me as if to say, 'What can you do?' Then she sees Edie rocking herself over the ruined game, sees her tears, and lets out a concerned sound. She starts across the room to sort out the new girl's table, which somehow seems to have become a terrible mess.

✤

I don't see Mrs Favell again until lunch. For the rest of the morning I spend as much time as I can with Edie, bringing her biscuits and orange juice and tea, which all sit beside her, untouched. I'm being extra kind to her and she knows it. It isn't helping. She keeps giving me smiles without any life in them and she's just as blank as she eats, swallowing the mouthfuls of chicken I cut for her, the soft-boiled cabbage and mushy potatoes. Her gaze is somewhere else, on the other side of the world perhaps. I wonder if I could reach her daughter on the phone. I could get them talking, cheer her up, but when I ask Nisha about it she pulls a face and shakes her head, as if she's tried all that already and found it hopeless.

I had half wondered if Mrs Favell would be too ashamed to come down for lunch, but of course she's no such thing. She marches in, heads straight to my table and stops in front of me. She holds something out. I notice that her hand, unlike so many of the residents', doesn't shake. The object she's holding is a letter. I recognise the handwriting at once.

'You wanted this,' she says, loud enough for everyone to hear, and conversations cease. The scrape of cutlery falls silent. Faces turn towards us, blurred shapes all around, and I can't look at them. There's only the letter, and her words, hanging in the air.

She thrusts it towards me and I take it. I open my mouth, wanting to explain to everyone that I didn't ask for this, didn't even want it, but the truth is, I *do* want it. I gather myself to say, 'Of course, I'll read it to you later, if you like.'

She cuts me off short. 'Take more care of it than the other.'

Then she walks away, and just like that, the murmuring of voices begins again. Plates are gathered in. Plastic aprons rustle. Somewhere, a fork or a knife falls to the floor. It's too late to protest and I'm left holding the letter. I can see from the first few lines that it's a new one, just for me this time, something I can read alone. I wonder why she gave it to me this way. At least she can't accuse me of stealing it, but the way she spoke – *you wanted this* – made it sound as if I'd asked her for it, even coerced her. And her, an old lady. Is that what people will think? Is that what she *wanted* them to think?

Suddenly I know they will. It's what they'll *choose* to think, despite my protest about reading to her. Everyone must know she doesn't really need me to do that. And I never did report her gift of the book. Now I can't. Patricia will want me to give it back, and how can I? There would be an even worse fuss.

I start to set down the letter, seeing just in time the pool of liquid spreading across the table where Edie has spilled her juice. The cup is still in her hand. She's shaking worse than ever and I reach out and steady it for her. She's never been this bad, not that I've seen. I don't suppose she'll be able to knit anything today. She won't manage the needles. I place her cup on the table and she stares as it slides around in the moisture. She doesn't watch me slip the letter into my pocket. I can't bring myself to fold it and it juts from my tunic like an accusation.

Take more care of it than the other.

I still feel the sting of her words. I want to tear the letter to pieces; I can't wait to read what it says.

17th September 1921

Dear Mr Gardner,

I dare say you did not expect another letter so soon after your own, but I could barely contain myself until your visit, which we now anticipate as a fixed event on the 21st. I have news to impart that would not wait, for we have triumphed – I have before me two photographs of the fairies!

I hope I do not delude myself when I say they are far better than any of us could have hoped. Some would say they are more nebulous and uncertain than those of Elsie Wright and Frances Griffiths, but I think in some peculiar way that has become their strength.

In the first you see the stream, with the little rock where I found the body. Do you make out the darting lights before it? Look closely and you will see tiny forms within – there is the merest suggestion of legs and arms, and the most brilliant points of brightness, you see, are in the form of wings. If you could only see their colours! Perhaps their brilliance is something connected with the speed of movement – although then every hummingbird must carry its own halo, so these must be quicker still.

The second shows my dear little Harriet. See how rapt she is about the sprite just approaching her from below! She looks almost afraid. She is a tentative little thing – but her fascination is plain. And the figure is clearer yet than in the first. Indeed, I believe it might even be the same pippin-faced fellow I saw before, though I cannot be certain of identifying individuals from among them. Indeed, I must hold the photograph close to my face to see the detail; I am afraid I have quite belied the spirit of Sherlock Holmes, for I have somehow mislaid my magnifying glass.

Still, I believe I can make out the fairy's form clearly enough, though to be sure, his movement has rendered it a little indistinct. Harriet was rather frozen in place, and so you see quite plainly her fair curls and long-lashed eyes, so like her father's. Along with these prints, I have also enclosed some photographs I took of the little skeleton. You may imagine how impatient I have been whilst I had them processed – I heard that Mr Wright has a darkroom under the stairs, but I have none, and had to send them out.

I dare say you will find the images of the skeleton the most interesting, not only for their clarity, but for the fact that you will have seen nothing like it in the whole course of your enquiries. I long to hear your response – though I am now caught up entirely in the thought of finding again the living creatures, for how gay and gladsome they look, engaged in their darting and dancing!

What the photographs lack in definition they make up for, I think, in the expression of that movement. Though of course your expert, Snelling, referred to some movement in the Wright photographs, I confess – and I trust you will not be offended – I found it difficult to detect. In these, it is unmistakeable. They are redolent of life.

Another difference is in the size of the little beings. In the previous photographs they appear to be about seventeen or eighteen inches high. Perhaps the girls were fortunate to meet with a higher order of fairy? These are much smaller, but very bright.

It is quite the stir in our household, and we are impatient to share our joy in the matter with the world at large. Do you really think Sir Arthur will be unable to come? Perhaps, with Harriet to accompany him, he might even glimpse the fairies himself! I am certain he would be thrilled by their presence, as we all are.

My daughter-in-law in particular is seized with fairy fervour, and often wends her way down to the glen. I should add that she took the enclosed photographs of the living fairies herself. I would have liked to have done it, but my old legs are less nimble of late, and I often remain at the house to keep company with Harriet whilst her mother plays the detective for us all.

Alas, I did not see the fairies this time. The descriptions and indeed the photographs are Charlotte's, though the excitement is my own. It scarcely surpasses hers, in recent days. As I said, she has quite thrown herself into the project. She will sit by the beck for an entire morning or afternoon, staring through the camera lens and waiting for a glimpse; and though the weather is turning rather chill, she says she does not feel it.

She had also of late grown desirous of borrowing my key to the outhouse, and would stand staring at the little skeleton for hours together, but she began to worry that something would happen to it, or that it might be 'stolen away'. I am sure, having kept silence on its existence with all outside the family save yourself and Sir Arthur, it is safe enough, but she has persuaded me to take it into the house. She placed the box under her bed herself, and says its proximity is a great relief to her.

To be entirely open and honest, I am somewhat relieved

that she no longer feels the need to constantly open the box and gaze at it. I have done so on only one further occasion, to take its photograph. Is it not a peculiar object? The decay has progressed no further, and it remains quite intact, as you will see.

But soon you may examine it for yourself. I anticipate the day. We shall not cease until then to obtain further evidence, but I am certain we already possess such that the world will fall before all your arguments.

It will be, as Sir Arthur so eloquently put it in his momentous article in *The Strand*, an epoch-making revelation.

Sincerely yours,
Lawrence H. Fenton

PS. It is interesting you say in your last that Elsie Wright also referred to the fairies being ugly, though it seems she witnessed some kind of transformation from beauty to ugliness all in an instant. I had thought that Harriet's use of the word could only be the insignificant outburst of a child. It is hard to imagine such beauty as the fairies possess dissolving to its opposite. But good and evil exist in all men, and so perhaps it is with these little beings. Perhaps it is only that they wear the honest reflection of their inner thoughts and feelings on the outside, rather than hiding them within, as we do! Harriet might merely have glimpsed some little aversion to our disruption of their lives, which would seem reasonable enough, since we were present at the passing of the tiny maid. That would explain, I suppose, how beauteous Charlotte has thought them since – they have forgotten all, as the mayfly forgets its mortality and flits gladsome in the sunshine, and are quite restored.

8

I read the letter twice. I don't have time and hope I haven't been missed, but I can't resist. If my phone wasn't shut away in my locker, as per regulations, I'd photograph it. I brought it to the only place I could think of to gain a little privacy – I'm in the loo, hoping no one else comes in. So far, they haven't.

How very strange the letter is, how redolent of another life, another time. I wish I could have met the writer – to know, at least, that he was real. I wish I could believe in the words, slanting in beautiful cursive across the page. How lovely, then, the story would have been.

And yet there are no photographs with the letter, no proof they ever existed. Perhaps Mrs Favell has them, and withheld them – is that why she put this into my hands? Does she want to taunt me with the possibility, to enjoy making me ask for them? After her behaviour over our card game I know her to be capable of it. It was just so bald; so vindictive. I try telling myself it was really Edie's daughter that had earned her frustration and she only wanted Edie to see the truth. Or that Mrs Favell has some reason for her bitterness, that she's alone in the world and not as content with that as she likes to appear. *People think their offspring will look after them. So glad I never troubled over it.* I have no concept of what her life was like before Sunnyside, how difficult it might have been. She might have been forced to be strong, to eradicate all signs of weakness to get where she wanted to be. In some odd way, she might think she's helping me to do the same. Maybe she thinks she was helping Edie.

This letter could be her way of making some apology. I almost wish, if it meant I could see the photographs too, that she'd said worse and been more sorry.

I can imagine the pictures so very clearly. I see a young girl with widened eyes, her lips parted with wonder – or is it fear? Her face is frozen but somehow I can't read her expression. Her grandfather had wanted to believe her fascinated, but had he only seen what he wanted to see? It's interesting that he had thought the Cottingley photographs lifeless; so that wasn't just the impression of my more modern and jaded eye. And yet he had believed in the truth of his own pictures, in their life, their movement, their reality. But he hadn't even seen them being taken at first hand. The photographer had been his daughter-in-law: Charlotte.

It is easy to picture her too, although that makes me uncomfortable, for somehow she has *my* Charlotte's face. I see her eyes, so coldly blue, staring down at a dusty, tiny skeleton, coffined in a wooden box. Enchanted by it, even obsessed. Was that the start of whatever had changed her? Was she so entirely caught by – what? Magic? Curiosity? The desire for something *more*?

Is that why Mrs Favell has shown this to me – because beneath her coldness, she shares some of those feelings?

I cast my eyes over the letter a third time, greedy for its words. After this, I might never see it again. She gave it to me in front of everyone but that doesn't mean I can keep it, or that I should. I'll take it back to her as soon as I'm done here. If anyone asks about it, I can say it was a mistake and that I've returned it. A part of me hopes she won't be in her room when I do, that I can leave it on her night table and quietly creep away. It isn't that I don't have questions. I just don't expect any answers, nothing that isn't a tease, some new way for her to feel superior.

For now I remain motionless. Then I hear the ladies' door open and the sound of footsteps. They don't go into a cubicle but stop where the mirrors must be. I know I can't stay in here any longer.

It's Mandy in front of the mirror. She's applying mascara; she wears too much, despite the regulations calling for minimal makeup. They all do, her and her friends, an insignia of their pack. She looks up and sees my reflection, gives a toss of her head in acknowledgement.

I match her look and wash my hands. As I dry them she says, 'All right, are we?'

She sounds offended at my silence, as if she hadn't been silent too. I smile and tell her that everything's fine.

'Getting on all right with the dragon lady?'

It's the first time she's asked and I await her mocking expression, but it doesn't come. Instead she smiles, and it looks like a real smile, almost apologetic. Have I passed some sort of test just by turning up day after day? I remember it was she who sent me to Mrs Favell in the first place. Maybe she's only being nice because we're alone, and she'll be back to her sly looks the minute she's with her friends. Still, there's warmth in her eyes, and something else: maybe even guilt.

'She's okay,' I answer. 'I mean, she's a little difficult. I'm not sure what to make of her some of the time. But I think we'll get along.'

'She's an old bag. I heard what she did to Edie.'

'I'm sure she didn't mean it.' I don't know why I'm defending her. If I liked Mandy more, if I trusted her, I don't suppose I would be; it's not as if I really believe it myself.

'Of course she did.' Mandy slips her mascara into her pocket and turns from the mirror, looking at me face to face. 'Look, I'm sorry if she's difficult. I know we threw you in it a bit. If you need some help—'

'I'll be fine.'

Her face closes up and she gives a single nod before walking out of the room, leaving me alone with my reflection. My face looks thin. I'm pale and I look tired and closed off, and I force a smile, smoothing down my hair, which is determined to tuft into spikes. At least Mandy didn't notice the letter sticking out of my pocket, its aged paper out of place against the crisp blue. And it won't be there much longer. I'm taking it back, right now.

I walk through the residents' lounge to the stairway, my keycard held in front of me, a shield against unwanted interruptions, but I don't need it. The door is propped open, as it often is – it saves time and hassle when the residents lose their entry cards or forget they're supposed to use them. I ignore the wide passageway leading to the ground-floor rooms and head up the stairs, each riser carefully marked along its edge to help prevent trips and slips. As I go, the air seems to darken. There is the sense that something has come awake: that I am being watched.

I shake my head, stepping into the first-floor corridor. The walls, painted with the same job-lot of peach paint as the rooms, are adorned with the kind of bland pictures that might be found in a cheap hotel, but it still doesn't feel right. I walk along it and stand in front of room ten. The bedroom doors don't lock – it wouldn't be safe if there was a fire or other emergency – but it strikes me that, although we sometimes find the wrong resident in the wrong room, no one ever wanders into Mrs Favell's by mistake.

Is that because they all feel what I'm feeling now?

I pause before giving a little knock, waiting longer than usual – *for what?* – and then push open the door. It looks as if I've got my wish: the room is empty. I walk into this space that's so clearly meant to look like it might be a room in someone's home and yet doesn't, not really. There is the neatly made bed, the blunt-edged wardrobe, the peach walls, only the shining bureau out of place – and my own reflection, caught for a moment in the mirror set upon the chest of drawers. Then, with a start, I see *her*. She is here after all, standing in the corner, perfectly still. Her gaze is fixed on the garden, or further than that, on the woods that lie beyond.

Without turning she says, 'You haven't yet told me what you think.'

I can't make out what her tone portends. 'No,' I force myself to answer, 'I suppose I haven't.' With a stab of spite I wonder if she means what I think of the letters, or of *her*.

Then she says, 'Oh, never mind *that*. I don't care about such things.'

'What do you—'

'I think you know, dear.' She turns to me, painting a bright smile across her features. I suddenly remember wondering what she would look like smiling. Now I don't want to see it any longer. It's as if vindictive thoughts and bad spirit are hiding just behind her stretched lips, the tips of her teeth. And what is she trying to suggest? Whatever game this is, I'm not playing.

'He wanted you to stay here, didn't he?' she says.

'What? Who?'

'Your – significant other, I believe you'd call him. Your amour, your knight-at-arms.'

That silences me. I haven't spoken of Paul to anyone here, even at my interview, other than to acknowledge the fact of his existence. 'How could you know that?'

She smiles again and this one isn't so nice, though it suits her better. 'Oh, it's in your eyes, dear. The longing to escape, the desire for other things – different things. There had to be something keeping you here. There had to be something that brought you back.'

I have a sudden image: not of Paul but my mother, though her face is blurry, seen through tears; mine, not hers. She's reading me my favourite story, Hans Christian Andersen's 'The Little Mermaid', and I'm crying. Sobbing in fact, because the mermaid gave up everything, just as she was supposed to do, for love, to find her handsome prince, but in the end he didn't love her back.

I blink. I don't know why I'm seeing this. It almost feels as if she's showing it to me; as if Mrs Favell could be in any way connected to my mother, as if she could exist in the same world. The cloying scent of lily of the valley hits my nostrils and I want to be sick.

But Paul does *love me*, I think fiercely, and I don't know why.

Mrs Favell smirks. *Your amour, your knight-at-arms.*

Another image: Paul pausing on the doorstep to wave a hand, not just at the house but the terrace, the street, the whole God-forsaken town in the dead end of nowhere: *Welcome home*, as if it's some kind of treasure, as if any of it matters.

Is he the prince in my fairy tale? If so he's in the wrong place and the wrong time: at the beginning instead of the end.

I open my mouth to reply, not sure what I'm going to say. What I find myself murmuring is, 'It's not for ever.' I'm not even sure what I mean. This job? This place? Or do I mean Paul?

Her lip twitches with amusement.

I take a deep breath, ready to remonstrate. We're encouraged to talk to the residents, but about their lives, not our own. None of this is her business. None of it is *hers*.

'Of course not, dear.' Her voice is mild and she turns to the window, so that all I can see is the curve of her cheek. It's as if she's no longer interested.

I try to defuse my anger. We're supposed to have patience, we who work at Sunnyside. We're supposed to care, having endless wells of kindness, sharing memories and dreams, *sharing* – an image again: curled up around a book, but instead of my mother it's Mrs Favell sitting in her place and I blink it away.

I shift my feet, wishing I could show her. I wish I could walk out right now and never come back. Sunnyside is nothing to me, or it will be. It's an in-between place, a nowhere place. I won't let it get its claws into me, with its burbling television and clink of cutlery, the rattle of jigsaw pieces in a box, the rolling of a die. The stink of adult shit and failure and giving up.

'You should learn how to give up hope, dear.'

Her words are so odd they're like a shock of cold water. I'm not even sure I really heard them.

She turns to me and she isn't smiling. Her eyes are sharp and they have a brightness I can't look away from, though there's no warmth in them, no humanity. She doesn't mean well and I know that and I shouldn't have spoken to her, not of Paul, not of anything connected to my life. I shouldn't even have thought about him in front of her, or my home, or my mother, where she could read all of it on my face.

Still, anger rises. 'What do you mean by that?'

'Oh, dear girl,' she says, '*dear* girl. He had hope, didn't he? Our friend Lawrence.'

She holds out her hand and I remember the letter. I'm glad to pull it from my pocket and hand it to her, breaking that tie at least. I'm not going to let her see that I'm interested. I won't read any more of them, even if she gives them to me; I won't look at her pictures.

'It's so sad to feel trapped,' she says, 'especially when you *are*, and it's far too late for regret, even when you haven't – even – realised it yet.'

Her words are so pointed I try to believe she's talking about herself, living here in her little eyrie at Sunnyside, but she slowly moves her gaze from my eyes and scans downwards, taking in everything: my neck, my uniform, my breasts – my belly – and she stops there, staring.

I look back at her, my eyes wide, as something blooms within. It's as if she's pushing a new idea into me, something I'd never thought of or imagined, and I turn cold. I rush from the room, hearing the echo of other words, ones she said at a different time:

Life decisions… No point in crying over them when it's already too late – is it, Rose?

It isn't right, can't be right. I lean against the wall, bending over, clutching at my belly, thinking, *Oh God.* I suddenly feel nauseous. I still have half a day to work but all I want to do is get into the car, drive home as fast as I can, go upstairs and count my pills. All I want is to be a hundred miles away.

9

Oh God, oh God, oh God. I mutter the words, my mind empty. The test shows positive. I'm pregnant, and if the little stick in my hand is to be trusted, by several weeks. I'm sitting on the bed, willing the tiny reading that means so much to disappear. It doesn't, but it still can't be true. I haven't missed a pill. I checked as soon as I got in, relieved that Paul is out on a job, that I'm home before him. Just buying the testing kit felt like stepping into an alien world. I couldn't look the pharmacist in the eye, though to him it was nothing, humdrum. Women do this every day.

Not me.

I remember the way Mrs Favell eyed my belly and feel sick all over again. She *didn't* know. She can't have known, not really, but it feels as if she's the one who told me and that makes everything worse. Even the memory of it makes me feel as if she's running her hand over my body. How *could* she have known? I hadn't even suspected. Now that feels like another failure.

I close my eyes and instead of Mrs Favell, I see my mother. What would she have said? She hadn't liked Paul, not at first. She'd have preferred someone else, a doctor or an accountant or someone in a suit, not a man with shaggy hair and strong arms and God forbid, tattoos. But she had known, in the end, that he was good for me. She had known he would look after me when she could not, and Paul had. He'd visited the funeral home and helped me choose a casket for her and organised the wake when I couldn't think or see or know how to feel. He'd held me while I cried. My handsome prince.

If she could have been here, she'd have been happy. She could have nestled her granddaughter in her lap and read to her. I wonder what story she would have chosen. Mum never did enjoy 'The Little Mermaid'. She hadn't altogether liked to read it to me. Is that why the book had vanished – because she hadn't wanted to see me cry?

I wish I could see her now, to tell her it's all right that I cried, that I had *wanted* to cry. That even if there never was a happy ending, at least it was magic. At least the sadness made it possible to *believe*.

I curl in on myself. I don't know what I'm thinking. I want to cry now, but I can't. The shock is too great.

It is only then that it hits me: I won't be leaving here. Perhaps I never will.

I look around the little room, the thin walls with their peeling wallpaper that echo with other people's lives, ordinary lives, and they loom over me, pressing in. For a fleeting instant I picture running away from it, leaving the house and the street and my job and Paul and my child far behind me. I don't have to have the baby – but I know I *do*. I can't contemplate getting rid of it. I see my mother's face again, and Paul's, imagine looking at the knowledge of it in my own eyes in the mirror, not even recognising the face staring back at me. I hear the whisper of Mrs Favell's voice: *Life decisions… No point in crying over them when it's already too late – is it, Rose?* And I think I hear the sound of a door clanging shut.

Except it doesn't. The bedroom door swings open and I turn but I can't focus. It takes me a moment to recognise Paul. He's staring down at me and I don't say a word and neither does he and I wonder why – can *everyone* see the pregnancy in my face? He reaches out and I only remember the testing stick when he lifts it from my hands. He must be looking at it, taking in what it means, but I only see the floor, an old thinning carpet with a pattern I would never have chosen. A weird sound escapes me.

He says, 'Oh my God, Rose. That's amazing.'

I can't look up. He moves around me, dropping to his knees, teasing my arms from my sides. He puts his hands on my cheeks and lifts my chin. He waits until I meet his eyes – his are wide and clear, and he's smiling.

I know what he's looking at. He is seeing our future stretching ahead, both of us together, walking the same paths on the same streets of the same town for years and years and years, and he's so happy he could die.

That night Paul says he's never going to get to sleep but he goes under quickly and lies with his back turned to me like a wall. I stare at the flaking paint of the ceiling. My mind can't assimilate the idea of a baby. It's unthinkable. I can't have it; I can't *not* have it. I think of it inside me, a part of us both. I tell myself I love Paul. I suppose one day I will love the baby too. I wonder what it looks like: a cluster of cells? A little curled form with arms and hands and legs? Does it have eyes, staring into the darkness inside me? I try to imagine holding it in my arms, gazing into its face and seeing my own eyes looking back at me. Maybe then I won't *want* to leave here any longer. With a stab of bitterness, I suppose that would make Paul happy. Is that what he wanted all along, what he's been counting on? I bend away from him, drawing up my knees, my hands forming into fists, and wonder if I'm echoing the shape of the baby inside me, curled up like a comma – or a full stop.

Before we went to bed, Paul said he'll take me to the doctor, that we'll get things checked out. The idea makes me cringe. I don't want to tell anyone about this. I don't even want to know myself. But then, the doctor might say the test I took was wrong. They can't be one hundred percent accurate, can they? I draw in a deep breath. Nothing's certain, not yet. The thing inside me might not even be real. I close my eyes and a face rises before me: Mrs Favell. I try to shake the image away.

I can't bear the prospect of seeing her tomorrow, her mocking triumph. *So glad I never troubled over it*, she'd said, as if it was so easy, something that could simply be brushed off. *Saved myself a world of bother.*

I hate her. I hate all of it: the stupid job I didn't want, this town, our house, Paul's indifferent back rising and falling with his breath. Most of all I hate myself. Why didn't I leave long ago?

As if to underline my thoughts, the thump-thump of next door's music starts up from beyond the walls. It sounds like a muffled heartbeat. I bury my face in my hands, feeling tears, hot and I suppose selfish. I don't care. I let myself cry, never making a sound.

Soon I won't be me any longer. I won't even be Rose. I'll be 'Mum'. I'll nurse and clean and cook and *care*, though it won't just be a job; it's never just a job. Maybe I'll still be at Sunnyside. If so my days and nights won't be all that different, apart from the age of the bodies I wash and feed and comfort.

I remember the way Mrs Favell had looked at me when I told her my name. The way she twisted her lip in scorn, as if she had already known it wouldn't belong to me for very much longer; as if she knew that wasn't really who I was.

10

As soon as Patricia sees me pouring double-strength coffee in the staff room, I can see she knows something is wrong. It's not surprising. My skin is washed out and my hair is lank and I have the unsteady, swimmy sense of not quite being in the room, of not quite being anywhere. There's a metallic taste in my mouth. I don't know if that's a symptom of being pregnant or my reaction to it. I suppose there will be a lot of that now, not knowing what's the baby and what's really me.

'Are you all right, Rose?' She moves to grab a mug herself. The room feels tinier than ever with the two of us in it.

I do the expected thing and tell her I'm fine. Of course I'm fine. I half turn to the counter, leaning over my drink, breathing in the steam. The mug halfway to my lips, I wonder if I'm allowed caffeine now. There's so much I don't know. What will Patricia say when she finds out? Will she have to keep me on? I never wanted the job, but the thought of being fired from it makes me cringe.

'I see that you've been watching over Mrs Favell.' She smiles, waiting for my response. I can't give one, not now. I can't smile back.

'I know she can be difficult.' Again, there's a pause I'm supposed to fill. 'Try to be understanding with her, all right? It's not easy, I know. But she's had a difficult life. And she's more vulnerable than you'd think – you wouldn't believe it to look at her. Sicker, too…'

I make a non-committal noise in the back of my throat.

'She's a very private woman, you know. She likes things confidential, doesn't like people talking, but I'm sure it's all right to tell you that her husband died. Of course she's not our only widow, we've plenty in that position, but this was years ago. Mrs Favell had to move in with her father-in-law, and – well, he did something terrible.'

That's what she says, *something terrible*, conjuring vague shadowy forms looming in doorways, a broad-shouldered man curling his hands into fists or pulling the belt from his waist. She doesn't explain and then she's gone, giving me a pat on the shoulder as if that could possibly help. I don't want to think of Mrs Favell just now. I don't care about her *terrible thing*. For her, whatever it was is over. Mine is here; it's all around and in front of me and inside me. I resolve to see the woman as little as possible, to get by with the bare minimum of contact, to pay no attention to anything she says.

I glance at the clock. I'm running late already and I need to help with breakfast. At least that will save me from thinking of other things. Paul, the house, the future – all of it can wait, time suspended for a while, as it is, I suppose, for everyone within these walls. Aren't we all just waiting – the residents for an ending, me for the beginning of something that might never come? It's a horrible thought, like something Mrs Favell might say, and her words echo in my mind: *The truth often is.*

I hurry along to breakfast, settle Alf into a chair and put a knife and fork into his hands while he peers into his plate, steer Reenie out of the kitchen and help her to cereal, then start adding thickener to cups of juice for those who have difficulty swallowing. Mandy is putting trays together to take to the less mobile residents; she looks up and scowls. Barry Pickerell is standing by the wall, staring blankly into a painting of a field of flowers, and I encourage him to turn from it; he looks at me as if he doesn't know who or what I am. Maryam Lal, one of the brighter ladies, thankfully takes him under her wing and leads him to her table. Still Mrs Favell doesn't come down. I wonder if she's pecking away at an apple in her room and at first I'm glad, then realise that, sooner or later, I'll have to go and check on her. None of my intentions matter; it feels as if she's thwarting me with her absence, showing me who's in charge.

Leaving the clatter and busyness behind me, walking up the stairs alone, I can't shake the feeling that, once again, I'm being watched. Perhaps it's only that I'm conscious of a new presence in my life; it isn't because of *her*. It isn't that she has a sense of being there even when she's not; it isn't that her room doesn't feel quite like anyone else's. Fiercely, I push such ideas away. They only serve to set her further apart – and she's *not*.

I turn the corner and the corridor is empty. It's *too* empty, like a lie; I tell myself this section is always this quiet at this time of day, since the residents who need breakfast in their rooms tend to be on the ground floor and plenty of others use the lift at the other end of the building. I tell myself it doesn't mean anything at all, though when I push open the door of room ten I'm not surprised to see her standing in the centre of it, facing me, as if she was waiting. Her blouse is the exact blue-grey of a baby's eyes and she's holding something in her hands, though I can't see what it is. She doesn't smell of lilies, not now; there's a fresh, sharp scent in the air and I see a hollowed-out core on her bedside table, stripped of its flesh. She has a seemingly endless supply of apples, although I never see them at breakfast or in the kitchen. No one else eats them: too much trouble for their dentures. I imagine her little teeth working at the fruit, scraping, biting.

'Dear me, what a face!' she says, and then adds, 'Of course I didn't miss breakfast, as you can see.'

I cross the room, pick up what remains of the apple by its stalk and toss it into the bin. The noise of it is too loud and the plastic liner billows, settling into the bottom along with the core.

'Dear me,' she says again. 'Facing what is to come with fortitude is not your métier, I take it?'

Again I ignore her, though her words stab into me. Does she truly *know*? I tell myself she can't.

She holds out her hand. In it she holds a bundle of letters, three or four, all softened with age and yellowed with time. An abundance; a generosity. I scowl at them. I don't care about her letters, not now. Perhaps she knows that. It's probably the very reason she's giving them to me.

But a creeping greed steals over me and despite my resolutions, despite the fact that it only binds me to her more closely, I reach out and take them. I expect her expression to change to one of triumph but it doesn't. She lets her hand fall and half turns away, glancing towards the window with a wistful eye. For the first time, her posture seems to wilt.

'Are you all right?' I ask what I should have asked at the beginning. 'Would you like to go and sit in the garden? It's a little grey, but—'

'Oh, it's never grey,' she says, 'not if you're really looking. The rampion has come early. See its little bells? The pea shoots are making curlicues around their stakes. They're never still, you know. The sap is rising, can't you hear it?' She closes her eyes as if she really can hear everything. I notice one of her fingers twitching, as if conducting an unseen orchestra. 'The cuckoo calls.'

I glance towards the window. I can't hear anything at all. 'We could go outside now, if you like.'

Her eyes open. 'It isn't what you want,' she says, 'but you can feel the life in it, can't you? There's no stopping it. No holding it back. It lasts as long as you want it to last.'

I catch my breath. I tell myself she's old – even having some kind of lapse. I can't think what she means, though perhaps that's because I don't want to.

She says, 'You can go.'

I bite my lip to keep from telling her I'd be glad to, and step back, and feel something small and hard beneath my shoe. I can't see what it is, though amid the institutional beige carpet fibres, something gleams.

'Be a dear,' she says. 'I think I dropped my earrings, but my back, you know.'

I'd swear her back's better than mine but I stoop and run my hand over the floor. I feel a hard object under my fingers and there's the cold glitter of a diamond stud. I can't see the other so I sweep my hand more widely, pushing aside the valance of the bed. There, just beyond reach, is a matching gleam. I lower myself to the floor and slide my hand under.

There is a box under the bed. It's made of wood, about twelve inches long and six inches wide. It's of ample size to conceal a fairy skeleton, tiny and delicate: wings transparent as an insect's, arms like a woman's, the knees, on close inspection, bending backwards. Ugly or beautiful? Perhaps it is both.

I tell myself it's only a box, probably placed there on purpose to taunt me, something she wanted me to find and made sure I did. I still itch to reach out and touch it. I want to open the lid and see what's inside. My desire to read the letters stirs within me. I want to read *all* the letters, though I'm suddenly certain that's not what she's given me.

'Are you finished?' Her voice cuts through my reverie. I leave the box and withdraw, clutching her earrings.

'Ah – victory,' she says as I hold them out, and we both look down at them. The earrings are not diamonds. They don't shine. The things in my hand are dull, tarnished; cheap.

She smiles and takes them from me, then bends to pick something up from her bedside table – her back is miraculously healed, I see – and she rubs the earrings with cotton wool, releasing the tang of antiseptic. They've been on the floor of course, though I half feel she's washing me off them. She puts one in her ear, then the other, no need for a mirror. Now that she's wearing them, they gleam. They're no longer tarnished, never cheap; she can't have managed that with simple antiseptic and yet as she tilts her head they shine out even more fiercely. They are no longer glitter; they are fire.

She says nothing, just stares at me as if in challenge. I was wrong, that's all there is to it. Of course they're diamonds: they're *hers*. It was only ever a trick of the light that could have made me think otherwise.

I turn from her and close her door behind me, clutching the letters to my chest. They felt like a boon when she handed them over; now they feel like a sop, a fraction of the riches she must have hidden away. I unfurl the bundle and examine them. The topmost is different to the rest, printed in black ink and on thinner paper. It almost falls to the floor but I catch it and read:

LONDON TELEGRAPH OFFICE
ORIG BRADFORD UNITED KINGDOM
19 SEPTEMBER 1921

MR E L GARDNER
MUST CANCEL VISIT -(STOP)- APOLOGIES FOR BREVITY
AND INCONVENIENCE -(STOP)- STRUCK BY SEVEREST
MISFORTUNE -(STOP)- LETTER TO FOLLOW WHEN ABLE
MR L H FENTON 8.54 PM

I bundle the letters together again, wondering what must have happened. Whatever it is, it will have to wait. I go to my locker, feeling brighter as I hide them away inside and slip the key into my pocket. No one's around, no one to see or ask any questions. I could almost forget they're *her* letters at all. It feels as if there are secrets waiting to be discovered within their lines, and for now, they're mine.

20th September 1921

Dear Mr Gardner,

I scarcely know how to begin. First, may I extend my deepest apologies for having to defer your visit. Please rest assured that we had anticipated it most keenly and would only ever have done so in the direst circumstance. There was certainly no rudeness intended; indeed, I am mortified to imagine what you must think. I trust, when I explain all, you will understand.

We have been struck by misfortune, not upon one count, but two. I shall begin, I suppose, and treat them chronologically, if not by the import with which we are affected.

First, the little skeleton you so particularly wished to examine is gone. I do not know whither or how, but I feel its loss most acutely, or did so until worse came to take its place. I discovered its absence myself. I cannot express to you my astonishment and distress. Indeed, my pulse became so rapid I feared the worst; it took some moments to compose myself enough to peer once more under Charlotte's bed.

I do not know what had carried me into the room to look at it – I suppose with your arrival growing imminent, I wished to be certain that all was prepared to your liking. And yet the box was not there, and I thought my old heart would burst at last.

I do not know how my daughter-in-law had not noticed the lack. She had been so assiduous in watching over it. I could not think what had happened, unless it was that she had decided its hiding place too precarious after all, and had found another. I comforted myself with that as best I could.

She was then in the kitchen and I hastened to ask her, though I could hardly form the words. I saw at once it was of no use. Her eyes opened wide with surprise, and I cannot adequately explain, but I *felt* the lack of it – that the fairy had blessed us with its presence, and had now gone from us, and would remain far beyond our reach.

I think I must have had a little turn, for Charlotte assisted me to a chair and helped me recover myself. I kept asking after the box, pushing aside the glass of water she held to my lips. I wanted nothing – only that which has become so precious to us! I tried all kinds of explanation, repeating that it must have been placed elsewhere. I think I even voiced suspicion of the photographer who had developed the skeleton's photographs, though I distinctly recall giving him some patched-together explanation that it was a created thing, a kind of game cobbled together from the bones of a wren and the wings of an insect, and he had seemed to find that satisfactory. And anyway, however would he have found us – and it?

All the time I rambled, Charlotte kept shaking her head and looking so sad – until her eyes filled with tears, as much with dismay at my wildness as at our terrible loss, I think. We had also roused Harriet from her accustomed place in the nursery. She delights at that time in sitting in the window seat deeply lost in a book, but I realised she was standing by me, quite stricken.

I endeavoured to compose myself, but my distress overcame my sense, for the only words I said were, 'Did you take it, Harriet – did you wish to play with the little maid under the bed?'

I saw at once from her expression that not only was she thoroughly upset by the imputation but found the idea abhorrent, as of course it should have been. What child would play with a skeleton?

Her demeanour at least had the effect of bringing me around and returning me to a care for those whom I love, at the expense of all the world and its beliefs and its knowledge. I comforted her, and in doing so in some measure comforted myself, though it sickens me to write of it still. I do believe I would grieve the creature as a human friend, if it were not that further misfortune has taken its place in all our hearts.

Although I was in some wise resolved to face the loss, and the possibility that it would expose me to censure from yourself and the great man we admire so well, my daughter-in-law could not allow it to rest. I curse myself for it! For it was in part her concern for me that must have driven her to put on her mackintosh and go to seek the little thing at once. Yet, I do not believe that to be the whole of it. I have previously mentioned her fascination; the little form always had exerted some pull over her.

Charlotte at once imagined not that some thief had stolen it away, but that the fairy had somehow been returned to the glen. I am not sure why she thought so. Perhaps she caught the idea from me that it had gone beyond us, to some world that we could not reach after – but she did reach after it. I would that she had not!

She insisted on it however, and to my great shame I did not press her to stay, for she raised some hope in me that all would be well. Perhaps she would find it lying on the rocks, or in some leafy bower – and so I let her go, and even wished her luck. I stood with Harriet and watched her hurrying away without so much as looking back, so intent was she upon her mission.

I sat with the child and leafed over her book with her (it was the Brothers Grimm, though I cringed inwardly to see it), and ruffled her curls – as much to reassure myself, I think, as her. Time passed. The grandfather clock marked out the minutes with its mellow ticking, and the chime marked the quarter hour and then the half, and then the hour. I realised we were no longer looking at the book. Harriet sat quite still, a pensive expression on her face, her lower lip pinched between her teeth. I stared out of the window, though all was a-blur, and I do not think I had been conscious of gazing at anything.

I examined the clock once more and found that another hour had begun. I stood and I paced. I prepared bread and butter for Harriet and she picked at it; I could eat none. We waited, and after a time Harriet went to her room. She slept, I think, or curled up on her bed and tried to.

The afternoon was fading towards evening. The days are growing short, and shadows were stretching and joining without. My unease grew. For I could not help but think of what Charlotte had said once, about following the sound of magical pipes all the way to Fairyland. I had lost my wife and my son, and could not bear the idea of Charlotte being lost to me too, following some fairy dance to a place where she could never again be reunited with Harry – my boy!

Grief overcame me. I did not put on my coat but rushed out as I was and started towards the beck.

As I went, I thought I discerned a darker shape at the edge of the verdure where the trees began. At first it blended into the gloaming, visible only by its odd and rather irregular movement. It was not like a man, nor any animal I had hitherto seen. It almost appeared to lurch along, feeling its way, and I hurried towards it, already feeling the presentiment of some dreadful tragedy. With equal parts relief and dismay, I saw as I grew closer that it was Charlotte. She was stumbling along with one arm outstretched, and the other clamped to her left eye.

I did not call out as I ran to her; I wanted only to reach her as quickly as I might. She looked up, staring at me with her one eye, and so it startled me beyond measure when I grasped her arms and she screamed in sudden terror. I cried out, calling her name, and tried to pull her hand from her face. I wanted to see what was the matter, but she drew back from me. 'I'm blind,' she said. 'Blind!'

I cannot describe my horror. I have no words sufficient for it even now; I have not the powers of a Conan Doyle or other great writer. My head swam and I could not speak, but she implored me to help her to the house and so I did; I supported her and guided her, though I did not understand. I found myself entirely unable to fathom what had happened, or how such a calamity had visited her in such a lovely place, with such lovely creatures in it. What did it mean?

She spoke little that night. I gave her a measure of brandy, which quieted her, and I settled her on the sofa, since she was unwilling to move; but she did at last uncover her left eye. I had dreaded what I might see, but to my great relief, it appeared normal. She only murmured one thing to me as she succumbed to the draught and fell into a doze.

'They spit in your eye,' she said. 'They spit in your eye, and it's gone. If I had not covered the other—'

She was blind, you see, but not in the eye she had covered. She had lost the sight in her right eye and had kept her hand over her left to protect it from them. I know not how such a thing could happen, or if she had become confused somehow about the cause and had mistaken the little creatures' intentions. I hardly dare to speculate, but something is terribly wrong.

I will try to write again soon.

Yours most sincerely,
Lawrence Fenton

11

I smooth out the letters, which are laid over my steering wheel. I don't know what to think of the one I've read. I'm sitting in my car, parked just off the High Street in town. It's not far from Sunnyside, though I can barely see anything outside the car; rain smears the windows, rapping on the roof, as loud as knuckles. It's lunch hour, for me anyway. Back at Sunnyside the residents will be settling into their sofas, sleeping theirs off. I wanted to be away from everything when I read the letters, to be alone, where no one could see.

I run my fingers over the paper again, feeling the texture of another age. I feel somehow bereft that the little fairy skeleton had vanished, and so completely, as if disintegrating into the lines between the ink. But of course it had to disappear; the skeleton could never have been inspected or tested, because it wasn't real. How could it have been? Yet it is strange to read of its disappearance just as I've discovered the box hidden under Charlotte Favell's bed.

But Mrs Favell is further away than ever from *this* Charlotte – who was struck blind, at least in one eye. I should feel sorry for her, but what I mostly feel is an odd kind of relief that Mrs Favell has no such impairment. Her gaze is too sharp; she would never tolerate such a thing.

I shake my head. Do I really need further proof that Mrs Favell can't be the same Charlotte as in the letters?

But perhaps I do, because while Mrs Favell was having lunch with the others, and when Patricia wasn't looking, I slipped out and went once more to her room.

This time I hadn't felt repelled so much as drawn to it, though that was surely because of the determination overspilling inside me: I'd decided I wasn't having it any longer. I wasn't going to put up with the way she'd made me feel. I wasn't hopeless; I wasn't worthless; I wasn't *tarnished*. I wouldn't stand for any of it.

As soon as I went in, I saw that she had left the bureau open. It seemed like a gift and so I began there, looking over its contents without touching anything; I wasn't going to do that. I wasn't like Theresa, the girl before me.

And yet the first thing I saw was an old-fashioned fountain pen, its black ebonite a little chipped, the gold fittings bearing a patina of age, and I hadn't been able to resist reaching out and uncapping it. Not wishing to mark her paper or leave any trace of my presence behind, I ran the nib across the palm of my hand. The ink was royal blue, bright and strong, nothing like the faded smoke of the letters, and it sank into the lines of my hand at once.

I had stared at it. Pulled a face. I stare at it now, but the mark remains imprinted on my skin.

Then, on a shelf inside the bureau, I saw a stack of writing paper. I reached out – with my clean hand, so as not to taint it – and touched its creamy surface. It didn't feel old. It was smoother than the letters had been; the sheets weren't darkened at the edges. Of course, ink could be changed and paper thrown away. Still, it felt as if whatever I had come to find was not there. But then, I already knew that.

If she'd written the letters herself, wouldn't she have called her fictional Charlotte Favell, not Fenton? Wouldn't she have addressed them to the more famous Doyle, not some little-known acquaintance?

Unless Fenton really was her maiden name. Patricia had said that she'd been married, and I wish now I'd questioned her about it. But perhaps even that wouldn't have been subtle enough for Mrs Favell's game.

And it does feel that some game is being played. Why else is she *feeding* me the letters like this, revealing her story a little at a time?

Had she even left the bureau open like that on purpose?

It had occurred to me then that she was laughing at me. Perhaps she even planned to send Patricia to her room on some pretext, ready to catch me snooping like a thief.

I had still lowered myself to my knees. I positioned myself next to her bed, ready to look beneath it, already picturing the box concealed there, surely the true reason I had gone poking around in the first place, breaking the rules, seeing what there was to discover.

I had reached out and pulled back the valance and then stared at it – seeing not the box but the little smudge of blue ink marring the clean, cream cotton.

Even now, I grimace at the memory. I hadn't been worried that someone would guess what I'd done. How would they work it out? This wasn't a fairy tale. Mrs Favell wasn't Bluebeard, surmising from the smudge of blood on a key that the young wife had trespassed into the forbidden chamber. I had thought I could easily wash the ink from my hand. I can still hide the stain somehow, or come up with some excuse for its being there. A leaking biro, maybe.

Would she know?

I shake my head at the thought. Whatever had run through my mind didn't matter: I had *awoken*.

I had let the valance fall back into place, keeping any secrets it held. I'd stood once more and hurried from the room. I'd told myself that isn't who I am.

Yet even as I sit here in the car, I'm still wondering if the box had been there, within my reach. I'm wondering what's inside. And I'm wondering if the fact of the bureau being open when I entered the room wasn't so much an opportunity as something else: a distraction, maybe. Even a feint.

I sigh, my breath adding to the mist clouding the windows, and sit back in my seat. Probably the box contains nothing of interest: jewellery, keepsakes, or as unlikely as it seems, old love tokens. At least this way I'm not disappointed.

I run my fingertips over the papers still in my hand. I don't want to return them to Mrs Favell's unfeeling ownership. If they were mine, I'd read them over and over. While I was lost in their words I didn't even think about anything else and now I don't want to. I let my thoughts drift, taking me back in time, away from the present, and I turn to the next letter and lose myself again.

24th September 1921

Dear Mr Gardner,

Thank you for your response, and indeed your good wishes. It is a salve to my heart, on one count at least, that you do not think badly of us for so precipitately deferring your visit.

I shall take up where I left off: with the question of Charlotte's sight. It is indeed the presiding concern of our household. Her right eye remains dark, and it is doubly unfortunate for she says her left eye is weaker, and so she has not only a shadow over all that she sees, but everything is less distinct than before.

I have tried, quietly and gently, to speak to her of what happened, but she will not be drawn on it, save for one thing, to which I will return.

I took her to Bradford to have her examined by an ophthalmologist. He could see nothing wrong and suggested it a kind of hysterical blindness brought on by extreme anxiety. I wonder if that is so? I hardly dare believe, for if such is the case her sight may be restored naturally. He said she would gradually see lights – but she shuddered at that, and he did not go on.

Indeed, the three of us pass our days sunk into gloom, for though I almost allow myself to hope for recovery, Charlotte is adamant it will not occur; and thus far, bitter experience has proved her correct.

Charlotte is resilient under her suffering, however. If I try to discuss it with her, or even if she catches me watching her, she smiles as if she is the one who needs to reassure me. She said to me, the key of her voice soft and low, that there are 'worse things in the world', and I knew that she was thinking of the loss of my son. How brave she is! He would have been proud of her forbearance. And at least she can still see little Harriet's face – I know she takes comfort in that. More than ever before, she likes nothing so much as to have the child sit on her knee, and to rest her cheek against her golden curls. Such a wistful look comes across her face then – ah, but it is full of love as well as sorrow, and the former, I must believe, shall always triumph over the latter.

It heals my heart to see them so, which is of inestimable relief, because I have worried incessantly. Charlotte does not wish to speak of the fairies, as I have stated, but I have pressed upon her that she must never return to the glen. If something else did befall her, how much more terrible would it be for something to happen to her good eye – how dreadful, to be cast altogether into the dark! And she says she will not go, but there is a terrible restlessness in her. I sense it beneath the surface, even when she sits over her sewing, tilting her head to see it the better, as if she were in thrall to something never far from her thoughts.

I should return, now, to the single occasion when Charlotte has spoken to me of the fairies. It was late one evening, when I had, as is the way of old men, nodded off before the fire. Charlotte had retired some time before, and Harriet of course had been long abed. It must have been late because the fire was reduced to only a few fitful embers, one moment setting the room agleam, then plunging all into darkness. Somewhere without, an owl hooted mournfully about the house.

I did not trouble with a lamp; I knew my way well enough. I went up the stairs, making sure not to knock the treads and make a noise about it. I did not wish to wake anyone, but it seemed someone was awake after all, for as I reached the passage the door halfway along it opened.

It was the door to Charlotte's room. I went towards it, and when I reached the opening I realised she was standing there, quite silently, staring out. Both her eyes were unblinking and fixed; none could have said that one of them was blank.

I began to apologise. I thought I must have frightened her, that she had heard some sound after all, and was looking out in terror of what might have come for her. But she leaned out and thrust something towards me. I closed my hand upon it; I did not at first recognise what it was.

'I saw them.' She spoke in a low voice, little more than a whisper, and yet it was full of a hoarse wildness. 'They took her back. I witnessed their solemnities.'

I opened my mouth to question her, to calm her, but she stepped inside and closed the door in my face. I stared at it; I thought I heard a bedspring settling. I decided it was best to leave her. I went to my room and lit the lamp at my bedside. It was only then that I made out what she had given me: it was the little cloth-bound volume, *The Science of Fairy Tales: An Inquiry into Fairy Mythology*. I had not even known she was reading it.

I leafed through it before I slept, finding within a peculiar mixture of curiosities. Some were obviously fiction, some intended to be fact, and some consisting of rather fantastical conclusions. Indeed, it should not have surprised me to discover a chapter headed 'Savage Ideas'.

I did not examine the book again until the morning. I slept ill – I think the odd thoughts it conjured had followed me into sleep. Still, I opened it the next day and confirmed my night-time impression of there being some very strange matter within. Have you read it? I wish I could ask directly – but no mind. I shall relate some of the phantasmagoria which passed before my eyes.

There are stories of midwives summoned to mansions filled with singing and dancing, to ease a fairy birth; others of the perils of eating fairy food, lest travellers in their realms become trapped there for ever; of the fluid passage of time in Fairyland, with a minute spent there taking years in the human world, or the opposite; and tales of terrible revenge for some accidental slight. Still more tell of changelings – children or adults carried away into Fairyland, replaced by worn-out fairies or stocks of wood, even fairy children, bewitched to resemble the stolen person. And there are stories that speak of the fairies' dislike of being observed, and their various retaliations.

And here is the point. Sometimes the person prying is magically deprived of their sight; sometimes the fairy plucks out their eye or pokes it out with a stick; others blow a mysterious powder into the face. Sometimes, however, that aim is accomplished by the fairy spitting in their eye. 'All water is wine,' they have been reported to say, 'And thy two eyes are mine.'

Whatever the means, it all has the same awful effect: the unfortunate person can see no more.

You will realise why I do not know what to think. Surely such benevolent creatures as we have seen would do no such thing. And what of Elsie Wright? She claims to have often met and played with them in the fairy glen. I wonder why such never happened to her?

But the same book tells me that fairies can choose to manifest themselves to humans. It is where people spy upon their private affairs that objection is encountered, and perhaps that is what we did, upon seeing the little dead body. I would that I had never taken it! It is possible that we have been punished – though the curse has not fallen to me or Harriet, but her mother.

Despite all, I continue to feel the loss of the little skeleton. It is like a constant ache. I wonder and wonder what became of it. We three – and you and Sir Arthur – are the only ones to know of its existence. And I think of the words that Charlotte whispered to me in the dark: 'They took her back.'

Perhaps the fairies did indeed break their bounds and trespass into the human world; and yet if so, the time of reclaiming the little maid is precisely when they have chosen to deal out such terrible punishment for her loss.

There is an image I carry in my mind: the prone body in the midst of all her fellows, moving in stately array in whatever rites and 'solemnities' they may possess. Perhaps they have ushered her into the next world – or welcomed her into their own again.

On a smaller matter, I am reminded that some odd happenings about the house could almost make me believe we are subject to some continuing fairy mischief. With more momentous issues to face, I had rather put them from my mind until this moment. You will notice, for example, that my letter is rather disfigured with blots. I have had much cause for my hand to shake, but I do not believe it to have done so to excess, and yet the ink constantly drips about. It is a disgrace next to your own type-written communications, and I cannot account for it at all.

My magnifying glass continues mysteriously vanished, as do a few other sundry items; flour is constantly spilt about the kitchen; and the milk rapidly turns sour, although it has not been left out, and the days have not been so very warm.

But these small inconveniences might somehow be the result of Charlotte's poor sight, and the anxious condition of her mind that must necessarily follow; and I can only apologise if my old hands are in a more agitated state of vexation than I am fully conscious of.

It only remains to sign myself,

Very sincerely yours,
Lawrence Fenton

❦

28th September 1921

Dear Mr Gardner,

Thank you for your last. Yes, we continue as well as could be anticipated, although in spite of all our wishes, the sight in Charlotte's right eye has not returned.

I have considered very carefully your suggestion that my daughter-in-law may have taken some hint from Mr Hartland's book. I suppose it is possible that some fancy has taken hold of her, resulting in a real impediment to her vision. It is the perennial question, I suppose, of which came first, the chicken or the egg.

After much thought, I rather decided it was beside the point. There is much supposition in these parts and beyond that fairies are the mere invention of children, yet I have held the little skeleton in my hand, and felt its weightlessness. I cannot doubt them to be real, and that being so, what other mysteries may exist?

The only point at question, then, is whether they are wicked and vengeful or innocent of wrongdoing. I would wish to hope – being part of God's creation, as I like to assume – they are blithe and good and mean us only well, but I wonder. Indeed, Hartland's book describes beings that are not purely benevolent but composed of 'caprice and vindictiveness, if not cruelty'. But how would he know? Perhaps they are neither good nor bad, being of some alternative line of evolution as you have proposed, and have no more morality than does an insect or a bird.

On another point, I can assure you that Charlotte's blindness is quite genuine. In order to do so, I have been sure to watch her carefully. Her eye looks perfectly normal, but I have many times seen her tilt her head and squint to see better with her one good eye, or to reach for some object and misjudge its distance without the aid of the other. If it is a pretence, it is a good one; and really, I cannot suspect her of any deception. She is of a steady, upright, honest, sober character, and I know if you saw her and conversed with her that you could not consider there was any trickery in it.

You mention that if there is no possibility of human falsity, you would be pleased to rearrange your visit. You ask if you may speak to her and examine her eye. She would pass any test, I am certain of that, but she remains reluctant to speak of the little folk or even hear anything said about them. She has undergone a dreadful experience, and I cannot at present subject her to it.

Perhaps a few more weeks will see her settled enough to consider it again. I am sure the results would be worthy of your patience. Though it strikes me that Sir Arthur is a trained ophthalmologist, is he not? If there was any medical advantage that may be gained, I could try to impress upon her the importance of a visit from you both. I am sure the thrill of meeting such a personage would outweigh any difficulty.

But we do continue a trifle unsettled. I have mentioned before some small incidents that, whilst of a mere domestic sphere, are really rather inconvenient. They have not ceased; if anything, they have worsened since my last. Charlotte cannot set down her needle without it seemingly vanishing into the air, and neither can she sew for pricking her fingers. Harriet constantly complains that her books have been moved or her place lost, or the pages spilled upon, even torn out. I know that some would raise their eyebrows and blame the child for the mischief, but really, she has never been prone to naughtiness. Besides which, she treasures her books, and I am sure she would do no such thing to any in her possession.

The dinner is often spoiled. Charlotte says the range can no longer be trusted. Sometimes it will not boil a kettle; at other times it will not draw and chokes us all with smoke. The smuts go everywhere, blackening our clothing and the walls. One can even taste it in our bread. It is most unpleasant. I see Harriet pulling faces over it, though bless the child, she eats it anyway, casting glances about the room as if concerned who might be watching.

Of course, all such things are explainable. I do not claim any particular supernatural agency; I have no reason to believe it to be the folk. And yet I wonder, and I have cause, as I will relate.

It is strange to say, after everything that has passed, that Harriet has begun to speak to me of returning to the glen. It very much surprised me at first, and I did not like to re-awaken her fears by questioning the wisdom of it, but I did ask whether she very much wished to go.

'Oh yes,' she said, 'I think we must, for Mama's sake.'

I did not like to probe her meaning. I suppose she wished to show her parent she was not afraid, but then she said, 'We need to stop them from being angry about the house.'

I gathered myself to respond, but she added, 'They don't really like us. They don't want to play. They don't really know how to dance. They only wish to make us want to be where they are.'

'And where is that, child?' I asked, but she would not say, or indeed utter another word. She continued silent all that afternoon, as if afraid of having said too much.

I cannot help thinking of Elsie and Frances, who loved to 'tice' the fairies and played so gaily among them, just as one imagines children doing. But Harriet has always been such a funny little thing. She prefers her books to the company of others, and then, she has found no suitable playmate. If I had not seen the fairies myself I could easily imagine her to have invented little companions to meet the deficiency.

Such is all my news.

Yours sincerely,
Lawrence Fenton

12

Indistinct forms pass through the rain running down the window. I see the red of a coat, the black whirl of an umbrella, tiny distorted faces. They merge and separate and I can't make them out with clarity. It's difficult to judge scale. The rain changes everything; those figures could be anything, even not quite human. Lawrence Fenton had said that his fairies were minuscule, smaller than the ones in the fake photographs. But if they stole people away and left changelings in their place they would have to be human-sized, so that no one could tell the difference. I suppose it is a part of their nature to be tricksters, always one step beyond our reach or understanding. Are they good or wicked? Angry or indifferent? Unhappy and sullen or gladsome and full of secret joy?

I remember Harriet's words: *They don't really know how to dance.* What did that mean? And shouldn't a child know the fairies best of all?

Perhaps they weren't fairies at all, not as we think of them:

not the gauzy creatures of Disney movies or even a young girl's photograph – unless they chose to appear that way. But what if there was *something*? Fairy stories of all kinds have been told across the world for hundreds of years, and they hardly ever have little winged creatures in them. Perhaps they are not so much stories as clues, snatches of something glimpsed and never really understood. The stories simply recount them in ways that people can understand, in accordance with their own beliefs or superstition or need, the particular shape of their fears.

Some thought of them as angels or demons. Some even conflated fairies with the spirits of the dead – all a part, perhaps, of Doyle's spiritual realm.

The little beings that live all about us and are usually unseen, which we have been pleased to name 'fairies'.

It strikes me that 'fairies' is a stupid, too-light name for them. There are other names that don't quite fit, other descriptions, but none that really encapsulate what they are. Perhaps there is no name that can do that. The way we see them now, light and gauzy, sweeter than sugar, beloved of children – *safe* – is perhaps the most cruel deception of all.

I shake my head. Whatever they are or were or are meant to be, they are always and ever a mystery, and surely the better for it. If there ever was a skeleton, it was much better lost. Some answers shouldn't be found; once they are, the magic would surely be gone.

I rest my chin on my hands. My head aches and images flit through my mind: Charlotte, *my* Charlotte, returning to the glen, witnessing the solemnities. Picking up the little body when the fairies aren't looking, cradling it to her breast like an infant. Stealing away with it, treasuring it, possessing it. *Caprice and vindictiveness, if not cruelty.* Those words certainly apply to Mrs Favell. Or is it only that she too has no more morality than a bird?

A soft beep calls me back to the present and I grab my mobile phone. There's a text from Paul: *Hi Mummy*, it begins, and I banish it with a quick swipe. Then I turn it off. I start the engine and run the windscreen wipers, revealing people; just men and women after all, some alone, some in little huddles, all of them hunched against the rain. People who are travelling through a world much like Paul's, having kids, raising them to be like them, to believe in the world they can see and nothing more.

I shake away the ungenerous thoughts. Paul's a good man, a decent man. I tell myself I love him. I'm no longer a child, clinging to stories; it's time to grow up. Perhaps my mother had known that. Perhaps that had prompted her to throw away my childhood books. I'm not Little Red Riding Hood wandering in the forest, a lost child trying to find her way, even if I do seem to have missed the path and I've already been knocked up by the wolf. *Woodcutter*, I correct myself. Paul would be the woodcutter, someone fine and noble who wouldn't abandon a *child*, and suddenly I'm fighting back tears.

It's only hormones, I tell myself. The rush of new chemicals coursing through my veins, changing the way I feel and think, changing who I am.

I just need a little more time to absorb the idea of a baby, that's all. Then I'll be able to face this. My future self will do better. She'll have courage, and – and *fortitude*, as Mrs Favell had so aptly put it.

➤•◄

I make my way back to Sunnyside before the clock can catch me out and, living up to its name, the sun makes an appearance, though colours are still deepened after the rain, the shrubbery alive with droplets sparkling from each leaf and bud. I rub my face as I walk towards the door. It's time to stop crying. I'll put the letters back and Mrs Favell will never know the effect they had on me.

Still, I feel that tug inside, the sadness of letting them go. They're a little piece of magic in a grey, rain-drenched world, and she surely doesn't deserve them. But none of it is real. I can't be like Sir Arthur Conan Doyle, seeking after things that never existed.

Surely a child must be miracle enough.

I show my face in the residents' lounge before heading upstairs. Edie is there, though at first I don't recognise her, because she's half drowned in a shapeless cardigan belonging to one of the other residents. Things get mixed up sometimes, in spite of the labels in everyone's possessions – except, I realise, those of Mrs Favell, who doesn't seem to need such precautions.

I don't go over to Edie, pretending instead not to see. I'll sort it out later; I don't want to get caught up. I hurry through the propped-open door and up the stairs, taking them two at a time. I stop outside room ten. I raise my hand to knock but somehow don't move. That sense of watchfulness is back, stronger than ever, boring its way through from the other side of the door.

Slowly, I turn my hand over. I stare at my palm, which is marred by a shadow: the stain of ink ingrained in my skin, marking each whorl and crease, darkening my lifeline, telling its story.

Nothing she can read, I tell myself, and curl my hand into a fist and rap three times. No answer comes. I force myself to push the door open and peer inside, scanning the room twice, making certain she isn't there.

I shove the door closed behind me. I'll put the letters on her bedside table. She's bound to see them there, though anyone else might too – I don't like to think of the other staff touching them or reading them, but after my earlier intrusion I don't even want to look at the bureau. Before I put it down, though, I see the ceramic bowl with the key inside it, and next to that, another letter. And so I reach out and pick it up.

➤·◄

30th September 1921

Dear Mr Gardner,

You will no doubt be surprised to hear from me so soon after my last, and without awaiting a reply in the interim. I shall tell you the reason at once.

I fell into rather a reverie yester-evening, and began thinking again of Elsie and Frances and their gladsome encounter with Fairyland, which seemed to bring them nothing but joy; and I contrasted it with our own household, fallen so deeply into a constant anxious silence.

And I thought how odd it was – now I must apologise, Mr Gardner, and trust you will not think me impertinent, but I only wish to express honestly what I felt – that Charlotte's photographs appeared so much more realistic than those published in *The Strand*.

I always thought they appeared rather flat, you see. I know that people wiser than I had examined them and detected signs that the fairies were moving, even your expert in photographic fakery, and yet I never could see it, not really. I blame my old eyes and my ignorance, of course; I am perfectly happy to be guided by wiser men than I. Indeed, I understand you to be the reference for lantern slides and images for the Theosophical Society, but still, I always somehow felt they had rather a cardboard cut-out quality that did not sit well with the living child next to them.

Then I thought of the missing skeleton, the incontrovertible proof that was so much needed, and I suddenly much desired to look upon our own photographs again.

I opened the bureau and took out the envelope. They had not disappeared; the plates are still in my keeping. I have checked them all several times and nothing has vanished, but despite that, something within them seems sadly changed.

The little living lights I had seen previously, with the suggestion of limbs and the bright haloes made by their wings, appear to have faded. Arms and legs are turned to clumsy lines; the motion of the wings no longer obscures their ornamented shapes, which I think look nothing like those of the fairy I held in my hands. Their hair almost appears coiffed, like that of the Wright girl's rather Parisienne-styled maids, and their dresses, now quite distinct, are as frilled and quilled as any lady's in a ballroom.

I have not ceased to be puzzled by the change. They no longer appear to be in motion but are sharply frozen; indeed, the little fellow pictured with Harriet is now more distinct than she. I cannot account for it at all. Have my eyes deceived me – were they always so?

I wished to ask Charlotte, but she refused to look at them, and it would be unfair to upset Harriet by pressing her. Instead my thoughts turned to you, and what you would think of it – what anyone would think.

You are in possession of copies of the earlier pictures, but how may we compare? Perhaps they never appeared to you as they did to me. Perhaps you thought me mad from the beginning and only humour what you see as the fancies of an old man. Pray tell me honestly what you think of them. I can only hope that yours continue as they once appeared, or you shall think me the most terrible confidence man – nothing but a trickster, when it is not I, but they! For the fairies must have changed them somehow, just as they have changed my home and my family; just as they adorn my words with ugly drips of ink; just as they have changed everything.

In truth, I would that I had never seen them. I would that Harriet had not gone poking into the hollows with her stick. I would that I had never come to Cottingley!

I anticipate your reply, in rather a state of agitation.

Most sincerely yours,
Lawrence Fenton

➤·◄

I set the letters down once more, the new one included, pushing their edges straight. This wasn't what I'd wanted to find. It's as if Lawrence Fenton's disappointment is an infection seeping from the page, filling my mind. If the whole thing was a hoax of course the skeleton had to disappear, that much was obvious, but for the photographs to change…

I see it happening as if the pictures are in front of me, magic dwindling from the world before my eyes, soon to be gone. I don't know why I feel so crushed. I've never seen the photographs. They probably never existed.

I turn to leave. The bed is neatly made, the corners squared, awaiting nightfall and the return of its occupant. It's all so normal – so ordinary. Is the box still there, hidden beneath?

She might have moved it as soon as I handed over her earrings, laughing at her little joke.

I kneel down next to it and lift the valance, ignoring the blue smudge marring the fabric, and the box is there, nestled in the shadows. I let the bedding fall back into place. My neck prickles and I glance about me, half expecting Mrs Favell to be there after all, standing by the window or in the middle of the room, but it is empty. When I listen, there are only distant, everyday sounds: the television, the scraping of a chair, a brief whistle – Jimmy, I expect. Some of the residents will be gathering to play games: i-Spy or Cluedo. They'll be wondering where I am.

Quickly, I lie down with my face pushed against the carpet and reach under the bed. The box is smooth under my fingers. I can't get a grip on it but I press downwards on the lid and pull it towards me and it slides easily. Then it's in my hands and I feel like a thief, like the girl who worked here before me.

The box is lighter than I'd anticipated. I turn it, looking for a keyhole, but there doesn't seem to be one. There's only a line where the lid joins the body. It isn't hinged. When I pull, the lid comes off.

The first thing I notice is the scent rising from within, sweet and evocative, like springtime. Bluebells? Of course, there's no skeleton. What did I expect? There is only a dried-out bundle of flowers, tinier than they should be, as if preserving has shrunk them somehow: little golden cups, minuscule orange trumpets, lacy white petals and yes, bluebells. Didn't people once believe that if bluebells rang out, they would summon the fairies?

But that's not all. Below the flowers are papers and I

wonder if here are more letters, but the stock is thicker. They're photographs, I realise, but not of fairies. Each picture, monochrome and bordered with white, shows a woman and her daughter. I know they must be related because their faces are a similar shape, a little like Charlotte Favell's. Their smiles are frozen. I leaf through them, trying to make out if one of them is *my* Charlotte, but the woman looks so young and fresh; the child is shown at different ages, up to about seven or eight. Then time seems to stop. I can't find any where she's grown any older.

From the corridor comes the distinct sound of footsteps. I try to replace the lid and fumble, rattling it against the box, and the footsteps stop. I swallow hard, replace the lid and shove it under the bed just as the door opens.

It's Patricia. She's carrying a clipboard and a cardigan I recognise as Edie's. She looks surprised and then she frowns. 'Whatever are you doing there?' she asks.

'I – I was looking for Mrs Favell. Then I thought I trod on something, an earring or something, but I couldn't find it.' I push myself to my feet and feel sweat prickle along my spine. Will she bend down and check? Will she see the box for herself?

She nods and says, 'Well if you do find anything, be sure to hand it in. Now, it's games hour. I believe Mrs Favell is already there. They need some juice. And Jimmy's misplaced his teeth; you could help look.'

'Of course. I'll head down now.'

She holds the door open for me and I slip out in front of her then listen as she follows me all the way down the corridor. Her gaze on my back makes me stiff and awkward. She stops when

I reach the top of the staircase and all I can think is, *Did I push the box far enough under the bed? Did I put it straight? If not, Mrs Favell will see. She'll know, and furthermore, she'll know the person who moved it was me.*

Another picture arises before me, not of the photographs, but the letters on the bedside table. There is something wrong with them and I remember the way I'd lifted the one she'd left there – *for me?* – and read it, becoming absorbed before replacing them once more. I see it as if I'm there again: positioning the little bundle of letters, then the new one – not beneath them, as it should have been, but on top.

She'll know I moved it. She'll know I read it, *her* letter, not yet granted to me.

I grimace. I can't do anything about it now.

A few more steps and I'm back among the residents. I sit next to Edie, who picks up something from her lap. It's a pair of baby's bootees, all finished, fresh and white. She holds them against my shoulder, pressing them there as if trying them for size. I force a smile, telling myself I'm relieved she's knitting again – I'd been half afraid that Mrs Favell's words would make her give up on everything – and then Mrs Favell herself is striding across the room, her eyes fixed on mine.

When she's standing directly in front of me, she slaps something down on the table: another letter.

'You only had to ask,' she says, and then she's gone.

I should protest. Everyone's looking, Edie blinking in bewilderment, but Patricia chooses that moment to walk in and I keep quiet. Did she hear? I shake my head, a non-specific gesture that could be taken to mean I don't know what Mrs Favell is talking about. But then, Patricia just saw me in her room.

How on earth did Mrs Favell find I'd been poking around and get here so quickly? Or had she already concealed this new letter on her person, knowing what I would do? She set me up. She's going to have me fired before I even know how the story ends. It isn't fair, none of it is, and tears fill my eyes.

'Oh dear,' says Edie. 'Don't you like them? They're for my daughter, you know.'

'She's not coming.' The words are out before I can stop myself and Edie sags in her seat. 'I mean – I didn't mean—'

But I see from her face that she knows I *did* mean it. She knows it's true. Her eyes are full of hurt as she crumples the bootees in her hands.

'I know,' she says, and her voice is small. 'I suppose I think if I do enough for her, if I try really hard, it'll bring her back. Isn't that silly? How very silly of me.'

I turn cold. How could I be so cruel? But they hadn't been my words – they were Mrs Favell's. La Belle Dame sans Merci, that's suddenly how I think of her, cold and yet alluring, impossible to break free of once she's cast her spell. Or in her case, does Belle Dame mean *beldam* – sounding so similar, yet meaning the opposite: a malicious old woman?

She hurt Edie too. She hurt her first and yet Edie didn't react like this, not when Mrs Favell said those things. It's hearing the truth from *my* lips that's made her look so beaten.

'I'm so sorry,' I say, and put my hand on her arm, but that only makes it worse. It only makes it more true. She doesn't look at me, doesn't react. Her rheumy eyes keep blinking, seeing whatever it is she's seeing, and I hate Mrs Favell with an intensity I've never felt for anyone. In a weird kind of way, I feel like it's her who's snatched my future from me. And what has she given in return? Not enough.

If I'm going to get in trouble for this new 'gift', at least I'm going to know what it says. I pat Edie's arm. Everyone else is focused on their game, and Edie doesn't notice when I straighten out the letter in my hands. It doesn't feel like a long missive. I hold it below the level of the table top and I begin to read.

5th October 1921

Dear Mr Gardner,

Thank you for your letter. It is true that it is very difficult to compare in writing one's impressions of photographs. To judge by your description, the fairies have remained in position, and yet I rather fear they have flattened somehow – that they are not so redolent of life as I felt they were.

But it is impossible to draw any conclusions without seeing. I do not know if they now appear quite dead, and you are being tactful; if they have become more like the Wright photographs, which have at least been accepted by experts; or if they remain as they once were.

I am considering going to the glen to get more pictures. At least then we should have some other point of comparison, but if the same thing happened again I think I might despair. What can one do against such subterfuge? And it is all around me… it is becoming difficult to consume a meal in our own home for finding the cheese mouldy or the meat maggoty. Against all our inclinations, we are driven out to eat. Indeed, I wonder if we may be driven out altogether.

I long to be a thousand miles from any mention of the word fairy, and yet I cannot escape it; it is in Harriet's anxious expression, constantly looking at me as if to say, 'Shall we go?', and in Charlotte's look of gentle sorrow as she bends closely over her work.

I have even begun to dream of them. They visit me each night in the darkest hours, and each time I am taken in, because the dream begins with a false waking. I hear them first. There are words I cannot make out, spoken in mellifluous tones followed by tinklings of silver laughter, and there is more of the clicking I heard by the stream. I open my eyes expecting to see them dancing in the air, and I do, but I am surprised at their proximity; the little green fellow is leaning right over me. I catch one glimpse of his tiny features before he reaches out, quicksilver fast, and all goes black.

I try to open my eyes again and see only the dark. I bat my hands before my face, afraid of what the fairies are doing, and my fingers close on nothing.

I reach up, feeling my own eyelids, dragging them upward. It is difficult to tell but I think they are already open. And that is when I wake, when the first terror of it closes upon me.

But it is only a dream, and many would doubtless claim that I have spent far too long lending such things credence already. As you said, Charlotte's condition may well be the result of suggestion – of, ironically, prying too far into the mysteries, upsetting the balance of her mind to the degree that she is physically affected.

I shall endeavour to learn from the spirit of Sherlock Holmes and take a more scientific approach. Indeed, I have fallen into some fanciful matter; I shall break off here and complete this letter later, when I hope I may be a correspondent of better sense.

Continuance – 7th October
I take up my pen once more rather late in the evening, for I have something new to impart, though whether it is of greater sense

than the last is, alas, somewhat questionable. That is difficult to achieve, however, whilst living in such a place. Indeed, I have further reason to think it benighted – but I shall explain. Driven, as I mentioned, for want of unspoiled food, we took dinner in the parlour of a local hostelry a few hours ago. It was not the first time we had been forced to do such a thing, and the novelty of it was somewhat tarnished; we spoke little, until the landlady came in and asked how we did.

We responded with the usual pleasantries. Then Harriet held up her glass of milk and said, 'The fairies don't like this. It's the special milk they want.'

The lady replied as one would expect, in the tones of humouring a child, and we went on quite dully until the end of our repast, when she bustled in with a little jug, which she set before Harriet.

'Beastlings,' she said with a wink. 'That's what the fairies like.'

My daughter-in-law looked up with some annoyance. I think we would have sent the stuff away, but Harriet seized the jug with such eagerness her mother could not have taken it from her. Indeed, the child appeared quite desperate at the idea of its loss, and although I felt considerable dismay at the woman's foolish meddling, I could not bear to remove it either.

Beastlings. It is the word for the first milk after a cow has calved, I believe; it has a peculiarly rich smell and an almost green tinge. I cannot say I altogether like it, and would not bring myself to taste it for the world. But then, that would have upset Harriet too much. She carried it home with the greatest reverence, and I believe would have gone running to the glen at once had I not told her it must be kept for the morrow; which, in the worst possible circumstance, is a Saturday, and so even school cannot prevent her.

I could not think what else to do, but I cannot imagine what possessed me to speak those words. For now she expects to go, and I do not know what I shall say to put the light of it out of her eyes.

I shall finish here. I think I shall walk to the postbox at once, in defiance of the dark; it might help me to straighten my thoughts.

Yours sincerely,
Lawrence Fenton

13

Put the light of it out of her eyes. The phrase is in my mind all the rest of the day. Whenever I can spare a minute I go to Edie, being solicitous, bringing her tea, seeing if there's anything she needs, her knitting needles maybe. She shakes her head and tries to smile. Each time I see that smile, something twists inside me. It's worse because I know she isn't doing it on purpose, there's nothing designed about it, not like it would be if it was Mrs Favell.

I suppose Mrs Favell must know I'm longing to find out what came of the promised trip to the glen. Did they really go? Did the fairies drink of what they gave? I almost don't want to know because of course they couldn't have, there's nothing left but to rend the dream in two, and yet I *must*.

What was it she said to me? *You only had to ask.*

I could ask now. She's upstairs, reading. She said that's what she was going to do, loudly, when some special visitors arrived with therapy dogs in bright little jackets. The animals are cute and fluffy and placid, all the better to be stroked and exclaimed over by the residents, hopefully lowering their blood pressures and bringing them a little joy. Exclamations rang out as the dogs were placed on the first waiting laps. None of them sat on Mrs Favell's knee, of course. She rose from her chair the moment they arrived, though for a time she stood and watched, as if she couldn't quite tear herself from the sight – though it disgusted her, that was clear from her expression. It was as if she was watching some arcane ritual, and she kept brushing at her skirt, as if it was covered in hair. Of course, it wasn't; it was spotless.

All the time I couldn't help thinking of Lawrence Fenton on his way to the glen, apprehensive and afraid. What else might he have felt – yearning? Curiosity?

I remind myself that it's all invention, perhaps even made up by *her*, but there's still a part of me that badly wants to believe there's something more to the world than slow afternoons and tea and talk of children and grandchildren who never come. Or do I only miss stories so very badly?

I nod to one of the ladies with the petting dogs and walk towards the stairs, half expecting someone to call me back, but nobody does. I open the door to the stairway and it closes again behind me with a sound like a whisper. The noise at my back is cut off: there's only silence and there's nothing to do but go on up, because I can't bring myself to open it again.

Mrs Favell is in her room, seated by the window, much as she was when I first saw her. Her blouse looks diaphanous in the light spilling through the glass, her pearls gleaming at her neck.

She isn't reading, doesn't have a book in her hand; there's an air about her of waiting. She might have been sitting there for years, and I wonder how old she is. Her neck is a little lined, but not too much. She's kept her figure, hasn't got jowly or bags under her eyes, and that makes her look younger than the others even as her clipped speech and formality make her seem older. I think of the way time is said to pass in Fairyland: fluid, malleable, a year flowing by for every human second, decades of summers swimming by as if in a dream.

'I knew you'd come,' she says. 'A fish on a hook, aren't you, young Rose? How old will *you* feel, I wonder – in a year, in three?'

She's reading my mind again. Her words have too much truth in them. I'm not used to so much truth and I squirm under it. I prefer quiet lies, the usual platitudes that make life tolerable. *It's a beautiful day. I'm fine. Your granddaughter will love them.*

'Let's not mess around,' she says. She stands abruptly and goes to the bureau, makes a point of placing the key in the lock, turning it, lowering the flap that keeps everything inside. She turns to me and smiles. It's a cruel smile, and I don't think she even meant it that way; it slipped from her before she could stop it. In the next moment she's smoothed it over.

With much deliberation, she selects something from within. I know she has more in there by the rustling, but when she withdraws there's a single letter in her hand. None of them were in the bureau when I searched it, but I can't admit to knowing that. She puts it down, closes the drawer, turns the key in the lock, removes it and places it once more in the bowl.

'I have it here,' she says. 'The secret. Everything you'd like to know, Rose: about me, about the world, about life. About the way it truly is.'

I can't quite believe she said those words, not even in reference to a fairy tale, but I nod. I wonder what she's waiting for. *You only had to ask*, she'd said, but she still hasn't given me the letter. I open my mouth to say *May I?* and she lets out a dry laugh and shakes her head.

'You don't want it,' she says.

I frown. Of course I want it, she knows I do. Before I can gainsay her she says, 'I don't mean the letter.'

I can't move. I can't speak; I feel as if I've been placed under some spell. The atmosphere is redolent with possibilities, things unsaid but known anyway, the past and the future coalescing into some new shape.

'Say it,' she says, and her eyes are greedy. She taps the letter in her hand as if offering it in return for something, some unholy exchange she can't even name. I think of Rapunzel – or rather her mother, young and pregnant, making her deal with the devil, or an enchantress at least; Hansel and Gretel, abandoned so that their parents could have more food to eat; the miller's daughter, promising her unborn child to Rumpelstiltskin. It's like she's a wicked stepmother, or a witch, or a—

I blink. She's a lonely old woman, that's all, just a human being with odd ways and an odder story to tell. There's nothing else to it, yet the impression remains that there's something beneath, a truth concealed behind the pearlescent blouses and scent of flowers.

'I don't have *infinite* time, Rose,' she says. 'I only want to hear the truth from your own lips. Tell me. Do you want it?'

I stand in the silence. Time passes. I think of Paul. I think of all the dreams and beliefs I'd had; I think of staying here for ever. And I think of the thing that's taking form inside me, the buds of its limbs, eyes forming behind membranous skin, the miniature torso curled in on itself as if tucked into a bird's nest, bones bending in unnatural ways, minuscule eyelashes, tiny fingernails, and I say, 'No.'

Her eyes suddenly shine, like sunshine spearing through clouds. Her smile clears into something transparent and she holds out the letter as if in reward, her arm perfectly straight. I reach out and take it. I don't feel that anything's changed; I don't know if I should. I suppose, one day, I'll regret saying that word, when I have a son or a daughter at my side, someone of my blood, someone I can never imagine being parted from. But they'll never know. It will be a private guilt, and anyway, it doesn't mean anything. No one need ever know. Even Mrs Favell seems to have lost interest, turning from me towards the window, looking out, as ever, towards the woods.

Without turning she says, 'Good day.'

I don't leave. I don't even move. It strikes me what a cruel thing it was to have me say, to push me to this point, to crystallise my selfishness. Even if no one else ever finds out, no one that matters, it's something I'll remember for ever.

And I want more: more in return than dry words in faded ink on crumpled paper.

'You're Charlotte,' I say, before I know I'm going to. I don't even know why, since the idea is ridiculous even to me. I'm tired and wrung out. I've been caught up in too many stories. I suppose I simply haven't wanted to think about my own.

No matter how silly it is, I wait for her answer. She doesn't provide one, doesn't even look at me, and anger rises. 'You are, aren't you? You're her.'

At last her voice drifts into the air, vague and distant, as if coming from a long way away. 'Of course I'm *a* Charlotte. But however could I be the same? What a funny idea, Rose.'

I think that's all, but she adds, 'No – *that* Charlotte is gone. She vanished long ago, and she's never, ever coming back again.'

The paper in my hand feels more dry and dead than ever. I feel as if I've lost something, though I don't know what. I turn and walk out of the room, half expecting to hear Mrs Favell's mad laughter ringing out behind me, but there's nothing; only a cold and fathomless silence.

14

The next morning, I don't go to work. Paul had made a doctor's appointment, texting me the details so I could arrange it with Patricia. He managed to get a cancellation, so we didn't have to wait too long. Patricia wasn't impressed, but after my encounter with Mrs Favell I couldn't bring myself to care too much. I told her I'd be an hour late starting my shift and now here I am, sitting in front of Dr Motram, answering questions about things I wouldn't have told my mother.

Yes, I'd still been bleeding.

Yes, I'd continued taking the pill.

Yes, I'd drunk wine.

Whatever my answer, he doesn't raise an eyebrow, doesn't change his blank expression. Is that deliberate, or is it all so commonplace? All he says is that any smoking or drinking has to stop now. Paul sits a short distance away, shuffling his feet, twisting his hands or placing his elbows on the back of his chair, always in motion. It's only when I say that no, I hadn't noticed anything out of the ordinary at all, that Paul sits up straight, as if trying to hide his incredulity.

He'll wonder why I ever took the test I suppose, but I don't care; I'll tell him something vague about how I just *knew*, and he'll be happy with that. Right now I'm uncomfortable and embarrassed and still have that feeling I'm not quite myself any longer, but underneath that I feel invigorated, full of energy, restored. I hardly slept – I stayed up reading *The Coming of the Fairies*, the name of it weirdly prophetic in the half dark – but I'm as refreshed as if I'd had eight hours straight. There's life in my step; it's fizzing inside me, right down to my fingertips. Even my hair looks better, gleaming, and my skin is clearer.

Paul grinned when I awoke and saw him watching. As soon as I did, he leaned in and rested his head on my belly, stroking it as if he couldn't wait for it to swell and change. Then he accused me of glowing. Is that a word only used for supposedly pregnant women? Now it seems a hundred years away, unable to affect me, not connected with me at all.

Then I hear the doctor explaining to Paul that over-the-counter tests are so good these days, so reliable, there really isn't much need to confirm anything, and I don't hear his words any longer: there's only the humming of the fan inside the computer on his desk, footsteps walking along the corridor, Paul's breathing, the sudden tap of computer keys as the doctor updates my records.

He says he's going to refer me to the Early Pregnancy Unit, that I'll need a scan. It's not usual to have one at this stage, he explains, but with the bleeding they just want to be on the safe side, even though it's fairly common, nothing to worry about. I have no idea how to respond. It's all too real again, everything crowding in. The thought of having a scan, of waving a photograph of blurry pixels at my friends, my colleagues – *but not my mum* – is surreal. It strikes me that I really am pregnant, and that there might be something wrong with it. It might even be because of something I've done. The very obliviousness I'm still trying to cling to could have damaged it, blighted its entire life. My body suddenly feels too light, as if made of feathers or dandelion seeds, something that at any moment could fly away.

It's because of *her*: Mrs Favell. It's because I told her that no, I didn't want the baby. Now it might really be gone, as if saying such a thing could have wished it away, and I don't know how to feel. I'm suspended between moments, between taps on a keyboard, the movement of the second hand on the cheap plastic clock on the wall.

Someone fumbles at my fingers. It's Paul, taking my hand. His palm feels hot and sweaty but I don't pull away.

'It's fine,' he says, 'you'll see.' His voice is tense, strung out on wires.

The doctor pushes leaflets into my hands. *You're pregnant: what now?* the uppermost says, and I want to cry. I want to see my mum, just once, for a little while. I want to tell her that this can't be me; I'm not ready.

Instead I shove the leaflets deep into my bag. As I do, I catch sight of the letter Mrs Favell gave me yesterday. I still haven't read it, haven't wanted to think about it. Is that who I am now, refusing to face up to anything?

I walk out of the surgery with Paul, nodding in thanks at the receptionist just like other people do. She doesn't notice. She's busy finding the key to the toilet for an old lady with a walker and thick ankles. Another, younger woman is sitting in the waiting room, a baby carrier in front of her. I can't see what's inside but she can't take her eyes off it, and she's smiling as if she'll never stop. She glances up briefly, seeking answering smiles, admiration of this thing she has made, and her eyes meet mine and her expression falters.

Some day soon, that will be me. I have an image of myself sitting in her place, but I'm not smiling. My eyes are dark and entirely blank.

Outside, Paul turns towards me, putting his hands on my shoulders and resting his head against mine. He's so much taller than me. I always thought he'd know what to do. He murmurs into my hair, saying he'll look after me. He says he'll drive me to work and pick me up again afterwards. I know he'll make a good father. I can see him comforting a child, making it smile, patching up an injured knee or a grazed palm.

I shake him off – I'm the one carrying the two of us, aren't I? I'm the one building a life for us, or I *was*. I lead the way towards the car, feeling as if I'm floating inches above the ground, but it's different now. The energy's gone, leaving me dizzy and wrung out. Can I smell burnt toast or is that another symptom of what's happening to me?

I'm not an hour late to work after all. I'm only forty-five minutes behind my time, though a hundred years might have passed.

It's easy to slough it off, though, that other world. I distribute nutritional milkshakes, selecting spouted cups or beakers, adding straws for those who find them easier, ready with more for when the paper goes gummy. I rush off in response to an alarm triggered by a frail resident's bedside pressure mat; just admitted for respite care, she'd tried to get up by herself. I smile brightly for Barry, who's increasingly showing signs of dementia and insists he hasn't shaved, must be shaved *now*, still confused even when I get him to stroke his own cheek; for Maryam, who's misplaced her glasses and can't see me properly, isn't it awful, I'm nothing but a blur; and at Edie, who isn't knitting but watching television with an expression of raptness, or emptiness, I'm not sure which. Guilt strikes me to the heart. At least Mandy and the others are taking no notice of me. It's as if I've wronged them by being late and they've already cut out the tainted presence in their midst.

That reminds me that once again Mrs Favell has kept herself aloof, and I know I should do my duty and see if she's all right. In a rush of perverseness I ask Mandy, in a loud voice that can't be ignored, if she's seen her. Without glancing up she says, 'She has a visitor. In the garden.'

I'm so surprised I don't answer. Mrs Favell with a visitor? It's just so *human* of her. I thought she must have alienated everyone she'd ever met, that she's embittered because she's alone, or perhaps the other way around. The visitor could be someone professional of course, a lawyer to go over her will or someone else who doesn't have a choice in the matter. Overcome by curiosity, I go to the French windows. I open them just enough to peek out and hear, 'Ah, Rose. There you are.'

I start. There's no one there, no one on the lawn, no one meandering the gravel paths. I lean out. She's sitting on a bench set against the side of the building a little to my right. Her face is half concealed by another person, whose back is turned. It's a woman. Her hair is golden, twisted into a chignon, not a strand out of place. A ruffle of lacy whiteness protrudes from the collar of her violet jacket. She is tall; I can see that even though she's sitting down.

I step outside and greet them.

'Well, chop-chop,' says Mrs Favell. 'You're just in time, Rose. I'd like you to meet my daughter.'

My mouth falls open. The woman on the bench does not turn as I walk up to her. Even so, I can see by her cheek that her skin is perfect; she could be twenty. Her posture is altogether self-possessed; she could be thirty. And then I see her eyes, and they are older still, and she stands and I look down and see that she is pregnant.

'This is Harriet.'

She smiles. It is sweet, that smile, and she puts out her hand and says, 'My dear, I'm so very pleased to meet you,' and her voice is music. It's all I can do not to gawp. She looks like Mrs Favell. I remember the photographs in the box of a mother and daughter, their faces alike, and I'm certain it's them, even though the pictures seemed to have been taken many decades ago. My mind does the sums and whirls and Harriet cries out in concern as I falter. She's still holding my hand, hers cool and smooth, and she puts her other hand on my arm and guides me to her place on the bench, so that I'm facing her mother. *Can* it be her mother?

The sickness I've been trying not to think about all morning rushes in upon me. How could I have imagined I was feeling better? I stare down at the narrow stretch of bench between us. The slats are peeling, shreds of paint scarcely concealing the dead grey beneath. Mrs Favell's eyes bore into me. Amusement seeps from her.

So glad I never troubled over it, she'd said. *I saved myself a world of bother.* Why had she lied? What game had she been playing? Or had she merely meant that she *had* had children, but didn't much care for it, hadn't spent time worrying or fussing over them? I wouldn't put it past her. I can't imagine her as a mother. A strict, starched Victorian one perhaps, foisting her offspring onto a governess and having them brought out for inspection, but not one who would hold a child, nurture it, love it.

And the name: Harriet. That had to be a part of the game. Despite any amount of confusion over her age, there's no way this woman could have been a child in the nineteen-twenties. And she's surely either too young to be Mrs Favell's daughter or too old to be having a baby now. Or is it simply that both of them are older mothers – like mother, like daughter? How old *is* she? Is Harriet even her real name? For whatever reason, she's playing along.

I turn to look at her. She's still smiling with those perfect lips, so redolent of sweetness, and yet her eyes, for a moment, are oddly blank. *Dressing*, I think, and then the warmth returns. She chafes my hands and says, 'There. You're feeling a little better.'

Without pause, she removes one hand and slides it along my forearm, and across, and rests it on my belly. I catch my breath, try to pull away, and feel the hardness of the bench at my back.

'It's all right,' she says. 'I know. I know.' She nods, and her expression is so full of sympathy that tears prickle at my eyes. 'Mummy told me all about it.'

It's a violation. I don't want her touching me. I've heard of this, strangers feeling they have the right to put their hands on the bump – not that I even have one – as if a pregnant woman's body is no longer her own. I wouldn't dream of doing it to her. Yet her voice is so soft, her touch so reassuring, that my discomfort begins to melt away. She means well, I tell myself. She has more understanding in her voice than I've felt in days. Her tone soothes me. I wonder if she's alone too, if she shares some of my fears, if that's why there's this connection. I no longer doubt she knows how it feels: the enormity of it, the terror. I'm not afraid now, though. It's as if she's draining it from me. A rush of strength returns and I remember for the first time in an age that I am in control of my life.

I straighten my posture. I'm not adrift any longer. I'm not a child, to sit here and cry and be comforted. I'm an adult, and whatever comes, it will be all right; I'll deal with it. I'll accept it.

'There – that's it,' she says. She gives a final stroke before withdrawing her hand and puts it instead to her own belly, the small, neat mound half hidden by her lovely jacket. Her eyes twinkle. I know it's a cliché even as the word comes to me, but that's exactly what they do.

I glance up at Mrs Favell. Her eyes are brighter too, shining with barely restrained laughter, full of what appears to be joy.

My mouth floods with a bitter taste and I suddenly feel cold all over my skin, right through to my centre. I'm empty, nothing inside but a hollow space, and her words whisper again in my ear. *Do you want it?*

I cry out, push myself up from the bench, stagger away from them.

'Oh,' Harriet says, her voice bell-like, though she doesn't sound surprised, not really.

Her mother says something too, in a low voice that still carries easily, loaded with meaning. 'She should be called Robyn.'

Is she speaking to her daughter? Yet the words go to the heart of me and lodge there. I don't know why; I don't know what they've done to me. I can't ask, can't even look at her again. I walk away from them both, my vision blurring so that I can hardly see. I feel glass under my outstretched hands and grasp for the handle, pulling myself inside, closing the door behind me. I stand there leaning against it, blinking. For a second, sound is distorted, as if my head is underwater, and then the sharp clear note of a blackbird rings out and everything returns.

'Are you all right?'

I can't place the voice. When I turn I see Mandy, her face up close to mine and full of concern.

'I am,' I say. 'I'm fine, I'm really fine.' I'm not sure who I'm trying to convince.

She nods and moves away from me. I turn and focus on the garden again, the lawn the brilliancy of emerald, the tulips vibrantly yellow, hyacinths of all colours waving their heads in the sun. And there are roses, crimson roses scattered everywhere. It's suddenly too bright to look at. I wonder if that's a symptom of my pregnancy, if everything is, and again the whole thing seems terribly unlikely. The doctor's well-worn words of this morning – that it really doesn't need to be confirmed – seem a thousand years ago. The coldness hasn't left me. I feel utterly and dreadfully empty.

15

An hour later I'm at home, sitting on the sofa. The TV is too loud, as if I've scarcely moved from Sunnyside. I'm still angry at Mandy. She must have been watching me – I don't think I fainted, not really, but she insisted I had. I found myself kneeling on the carpet, staring into its swirling pattern, right there in the lounge where anyone – everyone – could see. I don't know what happened. Maybe it was the temperature in there, always so warm. *Had* I fainted? Maybe I should be grateful for Mandy's interference, but there was a look in Patricia's eyes when they called her in, one that said *I knew you wouldn't last.*

Both Edie and Jimmy agreed that I'd passed out, but Patricia's look hadn't faded until Mrs Favell and Harriet came in. Mrs Favell took charge at once. She said, in a loud voice that carried across the lounge, that of course I'd been taken ill; I was working too hard; I looked quite dreadful. She added, 'There are rules about staff being ill, aren't there?'

It was then that Patricia said I should go home. I called Paul to come and fetch me, though quietly, not wanting to remind them I'd been to the doctors and that he must have driven me. Even though I was being sent home sick, I didn't want them speculating what might be wrong.

I still don't quite know what I'm doing here at home in broad daylight. Paul's behind me in the kitchen, making Horlicks – I didn't know we possessed such a thing, didn't like to tell him I hate the taste – but he keeps poking his head over the top of the sofa as if he's scared I'll vanish or collapse into its depths or maybe just die while his back's turned. I wonder if it's me or the baby he's worried about and push the thought away. If he knew what had been going through my head of late he'd probably hate me as much as I hate myself.

I stroke my belly. What had I been thinking? My fears seem surreal now I'm home. Harriet hasn't done anything to me. Nor has Mrs Favell; in fact, she was kind to me. The baby is inside me, growing, probably no bigger than one of my fingernails. Can it feel my feelings? Is it troubled by whatever stress hormones I've bathed it in? I can't allow my thoughts to run away like that. And I've left everyone at Sunnyside short-staffed. Guilt washes over me, bringing the taste of iron to the back of my throat, and I swallow hard. Paul passes me a mug and I sip despite my distaste; maybe the baby likes it even if I don't. My stomach groans at the milky warmth.

Paul's asked a hundred questions about how I am and he hovers over me now, shutting his mouth at my look. Instead he comes and sits on the sofa, putting his arm around me. I lean into the strength of him. He always seems so comfortable with himself, meeting anything that comes his way, never overwhelmed by the world. I imagine him playing with a little girl, laughing as she tries to kick a brightly coloured ball, picking her up and whirling her through the air as she giggles.

I try to imagine Harriet doing the same thing and I can't. Charlotte and Harriet: just like in the letters. Perhaps it's a coincidence, and Harriet's concern for me was genuine; she had no concept of playing some cruel joke. Still, the way Mrs Favell defended me seems as odd as everything else, perhaps even more so. Or maybe she wanted to be rid of me – after Harriet had touched me.

I touch my belly just as she had, finding the place, remembering the way she nestled in close, that horrible intimacy. I squirm at the thought of it and Paul strokes my hair, tilting his head, resting it on mine.

I know I shouldn't dwell on it – on *them* – but the questions keep coming. If Mrs Favell really had written the letters herself, working their own names into some fantastical story, why have the past Charlotte blinded by fairies? It doesn't make sense. If she *is* feeding those letters to me – and that's what it feels like, being fed, irresistible pieces of fairy food, as cursed as it is magical – she's also handed me the proof that none of it is real. Unless there's something in the next letter to explain everything – and I suddenly realise that it's still in my bag. I don't know how I could have forgotten it. I'm suddenly hungry for the words, for the end of the tale. The family was set to go to the glen once more, armed with nothing but a jug of milk. What could have become of that?

I wriggle out of Paul's arms, telling him I'm going to put my things away. He smiles and tells me to be careful, cutting off his words at my glare.

As soon as I'm alone I riffle through the papers in my bag, first finding the doctor's leaflets. The topmost has silhouettes of women at various stages of pregnancy and I grimace at their swelling shapes. I put my hand to my own belly, then pull up my tunic and look at my skin, and I am frozen in horror.

My belly is hardly mounded at all, and yet instead of the smooth, pale skin I've always known, always recognised as *me*, I am encircled by a series of little marks. They look like tiny footprints, as if I really have been touched by the folk – or danced upon, or around. *Widdershins*, I think. Anti-clockwise. They weren't there this morning, I'm sure of it. Did they blossom in the preceding hours or was it when Harriet touched me, claiming something of me – *inside* me – for her own?

I pull down my tunic, not wanting to see them any longer, telling myself they're stretch marks, nothing but that. But how, when I'm hardly showing? I sit on the bed and wrap my arms around my body. Has she really done something to me – to the baby? I can't shift my unease. I can't answer the question.

I drag the air into my lungs. For a moment, I just breathe. I won't let her get to me. I can choose not to listen – I can choose what to think. She is nothing to me. I find myself rubbing my arm, right over my tattoo: *Rose.* Claiming my own skin. I lean forward and grasp the letter.

In contrast with the slippery leaflets, the letter is thick and matte and reassuring under my fingers. It doesn't look like the others, though. The writing is untidy, words scratched into the page as if written in a terrible hurry. The ink is almost black in places, faded and ghost-like in others.

Not knowing if I'm moving on or trying to forget, to bury my fears and step into someone else's life, I begin to read.

➺⬟

8th October 1921

Dear Mr Gardner,

Forgive my rather untidy scrawl. I have more news to impart, and write in a state of considerable excitement.

Only a short time has passed since the worried-over visit to the glen. Harriet awoke full of fervent emotion and brimming with its importance, and to deny her – well, I somehow found no way to do so, though I could never have gone there again under any other compulsion. Harriet ran and seized her jug of green milk. And then she said her mother must come too.

Well, here was a difficulty. I said we must go alone and that I could not prevail upon her mother for anything, and Harriet behaved most unlike herself: she stamped, and shouted, and wailed; and her mother came all a-flurry to see what was amiss.

Harriet would not be quieted. She said her mother must and should go, and Charlotte only looked grave, and shuddered as if she were suddenly cold. I must confess that her reluctance spread itself to me; all I could think of was my dream, and that glimpse of an impish face before all went dark.

Then an idea struck me. Charlotte had said she was blinded when a fairy spat in her eye. What if she went to the glen, but kept her good eye covered somehow? I made the suggestion and Harriet fell silent at last, her face all raptness and hope.

Charlotte closed both her eyes. Then she rose and left the room.

Harriet and I looked at each other. We did not know if her mother would return, but after a few minutes she did, and she was dressed as I never thought to see her again. For she had

165

found her widow's bonnet with its finely meshed veil, the one she had worn when my son was lost to us.

I could not speak. I might have been transported back in time, to the very moment of opening the telegram with shaking hands – it had been sent to Charlotte, but she had been unable to look at it. It was I who had had to break the news.

'I think he will protect me from them,' she said simply, and began to put on her coat. And then she stopped and said, 'But it is not I who should wear this – it is Harriet!'

I put out a hand to stop her. She made a good point of course, but the idea of the child being dressed in such a thing – it seemed an abomination.

Harriet stepped back and said, 'I shall wear my hat with the low brim. And I will not let go of Grandpapa's hand.'

As if to demonstrate, she came to my side. Clutching the jug with one hand, she took mine in the other; and I thought at once of some little creature coming and spitting in her eyes, and her unable to throw up either hand to shield them.

But surely that could not be. She is a child; she is an innocent. On how many occasions did the Wright girl play with the fairies? She was perfectly unharmed by her experiences, was she not? And there was also a sense of – well, of being carried along; as if we were all half fallen into a dream, and following the course that we must take. It is fanciful to be sure, but I can think of no better way to describe it.

Still, I prevailed upon Harriet to allow me to carry the jug, and she reluctantly relinquished it, leaving her one hand free. Then we made to set out, but not without a last delay, for

Charlotte stopped at the threshold and would not go on.

Then she said, 'Thus I took the little skeleton. They were supposed to let me in – but it did not happen.'

I could not see her expression. I am not sure I could have looked into her eyes if it had been possible. I remained there fixed to the spot and unable to reply, and then she trembled and stepped out.

You may imagine my feelings. All the horror I had experienced at the loss of the skeleton was before me again – and here was the cause: not a fairy, but the woman who stood to me as a daughter. How could she have done it? But the 'why' soon came to outweigh the 'how'. For what must her feelings have been, to do such a thing? Had the fairies gained a hold over her? I remembered the way she used to hold the box in her hand and stare into it, as if fascinated. Was it only that she wished for nothing more than to go into Fairyland with them, that unknown and perhaps unknowable place? Now we were going straight to them, and holding another gift. Only think what had been her reward before!

Little wonder, then, that she had hesitated. Yet now she strode out boldly, as if to leave us behind. Harriet and I hurried after her. A thousand words crowded my mind, all the things I wanted to say to her mother; but I could not challenge her in front of the child, and we were already committed, and a part of me wished to know what would happen. My curiosity had been roused by the whole affair, and whilst I had come to long for the end of it, I somehow felt that the time was not yet.

Harriet was as good as her word and did not let go of my

hand. I was glad, as we went, that my own eye-glasses were in place. Blindness is perhaps the province of the old rather than the young, but believe me when I say that nobody is ever ready for that.

As we went, the sun was shut out by dense clouds which admitted no glimpse of the sky. It was not a bright day and soon it was darker yet for we stepped under the trees, Charlotte still walking ahead of us. She had not once looked back. Harriet and I had not exchanged a word. I felt her fingers close more tightly upon mine as we passed into deeper shadow.

I was surprised by how far autumn has progressed. It was not that there was anything unusual for the time of year, but I realised I had passed many of the preceding days ensconced inside. The air was cold and crisp, but with nothing enlivening in it. Everything was damp, but diminished; the beck had shrunk to a dull trickle. Leaves of russet and brown speckled the earth but all looked limp and rather dismal and it felt that way, too; there was a dead note to the place. It did not at all feel as when I had last seen it, and I wondered if that was because the fairies had gone.

The idea brought with it an odd sense of loss as well as relief. For they were a miracle, were they not? One such as man could marvel over for years to come. And I had seen them, but for everything I had grasped at, I had nothing to show. It reminded me suddenly of the tales I had read in Hartland's book, of fairy gold that turns to nothing but coal when spied upon too greedily.

Charlotte had continued on, and I still could not see her face. I suddenly wished to do so. I called to her and she halted, her head inclined as if focused upon the stream.

'Charlotte, perhaps you should cover your good eye,' I said. 'Here must do, I think.' I made to squeeze Harriet's hand as her fingers slipped from my own. I started, but she was at my side just as ever; she smiled as if in full agreement, and reached for the jug.

I peered into it with distaste, but I could no longer detect the greenish scent; it was lost in the tang of the stream that hung in the air all around us. I gave it to her. I wanted to clasp my hands over Harriet's eyes but she nodded at me so gravely, as if this is what must be, as if she saw everything.

She turned to the stream, where it fell into the little pool with a dull sound, and no birds sang, and no lights danced about her, and no words were spoken. I heard her breathy intake of air. And she held it high and, as if in a story, tapped her heels together. Then she held the jug over the stream and poured out the contents.

'The milk is free,' she said at last. 'And all shall see!'

I did not know where she had learned the words. The fluid whirled into the eddy, turning it cloudy for an instant, and was gone. Harriet watched, her lips almost forming a smile. I nodded to suggest that we had finished and may leave, but her expression did not change.

'All done,' I said, my voice falsely bright, and I turned to where Charlotte had been standing. She was not there.

'Mama!' Harriet had seen it too, for her voice lifted in sudden panic. She scrambled past me. I reached for her shoulder and felt it beneath my fingers; then she was running away. Too slow – is that not the way of the old? Too slow and too foolish.

She rushed into the trees. I caught glimpses of her pale

dress and flying hair, and then she stopped, because a figure stepped from behind a willow and leaned down and wrapped its arms about her.

It was dark, the figure, half drowned in shadow, and I opened my mouth to call out; then I saw it was only Charlotte, holding her bonnet, and I heard her say Harriet's name in delight.

Harriet froze. Then she squealed and threw her arms about her mother. Both turned and walked towards me, hand in hand, no sign of fear or concern on their faces; and something about Charlotte's expression was different.

'I can see,' she said, her voice full of gladness. 'I see everything!' She opened and closed both eyes as if to show me, and I think I only looked confused. How could anything have changed so quickly? This was too much, and too soon. It had been too easy. Were the fairies so grateful for a little milk they would bestow such a blessing so simply?

But Charlotte's joy was contagious, creeping from her to me, and she caught my hand in her younger, stronger fingers, and squeezed it, so hard that it almost pained me. She gave me such a wide smile I could not help smiling back.

'Is it true?' I peered at her more closely. Her eyes appeared just as they had before.

She did not answer; she only laughed.

'I want to go home,' Harriet said, reaching out for me.

I took her warm fingers in mine, but it was Charlotte who spoke. 'Yes,' she said, 'home,' and we turned towards the house, accompanied by the sound of the beck, Charlotte's footsteps following behind our own as Harriet skipped at my side.

So great a blessing, for so small a thing – but perhaps it wasn't so small a thing. Perhaps the fairies saw our offering as an apology. Perhaps they saw it as a promise; or perhaps there had been no fairies, and I was only an old fool. Charlotte really might have been struck by hysteria, and it was only a belief in her daughter's actions that had released her from whatever spell she had placed over her own mind.

Relief came over me at last. She had her sight – and if there were fairies, they were good after all! It might have been a mistake: they never meant to harm Charlotte's eye. They did not mean to sting Harriet's finger. And yet it felt too easy, too neat, almost as if some trick had been played upon me.

Harriet remained quiet all the way home. She smiled secret smiles to herself, no doubt of relief. Charlotte kept silence too, overwhelmed perhaps by her own good fortune and the sight of her child, the world rendered distinct once more, without any trace of a shadow to mar her vision.

It only struck me afterwards that I might have taken the camera. I had quite forgotten my resolve to get more pictures. Perhaps it is just as well. In all honesty, now that we are home together and safe, I hope that we might be done with the whole thing. I remain your humble servant and will answer any questions you require of me, of course, but I think my role as an amateur detective in this matter, such as it was, may well be behind me. I hope you will not mind it, after everything that has befallen us.

Yours sincerely,
Lawrence Fenton

16

I'm back at Sunnyside and, as if summoned by its name, light floods in at every window, dispelling any shadow that lingered there. I had dreaded coming back, half expecting Patricia to fire me after all, but she didn't even comment on my absence, which had stretched to two days. I'd felt adrift rather than ill but Paul had picked up on it and insisted, though I'd been glad of the rest, and part of me had been relieved. Every time I'd closed my eyes, images flooded in: overarching trees filtering the light, making everything wavering and uncertain; a jug of milk so fresh, so intense, I could smell it; a garden full of colours that were too vivid, like the one at Sunnyside and yet unlike, its emerald grass headache-bright, the sky an endless azure, the scattered rose petals like drops of fresh-spilt blood.

Now there is nothing to mar my vision; the garden is innocent in its normality. Daffodils sway in the breeze, interspersed with purple crocuses, and everywhere birds are singing. There is nothing odd about any of it. Even Mrs Favell looks different. She's still wearing her pearls and a silky blouse – today's is a pale spring green – and she still has her upright stance, but that *thing* in her expression has gone. She looks at me as if I'm just a care assistant, which of course I am, and nothing else. She doesn't seem especially interested in me at all and I tell myself I'm not interested in her. Everything feels ordinary, and yet flatter somehow, colour leached from the world despite the sunshine.

Occasionally I feel Mrs Favell's eyes on me, but when I turn she's bent over a book or helping Alf with his crossword and I'm not sure, when that happens, if I'm disappointed or relieved. The story is over. I don't think there can be any more letters. I kept the last one she gave me. I'm still waiting for her to ask for it back, but she hasn't mentioned it.

I've only kept it to spite her. Lawrence Fenton had made the right choice to distance himself from all of it, and I intend to do the same. Where could it lead? I doubt the Charlotte of the letters was really blinded at all. The whole thing was pure invention.

Yesterday, while I was resting with nothing else to do, I dipped into *The Science of Fairy Tales*, which is still on my laptop. I soon set that aside as well. It was indeed full of strange matter: stories of young women or their babies being stolen away by the folk, replaced by things that only looked the same – or almost. In reality they were the things that Lawrence had mentioned, bewitched stocks of wood or aged and worn-out fairies, transformed by a glamour or a spell to resemble the stolen person. Or they were fairy children, more fractious than the human kind, for whom the fairies wished to secure the milk and care of a human mother.

I shake my head. I wish I hadn't read it. I wish I hadn't allowed Harriet to put her hand on my belly. If she visits again, she's not coming near me; I won't let her. Either she's as bitter and twisted as her mother, playing some sort of game, or she's a pawn in Mrs Favell's. Even if it's over, I feel repulsed by the idea of her touching me. I don't want her thinking about my baby, let alone reaching for it – *probing* – through my flesh.

I try not to think about the scan tomorrow. At least it's fallen on my day off, so I don't need to upset my co-workers or tell Patricia I need more time. I bury myself in my duties, soaping old men with a sponge, rubbing lotion into sagging, age-spotted skin, scrubbing dentures, helping Alf lift the spoon to his mouth. Barry is having a bad day and stares at his breakfast without touching it. When I go to help he looks at me in much the same bewildered way, his eyes glazed, and I wonder how much longer he'll stay here. If his dementia gets worse – when he can't recognise anyone for who they are, possibly even his own reflection in a mirror – he'll be moved into a specialist home.

I'm not the only one keeping busy. When Paul dropped me off he said he was on his way into town to buy every job paper he can find. He promised, again, to look after me.

Edie puts her hand on mine and squeezes and I look up, startled. It's a relief to see the bundle of knitting tucked under her arm, to know she's working on it again, hopefully having forgotten what I said about her family. At first glance I take it for a yellow baby blanket, then she holds it out, all pride in what she has made, and I see only a mass of wool. Instead of careful lines of stitches there is a chaos of thread, so stirred about with her needles it's hopelessly tangled.

Still, there's no trace of her pain in her eyes when she says, 'I think there's something different about you, Rose. Don't you think so, Mrs Favell? Doesn't she look well?'

I wince at her appeal to Mrs Favell but the woman only smiles and there's nothing concealed behind it; nothing sly, nothing insinuating, nothing to make anyone think she's anything other than she appears.

'Of course there is,' she says. 'Very different.'

My unease rushes back but I brush it aside. I don't have to listen to her. That's not why I'm here. I'll finish my shift and Paul will be waiting, and he'll carry me away from it all, and tomorrow, *tomorrow*, for the first time, we'll be able to look at our child.

17

It feels as if we're going on some pleasure outing, just the two of us, until the hospital comes into view, a seventies box panelled in that peculiar shade of green so beloved of institutions. I can already smell the sterility of antiseptic and suddenly I'm cold right through. I suppose most women, when it comes to it, have a sudden panic that something is wrong with their child, that some carefully blank-faced nurse will take them aside, speaking in hushed tones, to tell them the worst. And yet this isn't quite like that, because even while I'm trying to picture myself holding my baby, trying to forget the way I felt when I saw that positive result on a plastic stick, I can still hear Mrs Favell's voice:

Tell me. Do you want it?

That evil bitch. I don't know how she's managed to take on such a presence in my life, or to cast such a shadow across it. What is she to me? Nothing. And yet I can still feel her daughter's hand finding its way along my tunic to my belly, maybe further, to what was nestled within.

Paul's hand suddenly lands in my lap, squeezing my thigh, and I catch my breath. 'Are you okay?'

Of course, I tell him. *Of course I am.* We're turning into the car park, the pale sky shining back from a hundred windscreens. Paul takes a ticket from a machine. He concentrates on slotting the car into a narrow space and by the time he's done, it's like he's forgotten the question.

From now on, for the length of a morning, I'll sit where they tell me and go into the rooms they choose at the times they want me. I'll lie back and have cold gel squeezed on my belly and I'll keep perfectly still. I'll do everything I'm supposed to do; I'll do everything *right*.

I'm sent upstairs, not to obstetrics as I'd expected but gynaecology, where the Early Pregnancy Unit is tucked away. No one here looks pregnant. I thought there'd be women with big clumsy bellies, perhaps with toddlers playing with giant plastic bricks or pulling fabric books to pieces, and I realise why: it's so that the women who come here won't have to look at them, if the news is bad.

There are only a few other patients, some of them looking younger than me. I can't read their stories in their faces, can't tell if they want to be mothers. They clutch various papers as they go from door to door, taking their histories with them so that doctors can write on them. When I'm called, it isn't into a white room with a reclining chair and stirrups as I'd imagined, but a consulting room. A brisk woman with a neat hijab covering her hair comes in and explains that she's a specialist nurse. She says it's probably too soon and sorry it's a little embarrassing but the scan will need to be internal; it's a bit uncomfortable but it's the best way to see. I'm going to have the external scan first in case they can avoid the other, but it's possible that nothing will show up and I shouldn't let that worry me. It doesn't mean anything, she says, and I'm sent to wait outside again.

Paul talks to me and I nod along, forcing myself to drink the copious amounts of water I need to get through before the scan. On the surface I'm as blank as the sky I can see through the windows. Beneath, all my fears are flooding back. It doesn't matter how hard I've pushed them away; I can feel Harriet's hand on me, hear my own voice saying I don't want the baby. I'm suddenly sure that it's gone. I turn to Paul and open my mouth then close it again. I don't think he'd listen to me. He'll hear it from the doctors soon enough; he'll have to listen to them. Sure enough, a second later another nurse steps out of a door and calls my name.

Paul helps me up as if I'm eight months along, big with a baby and ungainly, and I pull my arm free and stand. I walk ahead of him into the room.

This time there is a reclining seat. The nurse asks me to partially undress and lie down on it and I do. She dims the lights and adjusts her glasses, the better to see the screen. She doesn't comment on the stretch marks girdling my belly. Perhaps she thinks they're from gaining and losing weight. Perhaps she thinks they're normal. How would I know? The gel is a cold shock against my skin. I feel as if it's turning me transparent, like glass, and maybe it is. She keeps on talking, telling me what she's doing, but I don't really listen. This scan will come up empty. Then I'll have the other one, the *uncomfortable* one, the *embarrassing* one, even though it won't be any use because that will come up empty too. I don't know how to feel about it. I suppose I'll work that out afterwards.

She places a wand against my skin and a noise starts up, a constant loud humming, and a moment later there's a wet swishing sound. She moves the cold nub around, up and down then across. I don't know why she's taking so long. She leaves it in one place before moving it back and forth again, not saying a word.

Then she says, in a bright voice, 'Can you wait a moment? I'll just call the doctor in.'

Paul steps forward and holds my hand, though I don't look at him. I keep my gaze on the walls, at the posters covering every inch, the locations of sexual health clinics, the best technique for washing hands. I read them all, top to bottom and left to right, and I don't take in a word. The door opens and closes again. I barely look at the doctor, an older woman wearing blue scrubs and a distracted expression. When she murmurs something about how she'll just take a look I nod for a brief second so that she doesn't start fussing about how I am.

The noise has been going all the time, that humming and the sound like water sloshing around in a tank. She takes hold of the sensor wand and moves it as the nurse did. I wonder why she's so bothered if what they said was true, that they might not be able to see anything. She speaks to the nurse in a low voice and I catch, 'Yes, you're correct about the dates.' Then she's gone and we're alone with the nurse again.

She leans over me. She has very smooth skin and full lips and very bright, shining eyes. She says, 'Would you like to see?'

I don't know what I'm supposed to say. There isn't anything to look at. But she turns a screen around and I *do* see: a picture in black and white framed by its silver edge; a scattering of particles, like dust; a dark oval amid the paler fragments, and within it, the suggestion of something curled. And I realise what the sound is, that watery in-out, in-out. It's a baby's heartbeat.

I draw in a long breath and the rush of air makes me dizzy. I stare again at the image in front of me. I can't make sense of it. It's large/small, it's good/bad, it's everything and nothing. It's pixels on a screen, indistinct and impossible to read. It could be anything, and I'm more terrified of it and filled with joy than I can say.

The nurse passes me a paper towel to rub the gel off my skin. She tells me the other scan won't be necessary, they can see everything they need. She says I'm further along than I thought, that the baby inside me is about sixteen weeks old, and I want her to stop; I want to grab those lips and twist them so that she can't say any more. She's changing everything with her words. I can almost see it dissolving in front of me, rearranging its parts into something other, something strange to me. I can't be sixteen weeks pregnant. It isn't possible. I would have *known*.

I remember Harriet putting her hand on my belly then moving it to cradle her own. I remember the neat mound under her jacket. One of the leaflets I'd been given said that most women start to show by sixteen weeks, and she'd clearly been showing. Her baby was older than mine.

I think of the book I'd tried to read, *The Science of Fairy Tales*, and its strange matter. All the stolen babies, snatched away from their mothers and taken beneath the hollow hills. The changelings left in their place, changelings that quickly sickened and died, or voraciously demanded more and more food, that were content to eat and sleep and lie there, pretending they weren't already long worn out. Could changelings be placed in the mother's belly while the baby still grew? The book hadn't said. Maybe whoever wrote it didn't know. How could they?

I can't settle on any coherent thought. The nurse and Paul are still smiling at me, but the shine in their eyes is fading.

I realise I'm muttering under my breath, something about how it's not mine, can't be mine. At first I don't think the nurse has heard, then her expression changes and I realise she has.

Paul leans over me, kisses my cheek, maybe trying to stop me saying anything else. He hasn't shaved and his stubble is scratchy. When he speaks his voice is too loud; he's not talking to me at all. 'She's fine,' he says. 'It's just a bit of a surprise, that's all. For both of us.' He squeezes my hand a little too tightly, as if to say, *Shut up.*

I can't shut up. 'I didn't *know*,' I said. 'I would have known, wouldn't I?'

The idea strikes me that if I hadn't known I was pregnant when I started working at Sunnyside, *she* would have. Mrs Favell, with her sly looks and slyer smiles, would have known.

But there is a baby, and it's still inside me. To think she could have done anything to it is ridiculous. So I'm further along than I thought. That's not impossible, is it? I've heard of women having babies all of a sudden, never having realised they were pregnant at all.

I feel like I'm reaching after something that isn't there.

'It's quite possible,' the nurse says, echoing my thoughts. Her voice is chirpy again; she's brushed away any worries she'd had. 'You might have had some implantation bleeding. That confuses ladies sometimes. It's perfectly natural.'

Implantation. Perfectly natural. I think of the strange thing inside me, curled into its tiny nest. I suddenly want it, fiercely, and a rush of heat passes through me. I'm not sure if it's because I want to be a mother or because I don't want *her* to take it from me, but she can't take it from me, not if I don't allow it.

I push myself up from the horrible chair and remember. *I only want to hear the truth from your own lips. Tell me. Do you want it?*

And my reply, a single word, one I can't take back: *No.*

Had that only been denial – or had I granted her some kind of permission?

I sway and someone grabs my shoulder. It must be Paul because the nurse rushes around the chair and takes hold of the other. I'm caught between them and I can't move. I'll faint if I do. And I wish everything could stay like this, in their hands, so that I don't have to think any longer; so that I don't have to know what it is I've so unwittingly done.

18

'The roof leaked,' Mrs Favell says, 'every autumn. Every year my father-in-law would have a man come from the town and go over it, inch by inch. He'd stand there and smoke his pipe while he went all over the slates, tugging here, tapping there, and the very next month we'd have to put down buckets and chamber pots. Water dripped through the light fittings sometimes, and he'd stand underneath sniffing for gas with the drops falling into his eyes.'

I stand in the doorway and listen. I can almost see an older man with a beard, clad in tweed, blinking back the falling water. The room I envisage is small and dark with a low, beamed ceiling, smelling of tobacco and dust and time. I don't know what decade she's talking about – she's holding court to one of the other residents, discussing the 'old days' – but somehow I picture her wearing a print dress, not even a style from the nineteen-twenties but older still, sharply narrowed to a corseted waist, topped by a white Victorian apron.

That can't be right of course, despite the mention of gas fittings and chamber pots and the formal way she speaks. I close my eyes and see again the pages I read the night before, from *The Science of Fairy Tales*, archaic and strange. One way to banish a fairy, the author said, was to trick it into revealing its age, thereby exposing its true nature. I think of the scan, the too-large embryo growing inside me. Had we identified its correct age? Was it really sixteen weeks old? But Mrs Favell parades her knowledge of times gone by, not hiding it at all.

I tell myself not to be stupid, that everything isn't about me, just as her voice lifts. 'Oh, Rose dear, is that you?'

I grit my teeth and steal softly away, up the stairs. I won't slink into the lounge at her call like a beaten creature. I'm not hers to command; I'm nothing to her, or should be. I'm the hands that wipe and polish and fetch, doing the same things my predecessor did, only the faces changing. Soon I'll be gone too. The baby has put a time limit on that. It's due in September, at the end of the summer.

I put a hand on my belly, thinking of the little ticking clock inside me, the tiny chambers of its heart beating twice as fast as mine. My bump is plainly visible under my tunic now. It burgeoned just after the scan, as if seeing it suddenly made it real and it's not hiding any longer. Patricia didn't fire me after all. She tried to look pleased as she adjusted my duties, cutting out any heavy work or manual lifting.

After the baby is born, I needn't see Mrs Favell again. I'll never be her keyworker now; I don't need to know anything more about her or even come back here. She won't be able to put odd thoughts into my head and by then I'll have forgotten it all. I'll be far too busy with other things: changing nappies, feeding, wiping milk-spit from my clothes and raising mushy food on a spoon and other things I don't even know of yet.

And I will love my baby.

I think of times gone by, all the suggestions I read about for safeguarding an infant. Maybe I'll put an old iron horseshoe over the door to protect us from evil, telling Paul it's decorative. Maybe I'll open a pair of iron scissors into a cross and place it beneath the crib or keep a Bible wrapped in my daughter's baby blanket. It strikes me that such precautions aren't so very different from those used by people who feared devils and demons and possession; that the methods for casting a fairy out are a little like exorcisms in the kind of films Paul likes to watch.

But of course I won't do anything of the kind. I remind myself that those things are nothing but stories, not *evidence*, and shake away the strange tide of thoughts. I'm hormonal, not quite myself. I should listen to Paul, not Mrs Favell. He's the one full of stories now, of what it will be like. He got up first this morning to make breakfast, guiding me into a chair as if I'd become some delicate, brittle thing. His eyes were clear and bright and full of the future and I suspect he'd been awake for hours, waiting for me to stir so that he could lavish attention on me. His smile was different too, not a fleeting thing signifying nothing, but broad and full of the joy inside him. I could see the crow's feet forming around his eyes, and I wanted to kiss them. They're a sign that he smiles more readily than he frowns. The world rests lightly on his shoulders. Things don't *implant* themselves on him.

I am brought back to the present when a cry of unhappiness sounds from somewhere along the empty corridor. It's an odd sound, more raw than I'm used to hearing, and I can't tell if it was a man or a woman. I rush along it and almost collide with Nisha as she emerges from one of the rooms.

It's Edie Dawson's. Nisha doesn't say a word, just stands back against the wall to let me pass. What I see is almost exactly what I expect and sadness swells like something solid within my chest.

Edie sits in her high-seat armchair, her head bowed to reveal the scalp through her cloud of white hair. She wasn't knitting, or trying to. She has a book in her lap, though her head hangs so low she can't possibly be looking at it. The pages have slipped from her grasp, her place lost, and it strikes me as terribly sad to go in the middle of a book like that, to never know the end of the story. But I suppose there were worse things than that, for Edie. She will not now see her daughter again. She will not hold her grandchild. And Edie had known her hands would remain empty, no matter how she tried to occupy them.

Why linger, like this?

Perhaps she had accepted those words at last, and here was the result. I have a rush of feeling – not hatred of Mrs Favell, though that is there too – more a momentary longing for my own child, mingled with a pang of loss for my mother.

Mandy pushes past me into the room, closely followed by Nisha, who must have gone to fetch her while I stood staring. They make the expected noises and go through the expected motions, none of it any use now. Edie sits there, her small room crowded with visitors at last, and yet more alone than anyone could ever be. She is beyond any of us and I try to reach out to her with my feelings, but I know she's already gone.

The words that echo in my mind are the ones Mrs Favell gave to me:

And on thy cheeks a fading rose
Fast withereth too.

I touch my cheek. I suppose this is all it comes to in the end. Summer gives way to winter; sedge withers from the lake. Even birdsong has its end. Only hollow rooms remain, people going through the motions, the rituals of death, because that's all there is to do.

Mandy leaves the body – that's all it is now, a body – and goes to the window. She throws it wide, pushing the curtains back. When she sees me watching she looks away as if she's been caught doing something embarrassing and tells me to go downstairs and check on things in the residents' lounge.

I turn to leave, but Nisha catches up with me in the corridor. I've never seen her so rattled, but everyone loved Edie. I try to imagine Sunnyside without her in it and can't. It already feels odd, the atmosphere subtly changed somehow.

'It's to let the soul out,' she says. 'That's why they open the window.'

I stare after her as she hurries away. How long is it since anyone believed in such things? And yet the image is so vivid: Edie freed of her arthritic hands and bent spine, spreading her arms like a child playing aeroplanes and whooshing out of the open window, into the clean air and scent of flowers, leaving behind a trail of silver laughter that only she can hear. Maybe she'll go and live with the fairies, wherever they are. Maybe there really is some spiritual realm where they can exist, along with the dead. A sense of longing closes in on me and for a moment I can't breathe. When I close my eyes, it's my mother's face I see.

I hurry down the stairs, though as I go it strikes me that I don't know if I'm supposed to tell the other residents what happened or if I should leave that to Patricia. I feel like I'll be lying if I don't, but I'm not sure I ought to, so I imagine Edie somewhere free and happy, only those left behind with tears in our eyes any longer, and I paste a smile over my features.

When I walk in, Mrs Favell is standing in the middle of the lounge and I don't know how she knows or why it should fall to her, but I can tell by her expression that she's told them all already. Everyone turns towards me, a roomful of downcast faces, and my expression falters under their gaze; all of them knowing, and wondering how it is that only I can smile.

19

That evening I go upstairs alone, stooping to run my fingers over my mother's books, and I enter our room and sit down on the bed. The atmosphere of Sunnyside clings to me like grease on my skin: unhappy, drab, dismal with the knowledge of the thing that waits for us all. I wish we could simply reach out and touch the other side, as Arthur Conan Doyle had tried to do. I wish I could speak to my mum. I want to tell her that I'm afraid. There are no big bad wolves, I know that now; there's nothing hiding in the dark. It's all here and it's real and I'm not ready for it. But I have to be.

People die. They leave and they fail each other. They just aren't good enough. Stories don't turn out how anyone would have wanted.

I haven't mentioned Edie's death to Paul. He's circling job ads in the local papers, thinking of the future – our future. He's already polished up his CV. I doubt that even the depressed job market could stand in the way of his enthusiasm and I know it should make me feel better but I can sense him moving away from me. I had once thought that, with my influence, he would change; and now he has, though none of it is how I expected.

I'm letting things get to me. Feeling sorry for myself. *Failing*. I can't allow that. I'm the one who believes, aren't I? I'm the one who will move beyond this place. We both will. I should be glad that Paul's so focused. I breathe in deep, closing my eyes, picturing not a mansion or a castle but a simple, smart house in a nice, smart town. My life will still be an adventure. It's simply going to be a different one.

And there will be love. Isn't that all anyone should want? Look at Edie. All she had wished for was her family.

I reach into my bedside table drawer and take out the photograph of the scan. I don't look at it yet. I simply hold it, gently and by its edges, as if with reverence. I wonder if the little shape at its centre will visit me when I'm old. Maybe I'll learn how to knit and I'll make bootees and cluck over other people's babies. Would that be so bad? Many people would call that peace. They'd call it a happy ending. Family should be what remains after everything else has passed away, any number of jobs and experiences and adventures.

I lie back onto the pillow, raise the photograph before my face. And for a moment I can't breathe.

The dark ocean of my womb, revealed in speckled pixels like stars, is still there. It's definitely my picture. It couldn't have been replaced with anyone else's – why would it? But I know it's changed. The knowledge comes upon me all at once and gradually, seeping into my bones. Cold puts its hands inside me, as if the doctors are doing their scan after all, the embarrassing one, the uncomfortable one.

The thing curled up at the centre of the image is still there but it's different: flat and lifeless and unmoving. I try to tell myself it always was. How can a picture move, after all? But it's as if the letters were a warning, Lawrence Fenton's talk of living lights that faded, arms and legs reduced to nothing but clumsy lines. That's all that remains in front of me and I feel the emotion that binds me to it evaporate. It's nothing but ink. It's a clumsy rendering of something that might have been and nothing more.

The baby curls in upon itself like an insect or a bird. It is tiny and raw with fragile bones, like something desiccated. The head is too large with only the merest indication of an eye, and there is something *old* in its expression. It can't be a part of me. It can't be my baby.

I think of the Harriet in the letters, a little girl seeking out the fairies. I think of the *other* Harriet putting her hand to my belly, reaching for what lay inside. Words come to me: *The milk is free, and all shall see!* Except I don't, I don't see at all, and nor would anyone else. They'd think I was mad if I told them. I imagine taking greenish-smelling milk to Charlotte Favell and pouring it out in front of her at Sunnyside, soaking the carpet, the look on her face not one of disgust but amusement. But that's easy for her. She knows she's won already, doesn't she?

Tell me. Do you want it?

I clutch my hands to my belly, willing whatever was inside me to be all right, to come back to me. I won't complain again. I won't mourn the things I'm leaving behind. I'll never say I don't want it, not for anyone or anything.

I feel hands on my own, holding them tight. It takes me a moment to realise the voice that's murmuring is mine: *I'm sorry*, I'm saying, as if that will help. I open my eyes and Paul is there. He's looking down on me, his face crumpled with concern. His lips are moving, and I hear, 'Why are you sorry?'

I shake my head and tears well at my eyes. How to explain? I only say, 'I don't know,' because there isn't anything else.

He holds me and I lean into him. I feel his strength. He's better than me, I know. He's a good person.

And he starts to tell me a story. He speaks in soothing tones of how wonderful it will be when the baby comes. He says we'll be a family, mum and dad and little one, and we'll love each other for ever and ever. We'll play football in the park and eat ice cream and laugh.

I no longer know which story is the fairy tale.

He holds my hands as he talks and kisses the ends of my fingers. I pull free, looking down at the scan, which has fallen to the floor. It's blurred now; everything is.

'Hey,' he says, stooping to retrieve it. 'That's our baby, you see? Right there. My little boy or little girl.'

I can't focus on the dead pixels. I can't think. I only say, 'How do you *know* that, Paul?'

It's his silence that tells me something is wrong. His body is still pressed against me and he doesn't pull away, but tension spreads through him, from his torso, along his arms. Finally he moves away from me and the cold creeps into the space between us.

When I raise my head, he is looking at me with a blank expression. Even his eyes are empty, but something is forming there: a new knowledge, an awareness that wasn't there before, a new kind of hurt. It takes me a moment to realise what I've done, to recognise this thing I've created.

No trace of a smile touches his lips. No crow's feet crease the corners of his eyes. His forehead appears lined and I see the way his face could be sculpted in a new way, by new emotions.

I feel as if I've become transparent again, a woman made of glass, that he's examining me anew and doesn't much like what he sees. I hear my words again, this time the way he must have heard them. He doesn't know about Mrs Favell, the letters, the way I renounced our child, Harriet pressing greedy hands to my belly. He hasn't noticed how the scan has changed. I reach for it, suddenly desperate to show him, to make him see, but he jerks away from me as if I'm poison and it slips from his fingers.

He walks out of the room. He doesn't slam the door. I hear footsteps on the stairs and then there's nothing.

Is this what he thinks of me – that I've slept around? That the baby I'm carrying is someone else's, in the oldest and simplest and most faithless of ways?

He was with me through everything, through the death of my mother. And I stayed here to be with him, giving up everything I wanted to be, that *she* wanted me to be: all of the dreams, all of the stories.

The scan lies discarded on the floor. I try not to look at it directly. It is as Lawrence Fenton said – how can I prove the photograph has changed? The camera never lies, they say, and yet cameras lie all the time. The Cottingley photographs showed that, if nothing else.

I scoop it up, turn it upside down – *gone* – and open the bedside drawer, moving aside old lipsticks and boxes of hair clips and other stuff I never use, and shove it in deep. When I push the detritus back over the top I hear the metallic crackle of something I *had* used, at least until recently. Without looking, I pull the object free: a foil strip of contraceptive pills. I had taken one every day, I was sure of it, but they still hadn't worked. The thought comes to me, spiteful and no doubt unworthy, that Paul could have stolen one away, fooling me into thinking I hadn't missed any, so that he could get what he wanted. Maybe he replaced one with something that only looked the same.

In that moment I hear the scraping of the door against carpet as it opens once more. I don't turn but I hear Paul's voice. *Is* it Paul? He sounds different. *Everything* is different.

'I don't understand this,' he says. His step comes closer and the light changes as a shadow falls across my eyes. He bends and lifts the pills from my hands.

His tone, when he speaks again, is lower. 'What are you doing? Have you taken one of these?'

I find my voice. 'Of course not.'

The bed shifts under me as he sits down, making me lean into him. He's strong and warm, just as I know him to be, and I wish he'd put his arm around me and make everything the way it was before.

My fears melt and reality returns. My ideas have been ridiculous, my selfishness monstrous. The things I desired didn't mean anything. What were they, really – a new home, a new life? A house in a forest? I don't even know where such a happily-ever-after might be found. They're fading in my mind, those things, becoming smaller as they recede.

Paul says, 'Are you seeing someone else?'

I twitch.

'I never would have thought that of you – I mean, I *don't* think it. But why would you say…' His voice tails off.

I shudder. 'It's no one else's.' I can't quite bring myself to say, *It's yours.* I can't even say *it's mine.* I wonder suddenly if I'm ill. My mind must have slipped, giving way under whatever pressure I'm putting on myself. Who could think the baby growing inside them isn't their own?

'Are you leaving, Rosie?' Paul leaves his hand where it is, close to mine. Only his little finger moves as he strokes the side of my wrist. 'Is that it?'

I shake my head, barely.

I think that's all, but he draws in a breath, preparing to speak. 'I can't live like this.'

It's my turn to freeze.

'I can't be afraid of you. Not – *of* you. I mean I can't be afraid that one day you'll up and leave. We're having a baby, Rose. I know that's not what you wanted. But we'll be together, and I'll help you. I'll do anything for the both of you, you know that, don't you? But if you're even thinking of going – I need to know. I have to be with someone who wants this too. I need someone who'll love me – *us* – and stay with us, someone I can rely on. Rose, if you want to go, I'll try and live with that. But if you do, if that's what you really want, we can't ever go back to how things are now. It'll be over for good. I can't live my life wondering all the time if you're really with me.'

The words sink in deep. I get that feeling again that he can make out every thought going through my head and I don't like to imagine what he sees. I want to cry, but I know he's right; he's right and I'm wrong and always have been. I agreed to this. I moved into his house. I got pregnant. It's been my choice all along, not consciously perhaps, but that doesn't make any of this his fault.

Almost imperceptibly, I nod. He deserves more but I can't give it, not yet.

He says one more thing before he puts his arm around me, touching my cheek, inclining his head towards mine. 'Rose, I love you, yeah?'

And I lean into him, and I know that he does.

PART TWO

1

I wake and the baby is there. I blink against the fluorescent lights and feel the flailing limbs on my chest, the globe of a head. I don't at first recognise it; it's heavy – surely too heavy – with wisps of almost transparent hair, not as easy to make out as the web of blue veins running beneath the skin. Here and there it's streaked with blood, smeared with something white. My mind is full of fog. I don't know where I am and I breathe in and detect antiseptic, and something else: an animal smell, like something left under a hedgerow. I tell myself it's only blood and it comes back: the rush to the hospital, Paul clutching my bag and calling out soothing words and *laughing*, the sheer excitement of it bubbling up and out of him.

Someone strokes my arm and I realise a figure is standing over me, holding the baby in place. 'Careful,' someone says; I don't know the voice. 'She's still a bit groggy with the anaesthetic.'

I think they mean the baby and I look down at the head still streaked with blood – mine, I suppose – and into blue-grey eyes. They're wide and beautiful and a sudden emotion hits me, hard and without warning, and I smile. I reach out and the baby flails. I catch her tiny hand, soft with new skin, hard with barely covered bone. I run a finger over each knuckle. She looks back at me, into me. She's a perfect little baby and I'm suddenly terrified – she *is* perfect, isn't she? I wonder if I should be able to sense some golden tie connecting us. I can't, not really, but I've been warned that doesn't always happen, not straight away.

It returns to me in a flood. I'd anticipated hours of waiting, steady contractions deepening, an irresistible urge to push. The midwife nodding as the baby crowned. Sucking on gas and air to mask the pain, but there hadn't been any pain, not after the first ragged tearing that felt as if the baby was pulling me in two. There was the sense of being reduced to meat and bone, a half-faint ending in blackness. A series of images emerged from it: white walls and too-bright lights; Paul's face up close, visibly trembling; the terror of too many people in the room, uniforms in varying shades of blue, hair covered in plastic, thin rustling aprons; a raised voice, something about a heartbeat that was too slow. And moving, being rushed into another room, the brief glimpse of a skylight, there and then gone. Now this. Time has skipped. I feel I've missed it all, the minutes and seconds having flown by too quickly, snatched from me into a void. What did they do? I try to look down at the smooth dome of my belly, the one I've grown used to, but then I do feel pain and I sink back into heaped pillows.

'Don't try to sit up.' A woman wearing a mask puts her face

up close. 'You had to have a caesarean, so you need to lie flat for a while. It's all fine, but you'll be sore for a bit. Don't overdo it.'

The baby shifts, rubbing that domed head against me. A hand descends; it's Paul, smiling down. 'Isn't he gorgeous?'

I frown. 'She.'

He laughs as if everything is exactly as it should be. We had opted not to be told the baby's gender at the mid-pregnancy scan, but still, I had known. *She should be called Robyn*, Mrs Favell had said, and *she* had known. I had trusted her words, no matter how Paul crowed and teased me about having a son.

'Nope,' he says, and laughs again. It seems he can't stop laughing, though I remain numb. I don't think I've ever seen his eyes like this, so bright and alive and so very full of love. 'It's Daddy's little boy. I told you.'

I shake my head. Did Mrs Favell say *Robin*? But no: *She* should be called Robyn, those were her words. Has the hospital given me the wrong baby? It's happened before, I've heard of it, DNA tests confirming the swap years later so that nobody really knows who belongs with which family any more. But that couldn't happen now, could it? This is my child. *Mine*. No one can take her from me.

I have a sudden image of someone reaching for my belly, *into* me, a tugging sensation, an empty space left behind. I don't know if that was today or yesterday or further in the past. I shake my head again in confusion.

'He should have his dinner,' the midwife says. The mask is gone but I can't make out her expression. She's just a disembodied voice. 'He's had quite a day.'

Has he? I don't know what time it is. I don't know how many minutes flowed by while I was unaware. For me, it was seconds.

Paul looks pointedly at my chest and I realise they're waiting for me to do it – to be a mother. I fumble at the fabric, realise I'm wearing a hospital gown. The midwife helps me slip out of one arm and pull it down. It feels odd but she's all practicality, all routine as she adjusts the position of the baby's head. She says he may need a little help to latch on. She shows me how best to hold him and how to stroke his cheek, so that the baby – he – it doesn't matter, of course my baby's a *he*, Paul knew it even if I didn't – makes a snuffling sound and opens his mouth. It's a reflex, she says, the rooting instinct, he'll be able to smell the milk, and I feel something hard against my breast. I catch my breath, wriggling in spite of myself, trying to see. The baby looks up at me, ancient knowledge in his eyes, and he opens his mouth and I see the tooth jutting from it, jagged and discoloured, yellowed like an old man's. I pull away from him and let out a cry.

'Oh – it's all right,' the midwife says. She lifts the baby from me, making clucking noises and rocking it in her arms. Paul asks what is it, what's wrong, and there is the hint of something else beneath his concern: irritation.

The midwife comes back into view, cradling the baby's head against her shoulder. 'It's my fault.' She leans in between me and Paul. 'I should have told you – he has a couple of natal teeth. It's perfectly natural, they just form too close to the gum surface sometimes, though we may need to remove them if they're loose. The doctor will be in soon to check. Baby might end up swallowing them, otherwise.'

'Baby' makes gurgling sounds into her shoulder. He sounds happy to be where he is. She starts to lower him again, stopping when she sees my expression.

'It happens every so often. It can make it a little uncomfortable to feed, but he will be hungry – are you all right to give him something?'

I nod. She puts the weight on me again. He doesn't need any help to latch on at all; his wet mouth feels the way. There's a sharp tug and tingling warmth rushes through me, followed by deep-seated pain as his teeth delve into my flesh. I suddenly feel bruised: cut, stretched, beaten, reconfigured. I don't want to let them see how much it hurts. I don't look at him, don't want to see him *rooting*, so I close my eyes. What I do see is a wizened face; an old soul; a being born with teeth, wanting to eat and eat. This is what the book told me about, isn't it? Babies that appear just as they should – or almost.

If this is natural, would it seem so strange? Would it hurt so much? Would it feel like what it is – a violation? This baby – too big, too bold, too *male* – surely couldn't have come from me.

When I look into its face again its eyes are closed, fed, sated, a look of sleepy contentment stealing over it. But my knowledge is of blood and bone, and somewhere deep inside, in my flesh, I can feel the truth.

2

Our home is different now, strewn with brightly coloured items of smooth plastic, things I wouldn't have recognised in my previous life. The latest is mostly transparent, with a suction cup, handle and bottle attached: a breast pump. I couldn't keep on with the feeds, though it's important for the baby to have my milk. The post-natal midwife suggested it; she said that problems with breastfeeding could cause anxiety, tension, struggling to bond, all sorts of issues. They never did remove the baby's natal teeth and my breasts still bear purple indentations where they have made their mark.

I remember the last time I fed him myself. There was pain, although that has faded now, as pain does. And yet there had been that feeling, too: the deep, tingling pleasure of milk letting down, the sensation at the core of me as he drank, as if a door had been opened into my deepest being. It was the sight as he unlatched, more than anything, that made me decide that was enough: the drop of milky blood, warm against my dimpled skin. The tiny red smear that remained on his lips, the tips of his yellowed teeth.

I lie back on the sofa, telling myself I made the right choice for us both, that there's probably nothing about raising a child that doesn't come with accompanying guilt. I allow the ache from the caesarean incision fade to a background itch and try to enjoy the sensation of being myself for a while. The baby is sleeping. Paul is out at a job interview, having kissed me and the baby and left an hour ago. He looked odd in a suit, his hair smoothed back, making his features more prominent. I wonder how he's getting on. It's helped having him around but we'll be out of money soon, and we don't have any family who can help. Paul's brother's work is no steadier than his own. His mother came down for a day, but she's on benefits and Paul had to send her the train fare. Cribs and sterilisers and tiny clothes don't come cheap. Edie never did give me any of her knitting; it all went to strangers in the end.

My mother's books have gone to strangers too. The stairs had to be made safe for walking up and down them with the baby in our arms, and so Paul carted the lot away to Oxfam. I try not to wonder who has them now. I can't get used to the stairs, too wide and too empty, lending a hollow ring to my steps. Paul kept nagging at me to pick out some of the books to keep, but I couldn't face sorting through them, couldn't make that choice. Keeping just a few would have been worse. Now I'll never know if the fairy tales were somewhere among them after all, and I wonder if that's for the best.

Now there are other books: books with bright leaves that rattle or crinkle, books with pictures in black outlines and primary colours, single words on each page. Apple. Ball. Cat.

The baby shifts and fusses but doesn't wake. It's a little piece of freedom – he's constantly demanding food or time and attention – and he's so big, his limbs plump and heavy, fists waving, his face flushing even though he's asleep.

It still seems strange that he's separate from me, a new thing animated by his own will and his own desires. Part of me wants to go to him and kiss away whatever cares he has, but I don't want to wake him. It still wrenches on my wound to lift his weight, and besides, I need some time to think. My mind is so often clouded these days – maybe it's because the house is so warm, the heating turned up high to protect the baby from falling temperatures outside, and I'm just so tired. I try to grab some sleep when he sleeps but for now I'm wide awake, a little interval of clarity, and I have a decision to make.

Paul suggested calling the baby Alexander some time ago, though I kept putting him off. It was the name of a friend of his who died when he was a teenager and I don't really like the idea of naming him after a dead person I never knew. Of course, 'Alex' could also be a girl's name – but haven't I let that go now?

The thing is, when I look at the baby, he doesn't look like an Alexander. The name that comes to me – again – is Robin.

I pick up my phone and bring up the web browser. I'm not altogether sure what I'm thinking but I search for 'Robin' and the word 'fairies' then stare down at the screen. I hadn't really thought of it as a fairy name, but I find there are plenty of results;

they're just about paintings, not people.

The first image looks old, yet brilliant and jewel-like. It contains a host of little creatures, all of them beautiful or grotesque or mysterious. I can tell they're fairies by their size, since they're sitting among the flowers. In their midst is a robin and he wears a garland of blooms about his neck. The title of the painting is *The Captive Robin*. Not a garland then, but chains: the robin is their slave.

There's a paragraph about the artist. He was called John Anster Fitzgerald, or just 'Fairy' Fitzgerald. He loved to paint the little folk; his pictures of them apparently came out far more realistic than those of the people around him. I scroll down and see more of them. One in particular stands out, mainly because of its frame, which is made of real twigs formed into a rough rectangle. They resemble pale, knuckled bones, fingers reaching and grasping. It is called *Fairies in a Bird's Nest*. Of course it's really a nest within a nest, the frame forming the outer, another painted inside that. There are no birds sitting there, though: only fairies. Ousted from its home, thrust almost out of the picture, is an egg. One fairy holds it steady – though it looks more like a demon – while another tries to force its way inside through a hole in the shell.

I stare at that for a long time. The caption says the grotesque little creature is being hatched from the egg, but I know that it's not. It's trying to burrow its way inside, to take the place of the chick that should have grown there.

I close the browser. I'm not going to give my child the name that Mrs Favell chose. He isn't a Robin and never will be.

Still, he can't remain nameless for ever. Alexander, then. It isn't what I'd imagined, but how many things are? And I have nothing to replace it with.

I walk over to the baby and look down. He's sleeping peacefully, though his hands are curled into fists. 'Alexander,' I whisper. 'Alexander.' I tell myself that's who he is.

He opens his eyes, sees me looking at him and starts to cry.

Alexander won't stop screaming. He's in my arms but fighting me, wriggling and kicking, his movements sending stabs of pain through my caesarean wound. I've offered his bottle and changed him though he didn't need changing and he's still a hot little ball of fury, squirming and lashing out. His face has turned puce. I hadn't known that babies could be so angry. I tell myself he deserves to be angry, that he didn't even have a name until an hour ago, and I rock him and shush him and kiss his dampened scalp, but none of it helps. There's a constant ringing in my ears from the noise.

I try to comfort him, sitting him on my knee, bouncing him. Before I'd known I was going to, I start to sing. *Oranges and lemons...* but I can't remember the rest. *When I grow rich?* But that's not right, that comes later, and I can't think how to get there. *Here comes a candle to light you to bed... Here comes a chopper to chop off your head.*

I stand, swing him gently in my arms, start over. *Rock-a-bye baby, on the tree top... When the wind blows, the cradle will rock.* The words are all so odd; it never occurred to me before how strange they are. Alexander squirms. Shrieks. He is not comforted; it is as if he understands what I'm saying. *When the bough breaks, the cradle will fall… Down will come baby, cradle and all.* I stare down, my arms wrapped around him like branches and twigs, and the words echo in my head, but changed, almost threatening: *baby will fall…*

I barely hear the rattle of the front door but a moment later Paul barges in, his brows like thunder, his lips pressed into a line. I see at once it didn't go well and at the volume of his son's cries he only looks more exasperated. Wordlessly, he holds out his arms, though I hear what he doesn't say: *Why haven't you? When will you?* Or more accurately, *What did you do wrong?*

I hand the baby over, my arms suddenly light without his weight. The front of my shirt is damp with tears, or perhaps I'm clammy from his heat. For a second I wonder if it's milk. I've been warned that my breasts might leak, my body responding to his cries on an unconscious level, but it hasn't happened yet.

Paul nestles Alexander into his arms and at once, he quiets. One chubby fist goes to his curled lips and he starts to suck his knuckle.

'Didn't you feed him?' Paul demands.

'I *tried*. How did it go, Paul? How was your day?' I can't help the sarcasm. I can't help but think of the times when he looked at me the way he's looking at the baby. I should be happy to see it, but somehow it only makes me feel sad.

'Well, try again. He's hungry.'

'He can't be.'

Paul goes into the kitchen holding the baby in one arm, checks the bottle, warms it. A couple of minutes later Alexander is quietly drinking, his eyes drowsy with sleep. He makes little gulping sounds, more than usual, the aftermath of his sobs. Paul shoots me a look. He doesn't say anything else. Possibly he doesn't want to disturb the baby.

I glare at them both. It isn't long since I tried the bottle myself – it can't have been. We're a long way from Fairyland; time here isn't fluid and it certainly isn't magical. I wish I could make light of it, joke about the little traitor in his arms, but shadows still lurk in Paul's expression. I should ask about the interview, but first I try to brush everything away.

'Alexander,' I say brightly, offering the name like a gift. 'I've decided, Paul. Let's call him Alexander.'

He shoots me a look, but not one I'd anticipated. It's as if he's annoyed afresh that it's taken me this long, and what do I expect, a prize?

'You still like the name, don't you? Our little Alexander.'

Paul grunts. He sits and settles the baby on his lap. Alexander hasn't stopped feeding. He's nearly emptied the bottle. Is he so voracious? And Paul says, 'Did you ignore him?'

'What do you mean?' I say, but I know exactly what he means, can see it in his face. He thinks I was asleep or hiding away from the baby's screams – or maybe he suspects me of starving him on purpose. Why? To see what he would do?

I open my mouth – I don't know what words will emerge – when Paul lets out a long breath. 'Sorry, love. I didn't mean it.'

He says it in such a quiet, beaten voice that I suddenly envision everything that might have been: all of his dreams. The child magically transforming us into a unit, dad and mum and baby, all contented, all happy, wearing identical smiles. A bustling wife handing him a gurgling baby at the door, kissing him soundly before going to take an apple pie from the oven. I look around the room. The nappy I removed is screwed up on the table next to old mugs, coffee rings showing where others have been. My cardigan is crumpled over the back of the sofa, the remote control dropped to the floor. But I haven't had the chance to tidy up. I was rocking Alexander for so long – wasn't I? It felt so. I remember the time I spent googling his name – no, *not* his name – and feel new guilt. I scan the room for my phone, but it isn't there. I peer around the side of the sofa; it must have got pushed underneath. Or was I so disgusted with myself that I shoved it under there?

'How did the interview go?' I ask, wanting to know, though a smaller, meaner part of me relishes the chance to draw the subject from my shortcomings onto his. He doesn't answer. He sets down the bottle, not hiding a look of distaste when he sees the state of the table, tilts Alexander upright and starts rubbing his back.

'Paul?'

He shakes his head and his lip curls.

'Surely you can't know yet.'

'I can,' he says. 'They trashed my CV, then told me they were offering the job to someone in-house. Don't know why they bothered asking me in. Probably just ticking boxes.' He stares down at the floor as Alexander burps then makes little breathy sounds of satisfaction. 'That's my boy,' he croons, settling the child's head against his shoulder. And just like that, Alexander falls asleep.

You have the touch. I remember his mother's proud voice when she saw him with the baby, nestling against him in that same milk-sleepy way. She hadn't said much to me on her visit, though I'd been exhausted from the operation, had slept through much of it. A sudden memory: waking at some unknown time in the afternoon, hearing their voices echoing in the empty stairway, whispering, whispering.

Paul says, 'I've been thinking.' His tone takes me back to the moment he asked me if I was leaving him, and everything stops. I want to tell him I'll try harder, be better, that it will be easier when everything settles down, when we can sleep again. When we're ourselves again. I force myself to wait.

'I was thinking,' he repeats, more tentative this time. I smother the sound that rises in the back of my throat and he goes on. 'With me finding it difficult to find a job and all, and you feeling a bit depressed.'

A bit depressed. I try to hide my frown. No wonder I was thinking of his mother; I can feel her influence in the room, almost hear her whispers emerging from its corners. *Baby blues* – that's what she'd accused me of, isn't it?

Paul goes on. 'It might do you good. It is the twenty-first century, after all.' His grin is weak, the ghost of a real smile hidden somewhere inside it. I can't think what he means. I have absolutely no idea what he's going to say and so it comes as a shock when he adds, 'I could always look after the baby.'

For several seconds, I don't breathe. When I draw an audible gasp pain flashes across his features, his hopes already crushed.

'Sorry, love. I didn't mean it,' he mutters, and I realise this has been bubbling inside him, something he has tried to smother, not quite daring to believe it might actually happen. Is this what he and his mother had planned? The idea hangs between us, light and fragile, and I try not to smile.

I make myself pause, thinking of everything I'd be giving up. It isn't as if I don't love the baby. It isn't as if I don't love Paul. Somewhere, beneath everything, it is there: a pool of deep water, fathomless, full of layers and mysteries and things to discover, only obscured now and again by a film of unwholesome thoughts, coating the surface like oil.

'It's all right, Paul,' I say. Again, I force myself not to smile. That wouldn't be right, would it? It wouldn't be natural. I'm sure Paul wouldn't think so. I wonder if that will still be the case after a week, a month, a year. 'It's a good idea. We need the money. It makes sense. I'll call work and talk to them about going back.'

It's his turn to take a breath, and then the dam breaks. A jumble of words spills out – do I mean it, and he'll be so careful, and of course I'll still see Alexander *all the time* – and now we're allowed to smile, both of us, and Alexander lies there, peaceable for once, and he sleeps.

After a while I look for my phone. It's not on the sofa or under it. It's not on the kitchen tops, not on the floor, not in the hall. In the end, Paul rings it for me. I hear the tone, so quietly I think there must be something wrong with it, and I realise it's coming not from down here but upstairs. I follow the trail of sound into the bedroom. The tone grows louder. It leads me to my bedside table, to the top drawer, to a pile of make-up I don't bother with any longer, a little crackling packet of pills I haven't bothered with for a while either. I rummage beneath, find the phone, cancel Paul's call and shout absent-mindedly that I've found it.

And yet I didn't put it there. I know I didn't, and I wonder if I should be afraid. Even half dazed as I am, when could I have done so? And why would I hide it away like that? There's nothing in this drawer I needed. I cast my mind back over the afternoon. I don't think I went upstairs even once all the time I was waiting for Paul to come home.

We need to stop them from being angry about the house.

Charlotte cannot set down her needle without it seemingly vanishing into the air… Harriet constantly complains that her books have been moved.

And there is a book here too, I realise. There is one left to me, after all: the little ruined volume of Keats.

I shake my head. There's nothing odd about any of it. The phone is here, so I must have misplaced it. I'm tired and bruised and worn out from the pregnancy and it's made me forgetful. I've been distracted; I won't be so again. I find the number for Sunnyside – no point in waiting – and make the call, my voice suddenly hoarse, as if I haven't used it in a long time. I try not to sound desperate, keep it brief and professional. Patricia comes onto the line, sounding just as she always did, as if it might have been yesterday that we last spoke. She says she'll come back to me with the details and I imagine walking back into Sunnyside, stepping over the threshold in my uniform, but somehow it's the wrong one; it's the one I wore during my pregnancy, stretched by my bump but empty, *emptied*, hanging off my bony frame.

I shake away the image and grin. I don't care, not about any of it.

Downstairs, Alexander starts to cry. No: he's screaming, settling into his angry wails, and I imagine him waving his little fists. Paul calls my name. We must be out of milk. It's time to express more, but that's all right; it won't be for much longer. I start towards the stairs, wondering for a second how far my life has narrowed if the idea of returning to Sunnyside seems like such a breath of freedom.

3

The anticipated Monday breaks, and it's time. I'm out of bed early but Paul's up before me and he does everything, handing me a plate of scrambled eggs and toast when I go downstairs. He kisses me on the cheek and I know he feels guilty for getting the thing he wished for, but I don't care. I kiss him back and eat standing at the counter.

'I'll drive you,' he says, and I protest that there's no need, but he's all insistence and I picture how nice it will be, when my shift is over, to see him, to sink back and let him do the driving. So I grab my bag and I'm ready, though my muscles tighten with nerves. What will Mandy and the others think of me for going off and having a baby?

Paul starts pulling on Alexander's little jacket, one he doesn't wear often because it's so smart and babies are so messy. Paul's brother bought it for him – Marcus thrust it into my hands when he visited just after the birth, our house and not the pub for a change. He cooed over Alexander for five minutes, laughed at the size of him – *his father's son* – and went back to talking about football.

It hadn't occurred to me that if Paul's going to drive me, of course the baby has to come too. What kind of a mother am I? I protest again that it's too much bother, I'll take the car, but it's too late. Paul grins, says how much Alexander will enjoy his outing.

I want to say I don't think he'll notice the difference, but I keep quiet as we step out into a day that looks like any other and yet isn't, not for me. I'm not the same person who walked into Mrs Favell's room, who held out my hand and processed down the stairs at her side. I feel much older than that. A hundred years might have passed since I last saw her.

I shake my head. I won't think of Mrs Favell, not before I've even arrived. Still, I find myself wondering whether Harriet's given birth now too. I suppose she must have. I imagine her heating bottles in an ordered, neat, shining kitchen, her hair drawn back in a chignon, and pull a face.

'Why don't you drive?' Paul says. 'I'll squeeze in the back with the nipper.'

My eyes widen. Wasn't he supposed to be driving me? But he places Alexander into the baby seat and climbs in after him, pulling the passenger seat back into position. There's nothing left to do but get into the driver's side. I feel a twinge as I sink into the seat, the ghost of the caesarean. Knowing it would have been less comfortable for me in the back doesn't make me any less irritated.

I pull away sharply, ignoring Paul's pointed soothing of Alexander. It didn't bother the baby; he's fine. He doesn't start wailing until I pull up, oh so gently, into a parking space at Sunnyside. Is it because he knows I'm going to walk away from him? Does he think I don't love him enough to stay all of the time? A nameless longing suddenly aches within me, surprising and deep.

When I speak, my voice seems small. 'Bye, Paul. I'll see you later.'

'What? We're coming in, aren't we? It's your first day back.'

He's lifting Alexander from the baby seat. I see at once what he has in mind: a big reunion of me and my work friends, everyone exclaiming over the baby, saying how beautiful he is, how well we're doing, curious to see Paul, beaming over our budding family. It's too unlikely to contemplate. I think of Edie pressing some woollen gift upon me before I remember that she's gone, her soul flown from an open window.

None of it fits, or perhaps it's only me that doesn't. Maybe everything's fine and I should stop worrying, glide along with it all. For an instant an image rises: a painting, not of fairies but of Ophelia, lying in a stream; the one by Millais. Her face is white, her hands raised, her mind driven to madness and then left emptied, blank. She is surrounded by jewel-like flowers and I imagine tiny faces appearing from among them. I shake the thought away. That's not me. I'm not going to sigh myself into madness, to wait for things to happen. I'm working again. I'm going to be happy; I *am* happy.

Paul shushes his son, though Alexander isn't grizzling any longer. The air rushes in and out of him and he waves his fists at the world. His rounded cheeks are pink with unshed tears. He doesn't start to cry in earnest until we approach the door, though

Paul shuffles with him so carefully towards it along the wheelchair ramp. And so it is on a tide of shrieks, loud as a fire alarm, that I re-enter Sunnyside for the first time in months, feeling like a stranger. I don't know the receptionist. She must be new, or new to me, but she recognises my uniform and tells me Mrs Stott is in the residents' lounge. I'm so used to calling 'Mrs Stott' Patricia that I have to think for a moment who she means. Paul follows at my heels. I'm conscious that he's going to see, for the first time, that the other girls don't like me. Will he gossip about *that* on the phone to his mother? At least if Alexander keeps squalling, he might be too distracted to notice.

'Rose!' I hear Patricia before I see her. There's quite a crowd in the lounge; perhaps they've breakfasted early to allow for some activity. Mrs Favell is there too, her blouse a delicate sea green, her pearls lucent at her neck. She stands towards the back of the room but her presence demands notice, more imposing than anyone else's. She doesn't smile when she sees me. She has her back to the window, her face in shadow; it might almost be my first day, and this my first time of seeing her.

Mandy is kneeling on the floor, arranging board games in the cupboard, taking them out or putting them away, I'm not sure which. She straightens, scowling at the din that's pouring from the ball of fury that is Alexander. She smirks and I flush. It must be obvious to Paul what she thinks, but he's busy talking to Patricia. They're actually laughing together. She doesn't seem to notice his hair, which is neatly tied back this morning, or his tattoos, boldly on show. It's as if they're instant friends. She reaches out to stroke Alexander's cheek while Paul bounces him up and down. Still, he won't stop crying.

Jimmy whistles and calls out, 'What a little cracker.'

The residents shuffle into a circle around us or crane their necks from their seats, admiring as they're meant to do. Paul bathes in the baby's reflected glory. And a thinner voice cuts through it all, not loud but with a clarity that carries across the room, saying, 'Do let me try, dear.'

It's Mrs Favell. She makes it sound as if she's doing Paul a favour. I see the doubt in his eyes, probably worried for her immaculate blouse, and she adds, 'I'm good with babies.'

She looks like the last person in the world who'd want to hold one but Paul hands him over without a word. Mrs Favell's arms look too thin to support him but she lifts him easily and everything falls quiet. Alexander gives one last sniff and puts his thumb in his mouth, staring up at her with his blue-grey eyes. It strikes me suddenly that they might change soon, darkening to hazel or brown. Who will he look like then?

The baby's lips twitch. Is he *smiling*?

Mrs Favell doesn't rock or bounce him. She stands perfectly still, looking at Paul with a knowing expression.

He laughs, saying maybe she should take over because he isn't very good at it. Everyone laughs, but I don't. I try a smile but it doesn't feel right on my lips.

'Alexander,' Mrs Favell says, trying it out. I don't recall mentioning his name but I told it to Patricia when she asked on the phone and I suppose she's told everyone. Mrs Favell doesn't seem surprised that the child isn't called Robin. She doesn't accuse. There's nothing hidden in her tone and I feel an unaccountable relief that she's *accepted* his name, as if she knows he's ours, not connected with her at all.

Apart from the way he looks at her. Apart from the way he closes his eyes, quiescent at last, his skin luminous in the light from the windows, his face softening into peace. Maybe he's lulled by her touch, or maybe it's that fragrance she wears: lily of the valley. I can smell it from here. It crosses my mind that if he likes it so much, perhaps I should buy some.

The French doors open. A shape coalesces in the light, one I recognise, though I have met her only once before. Her hair is golden and she steps inside and seems brighter by the contrast, or perhaps it's the residents who have faded, with their grey hair and brown cardigans and beige trousers. With a start, I realise she's carrying a baby. I don't know how I failed to see it before; the child must have been hidden in her arms. It's so small and dainty. Harriet doesn't look at Alexander. She sees me and smiles, revealing perfect white teeth against her flawless skin, not a trace of tiredness on her.

'Another visitor,' she exclaims. 'How charming!'

I realise this is why everyone had gathered in here, to see Harriet and her child. They part to let her in and she approaches me. Her bundle is wrapped in snowy white wool: Edie's work? The baby is sweetly sleeping. Wisps of fine blonde hair curl over her forehead – I don't know how I know it's a girl, but I do. Her lips are curled like a rosebud.

Harriet leans towards me so that I can admire her better, one mother to another, but I haven't any words. The baby is beautiful. Suddenly I don't want her to see Alexander, don't want to see her expression when she does, although he's quiet now; content, in *her* arms.

'Her name is Robyn,' Harriet says, and I catch my breath. 'Oh – whatever is the matter? Are you quite well?'

Robyn. Of course that's her baby's name. Mrs Favell's words were always intended for Harriet. Why would she have been talking about naming *my* baby? And yet that hadn't been how it seemed.

'Robyn,' I whisper. I know it's perfect. *She's* perfect. I put out my hand and draw back the woollen blanket, just a little, and Robyn stirs with a breathy sigh. Her eyes open. I almost expect them to be like mine, dark brown, but of course they're blue-grey, like Alexander's, like any baby's. Who knows what they will reveal as they change?

Robyn lets out a cry; not so perfect then, just a baby, just like *mine*. Harriet adjusts her hold. 'She'll be hungry,' she says, and then, 'Oh!'

She's staring at me. Her expression changes: consternation? Disgust? I can't read it but I'm diminished by it anyway and I feel the warmth flooding the front of my uniform, trickling down my skin. I look down and realise with horror that my breasts are leaking – it's milk darkening my tunic, flowing in response to the baby's cry: *her* baby's cry.

'Oh,' is all I can manage, my tone different to hers. I hear the residents shuffling, some of them going back to their seats, the old men embarrassed, the old women embarrassed for me.

'It happens.' Harriet laughs brightly and the people around her laugh too, a rough echo. She's covering it over, making it better. All I can do is cross my arms over my chest. I realise Paul is staring, just standing there, and I hear Patricia asking if I have a spare uniform. I tell her that yes, of course I do. I shoved one in my bag this morning, ready to hang in my locker, just in case. Dealing with the old can be messy, like dealing with the young. The staff here always have spares.

Paul makes his apologies, exchanging goodbyes with everyone like old friends, and he's gone before I realise he never said goodbye to me, never offered Alexander's soft crown for one last kiss. Harriet has gone too; then I see her over in the corner, chatting with Maryam as if she's known her all her life. Robyn lies peaceably in her arms.

'You'd better change, Rose.' Mrs Favell is at my shoulder. 'Hadn't you?'

I don't acknowledge her before I walk away, hurrying to the loos to make myself presentable before my shift begins, conscious of the stains spreading from my breasts. Once I'm in a cubicle I yank off my tunic, peeling it from my milky skin, revolted by the smell of it. I wipe myself with toilet paper that disintegrates and clings, then take the other uniform out of my bag.

I realise my mistake as soon as I begin to pull it on. There's too much material. It's bigger than it should be, especially around the waist, and I close my eyes. It's just as I had seen it in my mind's eye: this is my maternity tunic. I grasp for the other, the milk-stained one, wondering if I can fix it using the hand-dryer, but I know it's hopeless.

My hands shake as I put on the tunic. I must have worn it when I was at my biggest because the tummy panel is stretched as wide as it will go and it bags into an empty belly of fabric in front of me. It feels like mockery. I'm the image of a woman who should be fruitful but isn't; one whose bump has been stolen away, left with nothing in her arms, nothing but an absence where her baby should be.

4

The day drags until it's time for Paul to pick me up, daylight finally yielding to the gathering dark and the nip of autumn in the air. The laundry was in use non-stop and by the time I managed to throw my soiled uniform into the washer it was barely worth changing into it again. It's still damp and I'm carrying it over my arm so that I can dry it properly at home. The one I'm wearing is still hanging off me. I feel like I can't quite breathe in it. The reason for that is the old belt I'd taken from the lost and found cupboard, stuff residents have forgotten they ever possessed, that lack their owners' names stitched into the inside of collars or ironed onto discreet corners, or maybe that relatives failed to claim after they died. I don't know who this could have belonged to – it's broad, dry, the leather cracked. I used to cinch in the excess fabric, pulling it aggressively tight, and even now the constriction around my middle feels like a triumph, though when I look down at the bunched-up fabric it reminds me of Reenie's cardigan: a nice try, but fastened on all the wrong buttons.

At least I didn't see Mrs Favell again, except at a distance. She was sitting with Harriet, the pair of them side by side, not looking at each other. Harriet was still holding the little golden child and I noticed that Mrs Favell didn't fuss over her, didn't take any notice of her at all, though she did have a new look in her eye, something like satisfaction. I didn't want to see it, or her. I didn't want to dwell on the way my body had responded to Robyn's cry.

Even now the hours have passed and the day is over, I don't know what to make of it. I feel as empty as my baggy tunic, as featureless as the sky. Everyone else on my shift has already left, shouting their goodbyes while I shrank back against the wall, watching the dark close in. It's remarkably quiet. The occasional car passes and that is all, until someone throws a window open in the kitchens and I hear the rattle of dropped cutlery, a staccato burst from a radio. Even so, I sense the silence waiting beneath. It almost feels as if it's emerging from the trees that loom behind Sunnyside, from the earth, the grass. Mrs Favell once spoke of listening to every tiny living thing and I almost understand what she meant, though now I know it is not sound they make, but silence; a living silence, a waiting silence.

Something bursts past my ear, a series of tiny clicks that quickly pass beyond range. Bats must be flying and I look up at the sky, searching out scraps of darker black flitting across it, but I can see nothing. Soon it will be too dark to make them out even if one flies right in front of me. More clicks: but when I look up there are only little lights confusing my vision, the first stars starting to emerge.

Paul is late. I look at my watch, an exaggerated gesture, hoping he'll pull around the corner in a blaze of headlights in time to see it. Then I shiver. I have grown accustomed to overheated rooms and I miss them now. Has he fallen asleep on the sofa? I imagine him snoozing in the warmth, lit by the television's flicker. He may have a baby to feed and bathe but I've lifted spoons to old men's mouths, sponged down their sagging skin. He's changed nappies and washed bibs; so have I. I've scrubbed bedpans until they gleam. Spitefully, I catalogue all the horrible jobs I've done, ready to throw them in his face. I'm a bad person, but just now I can't bring myself to be otherwise. The fact that I'd rather be here, that I chose to be here, only makes it worse.

I pull at the sagging belly of my tunic, remembering the sensation of warmth leaking from my breasts. We always tell the old not to be ashamed of their untrustworthy bodies – why should I be? It was natural. A mother's response. If it was something that happened to men, they'd probably boast about it.

That's not the reason it's troubling me.

I give in to my exasperation and rummage for my mobile phone. Paul's number rings for what seems a long time then goes to voicemail. He must be in the car, then. That's something, at least. Maybe Alexander refused his milk and made him late. But Alexander never refuses now, he wants more and more all the time. He always drains his bottle. I'm not sure I can satisfy him much longer. My breasts respond to that thought too, not with milk but with pain, the memory of his teeth.

I close my eyes. If only I could be like Harriet: neat, self-contained, composed, capable. An adult, not a self-pitying child.

The minutes slip by, viscous and reluctant to leave, and still Paul doesn't appear. It occurs to me that something is wrong. He might be in hospital. He could be rushing the *baby* into hospital.

Something inside me goes numb and I'm not sure if that's because I'm not a monster after all or because of the chill that's rising from the ground. I shiver in earnest. A breeze is picking up, one that must be coming from the woods because it smells of damp earth and leaves. What made me wait outside? I could go back into reception, but they've seen enough of my ballooning tunic. Better to stay here, in the dark.

Half an hour later, he pulls around the corner. I step forward, my legs stiffened with cold, as he throws open the door from the inside. His smile fades when he sees me. 'Sorry, love. The baby was restless. Couldn't find the keys anywhere, then it took ages to get him dressed and into his seat.' He grins again, something he can't help. He's talking about his son, after all. Even in the midst of remorse, contentment rolls off him.

I get in without saying anything.

'Aren't you going to say hello to little Alexander?'

I'm the bad person again. He's late and I'm the bitch, the wicked witch. I lean right over to peer into the baby seat, which faces backwards. Alexander returns my look. He's wearing his best coat. He's gumming his knuckles; a trail of drool has run down the arm, into the seat. It smells of sour milk – or is that me? I smother my sigh, blow him a kiss and face forward. Paul steadily, carefully, drives us home.

I never expected Paul to metamorphose into a meticulous house husband and when I think of Harriet's perfection I'm not sure I want him to, but I'm still shocked when I walk in. It looks as if someone's done battle with evil spirits. Baby clothes are everywhere. Was it really so hard to find Alexander's coat? And it's not just clothes. I cross the lounge and see into the kitchen.

I don't turn to Paul, not wanting him to see my anger. I'm not going to be that person. I tell myself it's a good thing he hasn't changed so very much that I can't recognise who he is any longer.

I hear the rustle as he takes off Alexander's coat, the smack of lips as he kisses his head. Then he's next to me and he freezes. He lets out a low whistle that tells me everything is not as I think, that Paul is as surprised as I am, and unease creeps along my veins.

'Woah. Sorry, hon.' He thrusts Alexander towards me and I grasp him awkwardly. 'For God's sake – I was sure I'd put all this in the washing basket.'

The basket's in the kitchen too, the lid on the floor. It was full to overflowing when I left this morning but there's nothing jutting from it now. The contents are scattered. Did Paul try to make a start on it? How did he make such a mess? The machine isn't even going. Then I see the worktops and fresh anger simmers inside me. Washing powder is everywhere, strewn across the counters, spilling to the floor, even in the sink. At first glance I'd thought it was only the light gleaming from the surfaces, but there isn't any light; it's full dark outside, nothing to be seen in the glass but my own reflection.

I go closer, Alexander wriggling in my arms. How on earth has he made such a mess? Why didn't he clean up? I would have. I know Alexander's difficult but I think again of my own day. An image: raising an old man's hand into the air, washing his armpits while he stares at the wall, the bulging belly of my uniform hanging between us, both trying not to see too much.

In the window, my lip twists into something ugly. I try to straighten my expression but I can't. Instead I go to the worktop and run my finger through the white powder. I frown. It isn't grainy, doesn't have flecks of blue in it as our washing powder does. It's too fine, doesn't cling to my skin in the same way. There's none of its sharp clean smell and I lift it to my lips. It's not washing powder but flour.

Flour is constantly spilt about the kitchen; and the milk rapidly turns sour, although it has not been left out...

I shake my head. I don't feel angry any more. I feel wrung out, empty; lost.

Paul is at my shoulder. 'How the hell did that happen?'

'Maybe you were baking me a cake.' My words emerge weakly, but the sarcasm is still there. He starts scooping up the flour, throwing it into the bin. Powder blooms into the air and he pats his hands together, making it worse. Alexander lets out a gurgle, a little like a laugh. I grip him tighter and he squirms in protest, so I force myself to loosen my fingers. What will he do if I don't? Cry, scream, or something else?

I go to put him in his bassinet. Paul is wiping down the tops, though more flour spills to the floor and when he rubs his hands on his jeans he leaves thick pale streaks on the denim. 'I must have got it out by mistake. Probably left the salt in the fridge too. Welcome home, love.'

He laughs. He isn't bothered by it, not in the least. And what can I say – that fairies are in the house? That we let them in? I wish I'd never listened to Mrs Favell. I wish I'd never taken that first letter from her hand. Now I can't banish her.

Still, I stalk over to the kitchen cupboards and yank one open. There is the little bag of flour, half empty, sagging, too much paper to enclose its wasted contents. I grab it, turn, reach the bin in one stride and dump it in. It's not like we're chefs; we won't miss it. No one's going to spill flour around my kitchen again. We're *done*.

Paul bustles about, picking up the washing, putting a pan of beans on the hob and slotting bread into the toaster, heating a bottle for Alexander. I offer to help but he insists and I sit on the sofa, let my head fall back and close my eyes. Still, the images come: Harriet, so capable, mature, *happy*. That lovely child in her arms. Perhaps she'll visit Mrs Favell again soon. Surely a grandchild will give her a reason to come more often. I might see her too: I might see the baby – *Robyn* – again.

Alexander shifts in his bassinet and starts to cry, a thin, hungry, exasperated sound. I sit there, waiting for my body to respond. Now that I've leaked milk once it might happen all the time, but when I look down at my chest, there's nothing there; not even an ache where my feelings should be.

5

I drive to work, carry out my duties, laugh and smile with the residents or cry and commiserate, doing whatever is required, the days blurring together. I go home and milk myself for Alexander and hold him on my lap and sit in front of the TV with Paul. Often we both fall asleep on the sofa before it all begins again. I don't think about where or who I am any more. The routine carries me. I run the steriliser, make sure that dribbly toys are washed, that clothes are put on the right shelves. My hands are deft even though it feels like they belong to someone else. My feet are still swollen from the pregnancy; my shoes don't seem to fit. Everything takes place at a distance, and I wonder if it's the same for Paul, though I don't ask him. I suppose this is what it's like, being a new parent. We're exhausted all the time and we don't talk and don't touch each other and we carry on. That's what people do. It will get easier; I wonder if it already has, scarcely without my noticing.

Until then, Sunnyside is my escape. At least Mrs Favell and I take little notice of each other. I tell myself she's just an unhappy old lady who wants to make other people unhappy too, and I'm glad I'm not like that and never will be. I try not to speak to her, concentrating on the nice ones, the ones who nod at all the platitudes: *How are you feeling, Lovely day, Nice to see so-and-so again, How's the family?* Until one day I go to Mrs Favell's room to see if she wants to take part in a trip to a stately home that Sandra is planning, and she isn't there, and an impulse takes hold of me and I look under her bed and see the box hiding in the shadows.

I don't think it's even been moved. It's still sitting where I must have left it, a little crooked. I'm not sure the lid's on straight. It's hard to tell without looking closer.

I lower my face to the carpet and reach for it, feel the familiar touch of wood made silky by the passage of years. I want to see the photographs again. Will they have changed? Will Charlotte and Harriet be holding a child in their arms, a pretty baby in an old-fashioned bonnet edged with lace? Will her face be shaped like theirs – or mine?

The box is in my hands. I take off the lid.

There are no photographs. At first, I'm not sure what I am seeing – it reminds me of a painting I once saw with a mass of twigs, but there are also clumps of moss and downy-soft feathers, and what I think of is a skeleton: fine bones, spindly legs bending backwards, the translucent filaments of wings. I blink. It's not a skeleton, not even a bird. But there is a nest, intricately woven. The hollow at its centre is tiny, smaller than a fist, and at its heart is an egg.

I stare at the perfect matte surface of its shell. It is the ivory of wedding dresses, though covered in numerous speckles like faded ink, their pattern reminiscent of handwriting. I pick it up and turn it in my hands, trying to see if there's some message there for me, but I can't read it. The egg is heavier than I expected it to be. *Robyn*, I think. *Robin*. I think of a grotesque little creature trying to push its way inside and it all comes back to me, more vivid and colourful than anything has been for months. I think of the baby inside me; Harriet's touch on my belly. And Mrs Favell's voice, seemingly years distant. *The sap is rising, can't you hear it? The cuckoo calls.*

The *cuckoo*. They lay their eggs in other birds' nests, don't they? They fool them into raising their chicks, too big and too voracious, while their own offspring are pushed out or starve to death.

And yet I don't think this is a cuckoo's egg. It isn't blue, but I think it's a robin's.

The egg yields at the same moment I realise I'm squeezing it. Shell fragments and something viscous and strangely warm spatter my skin. I cry out, expecting there to be blood, bone, hair, but there is only albumen on my fingers, glistening and foul. There is a smell but not what I expect, not rotten, not bad. I know what it is before I close my eyes and picture Alexander's fontanel: it is the perfume of his scalp.

Tears sting my eyes. I begin to wipe the remains of the egg from my hands as best I can, the fragments of shell turned sharp, and realise there is something else nestled within. I peer down and see something small and slender, a piece of eggshell gone bad perhaps, and then the light catches the edge of a glistening wing, the gleam of a dark eye.

I gasp and start back, spilling slime onto my tunic. I tell myself there's nothing there but when I look a second time I see the eye staring back at me, and something else: not feathers but lacy and impossibly delicate, albeit weighed down with albumen. An almost iridescent gleam flickers. It's an insect, that's all – I can't tell what kind. A dragonfly?

I can't wrap my mind around how it came to be here, inside the egg. And then I realise that this thing was never inside the egg; it couldn't have been. The insect had simply been caught in the box, a stray creature that had crawled or been trapped in there, probably accidentally, without even Mrs Favell's knowledge. I had scooped them up together, interloper and egg, and when I crushed them I had pressed them into one.

I rub my hands over the box, letting the ruined contents drip back inside. *There*, I think. *Witnessed their solemnities*. I tell myself I don't care what she'll think when she finds the mess; it serves her right. I replace the lid and shove it back under the bed and sit there for a second, staring at nothing, until the door scrapes back against the carpet and I turn to see Mrs Favell.

She stands over me, unmoving. Her lips are compressed, but she doesn't look angry so much as curious. It is as if she's *seen* me, really looked at me for the first time in a long while. I feel like a child caught nibbling the gingerbread house, about to be thrust into the oven by the witch; a trespasser in Baba Yaga's shack, as she flies through the window in her magical mortar and pestle; a bride hiding from her husband after peeking into the forbidden room, awaiting his punishment.

She doesn't need to say anything. She knows what I've done. It's written on my skin, would be even if my hands weren't sticky with albumen. It doesn't cross my mind until later to wonder how she'd come by the egg, whether it was even legal for her to possess it. I am diminished by her gaze, shrivelling away to nothing.

Slowly, she smiles. All she says is, 'I shall want you to read to me later, Rose.'

She doesn't need to say anything else. I'm dismissed and I know it. I get to my knees, then my feet. My movements are treacly and I can't move any faster. My limbs won't respond.

I leave the room. I don't think she troubles to turn and watch me go.

6

I know when it is time to read to Mrs Favell by the look she gives me from across the residents' lounge. She turns and walks out of the door and I know I'm supposed to follow. There's no point in putting it off and so I obey, keeping my eyes fixed on the stairs in front of my feet.

I find her waiting with her back to me, the cold autumn light limning her hair. The book is already held in her hand, her thumb marking the place. It has a worn cloth binding with a title printed on the spine, though I can't read it from here. Without turning, she holds it out.

Once I'd rebelled against the way she treats me like a servant, but now I don't care. I take the book, carefully so as to keep her place, and see the page she's chosen for me. I wonder if it's out of spite, but of course it is. She won't report me or say anything about prying into her private things, about how I smashed the bird's egg, but she will take her revenge.

I refuse to let her see that it bothers me. Anyway, there's not enough emotion inside me to protest or to cry. I tell myself I'm a shell, blank on the outside, empty inside. I won't rise to any of it – let that be *my* revenge.

The poem is by William Blake. It's from his *Songs of Innocence and Experience* – this one, I seem to think, is from *Experience*. It can't really be anything else.

'"The Sick Rose",' I begin.

'O Rose thou art sick.
The invisible worm,
That flies in the night
In the howling storm:

Has found out thy bed
Of crimson joy:
And his dark secret love
Does thy life destroy.'

When I look up at Mrs Favell, her shoulders are shuddering. What I can see of her expression is blank but it's all spilling out from behind the mask, mirth trying to burst free, and as I watch, it does. It floods from her; she makes high-pitched sounds and tears spring from her eyes.

'Oh, Rose,' she says. 'Oh, Rose!' She pulls a lace handkerchief from her lemon-yellow blouse, placed in the pocket for just such a moment, and wipes her eyes. 'He's taking everything from you, isn't he? And you – you give and you give.'

She moves suddenly and grasps my arm, her fingers digging in deep, wrapping about the bone. I offer no resistance as she pulls me in front of the mirror.

My hair is longer these days, no time to cut it, and it's pulled back into a tight ponytail that doesn't help hide how lifeless it is. My tunic, supposedly correctly fitted, sags from my frame. My face is thin – when did my cheeks sink like that? When did my skin get so dry and insipid, my eyes so dull? When did I last really *look*? It's as if someone's sucked the life from me. Is that what she's showing me?

For a second I feel Alexander's teeth grinding into my breast. Is that what's happening – he's draining me? I jerk my head as if I can escape the thought. Is that really how I see my own child: consuming my flesh, stealing my life away so that only a withered husk – a *shell* – remains?

'You look like a consumptive, Rose.'

It's an old-fashioned way of putting it but she's right, I do. I don't have the energy to protest. I can't even bring myself to move.

'He's hungry,' she says. 'He always will be. He'll drink and he'll *eat*.'

Something tugs inside me, a pull inescapable and deep. I want to cry, but damn it, I'm not going to. I *won't*. Besides, if I let her see that, I'm done for. I don't know why I should think so, but it's true. I try to tell myself she's nothing but a bitter old woman who had something terrible happen to her once, that she should be pitied, not feared. I tell myself I'm not as exhausted, as *denuded* as I look, but it isn't any use. Right at this moment, she's stronger than I am. Her will is keener. I can tell myself what to believe or not to believe, I can tell myself not to listen, but her stories are better than mine.

It will get easier, I tell myself for the hundredth, the thousandth time. *Of course it will.* She cuts in.

'Oh dear,' she says, and there's sympathy in her voice. It's worse than the mockery had been. 'So very tired.'

I swallow down the lump that rises to my throat. She draws something from her sleeve, a length of silk, like a stage conjuror at an outmoded end-of-pier show. It's another handkerchief, this one smelling of the rosewater I used to make in my mother's garden, crushing petals into a delicate scent that never would last. She raises it to her lips, touches it with her tongue. She *can't* be, but I'm unable to move as she steps closer, tilting her head, considering my reflection. She raises the handkerchief and I shut my eyes as she strokes my eyelids, twice each, with the damp fabric.

I hear her voice by my ear, a soft whisper. 'We don't need you any more, Rose.'

I'm not certain if I imagined it. What does she mean, *we*? Is she referring to everyone at Sunnyside, or she and Harriet? Maybe she means the baby too. I sway on my feet, thinking of her little sleeping face, so perfect. In my mind's eye she opens her mouth, but when she screams, it's Alexander's voice I hear.

My eyes snap open but I can't see. There's no room, no mirror, no reflection. There's nothing and I reach for my eyes, trying to open them, pulling at the lids, but I think they're open already—

'Goodness, what a fuss.' Mrs Favell's voice is distant again. She's moved away from me.

My eyes snap open and the room is just as it always was.

Was I dreaming on my feet? I'm still standing before the mirror and it tells me the truth. I look a mess, my hair dishevelled, my face pasty. I could never be the heroine of any story. I look like nothing more than a confused child.

'Perhaps you really should stay away from here,' she says. Her tone is softer, warmer, honeyed. It snags at something deep inside me, the place where a mother's love should be. Still I know that her voice is poison, and other words come to me, from another time: *And there I shut her wild wild eyes with kisses four.*

It's *her* poem, 'La Belle Dame sans Merci'. Is that what she just did to me with her handkerchief? But she won't close my eyes again. I won't be blind. It strikes me what an inadequate word 'fairy' is, or has become. She is something more, something for which I have no name, but still I recognise her for what she is. I won't forget again.

And she doesn't get to win.

'You're not going to make me leave,' I tell her. Then I walk out of the door and close it behind me. There's no need to slam it. If she really can see right through me, into me, she already knows that I mean it.

7

I don't see Mrs Favell for the rest of the day and I don't want to. There's anger in everything I do – I think of her as I stack the tea things, as I assist Alf in lifting spoonfuls of suet pudding to his lips, as I help the residents take their pills. Anyone can see it in me, I can tell, but they don't ask what's wrong and I don't try to explain. Why would I? Who here could understand, besides Mrs Favell?

I go home and the house is silent. Paul doesn't answer to my shout and the bassinet is empty. When I look in the hall cupboard, the pram's gone. He must have taken Alexander for a walk to help him settle. I picture him wrapping him up in blankets, holding him close, and pull a face, then hate myself for doing so. I go into the kitchen. Stuff is strewn everywhere, though no food, nothing ready, only dirty pots and the smell of something off. I run the hot tap, slam pots into the sink, go to the fridge and the cupboards and grab the first things I see: raw meat in a polystyrene tray, a few carrots, some potatoes beginning to soften, some milk for Alexander's return. I try to calm down, telling myself that Paul wouldn't be like this and Alexander is especially demanding just now, that it isn't for ever. An image flashes before me of Harriet, wearing a white blouse, brushing freshly washed hair from her face as she watches over Robyn, sweetly sleeping, and settling down to dinner with – whom? Is she married? Separated? I've never considered it.

I wash up, surprising myself by not breaking anything. I picture it though, plates cracking under my hands, glasses splintering into shards that pierce my skin, the brightness of blood spiralling through the water. I stare into it, seeing red against the white of soap suds, but when I blink there's only grey liquid, grease floating to the surface.

The front door opens and I hear Paul's shout. It's so bloody cheerful that I want to erase it, wipe away the expression I know he's wearing, the one that shows the crow's feet around his eyes. Footsteps sound behind me but I don't turn. My back stiffens and I hate myself for that too, for being the way I am, but I can't help it.

'Had a good day, love?' There's more in the tone than the question implies. He knows I'm pissed off and doesn't know why: he can't see it, which infuriates me even more.

He leans in and kisses my cheek. His hair is loose, rough against my skin.

'I took Alex to the park – he watched the ducks in the pond. Look, I'll do this. You're tired. Why don't you take him?'

'It's "Alex" now?'

My question brings a hurt silence and I'm not surprised. He's right, I *am* tired. I turn and hold out my arms and Alexander waves his fists at me. It's not deliberate, it can't be – he probably doesn't even know he's scowling.

Paul passes him over and I hold him close. His smell is unfamiliar – new fabric softener on his clothes? A different shampoo? Maybe he's just getting older. I rest my cheek against his, which is cool from being outside. He stiffens, throwing all his limbs out rigid, a solid block of resistance in my arms.

Paul takes the last few items from the sink. 'Sorry, love. Bit of a mess. Don't know where the time's gone. The days fly by so quick.'

Mine don't, I want to retort, but I swallow it down. The anger is fading and with it everything else, including the memory of what happened with Mrs Favell. Did she really say such things to me? Did she *blind* me? Suddenly I ache all over. Maybe she was right, I should move on, get another job, somewhere far away from her – but who would have me now?

'What the hell?' Paul says.

I soothe Alexander and turn to see. He's stopped washing up, is standing in front of the food laid out on the worktop, the carrots next to the bloody wrappings from the meat. I'm about to remind him to separate them when I realise what he's looking at.

Alexander's bottle, the lid off, is positioned by the window. It's still full. And in the milk—

Brightness spirals through the liquid, red against the white, already dissolving to pink as it is absorbed into the fluid: *my* fluid, the milk that came from me.

Paul reaches in, two fingers feeling into the narrow neck,

and I open my mouth to tell him it's sterile, don't touch it, and he withdraws them dripping, drawing something up out of the milk. It's meat: raw meat, milk slicking from it and running over Paul's hands to fall back into the bottle, my *baby's* bottle, tainted with blood.

'What the hell?' Paul can hardly speak. 'What *is* this, Rose?'

Alexander is a sandbag of weight in my arms. I think of my missing phone, of clothes strewn about the house, flour spilled everywhere. As if at my ear, a child's voice: *We need to stop them from being angry about the house.*

I don't know what has happened. I can't answer, can't meet Paul's fixed stare. I have no words to give. How can I say, *I didn't do it*? How can I say, *It was him*?

I can already see the look on Paul's face, hear the tone of his voice as he asks, *Who, Rose? Who exactly do you mean?*

But I know who he imagines *would* do it. What else is he supposed to think? The sting of it spreads its poison through my veins. Does he really suppose I would have fed that stuff to Alexander, holding it for him while he sucked it down?

I see from his expression that he does.

He's hungry. He always will be. He'll drink and he'll eat.

I push Mrs Favell's words away as Alexander is lifted – almost snatched – from me. Paul wraps his arms around him, greedy; or is he being protective? He doesn't say another word, only looks at me with eyes that are empty of warmth, empty of anything I want to see. I remember how I'd wanted to wipe the happiness from his expression when he walked in the door. Now I wish I could call it back again. I want everything to be how it was a moment ago.

I run up the stairs and into our room, throw myself down on the bed. I'm still wearing my uniform, as if I still belong to another place, and for a moment I wish I was back there. At least they need me.

I remember the way I'd stared into the washing-up water. The way I thought I'd seen red spreading through the white. But that had only ever been in my mind – hadn't it? I didn't do it, I know I didn't. I don't remember unwrapping the meat. I couldn't have hidden my own phone, could I? It wasn't me who threw flour around the kitchen. None of those things were me.

I bury my face in my hands and listen as Paul moves about downstairs, clattering pans, starting up the sterilizer. I imagine spoiled milk poured down the sink, meat thrown in the bin, everything cleared away and started afresh. Alexander for once isn't crying. Is he satisfied now? Or is it that he's content being with his dad, not his stupid, useless, depressed, *mad* mother?

I fling myself over on the bed and reach for my laptop, shoved into the space under my bedside table. I haven't read anything in what seems like a very long time. I haven't had the time or the energy and there's always something else to do, Alexander needing feeding or changing or soothing, and anyway, it only reminds me of the empty spaces leading all the way down the stairs.

I switch it on, open the book waiting there on the desktop, and stare at the words. It's the part about protecting a child from being stolen away. *A little late for that*, I think. A Bible in the cradle will stop a baby being snatched. Iron scissors opened into a cross offer double protection, since fairies hate iron and the sign of Christianity both. They cannot touch salt. A father's coat spread over an infant will fool the folk into thinking he's watching over it.

I scroll to the section on ways to rid the house of a changeling.

It's all superstition and foolishness but I can't stop myself from drinking in the words. As I do, I picture Alexander's screaming face. There's ringing in my ears and I don't know if it's real or an echo.

People would expose their baby in a field in the hope that the fairies would return their true child. They would summon the real mother to fetch it by making it cry, by beating or starving it. They would tip it from the cradle and sweep it out of the door. Dig a grave and leave it there all night. Hew off its head. Throw iron objects at it. Changelings fear water: the baby would be flung into a river. They fear fire: it would be suspended over the hearth, thrown onto hot coals. If the baby screams, it's a changeling; if it flies, shrieking, up the chimney.

I reach for my phone and search the internet for more. And more there is, stories from different times and places, from different cultures – as if everyone *knew*. As if they had heard the stories, seen the clues, followed the evidence. Just as if they had *believed*.

They doused the baby in a pool. They exposed it on a beach and ignored its cries as the waves drew near. They dosed it with foxglove, the fairy's own plant, to put the fairy out of it. Their charms all had one thing in common, I realise: the false child must first be cast out – sent back to the folk – before the true child can be returned.

I read on and find actual cases of it happening. There were families with children who didn't thrive or who had disabilities, unable to work but still a mouth to feed; one they couldn't afford or support, not back then. Changelings were often said to be weak and wizened, children who didn't grow as they should. I suppose it must have been a comfort to *those* people to tell tales of the fairies. But that was different: *they* were trapped. They must have gathered around the fire with furtive eyes, trying to justify the things they'd 'had' to do to be rid of their changeling child – the things they'd seized upon, the things they'd maybe even wanted to do all along.

The images in my mind multiply, sickening. They make me feel weary, sad, wrung out. *Enough.* Yet the image that lingers before me is that of the garden at Sunnyside. I see flowers pushing their way up through the soil, pea shoots twining around a stake as the sap rises. And in one forgotten corner, seeded perhaps from the woodland beyond, foxglove stems spire into the air, their purple bell-like flowers speckled with black, like splashes of ink. But that was in the summer, wasn't it? It wouldn't be growing now.

I can almost hear my mother's voice. We had been walking in the woods – I don't know where or when, only that I was small, and she was there. She was telling me the names of the flowers: campion, celandines, ragged robin. When she reached the foxglove, though, there was not just one name but many: fairy glove. Folk's glove. *Folk's love.*

I know that the plant is poisonous. But when used in the right way, in a special way, the drug within can help too, can't it? I'm sure one of the residents at Sunnyside has it in the medication for regulating his heart.

I shake my head, not sure what it is I'm thinking, and the door opens and my own heart flutters.

'It was just an accident.' Paul carries Alexander into the room, holding him out like a gift. 'I know you wouldn't hurt him.'

An accident? I wonder what kind of accident he thinks could have so tainted the milk, but I don't reply.

He bends, supporting Alexander's head so that I can kiss his scalp, which pulses faintly beneath my lips. Paul sits next to me, still holding his child. I don't know what I feel. Should I be grateful that his anger has softened? Angry that he thinks those words need to be spoken?

I realise the laptop is still open and shove the screen closed. I thrust it back under the bedside table before I reach out and take the baby onto my lap. I wrap my arms around him and lean in and nestle against them both. The baby gives little cries, fluting noises interspersed with breathy gasps. And Paul makes noises in return, meaningless, nothing but a series of empty clicks.

That night, I sleep badly. When Alexander screams, I get up before Paul wakes. I stand over the crib at the foot of our bed and the baby's face is pale in the dim light, his mouth a dark hole. For a moment he stops wailing and looks at me. I don't know if he can focus yet. I don't know what it is he sees. Still, his eyes seem to take in the entire world.

My vision speckles. Tiredness makes my bones heavy even while my mind feels too light. It's hard to fix on anything but Paul shifts and murmurs in his sleep so I bend and scoop up the baby. The boards of the stairs are cold against my bare feet as I pad downstairs. I step into the kitchen and he stirs, grabbing my hair, yanking tears from my eyes. I adjust my grip and hold him out, examine his wizened face. So much rage in such a tiny thing. His eyes are still the soft blue-grey of an infant's, but they don't look young. He opens his mouth, bawling, revealing an ugly yellow tooth.

I warm a bottle and sit on the sofa while I feed him, watching his lips pulling at the teat, a line of milk welling there. His eyes close, the lids almost transparent. I can see the blood running through them. I remove the bottle, notice the indentations in the rubber where his teeth have been. I tell myself he can't help it. I rest one finger on his lip, pulling on the slippery softness to see the natal teeth more clearly: ill-shapen, discoloured, slightly jagged at the tip. I stare into his eyes, which are wide, regarding me. I sit him up and rub his back. I feel the sudden warmth as he spills some of my own milk onto my shoulder and the smell turns my stomach. *The milk rapidly turns sour*, I think, and wonder that I can be so unnatural as to think he may not be mine.

All in my head, I tell myself.

He wriggles, wailing next to my ear. He's still hungry. He's always hungry. In the stories, that's why they do it, isn't it? Fairies want to steal human children to strengthen their line, but they don't always replace them with an enchanted stock of wood. Sometimes they leave a fairy child behind, to benefit from the care of the human mother, to drink her milk. Some even thought the false baby could imbibe a soul along with human milk, gaining a treasure the fairies don't possess by nature.

Is that why he's so hungry all of the time? Has he succeeded? I think of Fenton's letter, telling of eyes that are quite black, without a soul in them. I wonder if Alexander's will darken as he grows.

Is that why I feel so empty?

I shake my head and dab once more at his plump lips. They open in response, *rooting*, and a new picture rises: an everyday, ordinary picture of the shops, so short a distance away, and the quantities of baby formula lined up on their shelves. I know Paul wouldn't like it. He'd remind me that breastfeeding's important to give babies antibodies, resistance to disease, defence against allergies, to equip them for our world. Still, the image stays.

I pick him up. Usually I'm surprised at the solidity of him but he seems to weigh almost nothing as I carry him upstairs and lay him in the crib, then lie awake, listening to the breathy noises he makes, the little hiccups and gasps and exclamations, as if he's still crying out for more. The sounds are oddly articulate, as if they could easily become words and sentences if his undeveloped anatomy would enable him to form them properly; or if I only had the ability to understand.

8

When I awake to the sound of the baby wailing, the events of the night before seem as insubstantial as my movements as I change him and warm his bottle and do the things I need to do. Paul comes in stretching, grins, plants a kiss on my cheek. He takes the bottle and baby and starts the feed – do I only imagine the way he swirls the milk, examining the colour? He makes a comment about his clever boy sleeping through the night and I don't bother to enlighten him.

Time passes in skips: walking up the stairs, tilting my face into the shower's spray, willing myself awake, finding my car keys – did I really leave them in the bathroom? I settle into the car seat, wondering if I kissed Paul and Alexander goodbye. *Paul and Alexander*. The names are distant, people I heard of once, words that scarcely mean anything at all.

I help the residents with breakfast, more mouths that need

to be fed, like chicks in a nest. Mrs Favell is there and I check on her with no eye contact and little comment, and she behaves with similar coolness towards me. Why should she take the time to be rude? She's got what she wanted. I'm furniture to her now. I meet her smallest requirements and nothing more.

It isn't until I see Nisha heading outside with a mug of coffee that I am suddenly and fully awake.

Not entirely knowing why, I hurry after her, stepping into a garden now firmly in the grip of autumn. A few red berries, clinging to a shrub I cannot name, are the only colour. The smell is of dormant soil and mulch and, coming from the woods, a richer, fungal scent, a little tainted with rot. It isn't raining but the air feels damp.

Nisha stands at the end of the path, just beyond the furthest bench. She raises her mug, narrowing her eyes against the steam, but she doesn't drink. She delves in her pocket with her free hand as if she's forgotten something.

She doesn't look at me until I'm right next to her. I don't apologise for interrupting her break. Her habitual smile is replaced by a look of annoyance, almost suspicion. I don't care. 'I need to know about the girl who was here before me,' I say.

'Theresa?' She glances towards the French windows. Is she afraid someone might hear? 'I told you already.'

'I need to know where she is.'

She pushes away from the wall, distancing herself from me, shaking her head.

'You told me you were friendly. I have to talk to her – that's all I want, to talk. I think she might be able to help me.'

'What with?' Now she really looks at me.

'Just – nothing. There's something I need to know. I'm not going to upset her or anything.' I have no idea if this is true.

Nisha exhales, long and slow. 'Has Mrs Favell done something to upset you?'

I realise that this is what she expected to happen all along. She knew there was something wrong about her, they all did, and anger flashes through me. It quickly fades, leaving weariness behind: the residue of sleepless nights, the madness of the thoughts that weigh me down.

'Please, Nisha. I can't explain, but I need your help. I need Theresa's help. I just want to ask her a few questions. It won't come back to you.' I hope I'm not lying to her. If I can find this girl, if I learn what Mrs Favell did to her, it might make everything clear to me. I might be able to claw my way through the thorny forest of my thoughts.

'She works in the chemist,' Nisha says, 'on the High Street. That's all I know.' She throws what's left of her coffee into a rose bush, wilted and infected with black-spot, no flowers left. She edges around me and walks away, leaving clear footprints in the soft earth. In her haste to get away from me, she thought nothing of stepping into the dirt.

My hands shake on the steering wheel as I pull into the car park near the centre of town. Rain flecks the windscreen, not heavy, but leaving its mark. It feels like a warning. A few desultory souls walk past, stopping to put up umbrellas or fiddle with their hoods.

It's lunchtime and I wonder if she'll even be there, but I can't help that. Maybe she's sitting in a café. It could be her day off; she could be sick. She might have left. I don't even know what she looks like. I had imagined looking into her face and understanding everything, but now nothing in the world feels certain.

I throw coins into the pay and display machine then walk towards the High Street, feeling the same way I did when swollen with pregnancy – as if my centre of gravity has shifted, making the simple process of walking unfamiliar. I pass the bakery with its queue of office workers and builders in metal-tipped boots snaking out of the door; the Post Office, which is closed; a florist with a pretty window display but no one inside; a tiny boutique, its window filled with jewel-coloured sari fabrics. The chemist is an independent called Ainley's. I've been in there plenty of times. Perhaps it was Theresa who served me and I never knew. They have a jumble of items crammed into too small a space, a tiny pharmacy counter at the back.

I stop outside and peer through the window. A girl on the till rhythmically passes bottles of shampoo and packets of vitamins and bottles of orange juice across a barcode reader. Her hair is platinum blonde tipped with black, tied in a messy ponytail, and I wonder if this is the girl who was thrown out of Sunnyside because of Mrs Favell.

There's a queue at the till, so I can't just go up and ask her. I walk in, pick up a packet of mints and join the line. It doesn't take long before I'm close enough to read her name-badge: SUE. HAPPY TO HELP.

She doesn't look happy to help. I turn and thrust the mints

onto a shelf amid the chocolate bars and batteries and glance around. An older man in uniform is stacking shelves with cheap body spray and I look away from his smile. At the very back of the shop, the pharmacy is staffed by a young woman with pink-tinged hair, small-featured and hard-faced.

After a moment's hesitation I walk towards her and she meets my gaze and watches my approach. She doesn't smile. Maybe she can tell I'm not a customer. She has a name-badge too: THERESA. There's no HAPPY TO HELP, not this time. She wears the white tunic of a pharmacist; she must be trained and trusted, with the responsibility of handling drugs every day. Do her employers know what happened at Sunnyside? I try to picture her sobbing against a wall while the police search her locker and I can't. The pharmacy is on a higher level than the shop floor and I crane my neck to look at her.

'Do you have a prescription?' she asks.

I shake my head. I'm making her uncomfortable, I can tell. A rustling comes from the back room as if someone else is there, and I speak softly. 'I really need to talk to you for a minute. About Sunnyside. I think we have a mutual friend.'

That was supposed to make it sound less mysterious, but it only makes it worse. Her expression hardens and she casts a worried glance over her shoulder. I'm right, then: the matter of theft can't have been taken further or it would be on her record. A guilty little secret? Well, that can only work for me.

She steps back out of sight and I hear her say she'll only be a moment before she reappears through a side door. She grabs my arm, harder than she needs to. 'One minute,' she snaps.

I'm marched through the shop like a shoplifter and I don't say anything until we're in the street, a short distance away from the customers going in and out of the door. She's a head taller and she uses it, leaning over me. Her expression doesn't change. There's no trace of softness in her and I wonder that Mrs Favell could ever have singled her out – or has Theresa toughened up since then?

'What do you want?'

It's me who looks shifty, my gaze sliding away. 'I wanted to ask you about Mrs Favell.'

'*That's* your mutual friend?'

'Not exactly.'

'Seriously, what the hell do you want? It's not as if I was even there that long.' Despite the reference to her leaving, she seems less scared than angry.

'Look, I heard about what happened, okay? And I know what she's like. I'm working there now and I wondered if you could tell me anything about her.'

'What do you want to know?' She spits the words.

'Well – she's been saying things to me. She confuses me. I'm not sure who she is, not really.' I'm not sure *what* she is, that's what I want to say but can't.

She lets out a short bark of laughter. 'She's a witch. Is that what you want to know? I doubt you need me to tell you that. Why do you think she's there at all, at Sunnyside?'

I shake my head.

'Not frail, is she? Not like some of them. Not poor either. She doesn't have to live there. But if she lived alone she'd never have any fun, would she? You know what I think? She likes to watch people at the end of their lives. She enjoys it – just as if she won't reach the end of her own soon enough.' She sneers. 'There'd be no one to mess with, to play with their heads.'

I push aside the thought of Edie Dawson. This isn't why I'm here. 'Is that what she did to you? Mess with your head?' I must sound hopeful.

'What do you reckon? She says things to you, you know that. She plays tricks. It seems stupid afterwards, but when you're there, she knows how to get to you. She's clever like that. Had lots of practice.'

I nod. 'It's hard to explain to anyone else, but I – I'm not sure she's even—'

'She's not all there, that's for certain, but she's not mad. She enjoys it. Look, just stay away from her, okay? As much as you can.' Her expression softens and she leans in. 'I hardly knew what I was doing, you know – when I took the necklace. She had me so upset. I just wanted to hurt her, I think. I'm not a thief.'

I freeze. 'You *took* it?'

'I thought you said you knew what happened?'

'I did. I thought I did.'

'That's it: I'm done here. Leave me alone, okay? I've finished with the whole thing. I'm not talking about this ever again, understand?'

She walks off, leaving me standing in the street, not sure what happened. I haven't said any of the things I meant to, haven't asked the question I wanted to ask. Perhaps that in itself tells me all I need to know. Could I really have stood in the High Street and asked if she thinks Mrs Favell is a fairy? Or perhaps not that – but some nameless, strange, unnatural thing? Of course I couldn't. They'd have me locked up, even section me. It's not a normal thing to say.

I'm not a thief, Theresa had said. And yet it sounded as if she had been.

She says things to you.

Everything seems simpler and yet more complicated than I'd thought and I picture her going back to her counter, going on with her life, as if Sunnyside and everything in it had never existed. For a moment I envy her. I turn and walk back in the direction of the car. Lunchtime will be over before too long, and Patricia will be watching to see if anyone is late. It had better not be the girl who only just came back, the one who had a baby.

Still, there is something else I need to do before I face Mrs Favell again – and that means another quiet visit to her room.

>·<

11th September 1922

Dear Mr Gardner,

You will perhaps be surprised to hear from me again. It has been some time to be sure, and yet you cannot doubt my continued interest in this affair, no matter my silence. I have answered certain small queries you have sent; I hope I never failed you in that regard. And yet it is with the keenest sense of disappointment that I take up my pen.

I recently obtained a copy of Mr Doyle's book. Indeed, I opened *The Coming of the Fairies* with the greatest anticipation, as you may well imagine. You kindly informed me that a significant portion of the account would be taken up with further sightings and evidence of fairies, brought to light after the photographs taken in 1917 and the article in *The Strand* of 1920, and I did not deceive myself, I think, in expecting that my own was to be among them.

Imagine my feelings then, in leafing through it – and again, and indeed again – and finding nothing more than the same scant cases that were the subject of the secondary article in *The Strand* of March of last year.

I should tell you, I have no wish to convey my immediate impressions. Indeed, my emotions remain very high, though I shall endeavour to temper them.

The prime cause of my concern, needless to say, is that Sir Arthur may have disregarded my story because he believes it to be a fraud or imposture. Does he class us with the cases that were 'more or less ingenious practical jokes'? Has he truly dismissed us as such? I ask you directly, and I believe, after all my openness upon the matter, I am entitled to do so. Does he consider me a liar and a cheat?

But he can have no doubt, his own belief being what it is! He has many times stood accused of the most dreadful species of foolishness, if not mendacity, and it is difficult to countenance that being his first response to me.

I am a man of honour, Mr Gardner. I have always conducted myself as respectable in business and of decent character in all aspects of my life. I would challenge anyone to find a soul that would not speak for me in that regard. I have invented nothing. I can only mourn such proofs as I have held in my hand and that have gone from me, since they would have made my position unassailable and above reproach.

I have seen fairies. My daughter-in-law has been cruelly blighted for spying upon them and has been restored by their agency. I have held pictures of them in my hand. I have touched their earthly remains. Such is my testimony, stronger than many that are instanced in Sir Arthur's book, and yet my name is struck from the record as surely as if I had never existed.

It cannot be only because he has not made my acquaintance. He never saw Elsie Wright or Frances Griffiths, but has taken the word of others as to the unlikelihood of their having invented anything. He stakes his reputation on their photographs being genuine. And yet how great an argument in his favour would it be to show *other* photographs, captured in the same place but at different times and by different hands? It would reaffirm the existence of the sprites – demonstrating, at once and for ever, that theirs was no isolated case.

I know that through some misfortune my photographs had been rendered flattened and dull and without the traces of life they once held, but could they be entirely without purpose? For the ones printed in the book were no great demonstrations, as is evidenced by the public doubt and incomprehension that has greeted them.

Why, even within the text there was some little excuse made for them by an interested party, namely that the fairies' odd whiteness was a natural result of their lack of shadow. Such is nonsense! They have physicality – why, then, should they be without shadows? And elsewhere it is blamed upon the glow of ectoplasm. I am not even sure I believe in such stuff. And someone described their 'somewhat artificial-looking flatness' – that says everything, does not?

Yet I wonder if the images I sent to you have undergone some further deterioration that made them unfit to be seen even by the side of these? Those I keep here appear to be a match for them in my eyes, but can I trust them? I admit, it rather gives the lie to that old Yorkshire phrase that is referred to in the book – 'Ah'll believe what ah see.'

But you will forgive me the general tenor of my letter. Please understand that I am simply very distressed at the great opportunity that has been missed. I assure you that I have no desire for personal gain. I never have; I made that quite clear from the outset. I am a Seeker of Truth, and I know that in you and Sir Arthur I found fellow travellers along a similar road, and I cannot contemplate how we have somehow lost each other along the way.

Did Sir Arthur wish to keep the accounts of additional fairy sightings just as the secondary article had them, ignoring later developments? Had he so little time to commit to creating his new 'epoch' that he was unable to bring the section up to the present? Or did he wish only to protect us and leave us to our misery?

I must go further, for I feel my letter would be half incomplete if I did not mention not what is missing from the book, but some rather wild matter contained therein. I am no great writer, nor a philosopher. I am not possessed of any special wisdom that lifts me above other men, and yet in the name of common sense, I must address something that I cannot help but feel is disfiguring to the whole. My position as, I hope, your friend and would-be assistant speaks against it, but I must say it; I should feel dishonest if I did not.

I refer to the question of clairvoyance, and its use in detecting the presence of fairies not through the agency of the eye, but the mind. The 'observations' made by a Mr Sergeant (a pseudonymous name, I believe), not only of fairies but undines and wood elves, nymphs, brownies, gnomes and goblins, which fairly seem to have swarmed to Cottingley Glen to meet him in numbers worthy of an invading army, cannot but stretch credulity, particularly as they stand unsupported by any evidence save that of his avowed good character.

I recognise that Sir Arthur has a greater interest in the direction of spiritualism than in fairies, and that the clairvoyant in question is a friend of your own. I mean nothing ill. Rather, in reflecting the accusations that others will make, I hope I merely carry out some small service to the cause in which we are united, or ought to be.

Further – and here I take the risk, I know, of losing your regard entirely, but I must say it – I refer to the explanations provided of the nature and purpose of fairy existence that are put forward by the Theosophists.

Sir, I know that you are a noted member of that organisation, even serving as President of its Blavatsky Lodge, and I am sure they must do much good in the world; I apologise if my comments seem disrespectful. Perhaps it is my own ignorance or lack of understanding, but it seems to me that to describe in such detail the fairy business of making plants grow – with some tending to the leaves, others the roots, and some painting the flowers their various colours – is more than a little fanciful. We have scarcely proved the reality of fairies before unveiling them as the vital link between the sun's energy and the leaf!

Furthermore, the book explains the different species of fairy required for the numerous tasks involved in making a plant grow, and puts down their method to that mysterious concept of 'magnetism'. How could we know such things? We are describing the dark side of the moon by means of a match! It can surely withstand no serious questioning.

I do not wish to trample upon your beliefs – indeed, I am sure in other aspects it must be a very admirable system – but this is very wild, and surely has no place within a serious approach to the subject. And for the book to suggest, after all my experiences, that such beings possess no real material body

– even further, that the fairies do not die as humans do…!

But I will leave it there, at the risk of alienating you for ever. I hope you will forgive my consternation and give credence to my genuine intentions. I simply feel that something of a steadier and more closely observed nature would have had greater efficacy. But perhaps Sir Arthur felt, as he says somewhere, 'The human race does not deserve fresh evidence, since it has not troubled, as a rule, to examine that which already exists.'

Or – and do I dare hope? – he wishes to stretch the matter to a second volume, filled out with what has befallen us, to strike down the disbelieving critics of the first?

But again, I beg you to have patience with the length of my letter and indeed its manner, for my aim was never to displease you. And I beg you to reply – not only to give any hint of a reason which may be at your disposal as to the omission of my photographs, but to reassure me that I have not trespassed too far upon your tolerance as to be unable to sign myself,

Your humble servant,
Lawrence Fenton

9

I didn't come to Mrs Favell's bedroom searching for this. The letter was placed on top of the bureau, in plain view, as if waiting for me; as if she'd known I would be here at this moment. I hadn't come to take anything or to snoop. I hadn't even expected there to be more to the story. I came here with gifts; I tell myself they're gifts.

And Lawrence Fenton, that seeker after fairies, isn't shown in a good light. Suddenly I don't know what I'm doing here. It doesn't surprise me that he couldn't leave his encounter with the folk behind him, but I thought he'd been content with his family: Charlotte with her sight restored, everyone safe. Now he seems like a man who only wants his brush with fame – or notoriety. But surely he'd only wanted to be in the book because he thought he knew the fairies best?

It's as if she left this here to distract me. I came here with a purpose and even if that is nonsense too, there's no reason not to go on. What can I lose by it?

I grip my bag tighter. In it are the things I purchased at a little shop tucked away down a side street near the florist, before I headed back. I'd never been inside before. It was full of bric-a-brac and antiques, what my mum would have called jumble. The things I found weren't quite what I sought, but I think they will do. There's a small Bible, its leather cover worn to soft silkiness, the flyleaf covered in crabbed handwriting I can't read, and an old paperknife. I had wanted iron scissors that I could open into the shape of a cross, but the old man in the shop assured me that the knife is made of iron, that substance so repellent to the fairies. It feels rough and dry to my touch; it is old and blackened and cold.

There's also the item I brought from the pantry. That should have been easier, though the second chef had walked in as I was filling the container I'd had the foresight to lift from the staffroom. I explained that we needed sugar for our coffee and she nodded, but it wasn't sugar I'd taken: it was salt.

I open it and sprinkle the contents onto the carpet, trying to make a solid line across the bottom of the door. I rub it in a little with my foot. If anyone sees it I'll be in trouble, at least if they can connect it to me, but the line fragments and I'm not sure anyone would notice. I hope it will still be enough.

I wonder again what I'm doing. Isn't it madness to think this might work – even more so to act upon that belief? But I've begun and may as well go on.

Next is the paperknife. My choice seems more apt by the moment. I decide to be bold and place it in plain view and I put it down on top of the letter. If the missive was a message to me, here is mine in return. If she wants to put the letter away, she'll have to touch the knife. If she complains to anyone about finding it here, if she accuses me, I'll say I found it downstairs and assumed it was hers. They'll think one of the other residents misplaced it, or a visitor. Mrs Favell won't, but what can she say?

It's not as if I'm stealing.

That leaves the Bible. I look around. Hartland's book suggested placing it under a crib to ward away the fairies, but I lift her pillow and push the book underneath. I see at once it won't work. It's small, but still too bulky. I'd rather she didn't know it was there. I remove it and pause, looking down at the cross embossed into the cover, a little gilt still clinging to the leather.

Is that a footstep I hear in the corridor?

Without further thought I open the Bible and rip out a few of its pages. They're too thin to tear cleanly but are pulled in half and I stare down at them, catching the words, *Honour thy father and thy mother.* I grimace, hastily lift the mattress and place the loose pages underneath, right in the centre, hoping that housekeeping won't find them when they make the bed.

Another step – outside the door? I'm expecting her, of course. Her lunchtime is over and she won't long tolerate the conversation downstairs. That was the point. I need to see what happens when she tries to walk across the threshold.

I realise I'm still holding the Bible. I shove it under her pillow after all and turn to see two shadows breaking the line of light spilling underneath the door. I wait, holding my breath. For a moment I think I'm mistaken because those shadows don't move for what feels a long time, then the handle rattles and the door opens. The scrape of it against the carpet is too loud, *grainy*, and I catch my breath. Will it have broken the line of salt?

Mrs Favell stands there, her eyes narrowed, her face blank. I'm reminded of our first day again, but now our positions are reversed. I'm the one waiting to see who she is and what she will do, but her eyes are brightening by the moment, and she doesn't even look at me. Am I so unimportant to her – after what she's done? I curl my hands into fists.

She steps cleanly over the threshold and into the room.

'Did you require something, Rose?' Her voice is ice. Nothing about her has changed. The salt didn't stop her for a second, didn't even give her pause. Does that prove something? Have I lost my mind – or has my fear negated its power? Did I simply not use enough?

'I came to read to you.' I hold out the book I'd concealed in my pocket, the one I knew would fit because that's where I'd put it when she first gave it to me. It's the little ruined volume of Keats' poetry. 'La Belle Dame sans Merci'. 'I thought you might like that.'

She doesn't answer, just stalks into the room. The air shifts as she goes past me to the bureau and stares down at the letter, or at the knife positioned on top of it. She remains perfectly still and I wonder if that's because she wants to touch the paper but can't, not with the cold iron waiting there; then she reaches down and pinches the edge of the paper between her finger and thumb and slides it free. The paperknife clatters to the desk.

'Games,' she says.

I don't know how to answer. I couldn't speak if I did. Something bubbles up inside me, new knowledge perhaps, or triumph, and she reaches down without even looking and picks up the knife and holds it out.

Her skin doesn't burn. Smoke doesn't rise from the metal. She doesn't flinch at its touch. She only stands there, waiting for me to take it. My attempt to expose her feels pitiful. What did I think it could achieve? She adjusts her grip, turns it sideways and tosses it towards me. Awkwardly, I snatch it from the air.

'Yours, I believe.'

'I found it in the day room,' I say. 'I thought it was—'

'*Yours*,' she says again, and I am silenced. 'Did you read my letter, Rose?'

Blood rushes to my cheeks. She walks towards me and I think she's going to challenge me further and I can't take my eyes from her face – I don't think she's blinked even once. Maybe she doesn't need to. She tugs the Keats from my grasp.

'Did you like it? You miss a little poetry in your life, don't you?'

She leans in closer and I smell her scent: lily of the valley. I'm no longer certain it's the same one my mother used to dab behind her ears. This is richer, sweeter; redolent of real flowers, of springtime.

'Did you like his touch on your skin?' she asks. Her face is up close but even so, I can't see a single wrinkle or crease. She could be any age at all. She holds the book up between us, like a minister warding off evil with a Bible, or perhaps she just wants to remind me of the night I ruined it. She knew it was spoiled, though she'd barely glanced at it. I try to tell myself she'd only smelled the lingering trace of aftershave and stale wine beneath the cloying scent of flowers.

She takes another step and I retreat before her. 'A little advice. I suggest you leave things well enough alone.'

Her eyes have depths, I realise. Golden lights swim inside them. Images come to me: Alexander, his face purple as he screams with endless hunger. Mrs Favell showing me my own reflection: *You look like a consumptive, Rose.*

She moves aside, sitting on her bed as if we're done and all she wants to do is relax, as if I'm dismissed. Without turning she reaches beneath the pillow, takes out the Bible and holds that out too.

I swallow hard. I *am* consumed, with hatred for her. Salt didn't stop her; iron didn't burn her. The Bible didn't give her a moment's pause. Did I destroy its power over her by tearing it? Did I bring down a curse, rendering myself unable to see the truth?

Suddenly I'm exhausted. I've achieved nothing. I couldn't even stand in front of Theresa and say the word *fairy*. But perhaps that was a good thing, the right thing. I tell myself again that Mrs Favell is nothing but a spiteful old lady. She's bitter and she has too much perception and too little kindness, she's nasty and vindictive, but that is all. There is no other story to tell. I shouldn't hate her; I'm supposed to look after her. The salt, a Bible – all they mean is that I'm losing my mind. Perhaps Paul's mother was right, I have post-natal depression or I'm having some kind of breakdown, and I should get myself together because if I'm not careful someone will come and lock me away, probably somewhere not all that different to Sunnyside.

I reach out and take the Bible and the book of poetry, both of them as ruined as each other. I think of the word she said earlier: *games*. Theresa had mentioned that too. *She says things to you, you know that.* None of my tricks worked because there's nothing special about her – nothing magical, not in her or the world. I suddenly picture my mother's books, all of them gone now, not just the ones I'd sought but *everything*, and I feel a pang of sadness but I know that what remains is the truth.

Alexander is *mine*. Paul and me and our boy, we're a family. She can't ruin that, can't steal it from me. She can't poison it unless I let her, and I won't let her, ever again.

I don't know I'm going to say the words until I open my mouth. 'You won't make me give my baby up.'

Mrs Favell doesn't answer. She opens her mouth and laughs. She throws back her head and shakes with mirth.

I back away, rush from the room and slam the door behind me. I can still hear that awful laughter. I wonder if it will ever stop, if I will ever rid myself of it. She laughs as if she *knows*, as if she can see every thought passing through my head. She laughs as if that's what she'd longed for; as if my words were exactly the ones she'd most wished to hear.

10

It is the blink of an eye and a thousand years until I'm back at Sunnyside again. It's not that I can't remember the previous night – I ate; I sat with Paul; I expressed milk, despite all my resolutions to stop; I held Alexander in my arms and silently promised to love him. And yet somehow I was separate from it all. It passed in a haze, as if that was the fiction and this the only reality I know.

The weather is unseasonable, a displaced day of summer. There are clouds, but they are innocently white, moving swiftly by. Sunshine spears between them, chasing their shadows so that the ground almost appears to be moving.

The Activities Coordinator is here again, rallying everyone in her too-bright voice. A lovely day, she says, a *splendid* day, so why don't those who are able have a game of croquet? The lawn's not really big enough and there are only three hoops and the balls are big and brightly plastic like children's toys, but no one seems to mind. Sandra even persuades Mrs Favell, giving her the responsibility of helping Alf so that she can't make her excuses. She doesn't seem to want to be elsewhere though, not today. She stands in the shade of the wall, by an espaliered apple tree that has always looked spindly and bare but is suddenly bursting into fruit. The apples look tiny and hard and must be sour, yet Mrs Favell reaches out, plucks one and takes a bite.

Jimmy groans. His ball has hit the edge of the hoop and rolled away. Maryam cheers and Sandra claps as if he's done something clever. Clouds move across the sun and shadows shift. Sunshine pierces the furthest corner of the garden.

Mrs Favell suddenly stands in the fullness of its light. I stare, remembering something I'd read on the internet: that when the folk are exposed to sunlight, any glamour or deception is stripped away. They appear as they truly are.

The spell is broken. She isn't elegant. She isn't poised. The last time I saw her, her skin had seemed so unwrinkled she could have been any age. Not so now. Her face is lined, her lips thin, her cheeks sunken. Her hair is limp and despite the sun's brilliance it appears nothing but grey, untouched by silver or gold. Her soft blouse hangs from her bony arms, the claws of her hands. She looks worn-out and ancient. Only her eyes are fierce, gleaming with defiance as she looks at me.

She knows I've seen her – truly seen her. I can't swallow; my throat is dry. I can't move as she starts to walk towards me, her movements awkward, her limbs like sticks and too long. I almost think I can hear them clicking.

What will she do? Will she seize me in those claws, snatch me away?

She pauses, putting a hand to her back as if she is pained. I remember the torn pages of the Bible concealed beneath her mattress, too thin to feel them as she slept – but did she somehow feel them anyway? Did one of my tricks work after all?

A cloud passes across the sun and she is cast once more into shadow.

At once, she straightens. She half turns and calls out to Maryam, in a quite ordinary way, to 'Hurry up and finish him.' The curve of her cheek is smooth, her neck only slightly creased under her lovely pearls. She waves at someone seated across the lawn and there is no stiffness in her movement. I cannot hear her joints click; possibly I never could.

I shake my head. Did I only imagine it? No one else has noticed anything amiss. I imagine trying to explain it to them. Why should it seem strange for an old person to look old? What suspicion lies in an aching back or ungainly movements? She had taken a bite of a bitter apple and screwed up her face. The full light of the sun never flattered anyone. There is nothing strange or unusual in it, and yet I *saw*.

I watch her instruct Maryam in angling her shot. The ball passes cleanly through the hoop, to more cheers. Mrs Favell smiles and yet I suspect she's refusing to look at me. She's trying to show me I don't matter, that she doesn't care if I've seen the truth.

I turn and walk towards the French windows. She might not care now, but she *will*.

I hurry through the lounge, ignoring Barry, who sits alone

in the corner, nodding, with a blanket across his knees. I ascend the stairs two at a time. I reach her door and it's odd – I know she's outside, that she's behind me – but I automatically raise a hand to knock.

That sensation of being watched returns, redoubled. I picture Mrs Favell in the garden below, slowly turning her head from her game, towards her room; towards me. I haven't sensed this in a long time, I realise. Is that because she'd decided I didn't matter? Well, now perhaps I do.

I open the door and pause before entering. It occurs to me that it feels this way because she's set some ward of her own – protection against me entering her room again. Is it because my own tricks are troubling her at last? And yet she isn't going to stop me. I tell myself there is nothing preventing me from stepping across the threshold and after a moment, I do.

Everything inside is perfectly neat. It looks as if the room doesn't belong to anyone in particular. Only the bureau seems in any way connected to its occupant and I find that it's locked. I go to the china dish by her bedside, where once upon a time, she'd placed a key. It's empty.

Unlike the bureau with its rich grain and glowing wood, the chest of drawers is relentlessly ordinary. I pull open the top drawer and see sweaters in soft wool, neatly folded. I rummage inside, feeling for the hard stem of a key, anything that doesn't belong. There is only a drawer liner printed with rose petals, the faint remnant of scent rising from it.

The next drawer is slippery with silken nightgowns and full of underclothes rich with lace. They're fancier than my own; I picture the ugly nursing bra I bought during my pregnancy and grimace. I search through those too and find nothing. The last drawer contains slacks in thicker fabrics, all ready for the winter, smartly ironed. It's all so ordinary that I feel with renewed force what I'm doing. I'm a thief. I'm Theresa. How would it look to anyone who walked in? I have no reason to be here. Even if I came up with an excuse, the expression on my face would give me away.

Through the windowpane comes a faint cheer. Someone must have won the game. Have they finished or are there more rounds to play? I suppose I'll find out soon enough.

Will Mrs Favell come striding up the stairs, her aching back forgotten? At that thought I turn to the bed. I lift the mattress and see the torn pages, still there as they must have been all night as she slept, and next to them—

A key. It's *her* key, to her bureau.

I stare. Did she know about the Bible pages all along? Is this another one of her games – did her back ever hurt her at all?

Maybe I'd shoved the pages under her bed in such a hurry I hadn't seen the key. Or she had slipped it under there without feeling the touch of the misplaced papers.

I remind myself that whatever the answer, the key is within my grasp. I let the mattress fall into place and turn my back on it. The key fits smoothly into the little lock on the bureau and turns with a soft yet decisive sound.

As soon as I open it I see two stacks of letters, of the same creamy stock I've grown familiar with. They are pushed right to the back and I pull one of them towards me, bringing it into the light. I recognise the faded ink, the slanted handwriting.

Dear Sir Arthur Conan Doyle, Forgive the impertinence of my writing to you as a stranger and without introduction…

That was the first letter, one I've already read. I reach for the other bundle and see more letters, the one on top dated the nineteenth of September. Have I read that far? I can't remember the dates. I scan the first paragraph. *Dear Mr Gardner, Thank you, wholeheartedly, for your reply. There was no need to apologise for its brevity; the assurance of your continued friendship gave it an import more valuable than any longer missive could impart.*

My fingers tingle. This is new. Perhaps here I'll find the answers I need.

I check the bottom of the other pile and find the last letter I read. She's divided them according to me then, the ones I've read and the ones I haven't. Perhaps I matter to her after all. I grab the whole second bundle and this time I don't worry about folding the lovely paper. I crease them haphazardly, stuff them into my uniform pocket, lock the bureau and throw the key back under the mattress. These will be safe in my locker before anyone comes in from the garden.

Then, surely, I will know the truth.

➤◄

19th September 1922

Dear Mr Gardner,

Thank you, wholeheartedly, for your reply. There was no need to apologise for its brevity; the assurance of your continued friendship gave it an import more valuable than any longer missive could impart. I am glad to see that in at least one thing we can fully agree – that in such an enterprise we all must face the severest questioning, and to raise such issues amongst ourselves can be no obstacle compared to that of general disbelief.

But you also make reference to my use of the word 'misery' in my last. It was sharp-eyed of you, and indeed considerate. I thank you for your continuing interest in my little home.

You are right, of course. When I previously left off, all must have seemed quite content and happy. Charlotte was restored to us and as blithe and gladsome as may be wished. Harriet had her mother back, just the way she was. I was disappointed in my pictures and bereft of my skeleton but I had my family, and I accepted that – nay, was grateful for it, and anxious to do nothing else that would risk them. I resolved to never again go to the glen, or to permit them to go either.

Nevertheless, we are in misery; an insidious, creeping, low kind of misery that has stolen upon us, and it is all the more dark because I can see no way out of it.

I have been much thrown together with Harriet in these past months; indeed, when not in school she is ever at my side. She grows a sweet, thoughtful child, always anxious to please her grandpapa, and though I love to see her bent over her book or whispering in her dolly's ear, I would that she might prefer to spend a little more time in the company of her mother.

They have not argued. They have not had any quarrel that I know of. Indeed, Harriet is full young to have disagreements of any consequence, or to bear such things running on each day or week or even beyond, and yet to observe them is to know that something has come between them. And I must admit that I have felt a growing disinclination for Charlotte's company also, though she smiles if anything more sweetly than she ever did, and professes delight in everything about her.

She sees everything now, of course. There is no impediment to her vision, and yet it strikes me as a shallow sort of seeing, for the warmth of feeling that once accompanied those little glances is absent, and I do not know how to recover it.

She has suffered from her experience of the fairies, of course. I wonder sometimes if she has a variety of shell-shock such as that still faced by many survivors of the war. She no longer likes to sew; she does not read – I could not even persuade her to look over Sir Arthur's book, let alone a prayer book or her Bible. She picks at her food as if it is distasteful to her, and in consequence has grown rather thin and wasted. She sits quite still in the evenings and I believe would do so until she were in darkness if I did not suggest that we set a match to the gas-lights. And she gazes steadily out of the window, towards the place where the wind stirs the tops of the trees and describes its unknowable designs in the meadow grass.

If pressed, she tells me that she is happy. And yet – I cannot put it better than this – there is a blankness. I do not know what to make of it. Lines from Hartland come back to me: unwelcome lines about changelings and stocks of wood that I wish I had never read. They have planted images in my mind, and those images mock me and whirl and turn about until everything is confusion. She is *not* a changeling. She is unafraid of the fire; I have watched her most carefully. I have left iron scissors by her chair and she passed them to me when I asked for them. They did not burn her skin; she did not shiver at their touch. Could a changeling attend church? She was there with us even on Easter, that most holy of days, and she did not flinch. And yet…

Quite recently, I went again to see the woman in the village. Do you remember – the one who did not speak to me, but pushed Hartland's book into my hand? This time I thrust my foot into the door when she attempted to close it in my face. I asked her what she knew of changelings. Do you know what she said to me? 'Dun't dig,' she said. 'Dun't dig where tha dun't want buryin'.'

Burying. It makes me shudder to think of it. Fairies are said to dwell in the hollow hills, are they not? Their home is not in the sun but beneath the rocks, in utterly dark places, away from clean air and the sight of humanity or God.

When I returned I hurried to find Harriet, but I need not have worried – she had secreted herself behind the door as her mother busied herself about the kitchen. She still cooks, you see, though she eats so little. I myself taste the food carefully to see if she does anything differently now, and I do not detect a change, but how would I remember? It disturbs me to see her at table with us, raising the fork to her lips as she always did, hardly taking anything, smiling when she sees me watching.

It means she is staying with us, does it not – that she eats even a little of our food?

Harriet ran to my side at once and stood on tiptoe, as she does when she wants to whisper in my ear. 'She's wishing the butter,' she said, and scurried away as if suddenly afraid.

You see? I believe you have always said that children see the fairies better than anyone. Or has there simply been too much talk of fairies altogether in this house, and we are all cast half into a dream?

But I can tell you nothing definite, there is nothing certain, and so I will turn to Sir Arthur's book and relate some things that have occurred to me since my last reading. Indeed, there are several points that on closer inspection I do not like – things that disturb me greatly, in fact, and I believe it is my duty to bring them to your notice.

There are many mentions of the fairies dancing as an expression of their joy and carelessness, and indeed it is speculated that they only assume a human shape in order to do so, as if such a thing were merely some kind of holiday from their regular existence. I cannot tell you how this troubles me. Something about it makes me shudder, and I do not know what; only that I feel most strongly that it cannot be so.

There is an account given by one gentleman who claims to have followed a fairy, that it particularly noticed him and beckoned him onward. Why should a fairy show such interest in the affairs of man? And did it really mean to show him a flint arrowhead when it pointed at the ground? I wonder instead if it intended to lure him to some doorway into the other realm. And there is another case – one 'seen' in the mind by your clairvoyant, it is true, but he says a lovely fairy appeared to one of the girls, wearing an expression 'as if inviting Frances into Fairyland'. Why so? What did it want with her? And what is this land, if it lies beneath the ground?

I am reminded of something Harriet once said: 'They don't really know how to dance. They only wish to make us want to be where they are.'

Then there is the account to which you have referred previously, about the fairies whose beauteous faces became of a sudden as ugly as sin. Hartland speaks of that too, you know – people's grand and beautiful visions of the folk being torn away to reveal 'the most hideous imps of hell'.

When taken against the whole, these are hints, discordant notes in an otherwise harmonious symphony of pure and lovely beings, but do you not think we should listen to them? Who will hear, if we do not?

And yet that is not all – you know it is not. There is the case simply given as that of Mrs H., who said of a fairy that 'no soul looked through his eyes'. She saw – she saw! Is that what is so wrong when I look at Charlotte? I do not know, but I wonder.

You see, I think Sir Arthur selects what he will to support his cause and disregards the rest. He believes in the good of all creation. He does not wish to muddy the waters of spiritualism; he wishes the world to believe in a realm of goodness and beauty. He cannot admit the possibility that we have discovered something which is of creation – or perhaps not, as we understand it – but that is dark.

Yet these things creep in. They cannot help being seen in glimpses, like the fairies themselves. One witness even says, 'They are capable individually of becoming extremely attached to humans – or a human – but at any time they may bite you.'

I do not doubt the latter. It is the former I am struggling with. *Are* they capable of such attachment?

Charlotte dresses her daughter. She wipes her face; she directs and guides her. But does she *care* for her?

I will watch and I will write to you soon.

Yours,
Lawrence Fenton

11

I read the first letter standing in the locker room. The risk I'm taking is nothing next to my desire to know what happens. The bundle is thin – there can't be more than three or four letters left – and I feel so close to the end of the story I can't wait any longer.

And what a letter it is. Here is Charlotte, returned but changed, gladsome and yet cold. She looks the same but she is without feeling, without warmth; a mother, yet without love. The touch of iron did not reveal her for what she was. Even fire failed to do that. The church was as ineffectual as the Bible under Mrs Favell's pillow, and I wonder why that was. Did La Belle Dame sans Merci have them in thrall?

I can tell you nothing definite, there is nothing certain.

But he had, hadn't he? For the Charlotte of the letters had gone, just as Mrs Favell once said – *She vanished long ago, and she's never, ever coming back again* – and yet she was there, replaced.

Could Fenton's daughter-in-law and my Charlotte be the

same person after all? How long could the beings we like to name 'fairies' live? Perhaps they really don't die like humans do. They do not wither – unless they are glimpsed in the full light of the sun, when the truth of their age is revealed.

Fenton had known that a changeling could be dangerous. The writer of *The Science of Fairy Tales* had seen it too. Both learned, all too quickly, of the fairies' propensity to bite, their love of tricks. Of *games*. And Charlotte had been given the charge of little Harriet, just as *my* Harriet, in turn, has charge of Robyn. I wonder if she loves her at all. Is there any love in her?

But I haven't reached the end. And I've heard no one; I'm alone. Despite the earlier cheering, I don't think anyone has come back inside. I take the next letter from the top of the pile, see how brief the following one is, and start to read them both.

➤·◄

22nd September 1922

Dear Mr Gardner,

You will have been waiting, I am sure, for my letter, though I have not heard from you in the meantime. I shall not wait; I must tell you of my decision.

I have been drawn, night after night, to take up *The Coming of the Fairies* again. That title! In the dark, with nothing outside but the moon riding high and the bats clicking, it could be almost prophetic. Perhaps it is, but then, I have learned to fear other things than those which roam without; it is the ones within that must be watched.

The thing that draws me to the book is this. In your later investigations, you say – or Sir Arthur says – you paid visits to the New Forest and Scotland as well as Yorkshire, speaking to those who love and seek the fairies – you do not mention me, of course, but perhaps I no longer quite fitted that description.

You say that your part in revealing the Cottingley photographs to the world was the worst introduction possible, and that the pictures so used were considered an outrageous trespass and violation. You present this as a question of local attitude, not mentioning in the slightest my own findings; that the fairies do not like to be observed. But those who know, *know*. Why else would an old lady say to me that I should not dig where I do not wish to be buried?

I cannot bear what they have done to us. I cannot bear the hurt in Harriet's eyes when she turns from her mother, the way she tries and fails to elicit some small sign of love. What can I do, I have vainly asked myself? And yet now I see what was plain before me all along. I must trespass further upon the fairies; I shall publish.

Sir Arthur did not see fit to include my account within his own. What of that? I have no reputation in the literary line, no publishing contact, no idea of where to begin. But what I do have is a story of no less interest than your own, and the determination to see it presented before the world.

And so I have begun. I am currently preparing it. It is a fact that my photographs no longer hold true; they do not look so much like fairies as creations of the imagination, but that has not prevented others. And I still have the photographs I had the prescience to take of the little skeleton. Some will no doubt say it is nothing more than the partial remains of a tiny bird with a dragonfly's wings appended, but my character, my testimony, shall speak for the truth, as you did for the Wright girl.

I will warn people what they are really like. There shall be no talk of their gladsome frolics and dancing, only of their wickedness.

Charlotte sees what I am about. She thinks I cannot watch her as I once did, but I know! And I see Harriet, her little pensive face as she leans over her book, so pale from keeping indoors. The looks we exchange, when we think her mother does not see – it is all there, all evident.

The world will know. And if you do not believe my proofs are enough – why, I have heard her give herself away, with my own ears! It happened late at night, when I thought everyone was abed and I was going over my papers. Her voice came quite plainly from the passage outside my room, low and unlike herself, but perhaps like her true self; the one she hides from us.

'I stung you once,' she said. 'I'll have the rest soon enough.' And she made chewing sounds with her mouth, as if she was hungry at last – as if she was ravenous, and anticipating the sweet meat of her little daughter.

I rushed out upon the instant. She was too quick for me; she was not there.

She is a changeling, I know it now. Oh, I have moments when I doubt; weak moments when I merely think she will end her days in Bedlam with the other lunatics, or perhaps I will. But under such pressures, and quite alone with a child to protect, it is little wonder I experience some confusion. Why, sometimes I wonder if you are indeed who you claim to be, and if Sir Arthur Conan Doyle was ever in receipt of my letter; if you have not kept him apprised, as you promised to do, with all I have to say. I wonder if I have been cruelly deceived in everything – even led astray by a child's fancies, as some would say we all have.

But I must hold fast. For something else has struck me: a new idea which would explain all, and indeed show why Sir Arthur has not deigned to call upon me – why he would not dare to show his face!

He has set out to offer serious proofs of fairy existence. He has presented himself as describing all that science can bring to matters of a spiritual nature. And yet he has so subtly interwoven his facts with stuff so clearly discoverable as fiction as to deliberately undermine his own arguments.

The fairies, he says, appear stiff and frozen in the Cottingley photographs because they move so very slowly. I know this to be a blatant untruth. One of their apparently 'pencilled' faces is simply made to appear so by the outline of her hair. His eyewitnesses see them only in the derangement of the full sun or when they have been fasting.

He notes in passing the coincidence that the Wright girl's family was already 'inclined to occult study'. He happens to mention that the elder child is imaginative, even dreamy, that she often spent her leisure hours drawing fairies, and that she was apprenticed for a time to a firm of photographers. He states that even her father asked the girls how they faked the pictures.

One would almost think that he did not *wish* to be believed.

Of course, Sir Arthur does not overtly draw attention to these matters. He is too experienced for that. He simply presents them all, and indeed his own doubts, as things that could easily be overcome, and allows people to read into it what they will.

Here is the rub. Did he think no one would see through it? Did he imagine himself like his character, his Sherlock Holmes, building an unassailable wall of rationality? But I do see through it. I think Sir Arthur has purposely chosen examples of sightings that are poorer than mine. He has inserted passages of absurd surmise quite knowingly.

It all culminates in the half-crazed comments from Bishop Leadbeater. He talks of the orange and purple fairies of Sicily, black and white ones of the Dakotas, the sky blue ones of Australia, and, more risibly, the gleaming crimson fairies resembling the metal orichalcum – the *what*, sir? – of the Atlanteans.

Can anyone read this and not suspect? I see it now more clearly than ever. Why, when Sir Arthur writes that a high development of intellect is a bar to psychic perception, he must have been laughing down his sleeve!

It is pure nonsense, sir, and I tell you, I know the reason why. It is not some mischief that is at the root of it all, but fear!

Sir Arthur had taken on a sacred trust and was unequal to the task. And I think the key lies not with Elsie Wright and Frances Griffiths, but with another girl, and she, entirely blind.

The one I mean is, of course, Miss Eva Longbottom, of whom Sir Arthur writes at length. Her claims of seeing the little folk clairvoyantly, whilst being completely blind, make her particularly easy to dismiss, and yet I sense the truth in her words. That fairy music is something of itself and untranslatable has the unmistakeable ring of authenticity. For a person without sight to gain the impression of dancing 'without any tangles in it' has also, and if I do not deceive myself, her account of fairies singing 'in the tone of their colours' has enough of the peculiar to convince.

No: it is not her visions that I doubt, but the claim that the young lady was blind from birth.

That, I do not believe. How else would she know what colours are? I think that she was struck blind, sir, for spying upon the fairies; and it is that, more than any other threat, implied or obvious, that has made Sir Arthur draw back from a more convincing disclosure.

He has learned enough to discover that his fascination could come at a high cost and he has turned aside. He has glimpsed their true nature. Even as I write, I seem to recall something said in *The Strand* about their 'grotesque, unmeaning tricks', although I do not think he embellished the statement with any detail – that is telling in itself, is it not?

He had committed to publish, but he did not want to be believed; not because the fairies were not real, but because he knew they *were* – yet different to how he imagined them to be.

I cannot entirely blame him. What *are* these things we seek so heedlessly? I do not know and would not claim to. But they are loathsome creatures, and we have reason to fear them. Yes, I see through it: he *has* brought certain truths before the eyes of the world, even if they are not the ones he intended.

I, sir, shall not flinch from my undertaking to do the rest. I return to my books.

Yours sincerely,
Lawrence H. Fenton

➵•➴

26th September 1922

Dear Mr Gardner,

Sir, I must protest. You must know me too well by now, at least from my letters, to make such accusations, no matter how tactfully couched. Does Sir Arthur Conan Doyle know himself to be sane, despite the accusations he has brought down upon his head by publishing his book? Well, I know myself to be sane, and after all your investigations, you should know better than to call it into question.

I recognise that you were overwhelmed by a tide of fanciful reports following the article in *The Strand*. That is surely no response, nor an excuse for omitting an account of such importance. I realise that it was the great man's choice, but I question whether he has been entirely level in making it.

No matter. I realise I have unwittingly insulted you by questioning your integrity, and indeed that you are whom you claim to be. It was not my intention. I have simply been honest enough to relay every doubt that has assailed me; clearly, this was one I had long overcome. I see that conveying it to you has not illuminated the situation, and I would have better left it unsaid.

As for Miss Eva Longbottom really being blind from a baby, and the claim that she receives great joy from the fairy presences all about – well, perhaps that is what you have been told. Men (and women) said to be of equal character to mine are not immune to the occasional untruth; and it is possible they may be mistaken. I merely paraphrase your own words.

That is all I shall say, save this: no matter what there is

to fear or dread, no matter what ridicule I face from those who should know better, I will not be turned aside from this important work.

I shall trouble you no more.

Sincerely,
Mr L. H. Fenton

12

There are so many signs before me that fairies are nothing but pretence and imagination, I can almost feel the little skeleton crumbling in my hand. Perhaps the fairy remains were only ever the remnants of a decaying bird and insect wings. Harriet might have fabricated it, thinking it a charming game, never imagining how it would be seized upon. Hadn't Fenton mentioned that she loved poking into birds' nests? He had become too caught up in her game, seeing things that weren't there. And having set her grandfather on such a path, how could she go back on it? It would have been too daunting, too terrifying. She would not have wished to prove him a fool. She was a little girl – and wasn't that just what happened with the Cottingley photographs? Elsie Wright and Frances Griffiths played a harmless game with their painted fairies and were propelled before the scrutiny of the world. They made a great man, Arthur Conan Doyle, a believer. Finding themselves in such a situation, how could they admit it was all invention? How could anyone?

Yet even as Fenton spoke against their flat, lifeless images, he remained certain that the creatures he had found were very different. They brought pain, not delight. Was that the reason his discoveries felt real, where the original pictures did not? Even as the fairies dissolve into nothing, they rise again stronger than before. Anything nonsensical in Doyle's reports – the stuff about orichalcum and the rest – had been taken as signs of proof, not otherwise. Did Fenton have some prescient insight, or was that the very stuff of madness? Or only the height of the fairies' trickery and malice?

He could have imagined Charlotte's voice speaking to him in the night. His daughter-in-law might have been peacefully sleeping. He might have been sleeping himself and dreaming of her, not as she was in reality, but in his wildest thoughts.

What proof had he ever really possessed? What kind of impression must he have made on Gardner, that great proponent of fairies, for *him* to accuse Fenton of being insane? For I am certain that must be what had happened.

Was Fenton mad? Was I?

But Lawrence Fenton had a child to protect, and no matter what anyone else thought, no matter his own doubts, he had resolved to do what he must. He had refused to be afraid.

I cannot bear what they have done to us. I cannot bear the hurt in Harriet's eyes when she turns from her mother, the way she tries and fails to elicit some small sign of love.

I think of Robyn growing older under Harriet's elegant, cold gaze; the child trying to please her, make her laugh, to have her join in her childish games, to hold her when she cries. And I cannot bear it.

I remember something else I'd heard once – not in the letters or in any book, but a long time ago, standing at my mother's side in a darkened museum, looking into a glass case where a camera sat, untouched and unused for many years. Even after everything, even the girls' eventual admission of falsity, hadn't Frances always insisted that she *saw* fairies at the beck – that they were real, even if the photographs were fake? Or was that just a story my mother had told me?

Had she wanted so very badly for me to believe?

I leaf back to the preceding letter, scanning down the page until my eye snags on a phrase. *But they are loathsome creatures, and we have reason to fear them.*

That is when the door to the locker room opens and I turn to see Mrs Favell standing in the gap.

She barks, 'Come with me, Rose.' She gestures sharply towards the letters. 'And bring the last.'

As quickly as she came, she's gone. My cheeks burn. I want to sink into the wall, to hide, to walk out of this place and never come back, but I don't have a choice.

She's going to have me fired, and I still haven't read to the end. I look down at the final sheets, leaf through them, see the greeting and the signature, and I realise that Mrs Favell was correct: only one letter remains.

13

Mrs Favell is standing where I expect her to be, in front of the window in her room, gazing towards the wood. I wonder what it is she sees. Is the wind stirring the tops of the trees? Is it inscribing its unknowable designs in the meadow grass?

She gestures as if telling me to be quiet, or to stay where I am, and I do. The bureau is open. On its writing surface is the key, and next to it, mutilated pages from a Bible.

I don't want to see how much more angry she can become. She has always treated me like a servant or something to be toyed with. Now I have stolen from her, tried to trick her, even to hurt her.

I think of Theresa, cast out, the police making their search. And I am afraid – though I wonder what else she might do to me. Can it really be worse than what she has already done? I stand a little straighter.

Without turning she says, 'Are you ready to read it now, Rose?'

I look down and see I still have the last letter in my hand. This is exactly where I stood when I read the first one she gave me, summoned to her room for the purpose, and now here I am at the end of it.

This time, when I start to read, I do so silently.

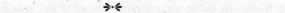

30th September 1922

My Dear Mr Gardner,

Pray, forgive the tone of my last. I regret it most earnestly. I dare say you did not expect to hear from me again, and you would not do so were it not a matter of the utmost urgency, indeed, possibly of life or death – or worse than either, as it may well turn out to be.

I have little time to waste, and yet I must leave a record in the event that some terrible thing may befall us. Indeed, I think it has already befallen us, and it is too late – but soon I shall don my coat and go once more to the glen, and see what I may, and end this where I must.

She is gone from me – little Harriet is gone. I shall try to restrain my feelings, and my rapidly scrawling pen, and explain myself in a rational manner.

It began this morning. Charlotte was in the kitchen as she so often is, and Harriet was peeping from behind the door. Charlotte was butchering a rabbit. She was making a stew, and humming some strange air, so quietly it was beyond recognition. She kept stopping – the strokes of her knife against the board would cease and the tune would pass beyond hearing, and after a few moments would begin again. Perhaps she was listening to the child breathing; who knows?

Of a sudden, I heard her stepping towards the door. Then she said, in a too-sweet voice, 'Do you watch me, child?'

I set down my pen at once. I hurried into the passage to see Harriet staring up at her mother, her eyes wide and not saying a word. Charlotte in turn stared at the child, her eyes a fixed gleam in her awful thin face. She never once shifted her gaze to me. She clutched the knife in her hand and blood dripped from it to the floor, but I think I was the only one who noticed.

Then Charlotte leaned over her daughter, and she raised the knife and said, 'I shall put both your eyes out of your head.'

I cannot describe the effect of her words. It was not just their intent but the way they were spoken, so cold, so *true* – but Harriet could not move. It was I who caught her arm and pulled her away, turning her from the sight of her mother's ugly staring, because she was entranced by it; I would almost say she was under some spell.

It broke when I pulled her back and knelt before her. She cried, then; indeed, you may only imagine her distress. I tried to soothe her, though I did not really know how, and with my shaking hands and unsteady voice – but I did what I could, which is all any of us can do.

I know what you will say. You will think Charlotte's words were suggested by her own experiences or by her fancies, and that the memory of them will fade. You will say she will one day be well again. But I heard the way she spoke and saw the way she looked, and I cannot doubt the truth.

All the time I comforted her child, I felt Charlotte watching us. And in her demeanour she betrayed – oh, from her stance I would have thought it amusement, but it was not even that; there was only the most terrible indifference.

If I had doubted before, I could not do so then. But she still held the knife, and I must confess that I was afraid.

I did not heat the poker and describe the sign of the cross upon her forehead. I did not slip a prayer book under her pillow or douse her with holy water or hold her before the fire to trick her into betraying herself. I did none of those things – curse my useless hands! I told Harriet to run along and read her book and not bother her mama, and I straightened to see that Charlotte had already gone. The sound of a knife on wood came once more from the kitchen, and I wondered what kind of stew she would *like* to make; I wondered if she would eat it all up.

I sat before my work, and looked upon it, and despaired. I do not know how time passed, but it was not until later that I thought to look in on Harriet. She was gone, of course.

She had left only a note behind:

They took my mama. I am going to find her.

And beneath:

I think I hurt the fairy lady with my stick.

At once I saw her in my mind's eye on that day in the glen, busying herself about the pool so brightly, so innocently, poking beneath each rock and branch to seek them out, only to meet with – what? I saw again that tiny figure of a man, a child's vision, the loveliness of him; I saw the perfection of his tiny, dark, brilliant eyes, lit with perfect rage. And I saw again the little maid at his feet. Had she been in health when Harriet came along and discovered her? But the child had meant no harm. Had Harriet truly caused the little fairy's death with her poking and prying – with her curiosity? It surely could not be!

If it was so, then all their mischief, all their revenge, would really be intended for the child. And she had gone once more to the glen – gone into their hands! What if, this time, she did not come back?

What if she *did* come back?

I cannot express to you my horror at the thought. Harriet, lost to me for ever – or Harriet returning, her feet browned with earth, scratching on the door perhaps at midnight, the eyes that were so like her father's as black as sloes. Harriet without the enlivening principle that makes her truly herself – without an ounce of love in her.

What might the wicked creatures do to my true grandchild if she had really done them such an injury as she suspected, and she fell into their hands?

You will see it all, I suppose. For perhaps this was the reason our encounter with the fairies was not like that of other people, or some of them. I do not know if they think like we do, if they have any system of morality we could recognise. I had not imagined that they discriminate: I thought their punishment had fallen to all of us, my son's wife more than anyone, but perhaps it is not yet finished.

It was Harriet who injured the fairy. It was I who carried off the little body. I cannot keep away from them, of course. I am going to seek them in the glen – the real Charlotte, with her eyes as soft and warm as they used to be, and my own sweet Harriet, unchanged, throwing her arms about my neck.

I fear it may be too late. For time is said to pass differently in the fairy realm, and if they have eaten of their food – what then?

Fairies are said to steal humans away and leave changelings in their place in order to strengthen their line. Will I find

Charlotte big with a fairy child? Or Harriet being raised a fairy? How would a human being ever become one of those frail creatures – or is there some race of fairy I have not yet seen? I cannot imagine it at all. For the thing that divides us is surely the possession of a soul, and how could that difference be surmounted, unless the fairies have by some means removed their souls from them?

I fear I am to go somewhere not of earth or of heaven or of hell, but somewhere that is different from them all. It is a terrible choice, and I pray you never have to make one like it. For I do not think I will ever see my son or my wife again, even in the next world, as has been the dearest hope of my life. A course lies ahead that is entirely new and strange and different to me. But I know my son would tell me, unhesitatingly, to go – to protect his daughter. And I will, for she is alone, and a child, and lost, and I can do no other thing.

I will try to follow where she has gone. I will take a Bible, and, I believe, the iron scissors. And if I find the false child first – then I can only trust that I shall know what to do.

Here before me is the price of my fascination. Sir Arthur has felt a little of it too, I think. His was the world's censure; mine – ah, but who knows what mine shall be? I do not know if I will be blinded or stolen away, or worse – for what could they want with an old man?

What could be more terrible than what they have already done?

How strange it is that I find you are the only one I can tell. I have almost finished my letter – all that stands between me and them – and when I set out I shall leave it on the table. Perchance someone will find it and post it to you. Perhaps that someone might even be me. Perhaps their hands, their face, will only look like mine. Who can say?

Nothing remains but to sign myself, now and I hope ever, your friend,

Lawrence

14

For a moment, I am lost. What did Lawrence Fenton do? Had he put the changeling to the iron scissors and received his own child back again? I think of Mrs Favell's daughter, Harriet, clutching a lovely baby girl in her arms. Is she the same Harriet as in the letters? But then she can't be human, or she would have died years and years ago.

I blink and look up. I think I see the truth in Mrs Favell's eyes, but perhaps that is also an illusion, for in the next moment there is only scorn, then that too is gone. She looks tired and a little old.

'It was very hard for him, don't you think, Rose?' she says.

Tears brim at her eyes and something in me twists. I don't know what is happening. *Of course*, I think. *Of course it was.*

'He went into the wood,' she says. 'He was limping, though he wouldn't have felt it. He would have held onto those iron scissors all the time, don't you think? His Bible too, for what protection that would give him.'

I am silent.

'Then he saw something brighter than the leaves, the long grass, the flowing water. It was her hair, shining amidst the branches as she stumbled towards him: Harriet, the little girl he wanted so badly to protect. What could he do? He longed to go to her, to take her in his arms and bear her home – but how could he *know*? This child, who had done the folk such harm – could she really have ventured into their domain without being changed?

'And so he did not go to her. Instead he waited for her: to call out for her grandpapa, to hold out her arms to him, perhaps to cry. She did none of those things. She only stared, her eyes full of fear, and said nothing. And what did *he* say, do you think?'

I shake my head. What would anybody say?

'He asked her if she recognised her grandpapa. And still the child did not answer. Perhaps there was only a little clicking, a sound made in the back of her throat, as children will when they swallow their sobs.

'He returned bathed in her blood, Rose. I wept for pity.'

I can only stare. *For pity?* Somehow that's the one thing I can't believe.

She turns towards the window again. I feel that she is seeing beyond the treetops, down through the branches, into the shadows and the deeps. Perhaps she sees little figures walking there, discovering who knew what; perhaps she sees only the past.

'She did look so very, very like her,' Mrs Favell murmurs. Her neck twists towards me as she adds, 'At least you know what *your* child looks like, don't you, Rose?'

Her tone, her expression, everything has changed. She's

brighter. She walks towards me rapidly and with purpose and I flinch as if she's about to attack me, but she only holds out her hand. It takes a second to realise I'm still holding her letters and when I hand them over she grasps them in claw-like fingers. Then she takes another step and I retreat before her, out through the door, into the hall.

She says, 'If you want the end of the story, Rose, there is one last place you need to look.'

The door closes behind me. I am cast out.

15

It's a good thing my shift's nearly over because I don't think I can keep my emotions inside while I go through all the ordinary routines. I don't think anyone notices – Jimmy gives me odd looks when I'm helping in the lounge, but the other carers don't even glance my way, which is fine with me. Eventually, the clock says I can go.

I grab my bag from my locker and leave almost at a run, jump into the car, grind the gears as I drive home. I go through the motions there too, hugging Paul, telling him that yes, it's great to be home again. I plant a kiss on Alexander's head. Paul nods, goes upstairs and I'm alone with the baby.

If you want the end of the story, Rose, there is one last place you need to look.

I put my face up close to his. Various people have commented that he looks like Paul or me, his nose, my chin, but I never know how they can tell. I try to see either one of us in the curve of his cheek. I hold my hands next to his short little fingers. He gazes at me steadily. I tell myself that all babies look as if they have old knowledge in their eyes, but I'm not sure I believe that's true.

When I first came home from the hospital, I read online that infants born with teeth in their heads were once put to death as demons. Back then, people didn't know any better. They're only teeth, as the nurse had said, and it's unusual but not that strange, even for them to be discoloured or jagged like Alexander's. Natal teeth can be caused by anything from trauma to malnutrition to the mother's exposure to toxins while the baby grows, so if anything, it's my fault.

I place him on the sofa next to me and undo the poppers down the front of his sleepsuit. I slip it from his shoulders as he jerks and kicks. I remember him doing that in my belly: the swipe of a hand or a heel rippling under my skin, the lumpy strangeness moving inside me.

The magic of it.

I ease the garment from his legs and peel the tape from his nappy, pulling that away too, and I stare at my baby.

He's perfect in his smooth, pale, marbled skin. There isn't a mark on him, but there wouldn't be, would there? It's me who's marked, those little footprints girdling my belly, like something claimed.

At least you know what your *child looks like, don't you, Rose?*

But how can I? He changes so fast. The layers of fat have thickened about his limbs, coating his bones, pushing out his tummy, covering the webbing of veins beneath the skin. His hair is thicker too, though it's still that indeterminate colour, almost transparent. He's different to the last time I really looked at him.

Tomorrow he might be different again.

'Isn't he gorgeous?' Paul stands in the doorway. He's been watching me watching Alexander and he's grinning at the sight. 'I sometimes just look at him like that. You know, you two should spend a bit of time together this weekend.'

I nod, though what I think of is Robyn. I've only ever caught glimpses of her. I've seen her sweet little face softened in sleep. I haven't really looked into her eyes. Isn't that what people say – that they looked into the eyes of their baby and they *knew*? But perhaps I always knew. My body had responded to her cries as it never has with Alexander.

Perhaps Harriet will bring her to visit Mrs Favell soon. That means I can see her again.

'... can meet Marcus there,' Paul goes on, and I realise he's making plans for us, ones I haven't heard.

He funnels his hands around his mouth, speaks in a squeaky voice. 'Earth to Rose,' he says, and I proffer the expected smile.

'Sorry. I was a bit distracted.'

'Understandable. I'm distracted by him too. I was saying, I haven't wet Alex's – Alexander's – head yet. I'm off to the Hart tomorrow aft, if that's all right with you. I'll see Marcus there, and it'll give you two a chance to bond.'

I realise several things. The first is that he's talking about bonding to make it sound like a favour to me that he's going out, but I don't care about that, nor the fact that it's a bit late for wetting the baby's head. The other is that tomorrow is a Saturday. That thought fills me with something like horror. Saturday: surely that is the day Harriet will visit. Sunnyside is always busiest at the weekends. It wouldn't normally matter — I work whatever days I'm needed — but this week is different because my days off coincide with the weekend.

I have to see her.

I tell myself it's fine and smile back at Paul, hiding the way my heart is hammering. 'Of course you should go,' I say. 'It'll be a good break for you.'

He plants another kiss on my cheek, one that feels real, a little like the ones we used to have. I think quickly and say, 'There's an errand I need to run in the morning though, something I said I'd do for work. You don't mind, do you?'

He's already stepping away, into the kitchen, though I catch his brief nod. He doesn't think anything of it, and I tell myself again it will be fine; that everything will.

16

I reach Sunnyside as the sun drags itself interminably upward in the sky. I was awake before six but forced myself to wait until now. Official visiting hours begin at ten thirty and at weekends people often come later. I couldn't risk arriving too soon and having no excuse to wait.

I'm not wearing my uniform. The receptionist – I've learned that her name is Lise, as in Lisa – also assists with admin and she'll know who's supposed to be working and who's not. So will the other girls. If they ask, I'm going to say I was just passing, that Mrs Favell has a slight cough and I wanted to check on her. Or someone else, perhaps; I doubt Mrs Favell has been ill a day in her life.

She told me there is one last place left to look and I know now that it must be here, where everything began. I don't know what or where, but she intended for me to reach the end; she must have.

Lise raises her eyebrows at the sight of me but I grin and wave
and she nods. She gestures towards the sign-in book – it's part of
the fire regulations to have a record of anyone in the building –
but when I walk past her she doesn't bother to call me back. I go
straight into the lounge. The residents are there. Jimmy's jowls
wobble as he chats to his son; Maryam smiles at the friend who's
come to see her; Reenie stares at nothing, the light catching in
her hair like a blessing. Alf bends over his jigsaw, his eyes mere
inches from the scattered pieces. Fondness washes over me. I
feel as if I'm never going to see any of them again, that they're
behind me already, and sorrow clogs my throat.

Of course I'll see them again. Why shouldn't I? I'll find the end
of the story and then, maybe, everything will go back to normal.

I check the room again in case I failed to notice Mrs Favell
among the rest, but I know I haven't. After all, she isn't one of
them; she never has been. I go to the French windows and look
out over the garden, although the day is grey, the lawn covered
with leaves blown in from the wood. Everything is drab and
colourless, the world turning towards winter. Perhaps that's why
everything inside me is shrinking too, but I won't let that stop me
from doing what I need to do.

Mrs Favell isn't here and nor is Harriet. I know where they'll
be and I turn towards the stairs. Will anyone think it odd if I head
up there in my jeans and crumpled shirt? No one's looking at
me. Still feeling strange, as if I'm learning to walk on unfamiliar
limbs, I go up.

The corridor is the same as it has always been, and silent. I listen,
unable to make out a word of conversation or the exclamation of

a child, the clatter of tea things or the tuneless whistling of a deaf old man, not even the endless burbling of the television.

Room ten is in front of me. Feeling as if I've gone back in time I raise my hand to knock then let it fall again. Do I detect a trace of lilies in the air?

I open the door. I go in and for a second I see her, standing where she always does. She's looking out across the trees, the edges of her silver hair turned to gold in the autumn light.

I blink and she's gone.

The bed is stripped bare. Housekeeping must have been, but they've neglected to put on fresh sheets. Then I see that the bureau is missing. There's no gleaming wood, no books, no pens, no envelopes, no stamps; no letters. For a moment I think I've walked into the wrong room – it might be anyone's now, so plain without her in it – yet the imprints left by the bureau are still pressed into the carpet.

The mirror has disappeared from its place on the chest of drawers too and I can't even see my own reflection as I pull open the drawers one by one. There's nothing inside but pieces of curling drawer liner, each adorned with a faded pattern of flowers and smelling of nothing at all.

The wardrobe too is bare. All of her blouses, soft and pliant as dead rose petals, are missing. The hangers rattle under my hands, as empty as bones.

Mrs Favell has gone. *Dead?*

The word won't connect with anything else. She can't have died. There would have been a fuss. Someone would have told me. I'd have seen it on the receptionist's face, on the faces of the residents, even the visitors. Death does not visit quietly. It does not leave everything so neat. The window of Mrs Favell's room is closed.

But she is gone. She made her one last mocking statement, making me believe she would show me everything, before vanishing into the air. Did she fly, shrieking, up the chimney? Did she walk barefoot through leaf-strewn grass and enter the woods at last?

When I close my eyes I see her face, the brightness of her eyes, her smile. I hate her more than I've ever hated anyone. I think of Alexander – of *Robyn* – and imagine tearing into her face with my nails.

It's difficult to think. I haven't slept and everything has gone from me and I don't know what to do. Is there some way I can follow her? Like Lawrence Fenton, should I take up my Bible and iron knife and enter the woods?

I go to the window. The massy crowns of trees form a barrier, opaque and impenetrable. The remaining leaves are softened to grey under the sunless sky, untouched by any breeze, motionless, waiting. What might be hiding beneath? Magic perhaps, in the dark and secret places? Or other stories, stories that would make everything clear instead of only more confused?

I squeeze the bridge of my nose between my fingers. Mrs Favell doesn't need the woods. She never did. I think of her neatness, her pearls, her cultivated smile. Could she resist leaving some final message for me?

I examine the room again. And I see what must have snagged at my thoughts, in plain view all the time I stood here: her pictures, the black-and-white faces in their silver frames, are still there. I suppose I hadn't noticed them until now because they were as I expected to find them; it was everything else that was wrong.

I can't think why she's left them behind. Residents don't put up their own pictures – the caretaker does that, on an allocated section of wall which can be painted over when they leave, ready for a new occupant. Did she forget to ask him to take these down? Are they being sent on to her? It surely can't have been so very difficult to have them removed, certainly not in comparison with the bureau. Perhaps they were only *dressing* after all and she didn't care enough to keep them. Or did she leave them here on purpose – even, perhaps, for me?

I examine them more minutely, realising I have never done so before. I had neglected my duty in that. Patricia had told me to chat to the residents about the past, to go over old albums with them, to *listen*. I didn't do so with Mrs Favell. Instead I'd turned away, but I look at them now, a string of faces, long forgotten and surely irrelevant. The only one I'd ever really noticed was the smiling young girl and she's smiling still, though it's fixed and frozen, transformed by the camera into something lifeless. With a start, I think I recognise a younger Mrs Favell.

Then I see Alexander.

Suddenly I can't breathe. This frame is ornate like the others, and old, surrounded by a gleaming wreath of silver leaves, but I'm almost sure it's him. He's wearing an old-fashioned white dress, a Christening gown, and lying in an ancient pram – one with a huge arched hood, the fittings made of shining metal. I tell myself it could be any child, but it's not. He stares into my eyes. His expression is sly, his demeanour musing, as if he knew when that picture was taken that one day I would be standing in front of it.

I close my eyes. I should have trusted my instincts. I had known it, *felt* it when Harriet put her hands on me, draining my womb, stealing my baby from inside me. I had known myself to be empty.

And I know they've done this before, probably many times. They must have. Alexander might be ancient; he could have been given to who knows how many families before me, growing up, wearing out, only to become something that looks like a child once more. How old are Harriet and Charlotte, truly? How long have they lived? How many children have they borne, ones they didn't bother with, never troubled over, because they were put as changelings into someone else's belly?

And the real babies, the ones they stole – what happens to them? I think of Robyn sleeping so peacefully in Harriet's arms. Was she under some spell to quiet her? Did she know her true mother was near? My body had known the truth. Why hadn't I acted? I could have saved her.

I turn and grab the door, yank it open, but force myself to stop. Something is telling me to wait.

If you want the end of the story, Rose, there is one last place you need to look.

I've looked already, haven't I? The picture was waiting for me, its message plain. Yet I can't help feeling there's something more.

I go back into the room. It remains bare, there's nothing else, and then I remember and kneel by the bed. Beneath it, where it has always been, is the little wooden box.

She left it there for me, I know that. She would never have

forgotten it. Warmth rushes through me as I realise this is it: the one thing I was supposed to find.

I pull it towards me, the wood slightly warm under my fingers, like something alive. Whatever she concealed within, it isn't heavy. For an instant I imagine opening the lid and finding nothing, just another empty space where she has been, the echo of mocking laughter. That can't be the end of it all. It *can't*.

The box is in my hands. I sit with my back to the bed and place it in my lap. I can't afford to wait but I stare down at it, looking into the depths of the grain, beyond the gleaming surface. I already know the ruined egg will have gone, but when I remove the lid my eyes open wide.

The box is full of flowers, as it was the first time I looked into it, though I'm sure they have changed and this time there are no photographs hiding beneath. I can't think how I hadn't noticed the smell because it is strong and musky, half rotten, and I see that the petals are wilted and limp. Beneath the cloying decay, though, I detect another scent: that of summer, of sunshine, fresh breezes and lilies.

There aren't any lilies, though. I recognise the bell-like flowers at once, supported by once straight stems. They would have been a rich purple, though the petals are faded now to a colour a little like meat.

She didn't leave lily of the valley or roses or any such thing. The flowers she meant for me to find are foxgloves.

17

I must look like a normal person as I walk down the stairs to the residents' lounge. I know this, because when I step around the corner at the bottom there is Mandy, an activity sign-up sheet in her hands, and she stops and looks at me. She betrays no surprise and her eyes hold no suspicion. She can't see the turmoil of my thoughts.

'Came to see her off, did you? Bit late.' She smirks, pleased to have thought up a new way to be unkind.

I ignore her, make to go past, and change my mind. 'You knew she was going, then?' I keep my tone low and careful. I don't think I've betrayed my feelings but she laughs and I feel myself redden.

'What, didn't *you*? Her best friend and all? Don't tell me you didn't know.'

Mrs Favell planned it, then. She had known all along she was leaving.

'She went early this morning. She only packed last night – didn't have much to take, as it happens.'

I reach out as Mandy moves to leave and grab her arm. She scowls at me, trying to shake me off, but I grip tighter. Does she see something in my face now? If she does, I don't care. 'Where did she go?'

She squirms. 'All right! I didn't know you were so upset about it. Who'd be upset about *her* leaving? You should be celebrating, love.'

She means to be patronising and I see the unease when I refuse to be intimidated. *Never again.* 'Where?' I demand.

'Godsakes. She went with her daughter, with Harriet. You didn't think she was staying here for good, did you? Not that one. It was only ever till the house was ready, and now it is. Didn't even say thank you. Not to me and not to you either, I reckon. You want to watch who you get so friendly with.'

Does she mean I should have tried to be friends with her and the other girls instead? I don't want their friendship, not now. I remember the way Mandy had rebuffed me, the way she'd sneered, the way she'd sent me to *her*.

'This house – where is it?'

'I don't know, do I? If you wanted to keep in touch so badly you should have asked her for an address. Or maybe she didn't want you to have it?'

Mandy walks away from me and this time I let her go. I hope to never see her again. The chances are good that I won't.

I walk towards reception. Despite my hopes that she'll have wandered off, Lise sits at the desk, tapping at a half-concealed mobile phone with her pink-painted nails. Her sidelong glance doesn't invite conversation and I don't provide any. I step past her, taking confident strides as if I know exactly where I'm going. I hold my keycard against the door that leads to the staff areas.

She swivels in her chair but I don't stop to answer the half-hearted question in her eyes. She has no real authority. I don't think she's likely to protest and she doesn't as I head towards the manager's office, peering through its windows at the filing cabinets ranked against the back wall. That's where I'll find the information I need. There would have been forms to fill in, red tape to satisfy. Mrs Favell wouldn't have wanted to raise questions by refusing to provide a forwarding address. She'd have known I'm not supposed to have access to the file.

It strikes me that the office might be locked. Patricia doesn't often come in on weekends. Or would it be left open in case of emergencies? I've never had cause to find out. Possibly there'll be some procedure and she's given a key to someone else. Whichever is the case, the office is empty.

I try the handle and it doesn't turn, then it gives and I stumble through the door. I'm inside, just like that. I'm also exposed behind all the glass, can't hide what I'm doing, not in here. But Lise hasn't followed and who else would have reason to come in? I have time.

I ignore the computers, darkly sleeping – I don't have any passwords or login details, and I suppose even Sunnyside will have that much security – and turn to the filing cabinets. I grab the handle on the first and pull. It doesn't move, doesn't even rattle.

I hadn't noticed the little keyholes set above each drawer, but I do now. I can almost feel the information within, so close and so out of reach. I try the rest of the drawers but not a single one will move.

The desk, then. Would Patricia really be so careful that she takes the keys away? I think back to her giving me the entry code for the front door, printing it out rather than making me memorise it. The way that doors are so often propped open here, convenience coming before security. There would be issues around patient confidentiality if she left a key lying around, but it's not as if even Lise would allow any stranger to wander back here.

I try the top drawer of the desk, the shallowest, the kind that will have a little tray where all sorts of small items can be placed. It slides open at my touch and there is a key-ring, standing out from the biros and erasers and staplers. It's well used, the little furry white poodle appended to it greyed with time.

There are several keys attached. I try the first in the leftmost filing cabinet, metal scratching against metal as my hands shake. It doesn't take long; the second key I try fits. I pull the drawer open to reveal a series of suspension files with tabs marked AA–AL, AM–AZ, BA–BE and so on.

The letters must be for patient's surnames. I glance into the first and see a file headed Mrs Abbott, someone I don't know, dead, perhaps, or moved elsewhere, or maybe she too was taken home by family.

I must need the next drawer down. I fumble the keys again and they scratch like something trying to get in, which I suppose I am. This time it's the very last key that turns and I drag the drawer open until it slams against its rail. I find the suspension file marked FA–FE, lift it from the cabinet, and the door opens and Patricia walks in.

My first thought is that I could have seen her. If I'd angled myself a little more towards the glass, I would have. Now I'm frozen in front of her stare. I open my mouth to offer some excuse for my presence – perhaps she doesn't realise I'm not supposed to be in today? I could give her a half-truth, that I'm searching for Mrs Favell's address to send something on to her. I think of the wooden box or the pictures, but it's too late. She's seen my expression. She knows anything I say will be a lie.

I feel five years old again, caught in the act of stealing my mother's perfume. The scent of lily of the valley is suddenly all around me, heady and overpowering.

'Are you going to tell me what you're doing, Rose?' She shifts her gaze to the cabinet, where her silly bunch of keys with its ball of fluff hangs from the lock. She gestures towards the suspension file in my hands. 'Whose is that?'

I find I am breathing normally. My heart doesn't race. I'm doing what I'm supposed to do, what I need to do, and I feel calmer than I have in days.

I shift my grip on the file to open it without spilling the contents. I glance at the names within, then at her as if to say *yes, I'll do what you want, I'll show you what you asked to see* – buying time. Mrs Favell's file is there and I pull it free, allowing the others to drop to the floor.

'Rose?' Her voice remains low but there's an edge to it, the hint of a threat.

The file is in my hands. The *answer* is in my hands. I know it and at last my heart gives an arrhythmic stutter.

Patricia stands between me and the door. 'I don't know what's happened to you, Rose,' she says, 'but I know you're a good girl.'

A good girl? I'm a woman. I had a *baby*. Doesn't that prove anything – didn't it change everything?

She seems encouraged by my inability to speak. 'I don't know what you think you're doing, but those files are confidential. What is it you're looking for?'

I open my mouth, all the excuses I can think of floating somewhere out of reach, and anyway, I have no voice. Words have gone from me. They wouldn't work on her anyway: she'd see through them at once.

She holds out her hand, palm upwards, and waits for me to put the file into it. To give up, to say sorry, perhaps to weep. I do none of those things.

She catches her breath. 'If you don't give it to me, Rose, if you don't explain yourself, there's nothing I can do. This is an invasion of the patients' privacy and if you insist on intruding in this way, I can't save you.'

I can't save you. That's not what she means, not really. She means she won't try. She'll fire me, and worse: she'll call the police and accuse me of stealing. They'll riffle through my things as they did with Theresa. None of it seems important now.

'I'm waiting.' She's gone past the talk-down stage and into coercion, but she's still just talking, I realise. She's not going to block me. She can't stop me from leaving, not unless I let her.

For an instant, I see the disappointment on Paul's face when he hears I've lost my job. I suppose it should trouble me more. There won't even be a reference. I might have a police record. I struggled to find this job and won't get another, and no one is queuing up to hire Paul. We'll have no money, no prospects, no happily ever after. And yet I can't see an 'after'. There is only now; there is only *her*.

I stand taller and clear my throat before saying, 'You need to get out of my way.'

Now it's me who sounds threatening and dismay spreads across her features. I have to use that to my advantage, before she gathers herself. I step forward and, as if pushed, she steps aside, away from the door. I remember Mrs Favell doing this to me: stepping forwards, making me back away. Perhaps I've learned something from her after all.

There's anger in Patricia's eyes but I don't give her the chance to let it out. Still gripping the file, I brush past her. I expect her to grasp my arm or my shoulder but she doesn't move, doesn't shout or shriek or reach for the phone, not yet.

When I glance back through the glass I see her standing quite motionless, her expression flat. She watches me leave with narrowed eyes.

18

I don't stop to read the file. I can't. I have to get away from Sunnyside, though the contents pull at me from where I've thrown it on the passenger seat. I want to stamp on the accelerator but I force myself to be careful, keeping each move deliberate, one eye on the speedometer. I can't be pulled over by the police only to have the alert go out for me while they're running my number plate through whatever checks they have.

For a change there's a long stretch of empty kerb outside our house and I pull up and yank on the handbrake. When the driver's door flies open I nearly shriek but it's Paul leaning over me, Alexander wrapped in a blanket in his arms. Paul doesn't notice my shock. He doesn't read in my eyes what I've done: thrown away my job; stolen confidential patient information; burned any future we had.

'Where have you been?' he snaps. 'I thought you weren't going to be long.'

Has it been that long? I blink. It felt like moments. I realise I've made him late for the pub, as if that's what matters.

'Here – take him.' He thrusts Alexander at me before I'm fully out of the car. Then he softens. 'Look, sorry to dash off. Marcus is at the Hart already, he's bugging me for being late, and Alex just spit up everywhere. He'll be hungry, all right? I'll see you later.'

Alexander isn't even dressed under the blanket. He smells sour. I don't have time for this, to wash and dress him, to be his mother. I have to read the file, but Paul is walking away.

I watch him go. He doesn't look back, doesn't wave to me over his shoulder. He no doubt expects that he'll come home in a few hours to find me there and we'll curl up on the sofa, watch something crap on TV. Or maybe he's not thinking that at all. He's anticipating his first pint, rehearsing some joke he's going to tell his brother. He's already put me from his mind.

You know what's different about you, Rose? What I love about you? You believe.

And suddenly I know that the thing Paul said he loved about me was never the thing he loved at all, and I want to cry. There's a weight in my gut, a cold stone.

I heft Alexander onto my shoulder, go around the car and retrieve my bag and the file from the passenger seat, shove the door closed with my hip. I can't cry now. I don't have time. I can't think about any of this.

Paul left the front door ajar, knowing I'd have my hands full when I came in, knowing he planned to shove Alexander into my arms in the street. The tears brimming at my eyes give way to anger as I go inside. It was only a few minutes. It's only the pub.

I place Alexander in his bassinet as he is, blanket and sour smell and all. He doesn't bother to cry. He opens and closes his lips and I see the tips of his yellow teeth.

Paul has left his milk out ready on the kitchen counter. I touch the side of the bottle; it's slightly warm. Perhaps he was about to feed the baby when he heard me pull up outside. As he said, Alexander will be hungry, but he still isn't screaming. Soft sounds come from the bassinet: mouthy, sucking sounds.

I set down the file. I open my bag and stare at what else I brought from Sunnyside. After a moment I tip it out, shaking the contents onto the counter. Dead leaves, wilting stems, bell-shaped blooms. They are the exact colour of drying blood: the fairies' own flower. Fairy glove. Folk's glove. *Folk's love.* I stand in front of them, entirely blank, an empty skin. I tell myself I don't know why I brought them here, then I tell myself I do.

I turn my back on them and pick up the file. I need to find out where she is. I open it and start to read. As I do, finally, Alexander begins to cry.

There's a cover sheet filled out neatly in black ink, the bottom corner initialled, though I can't make out the letters. It has all the basic facts: name, height, weight, the name of her doctor. They think she was born in 1943. The details mean nothing to me. Did they really think she could be categorised like this – reduced? Everything about her put neatly in boxes, like anybody else? I scan down and see a section labelled *Next of kin.*

Harriet is there. She's Harriet Gorman, Mrs. And there's an address.

I flick through the rest of the papers. Mrs Favell's Individual

Care Plan, with her preferred routines and diet, I've seen before. There are plenty of other things I haven't and don't care about: eye tests, hearing tests, records of flu jabs, a slew of medical papers in tiny print. *Flu jabs?* Why would she need such a thing? Sunnyside must have insisted on those. She would never admit such vulnerability.

I flick past the pages and find a sheet tucked behind the rest. This, I didn't expect: it speaks of the greatest vulnerability of all. It's a Power of Attorney, entitling someone else to manage her affairs should she become unable to do so – as if that would ever happen. Would that too have been suggested by the staff? And I see the person's name, the one responsible for taking over her life, the words printed next to it, and I can't take it in. It doesn't make any sense.

There are no other address details. I leaf back to the next of kin. What had Mandy said? *It was only ever till the house was ready.* And her daughter had come to collect her. She had prepared a home for her: Charlotte and Harriet, together again.

I imagine them nestled in some ancient, low-ceilinged cottage, somewhere they've kept and passed down, one to the other and back again, when it came time to pretend their long life was finally at an end. Crumbling plaster that has been patched and patched again, the floors polished to a new gleam, the walls freshly painted, layer over layer.

I read the address again, see that the house is in Cottingley, and I know that I've found them.

19

I want to leave straight away but of course I can't. There are things I have to do first, the most important of which is to feed Alexander. I wrap one arm around him and hold the bottle with the other. Willing him to drink won't make it any quicker and so I rock him and watch the line of milk welling around his lips as the level goes down. He brushes at the bottle with tiny, dimpled fingers, as if longing for the day he can hold it himself.

My heart isn't knocking against my chest any more. I can't even feel it; there's an empty space where it's supposed to be.

After a time, the baby is done and I tilt him against me, his head resting against my shoulder, and I rub his back. His damp fingers clutch my shirt. At last he becomes still and I settle him into the bassinet. I couldn't leave him hungry. I know he'll sleep now.

It's almost time to go, but there's something else I need. I run up to the bedroom, glancing at the crumpled sheets where Paul and I slept only last night, so familiar and yet already so strange.

How could it all have become so alien to me so quickly?

Before I go I pull the creased, milk-damp shirt over my head, wiping myself with it before throwing it into a corner. I have plenty of similar shirts, ready for milk-spit and worse, but I open the wardrobe and pick something else: something smarter, a blouse I once wore for a job interview. It's more elegant than my usual clothes and when I fasten the buttons I feel better, as if I've donned armour.

As I rush out of the door, I grab the page from the file with Harriet's address and punch her postcode into my phone. The house already feels empty. Alexander isn't crying any longer. Paul will be well into his second pint down at the pub. Now I'm leaving too; the one who should be here, watching over our home.

But it isn't my home. Not without my baby in it.

I think of Robyn. She is the one I need to focus on. *I'm coming, sweet girl*, I think. *Mummy's coming*.

I rest one hand on my belly as I drive, navigating through the uniform rows of terraces. The little footprints that marked me during my pregnancy are still there, not faded a bit despite the aloe vera I've been rubbing on. They may have marked me, but they can't claim me, not for ever. They can't take what's mine. Fierce longing runs through me, a golden thread tugging at the very centre of my being, connecting me to my child. Can Robyn feel it too? I'm confident she will. They never did manage to sever it, no matter how they separated us.

The houses around me grow bigger and grander before giving way to fields spanning either side of the road. Then there are only occasional farm buildings and the way ahead, winding between them. There are a few cars on the road, mainly heading in the opposite direction to mine. In the distance it must be raining: the land is closed in by heavy, louring clouds, massing like a battle, the horizon smearing into the sky.

I can still see the words I read earlier, set out so clearly, making no sense. Of course the Power of Attorney had been made out in favour of Harriet. It was the little printed statement by her name that I hadn't expected:

Harriet Gorman. Daughter (adoptive).

She can't be adopted. She looks like Mrs Favell, moves like her, acts like her. Whatever Mrs Favell is, Harriet is too. No matter where they came from, I can't doubt that they are mother and daughter.

I tell myself it must only be another trick, perhaps to disguise how long they live. No one could go on indefinitely without raising suspicion. Each in turn might have to fake her own death, ensuring the other is their heir, no matter who is the elder or younger. How far back do they go? They might themselves have eventually become worn out and left in human cribs in place of real children, becoming changelings to begin again. They could be any age. Could Harriet actually be Charlotte's mother? They could have taken on many different identities over the years. That might be why Charlotte is now named Favell, not Fenton.

My phone chirps from my pocket and I catch my breath, thinking of Paul, but it's only the automated voice of my satnav telling me where to turn. I make a tight left onto a smaller, quieter road, which winds over the tops of undulating hills. I can't see a town in the distance or any indication of where it could be. Cottingley might be a ghost village.

I drive on, noticing a tiny overgrown lane dropping sharply into a dip, signposted *Beck Foot*. Does that mean the famous Cottingley Beck – am I close?

Soon the road widens out, stone walls and overhanging branches giving way to junctions, traffic lights, bus stops. Cars swarm everywhere, full of purpose. I pass what appears to be a grand hall surrounded by well-tended lawns, glimpse tennis courts and signposts for a health club. I see a sign for a business park, an academy, a crèche, and realise I'm close to the centre of the town, though my satnav remains silent. I cross some mini-roundabouts, seeing pleasant stone houses, surely too new. A pub proclaims *Live sport here.*

This can't be the place. I flick on my indicator and turn off the main road so that I can check the map, glimpsing the 'dead end' sign too late. Still, at last, I'm somewhere that feels right. The sign at the bottom says MAIN STREET but the lane is tiny, narrowing as it leads steeply uphill. It's edged by cottages built in mellow Yorkshire stone, though the windows look new and wheelie bins crowd the little front yards. This road was surely designed for horses and carts rather than motor traffic. Was it once the centre of Cottingley? It's too small for the people who have come to fill it. It doesn't match the place Lawrence Fenton described; it's too built-up, too close, but then he'd lived just outside the town, hadn't he? Further along the beck.

The name 'Main Street' connects with something in my mind and I realise where I am. This is the place not where Fenton lived, but Elsie Wright and her cousin, Frances Griffiths. I picture two girls standing in the middle of the street, everything faded to monochrome, even their faces. The youngest wears a white pinafore, smeared from her dirty hands; Frances has been running and playing, though she doesn't want to get marks on the lens of the camera she carries. It's borrowed from Elsie's father. She is going to the beck; she's going to meet the fairies. She doesn't yet know the debate and speculation that will follow. She can't imagine the furore she will cause. One of the greatest hoaxes in history – what would she have said if she knew? Would she smile at me or would she hide her face? Perhaps she'd never have played by the beck again.

I wonder which of the cottages was theirs. I try to peer behind them as I pass, to see the stream running by their back gardens. I can't see anything past the parked cars and walls and sheds. There's a space at the kerb and I pull in. I don't have time to find the beck; that's not why I'm here. I check the map and see that Harriet's house lies a little beyond Cottingley, where higgledy-piggledy lanes give way to long patches of green. Perhaps it is near to where Lawrence Fenton made his home.

I use an even tinier side street to turn around before rolling back down the hill. From this direction it's easier to make out the large, somewhat intimidating building near the bottom of the road: the old town hall. There's an open driveway at its side, leading towards the cutting that runs behind the houses.

I don't want to waste time but in spite of myself, I stop the car once more. When I step out I can't detect the ozone scent of water, can't hear the babble of the beck, but I know it's there. I can tell by the profusion of ferns that nod their heads over the banking. And I can *feel* it.

At this point on its course, there is no glen. Cottingley Beck trickles over a flat bed of stones, the water clear and clean. Opposite, the banking is thick with verdure, trees reaching their limbs over the stream. To my right I can see the backs of all the houses. Their gardens are on a higher level, separated from the water by a stone wall. I could paddle up the stream behind them if I chose. I couldn't do so in the other direction; to my left, a razor-topped fence bars the way. The water passes beneath it and is gone.

Quickly, I kick off my shoes before stepping into the water. There's a shock of cold, the smooth touch of mossy stones. I imagine a little girl poking into nooks and crevices, hunting fairies, turning to me and smiling. The sight of her presses on my heart. There's no time for this, there never was, and yet I feel a rush of strength, as if receiving a benison for my pilgrimage.

I pull my shoes over my wet feet and hurry back to the car. I drive more quickly, as if the cold has renewed my sense of purpose. When I turn onto the main road I know the exact moment when it bridges the beck, though I can't see it any longer; it was so quickly hidden from view.

I sense that they're close now, and not only because I've looked at the map. I feel everything: not only the history stretching away beneath me but Charlotte, Harriet, and most of all, my daughter. My body aches, as if it knows it will soon be reunited with a piece of itself.

The road rises, climbing away from the place that started it all. Houses give way to open fields, patches of trees, long views. I wonder if the beck is there too, winding away in a path it has worn into the fields, but if so, I cannot see it.

The road sweeps around a corner, demanding my attention, and I glimpse a narrow opening. I recognise it at once, though I've never seen it before; it is so very beautiful. This lane is beyond the reach of the town. There are no other buildings in view, no crammed cottages, no windows peering down. Here are only hedgerows of tangled, wiry hawthorn that brush the sides of my car as I turn into it, their dark green softened by the lace of cow parsley, and suddenly there is colour: yellow trefoil, pink campion, blue cornflowers and harebells, even spires of foxglove. Life lingers here still, as if it has chosen to stay in this narrow lane, autumn forbidden from taking hold.

I turn a corner and see the house nestled into the hillside. It is small and neat, built of mellow stone, almost appearing to have grown where it stands. Mosses creep across the slate roof and window boxes are laden with flowers. Roses grow in an arch over the garden gate, still heavy with crimson blooms. As I watch, sunshine penetrates the clouds, and its rays touch each flower with light.

When I turn off the engine I realise how quiet it is. This place is sheltered from passing traffic, from other people, from the world. It feels like a land where it is always summer.

I get out of the car and approach the gate. It isn't entirely quiet, I realise. An old song is playing, plaintive with the hiss and crackle of a gramophone. It strikes me that this might be Lawrence Fenton's house. It might be a hundred years ago. At any moment he might step from the door, a child clinging to his hand, Charlotte following in her widow's bonnet. Or perhaps they are inside, dancing to the soft music – and I think: *They don't really know how to dance. They only wish to make us want to be where they are.*

And I *do* long to be where they are.

That is when I see the crib. It stands in the middle of the garden as if waiting for me, an old, carved thing, substantial and sturdy, covered with cotton hangings. The clean white fabric is brilliant against the emerald of the grass. It looks like something from a fairy tale.

There is nothing else. Charlotte and Harriet are nowhere to be seen. Perhaps they have left the child, knowing I was coming for her: a mother's love, driving them away.

Perhaps the crib is empty.

My fingertips numb, I let myself in at the gate, wincing at its creak. My chest is so hollow with longing it hurts. Soon Robyn will be in my arms and that will mend it all. They say that a baby changes everything – and she will.

I listen for her as I step quietly towards the crib. The emotion rising in my throat isn't just excitement: it's fear. What if I peer under the hangings and she isn't there? What if there is only Charlotte's laughter, ringing in my ears?

A breathy sigh rises from the crib, a sweet and lovely sound. I pray there will be no more tricks, that I won't look inside and find an ugly little troll with misshapen limbs and sloe-black eyes. I pray I won't see Alexander, the weight of him, his curled fists.

I peek in and she is there, as lovely as I have imagined her so many times. Her golden hair is fine as silk. Her dress is long and white, like the one in the photograph on Mrs Favell's wall. I cannot see her eyes because they remain closed, though I see the veins running through them, the luminosity of her skin. One hand is raised by her face, not formed into a fist, not lashing out or waving in anger but gently curled, her fingernails like lucent shells. They're a little uneven, as if someone has kept them short by nibbling them rather than risking scissors. Did Harriet do that? I think of her holding my daughter to her breast, suckling her, and rage steals my breath. I have missed so much; so many moments have been stolen from me. I can't bring myself to believe I ever said I didn't want her. I do. I'm here. That's what matters now, not the past.

Then I see the thing in the crib next to her and I am frozen.

'What are you doing?'

The voice cuts through the air, sharp with indignation. Harriet rushes from the back door, brushing something from her hands – flour? I picture myself grabbing my daughter, running away, trailing soft lace, but somehow I can't move. Has she cast some spell on me? I tell myself it's only because I *won't* run from them, won't let them intimidate me again. Besides, there was something in her cry that I hadn't expected from her: fear.

'She's mine,' I say. 'She's my child. I'm taking her home.'

She stops halfway across the lawn, her eyes wide. 'Whatever are you talking about? That's not your baby. You know it's not. Where is he?'

I can't answer that and I'm not going to. I won't let her trick me into saying Alexander was ever mine. I won't give them that power. They know he's *not*.

'Robyn is my baby,' I say. 'Charlotte showed me everything. You took her and you left me with *him*. I know what he is, I've always known. You're not going to keep her away from me any longer. She needs me.'

Harriet gawps. Then she says, 'Are you crazy? Get away from my baby. Now. Or I'll call the police.'

I stare at her, defiant, daring her to move. Let her try. Now that Robyn is within my reach, I'll never let them take her from me again. If Harriet moves to make a phone call I'll be gone before she can dial.

And she knows it. She takes a single hesitant step towards the crib and instinctively I lean over my baby. I see again the thing they have placed next to her: a roughly carved doll, its face barely formed, only half emerging from the oval of its head. It's obviously hand-made. It wears a small white christening gown, an echo of the one they've put on Robyn. *A stock of wood.* I can't think what it's doing here. Have I returned the changeling child – Alexander? Is this what he was all along, this ugly, misshapen thing lying next to the baby? Or is it only what it appears to be – a doll?

She holds out her hands in a placatory gesture. 'Don't hurt her.'

Hurt her? Indignation makes my mouth fall open.

She looks as if she's fighting back her own anger, or her fear; she can't get her breath. 'Look, I might have some idea why you're so upset.' She glances over her shoulder as if indicating the person who must be close by, somewhere in the house, listening perhaps. 'We can talk about this.'

'I'm not going to listen to you. You – *she* – you've talked enough. It's all tricks and lies.' I can't allow them to twist everything. That's what they do, what they love doing.

Something like understanding is dawning on her face. Soon she'll have to accept it. She'll realise she's lost.

Then a distorted shape rushes from the house.

Her nightgown is too short to cover her stick-thin legs or her bony, clicking arms. There's no need to cover the truth now; there's no glamour or disguise. Grey hair is disarrayed about her face but I catch glimpses of her hook nose, hollowed cheeks, witch's chin. She has always been thin but now she looks emaciated, the goblin revealed. She shrieks as she comes, flying barefoot across the grass, and I can do nothing but watch. It's Harriet who moves, snapping out a hand to grasp her mother's bony wrist, bringing her to a halt beside her.

Charlotte doesn't look away from me. Her eyes are bright points of concentrated fury, but still, they are black; there is no soul in them. I see that now. No heart beats in her chest.

And yet Harriet turns to her as if the answers aren't already plainly revealed all around us, and says, 'Mother, what have you done?'

Charlotte's chest, heaving with each panting breath, stills. Is she even breathing any longer? Her words emerge in a hiss. 'How is she here? How did she—'

Harriet doesn't try to explain and nor do I. She only repeats, 'What have you *done*?'

Charlotte's lips draw back from her teeth, as yellow and misshapen as Alexander's. A family trait? She tries to compose herself, standing taller, transforming her features into a semblance of the woman I first met. She lifts her chin and looks defiantly at her daughter.

'All right.' Harriet's tone is low. 'Your name is Rose, isn't it? Well, I'll tell you then, Rose – I'll tell you all about my *mother*.'

Is this a story? Does she think I'll stand here and listen, wait for her to bewitch me? But her next words stop my breath.

'You think Robyn's your baby? All right. I can see my mother's been playing her games. I can tell you about those. I've played them before. She made me think I was a *changeling*, once.'

She nods as her words take effect. 'Of course, *I* was only a kid. I was young enough to listen to such tales.'

Poison, I think. Still, they're only words. They can only harm me if I let them.

'Oh, she was disturbed, more than anyone realised. She had a right to be. Her father-in-law did something…'

Patricia's voice: *Mrs Favell had to move in with her father-in-law, and – well, he did something terrible.*

'She never could get over it.' Harriet glances at her mother as if awaiting permission to go on. Charlotte doesn't give it. She keeps glaring at me through narrowed eyes. She looks as if she'd like to tear me apart with her teeth.

'Her father-in-law murdered her real daughter,' Harriet says. 'He was disturbed. He had some odd idea that she wasn't a normal child and he took a blade to her. I didn't know it then, of course. I couldn't possibly.

'She got it into her head that another child would come and take the place of the one who was taken, you see. But that child never came, so Mother went to seek her out. And after a time, she found just the right one: she found me. I was the right age; and I looked just like her.

'I wasn't christened Harriet, of course. She gave me that name when she adopted me, like she gave me everything else. I was just a little girl, living in a children's home. When Mother came and found me there, when she took me away, I was grateful. I only learned afterwards that Harriet was the name of her own child, the dead one. I didn't know I was nothing but her replacement.'

She pauses. 'By the time I found out, I was used to it. It *was* my name.'

She stares at the crib for a moment. 'She used to tell me I wasn't her real baby, though. She called me her little changeling. I didn't understand, not really. She may have adopted me, but it was never me she wanted. It never really made me yours, did it, *Mother*? I was never good enough, never the same.'

There is pain in her eyes as she addresses Charlotte, years of it, all the pain a little girl could feel. For a moment I think I glimpse its echo in Mrs Favell's.

Harriet's expression clears. 'We got past all that years ago,' she says, 'or I thought we did. She had therapy. They called it a form of Capgras Syndrome, Impostor Syndrome: the delusion that someone close to her had been replaced by a double. It seemed to help, giving it a name, some kind of diagnosis. It helped *me*, though I sometimes think that's the reason I left it so late to have my own child. And the problem was that it remained true, in a sense. Her daughter *had* been replaced.

'Now she's ill and she's always been bitter, and we're there again, aren't we, Mother? Or is it just that you've hidden it all these years and it's only now that you're being honest?'

Charlotte doesn't answer.

'So what has she done to *you*?' Harriet looks at me and it's a simple question but I can't reply. How do I explain? Charlotte's done nothing but tell me the truth.

I only want to hear the truth from your own lips. Tell me. Do you want it?

I shake my head. She made me tell the truth, too – but the truth can change. The truth can be wrong.

Harriet speaks more brightly. She thinks her words have changed things, formed them into something else. 'My mother always hated seeing other women with their children. She hated seeing them happy where she couldn't be. I think she wanted them to feel how she felt. I was supposed to fix that of course, but I failed. I was only a child. I didn't understand. How could I? She'd drag me away from the park, crying, because she couldn't bear to watch the families playing there. To see them smiling, laughing – *together*, in a way that we never were. As she wasn't allowed to be with her own daughter.'

I don't believe her. I can't see it. I can't imagine Charlotte acting out of weakness, out of jealousy. Is Harriet trying to imply that Mrs Favell had been jealous of *me* – a young woman with a baby on the way? Had she so envied me my child – could I really have had everything she ever wanted?

I think of photographs in a box under the bed, a mother and her child, never any older than seven or eight. I shake my head. Was that her real daughter? Could she really have replaced her – when she'd managed to seek out the right child, the one she imagined must be meant for her? Is Harriet the only kind of changeling she ever had?

An image rises, though not of Alexander or even Paul. It's

Edie, sitting at a table with cards in front of her, knowing she will never see her own daughter again, knowing she won't see her grandchild. And Charlotte had done that. She had relished seeing the pain of Edie's family too, had triumphed over her when she said, *She's never coming back.*

But that doesn't matter now. It doesn't change anything. There may be some truth in Harriet's words, but one truth doesn't make everything a lie.

'I really thought you were over it.' Harriet's voice breaks and I look at her in surprise, but she's not talking to me. It's almost as if she's forgotten I'm here. There are tears in her eyes, as if she really is crying.

'I thought when I told you I was pregnant that this was all in the past. I thought you'd be happy again, truly happy this time. I thought Robyn would be enough.'

She wipes away the tears. Are they real or only another glamour? They glitter like diamonds. She looks up at me through her eyelashes. 'Mother has cancer,' she says. 'It's early days, but they can't operate. You must have known that. She's dying.'

I can't take it in. *The fairies do not die as humans do.* I think of the bundle of papers I stole from Patricia, the way I'd leafed past the medical records along with the routine tests, the flu jabs, everything that hadn't seemed to matter. Was this there too, and I had cast the information aside? Had I seen only what I wanted to see?

'That's why I prepared this place for her,' Harriet says, 'and brought her home. I thought she could spend some time with her granddaughter, enjoy being with Robyn, before—'

Her words distort and dissolve, then she gathers herself. 'But you won't, will you, Mother? You know she isn't really your blood. You know you won't get to enjoy her and love her, so – this? You spin some stupid story to this girl, and make her think whatever crazy things you can?' She tails off into a bitter laugh.

There is silence as time stops. Everything waits; even the breeze falls still. Charlotte doesn't answer, and I think to myself what a pair they make; how beautifully they have orchestrated everything.

And I think of ink in a bottle. Mrs Favell bending over it, a fountain pen in her hand, a sly smile on her face. Had she really written the letters herself? Or were they a kind of heirloom, the story of a delusion that hadn't only been hers – had her family had some propensity for it? Perhaps she'd simply sought out the relics of ideas that were similar to her own. Then she'd carried them down through the years, until she found the right recipient for her stories.

Is she only a bitter, dying old woman without any love in her, as Harriet suggested, or something else – a monster?

Which story do I choose to believe?

I close my eyes and see Alexander: the last glimpse I took of him before I left the house. His eyes are closed, his fists unmoving. He lies in his bassinet, quiescent at last, as still and quiet as a baby in a photograph.

Which story can I possibly choose to believe?

I look down and see Robyn, so delicately formed, so sweetly breathing, so golden. She always rested so gently in Harriet's arms, the two of them so elegant. She had looked, I realised, as if she belonged there, the two of them perfect together.

It should have been me.

I hear a sound and my eyes snap open. Mrs Favell has moved; she stands just on the other side of the crib, unblinking. She reaches for the baby, her fingers like bones. My hand goes to my pocket and I withdraw it, holding the thing I'd retrieved from my bedroom before I left: an old blackened paperknife. It is blunt, but I think it will do.

Harriet lets out a strangled sound and Charlotte remains motionless. Something Harriet said passes through my mind, sharp and with new clarity.

I thought you'd be happy again, truly happy this time. I thought Robyn would be enough.

And I know they don't deserve her. Robyn should be with her mother, the one who loves her; not cold, distant Harriet, nor someone who can only think of her as just another shadow.

I gesture with the knife and they step back, like one creature now. Their words are nothing but little cries, meaningless to me, the sounds inhuman.

Their reaction does not surprise me. They recognise a true mother's love and are afraid of it. They know I would never do anything that wasn't out of care for her, though the knife is ugly against the innocent white hangings, the lacy dress. Part of me recoils from it but I can't listen. The sounds they make are poison. I reach for her, the perfect baby, *my* baby, the one I so badly wanted, and I turn and run in the direction of the lane, leaving the beautiful garden and their shrieks behind me.

20

Their cries ring in my ears as I drive away from the cottage, long after they pass beyond the range of hearing. I'm on the main road again, cars jostling and pouring forth their fumes, virulent yellow and black signage pointing the way. Passers-by walk with their heads down, following some preordained path they can't even see. I'm cast out of the lovely garden, banished from the summer that lingered in the grass and the gentle air, from the crimson roses that blossomed there.

I recognise the road I have travelled before. I've reached the place where it spans Cottingley Beck and I imagine the bright water below, unheard and unseen by anyone. My car passes over it, the changing tone barely noticeable as it crosses the bridge, and we continue on our way.

I should feel happy. I've got what I came for but my mind is blank. I turn off at random in a new direction, a quiet road, wanting to get away from the other motorists and anyone I can see, or perhaps to escape their view. I tell myself that no one's looking at me, they don't know anything, but still the sight of them makes me anxious. I need to be alone. I have to be with Robyn; I need to think.

I try to look over my shoulder, glimpse the back of the baby seat, a spill of white blanket. The car drifts left and I straighten, adjusting the wheel. She's fine. She isn't crying, isn't fretting. She doesn't miss the woman who'd posed as her mother. Soon she won't even remember her.

I wish she'd fade as quickly from my own mind. Harriet's words are still whispering somewhere deep inside me, sour, poisonous. I can't allow myself to listen. If I hadn't listened to Mrs Favell I'd never have been in this situation. I would be with Paul and my daughter, happy, the three of us. I would surely never have wanted anything else.

The landscape around me changes as the road climbs. I'm heading onto the hills, into the open, and I feel better with only the sky around me. Safer. No one is near. I can be myself again, breathe again, stop the awful litany of thoughts crowding my head. But still they haunt me. I screw up my eyes against them, beat my hands against the wheel. The pain in my palms brings me back, though for a moment everything is a blur. I won't give way. I can't show weakness. I'm a mother, a real one now, and I'll do everything a mother needs to do, and I have; I've begun. I have my daughter back.

I've reached silence now. I feel it waiting beneath the hum of the wheels, all around me, emerging from the hills. The land undulates into the distance, nothing crossing it but dry-stone walls. Exhaustion comes over me in waves, weighing down my limbs. Did I really fight off Charlotte and Harriet with an old paperknife? The image is too surreal to be true.

There's a lay-by ahead and I ease off the accelerator and pull into it. The car sways like a boat over the pitted surface. I will catch my breath, take stock, decide what to do, where to go. But first I will hold my baby.

I release my seatbelt, turn and pull myself half over the centre console so that I can see into the baby seat. When I do, I am frozen. I can't believe what's in front of me but I blink and it doesn't change.

The seat is empty.

I lunge over it, reaching for her, running my fingers over the straps that should have secured her there. Has she somehow fallen out – will there be a tiny body crushed behind my seat? I climb fully into the back and reach into the space where she should be and realise there is something there after all.

The thing is a doll. A stock of wood. It is nestled into the bottom of the baby seat, its face hideous, its body motionless and stiff. I can barely bring myself to touch it, but I do; I lift it up before my face.

I can still see my child, the perfection of her, but she's beyond my reach. The vision is gone, all of it is, and I let out an odd sound of loss and rage and despair. Did I really think I could win? They are stronger. They always have been. Harriet with her sweet face and her honeyed tongue, Charlotte laughing at my hope, plucking my child from the air with bony fingers, stealing her back again. Exchanging her for *this*.

Because I'd said *no*, hadn't I? She'd asked me the question and I said I didn't want her and that was it: the only chance I'd had was gone. Everything after that was already too late, the pact made, the agreement sealed. And they had known that, even while I trespassed in their garden, doused myself in the beck, drove towards them – *who's that trip-trapping over my bridge?* Their fear had been nothing but pretence, had only ever been mockery. To them, it never was anything but a game.

Had the baby in the crib ever been real, or was that only another illusion – a glamour?

And I bury my face in my hands. I had *forgotten*. How could I have forgotten? Something I had read about changelings comes back to me: their dislike of water. That was why some immersed them in a pool or left them for the sea. But *running* water – that was another kind of spell against them, wasn't it? Because a changeling couldn't cross it. But I had driven Robyn straight over Cottingley Beck, the most powerful water of all.

Did that mean the lovely baby in the garden had only ever been a changeling? When we reached the running water, had she melted away into the air? Or was she really my daughter, but it was too late and they had already made a fairy of her – removed her soul?

I never had seen her eyes open, all the time we had fought over her crib. She never once looked up at me.

Something breaks inside me, a golden tie severed, turning black. I don't know what I feel. Nothing has any weight. Not even her, I realise – I don't remember the solidity of her in my arms. I can't recall the awkwardness of gripping her as I ran, the way she must have squirmed as I put her in the car seat. I don't remember any of it. It's all dissolved, like words into the air.

Yet words feel heavier now than anything else.

Tell me. Do you want it?

My answer is bitter on my tongue. And more questions surface, ones that were waiting there all along; the ones I had buried somehow, keeping them *beneath*. Where exactly had I thought I was going? What had I imagined I was going to do with her?

I have nowhere to go. There is no one I can run to. I do not even have a home where I could take her, not any longer. Paul would think I'd gone mad if he saw me with Robyn. How could I make him believe she's his daughter? He'd call the police himself. They'd call me crazy. They'd drag me off and lock me away.

Paul has only ever wanted his son.

Alexander. I close my eyes and see him, his chubby fists, his purple face, his constant screaming. Is it really possible that Robyn was Harriet's after all? If she is, that means Alexander is mine. But I've never felt it to be so. I've never sensed any golden thread connecting him to me. He never slept sweetly in my arms. Or is it only that I never gave him the chance?

He was sleeping when I left, though. Sleeping more soundly and deeply than he ever had...

I think of him lying motionless in the bassinet, finally at peace. It is all suddenly so clear: a little centre of quiet amid the grimy lounge, strewn with chaos. I hadn't looked back at him for long. I had only wanted to go. And everything had been so ordinary. There was the kitchen counter strewn with pots to be washed, the kettle, the microwave, the bottle of milk – drained. And yet there is something out of place, something that snags at me, that doesn't belong. I scan along the worktops as if they are before me again and I see the limp petals of decaying foxglove.

Suddenly I can't breathe. How was it that I thought the spell worked – the one to banish a changeling, so that the true child would be restored, reunited with its mother?

I close my eyes. I know I fed Alexander. I can still feel the weight of him. The line of milk welling at his lip – had it been white?

As white as snow, I think. *As white as snow, as black as ebony, as red as—*

I open my eyes.

No. This isn't the true story and I push it all away. It can't be. The first time the milk was tainted, I hadn't even done it by my own hand; that was only another trick, played by the fairies. It was Alexander, carrying out a nasty prank to make Paul angry with me; capricious and cruel. And anyway, he had wanted the meat, had *needed* the meat—

He had to eat and eat. He had to regain his vitality, drawing it in along with the life he was draining from me.

You look like a consumptive, Rose.

I cover my eyes. Why hadn't I listened to the stories in the first place? I should have put a rusty horseshoe over his crib, a Bible under his blanket. I find myself hunting for something, checking the car seats and the footwells, even though it was always too late; my baby was taken long before he ever slept in a crib.

I replay the events of the last few hours. I think of the way I'd held out an ancient iron knife over another crib, another child. Harriet's eyes had widened in horror at the sight. She and her mother had backed away, repulsed by the cold iron, as they should have been. And I'd reached for the baby. *Her blanket as white as snow. The knife as black as ebony. My love for her as vivid as a blood-red rose...*

I shake the images away. I don't truly remember any of it, it feels like nothing but a story, and I let it drain from me, leaving my mind empty. I had left the garden behind me, that much was certain. *Had* I felt the weight of her in my arms? Or on some level, had Harriet actually convinced me? Perhaps I hadn't snatched her up at all. Perhaps I hadn't saved her because I had never wanted a baby. That had been the truth as I had spoken it and it was still the truth and always the truth and that is something I cannot change.

I shake my head. *No.* I reached out for her – why? To save her – or to let her go? And yet this thing is here, a false child. Had I been so bewitched that instead I'd grasped at nothing but a stock of wood?

I climb out of the car, slam the door behind me. A cold breeze lifts the hair from my neck, indifferent and merciless, and I shiver. Summer is long behind me now. I feel it in the air, taste the loss of it all around me. The road stretches away in either direction, featureless and grey, across the heath. At one side a grassy bank slopes downward, a few sparse trees clinging to the earth, slanting away from the prevailing wind. Beyond them is a little flash of bright water. It gleams coldly, shining back a wintry light, but when I look up I cannot see the sun. There is only a white blankness where it should be – or can I not see it because I am cursed?

I walk away from the car, towards the pool. I see now that

it's a small lake, the edges rippling silver where water meets the reeds. It's abandoned, I know that at once. No one would cast a fishing line over this water; no one would sit by its banks or try to warm themselves by its gleam. It is still and silent. There is no life about it. If summer lingered in Charlotte Favell's garden, here is where winter holds sway. Perhaps it is even an offshoot of Cottingley Beck, long since cut off from the stream, turning toxic and sour. The sedge has withered from the lake; no birds sing.

It is the place she told me of with her poem. And so I look for her, standing under the trees in some delicately coloured gown, lavender or mauve or baby blue; a graceful woman, so much more poised than I, so much more elegant. She will be wearing a new face of course, not the one she showed to the world or even the one I glimpsed under the full sun, but the one she hides beneath them all; she will be her true self at last – La Belle Dame sans Merci.

It's an important poem… It's for you.

She had poured her words into my ear. They were like worms, eating their way into me like a canker, finding out my bed of crimson joy, rotting me from the inside with their dark and secret love.

O Rose thou art sick.

She had told me all along what she was doing. She had told me what I *was*. And I see it at last. I remember my impatience with it all, my longing to get away. The way I'd resented the times I'd had to wash them, feed them, change them. I'd seen only the surface of things: the false teeth and incontinence and bedsores and being asked the same questions over and over again because they couldn't remember the answers. I hadn't seen *beneath*. I hadn't seen because I hadn't troubled to look and my punishment was that Mrs Favell had seen *me*.

I had been a carer, but I hadn't, had I? I hadn't really cared about anything.

I abandoned my son. I left the man who loved me. I gave them up for nothing but a story. And I know that Charlotte is not here, that she never will be here again, and I am bereft.

It's for you.

I am the only one standing here by this lifeless lake. Why should I look for anyone else? This is *my* place. I look down at myself, holding out my arms, seeing the garment I'd chosen to wear, as if I'd known. My blouse is silky, pearlescent, and the faintest, softest green.

You remind me of me, Rose.

But of course I had. Because it was never her, was it? *I* am La Belle Dame sans Merci, the woman without mercy; the woman without love. It was always me.

I picture myself walking away from here, getting back into the car and going – where? There is no place for me now. She has seen to that, or I have. I am not a wife, not a mother. And I realise: this is my happily ever after, the one I had wished for. I am free. I can go anywhere; I can be anyone.

The knowledge creeps into me, along my bones, through my veins, layers of it going down and down as if into deep water. It is cold, turning me numb as it bleeds through me. There are no ties left. There is nothing to keep me from my future. I have my wish, and it is Mrs Favell who has given it to me. She was my fairy godmother all along. She granted my desires, everything I ever wanted; I just had to give her a little something in exchange.

I step towards the abandoned and lonely lake, no life in it, as the sun recedes from the world. I look down into the darkened water at my reflection, shimmering in the surface: my pale form, my eyes staring back at me, always and entirely black.

No. She cannot win; I cannot finish this way. It isn't the end. I have my happy ending, but at the wrong time, when I no longer want it. I only want my *life*.

Have you ever been in love, Rose? – that had been her question, and I know now that I have. I felt my child growing inside me, his skin and bones forming within, his translucent eyelids opening and closing in the dark of me, his heart beating so much more rapidly than mine. She cannot take that from me. I turn my back on the lake where no sedge grows, where no birds sing – the one she meant for me to find – and I run back towards the car.

It takes for ever and is gone in the blink of an eye, but I reach the ending. Time is flowing differently now, slipping away all around me as if I'm in Fairyland, but this is real: this is *mine*. I look up at the narrow dirty-brick terrace, trying to read in the blankness of its windows what lies within. Is Paul already back? Has he found Alexander there alone? Is he even now cradling his son to him – that, and his own bitterness?

He can't be. I will him away with my mind. He *won't* be. Mrs Favell's story has finished, the one she wanted to tell. I listened too long; now I will write my own.

I already know what I will find as I step out of the car, hurry along the path and turn my key in the lock, the mechanism so worn it does not make a sound. I pause for a moment in the hall. Here are no snaking words to find their way beneath my skin; they are banished now. There is silence within, silence without. This is my home.

And I see it all.

Alexander is lying quite still in his bassinet. I lift him, hold him to my breast, close my eyes, breathe him in. A breathy sigh – his or my own? – fills my mind, my heart. He does not wriggle; he does not fight. He must know I have decided to be his mother at last.

I tell myself I never could have hurt him. I never could have cast him away. Even when I'd seen that hideous carving in another baby's crib and wondered if it somehow represented Alexander, a changeling returned to the fairies, some part of me had still chosen it in preference to any other child.

My arms begin to shake – with relief perhaps, or with spent adrenaline for dangers past. He is *mine*. My son. He must be hungry. I will hold him for a while longer, feeling the weight of him, the solidity. I will breathe his breath. I'll feed him the milk my body has made, nurture and comfort him, and soon his father will come home and he'll forgive the things he doesn't know he needs to forgive and it will be as it always was. Better, even, because I will never want to leave again.

I refuse to see the kitchen, to think of the chaos strewn across the worktops, the history of the things I have or haven't done. I will not see the stolen papers abandoned on the floor. None of that matters, not any longer. Patricia will forgive me. Perhaps

Harriet will even vouch for me. She knows what her mother is, after all. They won't press charges. They already know I won't go back: I've made my choice.

I close my eyes once more and tell myself a new story.

We will be mother, father and baby. The three of us will walk in the park, doing everything Paul had spoken of. All the stories he told me once – they are the ones that will come to be. We'll swing Alexander in our arms between us as he grows. We will watch his clumsy movements as he tries to kick a ball and we'll laugh together. We will have matching smiles and matching dreams, and somewhere not too far distant another mother will hold her child, a little girl, and she too will tell her stories. She'll tell her she will always be hers, and wanted, and loved.

Paul will be happy and so shall I. He won't need to speak to me again about coming around, because he'll never need to. We'll find the work we need to get through this and we'll do it together. There will be new choices to make, and this time we'll make all the right ones. I could even return to my studies. I'll finish what I once began; I can still be the person I have always wanted to be.

And one day, when my family is ready, we will leave. When we do, it will be to a new reality: one we have chosen, one we have built, one we will create with our own hands. I can achieve every dream I've ever had. They will become real, surrounding us like a fairy materialising in a photograph. Surely, after these last months, anything else will be easy. I'll take Alexander and Paul with me, somehow. I'll find a way. I always have.

And we will be together.

You believe, he had always said to me. And he was right. I do believe. Mrs Favell had tried to take that and warp it and twist it into something I could no longer recognise, but I see that now. It doesn't mean I have to stop believing in anything; it doesn't mean I can't try again.

I hold on to it all, everything I have gained – a new ending. This is the future: it is beautiful; it is life, and it is my own.

Alex doesn't stir, though I'm holding him so tightly. He sleeps on, peaceful in my arms, trusting me at last. He knows I will take care of him; he knows I will take care of us all.

ACKNOWLEDGEMENTS

Thank you so much to the vibrant, enthusiastic and always awesome Team Titan, particularly Cat Camacho and George Sandison, for shepherding this book into publication. Thank you too to my agent Oli Munson of A. M. Heath, for setting it all in train. I'm also grateful to designer Natasha MacKenzie for such an incredible cover and to Wayne McManus for taking care of my website.

This book owes a large debt of gratitude to Ian Whates, who asked me a few years ago if I'd write a novella for his independent press, NewCon. The result was *Cottingley*, a story told entirely in the form of letters, released under the name Alison Littlewood. Thank you, Ian, not only for publishing that novella, but for being so supportive when I decided to revise and interweave those letters into the new and rather longer contemporary story that became *The Cottingley Cuckoo*.

Thank you to the incredibly talented writer Priya Sharma, for support and friendship as well as help with my research questions – any errors remain entirely my own. This book is dedicated to you and Mark Greenwood, fabulous people both, not to mention fiendish Cards Against Humanity players.

A big shout out to my writing friends, and the giant genre family formed by events like Edge-Lit and FantasyCon. I miss you, and I'm looking forward to a time when everything becomes possible again.

Fergus, thank you for being there. Thanks too for that trip to Cottingley where you waited, not even a little bit bemused, while I insisted on kicking off my shoes and paddling in the beck. It just had to be done, in memory of a hoax that by turns delighted, entranced and puzzled the world.

One hundred years ago, when Elsie and Frances took their startling photographs, they pictured a very Victorian kind of fairy. Such pretty winged creations, flitting among the flowers, had largely replaced the older tales of darker, more dangerous creatures, who played nasty tricks and might even steal humans away. This book brings the different strands of lore together, and I'm grateful for the work of the numerous folklorists and researchers who have made it possible. I am also indebted to *The Science of Fairy Tales: An Inquiry into Fairy Mythology* by Edwin Sidney Hartland (1891), *The Coming of the Fairies* by Sir Arthur Conan Doyle (1922) and the poetry of Keats and of William Blake – who, in a delightful piece of symmetry, once claimed to have witnessed a fairy funeral.

Many are surprised that Doyle, creator of the ever-rational Sherlock Holmes, also argued for the existence of fairies. As

Rose surmises, his was an attempt to apply scientific methods to unscientific matters, and his aims were really rather noble. He wished to increase the world's knowledge, to provide comfort against the fear of death and ultimately, to better the lot of humankind. He was a dreamer as well as a rationalist – and who isn't the better for that?

Finally, I would like to thank my parents, Ann and Trevor, for the love and fairy tales – always.

ABOUT THE AUTHOR

A. J. Elwood studied literature and history, which everyone assured her would never have any direct relevance to what she ended up doing with her life. She remains fascinated by those times when people could believe in things we think of as madness and have perfectly good reasons for doing so. An early obsession with fairy tales has stayed with her and she loves to pen stories that hopefully contain a little bit of magic and often more than a little of the strange.

Elwood lives in a three-hundred-year-old house where floorboards creak, doors open of their own accord and rooms seem to spontaneously transform into libraries. She enjoys travel, particularly to cold places; she dreams of living above the Arctic Circle with mysterious lights and the silence of the snow. For now, her beloved dogs wouldn't let her. She's happy to remain in Yorkshire with her partner, a growing collection of fountain pens and increasingly inky fingers. She also writes as Alison Littlewood.

For more fantastic fiction, author events,
exclusive excerpts, competitions, limited editions and more

VISIT OUR WEBSITE
titanbooks.com

LIKE US ON FACEBOOK
facebook.com/titanbooks

FOLLOW US ON TWITTER AND INSTAGRAM
@TitanBooks

EMAIL US
readerfeedback@titanemail.com